"You'll find me easy to please, Jessica," he said. "All you have to do is smile in my direction."

Such foolishness! "A smile will do it?" she asked.

"Just looking at you gives me pleasure," he told her, and she laughed, a quick, harsh sound.

"I'll put some stock in that if I didn't know how I look these days, Finn." She set her jaw, deliberately acknowledging her own shortcomings.

He laughed at her. The man had the audacity to touch his fingers to her cheek and then bend to kiss the tip of her nose. "You don't know what you're talking about, Miss Jessica."

Then he was laughing no longer, his mouth taking hers fiercely, his need powerful, elemental. And then they lurched, almost in unison, as the baby made its presence known to them both, a tiny hand or foot poking indiscriminately in protest…!

* * *

Colorado Courtship
Harlequin Historical #691—February 2004

Acclaim for Carolyn Davidson's recent titles

The Texan
"…heart-touching characters
and a vivid, mythic setting…"
—*Romantic Times*

A Marriage by Chance
"This deftly written novel about loss and recovery
is a skillful handling of the traditional Western,
with the added elements of family conflict
and a moving love story."
—*Romantic Times*

A Convenient Wife
"Carolyn Davidson creates an engaging,
complex plot with a hero to die for."
—*Romantic Times*

The Tender Stranger
"Davidson wonderfully captures gentleness in the
midst of heart-wrenching challenges, portraying the
extraordinary possibilities that exist within
ordinary marital love."
—*Publishers Weekly*

COLORADO COURTSHIP

CAROLYN DAVIDSON

HARLEQUIN®

TORONTO • NEW YORK • LONDON
AMSTERDAM • PARIS • SYDNEY • HAMBURG
STOCKHOLM • ATHENS • TOKYO • MILAN • MADRID
PRAGUE • WARSAW • BUDAPEST • AUCKLAND

Special thanks and acknowledgment are given to Carolyn Davidson for her contribution to the COLORADO CONFIDENTIAL series.

ISBN 0-373-29291-0

COLORADO COURTSHIP

Please address questions and book requests to:
Harlequin Reader Service
U.S.: 3010 Walden Ave., P.O. Box 1325, Buffalo, NY 14269
Canadian: P.O. Box 609, Fort Erie, Ont. L2A 5X3

Sometimes those who point out our faults are not truly appreciated. But if the truth be known, I owe an enormous debt of gratitude to the women who read and critique my work and let me know when and where I have fallen short of the goal. They do their best to make me look good in front of my editors, and to those ladies I offer my heartfelt thanks for their efforts on my behalf. Brenda Rollins and Betty Barrs, this book is dedicated to you, with love.

And as always, to Mr. Ed, who loves me.

Prologue

Saint Louis, April 1862

He wanted her.

With but a single glance he acknowledged the desire flaring within him, knew instinctively she would fit neatly into his arms should he lift her against himself. His mouth tightened, as did the pressure of his knees against the sides of the horse he rode, and the black gelding sidestepped, tossing his head impatiently.

Appearing small and fragile beside the tall wagon, the woman's face was in profile, her features finely drawn. Woman? She seemed but a girl, clad in a poorly fitting, voluminous dress. From beneath her sunbonnet, dark hair hung in a long braid down her back, the end tied with a bit of ribbon. It was a feminine touch, almost an aching reminder to the watching eye that, no matter the adversity, a woman's need for such small fripperies would prevail.

To Finley Carson's narrowed gaze, she appeared too delicate for the rigors of traveling across prairies toward the mountains that beckoned the unwary. Silently she stood looking upward at the seat, and then placed a slender hand on the wooden vehicle, hesitant, obviously fearful of climbing upward, lest she fall.

"Get in, Jessica." The order was growled impatiently, the man standing beside the pair of oxen apparently not given to gallantry. Harsh syllables that offered no leniency to her smaller stature, her obvious fear.

"I'm not sure I can," the young woman answered. "There's nothing for me to step up on." Her voice was husky, that of a woman full grown, but laced now with frustration only too clear to a bystander.

And a bystander was exactly what he must be, Finley Carson reminded himself. No matter that the man muttered an obscenity as he stalked back to where the young woman stood, it was not *his* concern that she was lifted and tossed with careless movements to sit atop the seat. Not his affair to wonder at her rough treatment by the man whose actions brought quick tears to her eyes and caused her to cringe from his uncaring hands.

Yet, the aching awareness of dark hair and fragile-boned femininity made Finn frown. The urge to rest callused palms upon her narrow shoulders, to look into those wary eyes, tugged at him. For a single moment he knew envy of another man, such as had never possessed him in his twenty-six years.

His hands tightened on the reins of his mount and moved with an almost unseen signal, turning his horse aside. The black gelding obeyed with a toss of his head, and Finn caught a glimpse of the woman's face as she turned her head in his direction. Unsmiling, she nodded, a simple acknowledgment of his presence, and he felt a lurch in his chest as controlled anger gripped him.

He wanted her. Ached to lift her from where she huddled on the high seat. Yearned for a long moment to feel her softness against his body. The thought possessed him and he turned aside, his heels again nudging the barrel of his mount, urging him into an easy lope.

With a discipline gained from his years as an army scout, Finn Carson put the dark-eyed female from his mind, his jaw firm as he rode down the line of wagons. His gaze surveyed the men who performed last-minute chores, readying the train for its imminent departure from Saint Louis, heading for Independence, Missouri.

This was an assignment he almost relished, one that must be uppermost in his mind over the next months. Taking his place on this wagon train as a guide, using his skills to find the man who was a cheat—a murderer who had stolen the deed to a homestead. One hundred sixty acres of land that lay in the shadow of Pike's Peak—a speck of wilderness that held a fortune in gold in its depths, if the assayer's office could be relied upon.

Lyle Beaumont. The man was here, his presence a canker, his very existence a stain on the essence of decency Finn had been raised to believe in. Lyle Beaumont—the man who had cheated Finn's brother, Aaron Carson, of his rightful claim to land and then killed him to conceal the theft.

Lyle Beaumont—who even now possessed the deed to those 160 acres in Colorado.

It was toward that man his mind must focus, that man Finn must identify and pursue, even as he hid his own identity on this train. With regret, he set aside the moment of yearning he'd suffered, acknowledging his purpose would not—could not—include a dalliance of any sort on the journey. Certainly not with a woman who so obviously was already possessed of a husband.

There were only a dozen or so females counted among the group. Most of the men were miners who traveled toward the promised land of gold and silver that courted their interest. More of an obsession, actually, Finn decided with a shake of his head. Men who lusted after gold were a breed apart. Willing to sacrifice everything they possessed on the altar of greed.

Even a woman—a woman obliged to follow the path her husband took. A woman who was off-limits to other men, he reminded himself. A woman bound to the man who had placed a ring on her finger and fear in her heart.

Chapter One

June 1862

It was a scar on the landscape—a raw wound against the backdrop of prairie flowers and lush grasses. The earth was mounded over the narrow plot of ground, and beside it Jessica stood in silence. The man she'd lived with for most of her adult life lay beneath several feet of hardscrabble soil.

Her last memory of him was the look of surprise he'd worn as a bullet tore through his chest only hours before, a recollection she suspected she'd live through again, more than once, during the long nights to come.

"Mrs. Beaumont?" The wagon master stood at her side, his palm cupped beneath her elbow, and she glanced up as he spoke her name.

"We've got to get rolling, ma'am," Jonas McMasters said, his words spoken firmly as he nudged her from the graveside. Beside him, the kindly minister who was heading for Santa Fe with his family closed his Bible and offered her a final nod. At least Lyle had had a real funeral, Jessica thought, even though he'd said more than once that he had no belief in anything he couldn't lay hands on.

And that included the God she worshiped.

Now Jessica nodded at Jonas, aware as they turned from the grave that a huddled group of men waited next to Lyle's wagon. Her wagon, she amended silently. The bullet that had shattered Lyle's heart had effectively robbed her of her position as his wife, as a woman under a man's protection. Now she was on her own, yet not alone, she thought, as the child within her reminded her of its presence with a rolling motion.

"I'm ready," she told Jonas quietly, aware that she did not present the appearance of a grieving widow, that her tearless eyes made her seem uncaring. And yet, she could not mourn Lyle. At least not as she might have if he'd endeared himself to her in any way over the past years.

He was dead, and she faced an uncertain future. But for today she had only to sort out what she would do for the next few hours. Tomorrow morning would bring problems enough to worry about for one day. There was no point in thinking too far ahead.

"Mrs. Beaumont." Another voice broke her reverie as she made her way toward the wagon. Finley Carson stood before her and she looked up at him, met his gaze and felt a shiver of awareness. "I'll walk with your oxen this afternoon," he said. "Why don't you ride in the wagon and get some rest. You're looking a little peaked."

And then his mouth twisted in a grimace. "And wasn't that a kind remark to make," he said with a shake of his head. "I only meant that you've had a shock, and in your condition…" His voice trailed off, as if he were aware that her obvious pregnancy was a topic not fit for discussion between strangers, especially when one of them was an unattached male and the other a woman who had been, only hours before, cast into the role of widowhood.

"I'll leave you to tend to her, Finn," the wagon master said with a quick nod of his head in the other man's direction. "We need to make another three miles or so before sunset."

Finn Carson's hand touched Jessica's back, his wide palm warm against flesh that felt chilled from within, and she shivered. He bent to peer beneath the brim of her sunbonnet. "Can I help you up onto the wagon seat?"

"If you don't mind," she said, aware that the step was too high for her to reach. Lyle had made it plain he had no patience with her, just providing a box for her to climb up on in order to get into the back of the wagon and then find her way to the front. It seemed that Mr. Carson had more finely honed manners than Lyle, she thought as the man supported her, lifting her, his hands firm around her middle, then easing her onto the wagon seat.

"Thank you," she whispered, breathless as she arranged her skirts and settled herself. He was strong, there was no doubt about that, and mannerly to boot, his index finger lifting to touch his hat brim in a small salute.

She sat stiffly, barely able to focus her thoughts, yet aware of the men who sorted out their families, the miners who lined up the wagons, and the womenfolk who cast her looks of sympathy as they gathered their children up and hastened to ready themselves for departure.

The shot had come out of nowhere, it seemed, felling Lyle as if lightning had struck and taken his life in a single instant. He'd turned halfway toward her from his position near the oxen, and the light in his eyes had gone out as though a puff of air had extinguished a candle. He'd fallen and, in moments, had been lying in a pool of blood that spread beneath him like a scarlet cape.

Three men had ridden out, intent on seeking the gunman, and had come back empty-handed an hour later, shrugging helplessly as they stood before her, hats in hand, sweaty and weary from their efforts.

Now she watched dully as the oxen leaned forward and the wagon was set into motion, Finn Carson walking to the right of her team. He glanced back at her, his blue eyes darkening with concern as she lifted her hand in acknowledgment of his unspoken message. And then she relaxed on the seat, knowing that the jouncing of the wagon was easier to survive if she rolled with the rocking motion.

Finn walked at a steady pace, conscious of the woman atop the wagon seat behind him. As he'd been aware of her daily ever since the wagon train had left Independence long weeks ago. He'd dreamed of her, had imagined touching her dark hair, had envisioned holding her in his arms. Since the day in Saint Louis when he'd first seen her, she'd stuck in his mind like a burr beneath his saddle. And though his good sense had bade him forget the woman existed, he'd hoarded the vision of her wide-set eyes, her gleaming hair, and the memory of her gentle profile as she walked the trail.

She was married. He'd repeated the words over and over, even as he'd chafed when Lyle Beaumont treated her uncaringly, when the man had ignored her needs and been unkind in a hundred ways. Finn's stride was long, his mind working in time with the pace set by the oxen who plodded beside him.

Jessica Beaumont was a widow, available…and in dire need of a man to take care of her. Tonight, after they set up camp, when the wagons were circled and fires lit, he'd go to Jonas and speak his mind. And if the unwritten laws of the wagon train were to be observed, Jessica would accept a husband from among the available men in the group, or be sent back to civilization at the first opportunity.

She'd not been treated so well since Saint Louis, Jessica thought. Never had Lyle lifted her from the wagon, carried firewood or asked after her well-being while she cooked the evening meal. Now Finn watched her from beside the wagon, his gaze intent on her as she bent over the campfire and rescued her kettle from the flames. She stirred the rabbit stew once and her stomach rebelled as the rich scent rose on a cloud of steam.

"If you're ready to eat, I'll dish you up a serving," she said quietly, turning to face him. He stood upright from where he'd leaned against her wagon and stepped closer, taking the kettle from her, gripping it firmly over her protests.

"I'm not used to being waited on," she said. "I don't mind—"

"But I do," he returned curtly, cutting off her objections to his lending a hand. "You've had a rough day, Mrs. Beaumont. I'm here to look after you this evening. Jonas gave me leave to skip my duties for a day or so until we get you some help lined up."

"I can take care of myself," she told him, lifting her chin in defiance of his words. "I watched Lyle tend the oxen for the past weeks. I'm sure I can learn well enough how to stake them out at night and get rolling in the mornings."

"I'm sure you can," Finn said agreeably. "But it isn't necessary. Not while I'm here, anyway." And making himself indispensable to her was the name of the game, he'd decided during the last four miles they'd traveled today. Jonas had agreed—halfheartedly to be sure—but had finally given a curt nod in response to Finn's suggestion.

"You got any more of that stuff?" Jonas asked, as if in answer to Finn's thoughts. He squatted beside his guide and looked up at Jessica. "How you doin', Mrs. Beaumont?" he asked.

"I'm all right," Jessica told him. "I'll fix you a bowl right away, Mr. McMasters."

"You need to eat, too," Finn reminded her quietly.

She only nodded as she dug through the small keg in which she kept her dishes and silverware, seeking out a bowl for Jonas. Filling it to the brim, she offered it to him, handed him a spoon, then returned to dish out a portion for herself.

"I know I have to eat," she said, her gaze meeting Finn's. With care, she lowered herself to sit on the ground, her skirts surrounding her, her legs tucked up beneath her, and felt herself the focus of those who watched from various campfires around the circle. And then she poked at the savory stew, forcing herself to lift a spoonful to her mouth.

"Ma'am?" Jonas's voice caught her attention and she looked in his direction.

"I know this ain't a good time to be talkin' to you about this, but there ain't gonna be any better time, so far as I can see, in the next couple of weeks," he said glumly. "The hard fact is that a woman alone can't travel with the train, Mrs. Beaumont. You're gonna have to either find a husband or leave the train when we reach Council Grove. And that's less than two weeks from now."

"I'm not leaving the train," she said firmly, her jaw set, as if that alone would convince him of her intent. "My husband has—had, I mean—a deed to property near Pike's Peak, and that's where I'm going. It belongs to me now." Her hand rested in an automatic gesture against the rounding of her belly as she spoke. "It's all I have, Mr. Mc-Masters, and I'm not walking away from it."

"Well, it'll take a man to work the land and build a place for you to live," he told her bluntly. "A woman alone can't handle something like that."

"There's a cabin there, according to what Lyle heard of the place. Not much, but enough for shelter. And he said there was a chance that gold could be found there." She lowered her voice, lest the words carry to the adjacent campfire. Gold was a powerful incentive, its presence inciting men to lie and steal. Even to murder.

Lyle's life's blood had been shed today, and unless she missed her guess, the claim to land in Colorado had something to do with it. Lyle had bragged one night, after he'd consumed half a bottle of whiskey, telling her of gold to be found, and then left bruises as he threatened her lest she repeat his words to anyone.

Now the land was hers, and sharing it with a man was not her first choice.

"Ma'am, you'll have to be thinking about accepting one of the available men on the train as your husband," Jonas said, his dark eyes holding not a shred of doubt as to his ultimatum. "It's just the way it is, ma'am. I'll give you till we get to Council Grove to make a choice."

He looked around the circle to where more than a dozen men watched the drama going on, with Jessica as its focus. "You won't have any lack of suitors," he said with a grimace. "There's already talk about who you'll pick." He grinned briefly, shaking his head. "There's never enough women to go around in the West, and these men are already plottin' to come courtin' you."

Jessica glanced at him, then shot a look at Finn. He returned it with a nod. "Jonas is right, you know," he said. "Any one of those men—" He tilted his head, lifting an eyebrow for emphasis as he spoke. "Any one of them would be on you like flies on honey if you give them a nod. You're a good-looking woman, and you've got a wagon and a team of oxen, and, as you said yourself, your husband had a deed to a piece of property."

He smiled, looking into the depths of the fire for a moment. "You're going to be in demand, Mrs. Beaumont. I'm not the only bachelor who'll be coming to call. And, as harsh as it sounds to a woman newly widowed, you're going to have to make up your mind in a hurry."

Jessica nodded, aware that the truth was staring her in the face, and the man delivering the message was no doubt presenting himself as one of those offering for her hand.

"I expect you're right, Mr. Carson. But not tonight, please. I can't think straight right now, and by the time I get my supper mess cleared up, I won't be fit company for anyone.'' If Finn Carson meant to make her an offer, he'd have to wait until her head was clear and she was able to consider all of her options.

An hour later she was settled atop her feather tick on the wagon floor, her mind racing with the events of the day. And for the first time, tears came to her eyes. Not grief at Lyle's death, although she supposed she should feel some small amount of remorse, at least, at leaving him by the side of the trail in a poorly marked grave.

But the past years had hardened her heart to his cunning smiles, and she'd long since lost any love she'd ever harbored in her heart for the man. He'd been mean. There was no other word for it. The man had been uncaring at times, harsh when she didn't oblige him to his specifications, and too handy with hands that hurt and bruised her on occasion.

No, she didn't mourn him, only the loss of those long years she'd spent trying to hold together a marriage that was doomed from the beginning. Her father had been right. Lyle Beaumont was a taker, a man without scruples. And Jessica had been blind to that side of him…until it was too late.

She curled on her side beneath a quilt, and a succession of faces appeared behind her closed eyelids. Miners, both young and in their middle years, at least half a dozen that she knew of, who had offered their condolences today as they eyed her with narrowed gazes, as if they considered her ripe for the taking.

She shivered. There were only two unattached men on the train she would even consider if push came to shove and she was forced by circumstances to choose a husband. Finn Carson, one of the guides, was one of them. The other, a miner named Gage Morgan, was a tall, husky man, older than Finn by few years. He was quiet, a good-looking specimen with dark hair and smoky-gray eyes. He'd offered his hand and had engulfed her own in his palm, just for a moment as he passed by the open grave this afternoon.

"Ma'am," he'd said quietly, and his piercing eyes had darkened, taking her measure, a hint of admiration in their depths as he offered silent condolences. On the surface, he was all that a woman could ask for, she thought, and wondered what there was about him that made her stomach clench. Not that he had offered any disrespect. Never had he been anything but courteous the few times she'd nodded in his direction during the weeks they'd been following the trail.

Now she wondered at him, her fists clenching as she thought of what it would mean, should she take either of those two men as her husband. Eventually they would want to claim their rights, and she would be obliged to comply.

Shivering, she pushed aside the memories of nights filled with fear. Sleepless hours when she dreaded Lyle's homecoming, those times when he was out at a saloon or gambling at a poker table.

Taking a man into her bed was a daunting prospect. Offering her body before the baby was born was out of the question. She was misshapen, her body swollen with the babe she carried. Not that she cared—in fact, she gloried in the heavy weight of the child within her. But to a man, especially one who'd had his share of voluptuous women, she might be more than a bit off-putting. But then, most of these men were hungry for female companionship, and that fact alone would probably make her more appealing to them.

She smothered a giggle under the quilt, and then felt a stab of shame that she could lie in her bed less than a dozen hours since Lyle's body had turned cold in death and laugh at the prospect of another man climbing into her wagon and taking his place at her side. She needn't fear turning a man's head, she decided, punching her pillow as she tucked it beneath her head.

The deed to land near Pike's Peak was another matter. It was enough to lure any man into her clutches, given the steady stream of miners heading west, hoping to find just such a claim to work. If Lyle was right, if the land were indeed worth—

She sat upright. If the deed was worth what Lyle had claimed, perhaps someone had killed him in order to lay hands on it. Shivering, she pulled the quilt up around herself and leaned against a trunk. Someone might be, this very moment, planning on finding the deed.

And she didn't even know herself where it was. Only that Lyle had hidden it and laughed when she'd asked its location. *"You don't need to know,"* he'd said harshly.

"Mrs. Beaumont? Jessica?" The voice was low, its tones pitched so as not to carry beyond her hearing, and she caught her breath sharply as she saw the shadow of a man standing at the back of her wagon. Standing head and shoulders above most of the men on the train, he was easy enough to recognize. Finn Carson, himself, come to call. She drew the quilt closer about her shoulders and felt the beating of her heart like a bass drum in her ears.

"Yes, Mr. Carson," she answered, her whisper carrying to where he stood.

"Are you all right, ma'am?" he asked. "I'm going to crawl under your wagon to sleep tonight, and I wanted to know if you need anything before I settle down."

"Are you by chance staking a claim, Mr. Carson?" she wanted to know, aware that her voice held a brittle note. He might as well put up a sign, she thought. *This woman taken.*

And then his words verified her thoughts, and she heard amusement color the syllables. "You might say that, ma'am." He was unmoving and she shifted, rising to her knees, the better to catch the expression on his face.

"I hope you know that Jonas wasn't pulling your leg, Mrs. Beaumont," Finn said. "You don't have a choice. Either you marry one of us, or you get sent back East when we reach Council Grove.'' He stood without moving, as if he awaited a reply, and then he held out a hand to her.

"Will you come over here and talk to me?"

"No." She didn't believe in mincing words, could not countenance a clandestine meeting on the very day she'd buried her husband, and her cheeks burned with embarrassment as she wondered that he would expect it of her.

"Will you take a word of advice, then?" he asked quietly.

"Talk to me tomorrow," she said sharply. "I'm a newly widowed woman, Mr. Carson. At least give me tonight to mourn before you make your bid for me."

He was silent for a moment, and then he propped his forearms on the side of the wagon and leaned forward a bit. "I saw you in Saint Louis, *Jessica.*" As though he owned the right to it, he used her name deliberately. "I watched the way the bastard treated you that day when the first wagons loaded up and pulled out toward Independence. You can't know how badly I wanted to knock him flat on his back."

"You saw me? In Saint Louis?" She was stunned by his words, not that he'd seen her, but that his reaction to Lyle's behaviour had been so strong. "Why should you care about the way Lyle treated me?"

"I've watched your wagon, him especially, for the past weeks, ever since we left Independence, and he did nothing to impress me with his...his ability to perform as a man." He chose his words carefully, and Jessica heard the bitter tinge they carried.

"Who are you?" she asked, whispering the words as a shiver of apprehension swept over her. "Have you been keeping an eye on me all along?"

"No." It was one syllable, one word, muttered harshly, and she knew it for a lie.

"Good night, Mr. Carson," she said, drawing the quilt over her shoulder again as she placed her head carefully on her pillow. She heard him move after a moment, heard the muffled rattle of a metal bucket beneath the wagon as he found his place on the ground. And knew that Finn Carson was a man to be reckoned with.

He'd botched it. He'd pushed her too hard, said too much. He'd backtrack, let her stew a bit and then choose his time. The ground was hard beneath him, but Finn was used to sleeping wherever darkness found him. He'd shared feather ticks in his time, slept on cotton mattresses more times than he could count, and spent more nights under the stars than he could shake a stick at.

Sleeping beneath Jessica's wagon was, after all, akin to staking a claim, as the lady herself had said. And somewhere in that wagon was the deed to a claim that Aaron Carson had died for. Finn's mouth flattened as he thought of his older brother.

Aaron's mercantile had held the man captive as surely as if it had wrapped chains around him for almost ten years. He'd been tied to making a living, when his heart had yearned for adventure, and his feet had itched to travel toward the goldfields. Aaron's letter to Finn in April had been filled to the edges of each page with his excitement.

A customer, a man Aaron had outfitted and sent on his way four years before, was dying and had sent the deed to his claim back to Saint Louis, addressed to Aaron, the storekeeper, with a description of the location of Carson's Retail Establishment.

Becuz you give me a hand when I needed it, the letter had said. *Now I'm dying and here's yer payback.* The miner had signed it with a shaky hand, and sent the letter, the deed, and the assayer's report with it to Saint Louis. Aaron's life had changed forever.

It was a rich claim, according to the assayer's report that had been included in the envelope, and the deed had been proclaimed valid by a lawyer. Aaron's soul had thrilled to the news. He'd written to Finn, inviting his brother to join in the trek to the goldfields, offering to share the gold they would mine together.

And then he had been killed for a piece of paper, one that promised riches beyond belief. Standing by Aaron's grave, Finn had sworn to avenge his death and set off to find Lyle Beaumont, the man he'd been told was the thief and murderer who'd pulled the trigger and stolen the deed.

Only to find that Lyle Beaumont had something infinitely more precious than the deed to a piece of land.

A woman—a heavily pregnant, defenseless female named Jessica Beaumont. A woman who had, from the first, touched a chord in Finn's heart. A woman who even now held the deed he'd vowed to regain.

He would have them—Jessica Beaumont *and* the deed to the piece of land Aaron had died for. No matter the price, Finn would possess both.

The woman didn't stand a chance.

Chapter Two

"Good morning, Mrs. Beaumont." Jessica knew without looking from the back of the wagon that her visitor was Gage Morgan. His voice was distinctive, deep, and with a touch of the South in each syllable. Hastily she fastened the remaining buttons on her dress and snatched up her brush, bending as she reached the opening where he stood.

"I'm not ready for company this morning," she said quietly, looking out on the circle of wagons, and then to the man who watched her. Close enough to see within, yet far enough distant to appear discreet to the passersby, he smiled as she glanced in his direction.

"Can I help you from your wagon?" he asked, extending a hand as she considered the ungainly chore of climbing over the rear opening.

It was too good an offer to pass up, she decided, having found over the past couple of weeks that her balance was decidedly off center. His palm was broad, his hands callused and strong, and he gripped her firmly, long fingers at her elbows as she carefully climbed to the ground.

"Thank you, Mr. Morgan," she murmured, feeling at a distinct disadvantage, off balance with the added weight of the baby and her hair disheveled from a restless night's sleep. Her face was still unwashed, and it was embarrassing to have a stranger see her without the benefit of time alone to put herself together for the day. On top of that, she felt other eyes watching her, probably making her the topic of gossip over every campfire.

"My pleasure, ma'am," Gage said, smiling lazily, his gaze fastened on her as she wobbled a bit, unwillingly thankful for his steadying hands, hands that caressed her arms lightly before he released his grip. "I brought you warm water from the campfire by our wagon," he said. "I thought it might be welcome."

And it was, she realized. Yet, there was a degree of hesitance as she nodded her thanks, and the obligation she felt to the man made her uneasy. If Finn had done the good deed, she'd have no doubt welcomed his help. But coming from Gage Morgan, it didn't sit well, and she had to force the smile he no doubt expected.

"I'll leave you to it, ma'am," Morgan said, tipping his hat, his gaze narrowing as his eyes took a survey of her face and form. "If there's anything at all I can do for you, just give me a wave and I'll be here. I hope you realize you can depend on me to lend a hand when you need it."

"Thank you, Mr. Morgan." Turning from him, she reached inside the wagon and found the towel she'd left on a box, handy for her morning ablutions. When she looked back to where he'd placed the bucket of water, she found he'd filled the basin for her use, and she felt her mouth tighten. It smacked of intimacy, tending to her needs this way, and she felt he'd ventured too close for comfort.

But the water was warm, refreshing against her skin and she used it lavishly, appreciating the luxury of the early-morning wash without having to first light a fire. Her hair required daily brushing before she braided it, and it didn't seem she would have the time available this morning to perform the task. A quick swipe of the brush through the dark waves would suffice, she decided, as she reached for her sunbonnet.

More than one man spoke as she made her way to a
secluded area that had been set aside for the women's use
last evening, and assessing eyes took note of her, much to
her discomfort. It seemed that marriage had, before today,
provided a barrier, protecting her from the attentions of
other men, and now that Lyle was no longer in the picture,
she was open game for the available men on the train. Jonas
had warned her it would be so, but the reality was almost
overwhelming.

In a few minutes, she returned to her wagon and found
Finn there, tending a small blaze, her skillet in his hand,
bacon waiting on its surface for the burning wood to heat
sufficiently. He glanced up at her and grinned. His hair
looked like morning sunshine, she thought, and his eyes
were warm. It was unfair to compare men, one to another.
It was like apples and oranges, her mother had always said.
Yet, the difference between Finn and the darkly handsome
Morgan was a night-and-day variation.

Finn watched her, his good mood apparent, and she
found herself returning his smile as he welcomed her back
to her own campfire. "Good morning," he said with a hint
of teasing edging the greeting. "I didn't mean to neglect
you this morning, but I had to leave early on, just before
sunrise. Jonas asked me to ride out and take a gander at
the trail up ahead. I'm sorry I wasn't here to lend a hand,
but I promise you I'll have a real treat in store for you
tonight when we circle the wagons."

"A treat?" she asked, and he shook his head.

"I'll say no more till tonight," he said.

The man was clean shaven this morning, his clothing
neat, his hair showing the line where his hat had perched
as he rode. An altogether presentable appearance, one she
could envision taking pleasure in viewing in the days to
come. And with an indrawn breath, she recognized that she
was very near to making her choice, no matter the suit-
ability of Gage Morgan.

"I missed you earlier," she said in answer to his apology. "I was about to set a match to my fire and fix some breakfast."

"I beat you to it, and saved you a bit of time," he told her. "Now, I expect some food for my trouble. But I'll bet you've already figured that out."

He was crowding her, and she recognized his methods, knew he meant to gain a foothold, but she was onto his shenanigans. Her smile came easily as she nodded, waving a hand at the skillet he held. "I'll do that. Give me a few minutes and I'll mix together some biscuits and get them baking in the coals, then I'll tend to the bacon."

Turning back to the opening, she lifted the wooden box, settling it in place so that she could climb into the wagon bed, only to find him at her side. "Here, you take this," he said, giving her no choice as he pressed the skillet into her hands. "I'll climb up and get you a measure of flour from your barrel."

Flustered, she took the iron pan and then watched as he made short work of what would have taken considerable time and effort on her part. In moments, he had the bowl of flour handed out to her, and she took it in her free hand and placed it on a precious chunk of wood by the fire. The lard can and her jars of salt and soda clutched to his chest, he climbed down and placed the bits and pieces next to the bowl of flour.

"All right. I'll switch with you," he said cheerfully, spreading the coals a bit as the wood burned down to permit the skillet's placement atop the heat. "We're going to have to resort to buffalo chips soon," he said. "There won't be much more wood available until we reach Council Grove."

Jessica nodded. "I thought I might gather some during the day and fill a burlap sack full while I'm walking by the oxen."

"Probably be a good idea," Finn agreed, placing the bacon to fry atop the coals.

With deft movements, Jessica mixed lard into the flour, added salt and soda and then formed the biscuits while Finn turned the bacon as it cooked. The shallow stone she used for baking was already hot beneath the coals and Finn poked it from the fire, then wiped it clean with swift movements, readying it for her use.

The biscuits sizzled in a bit of lard and within ten minutes the small, flat bits of bread were ready to eat. "These don't look like what I made back home in Saint Louis," she said, placing bacon between two layers of the makeshift bread. "But they don't taste half bad when you're hungry."

"It's enough to keep us going till nooning," Finn told her as he gingerly lifted two more from the stone, tossing them from hand to hand to cool them down. She smiled at his antics, aware that his actions were designed to amuse her. Hers were not the only eyes focused on Finn, but he seemed oblivious to the frankly envious looks from several men aimed in his direction.

And then he settled down to finish his breakfast and sat cross-legged on the ground, his gaze assessing Jessica, lingering on her face as if he gauged her well-being by the color of her skin, the circles she knew lingered beneath her eyes.

"Thank you for sleeping under my wagon last night," she said as she brushed the crumbs from her fingers. "I know I was less than gracious to you, and I apologize."

"When I consider the day you lived through, I'm surprised you didn't reach out and toss me on my—" He grinned suddenly. "Sorry. I forgot myself for a moment there."

He was a scamp, she decided, his eyes twinkling, his mouth curving in a smile. And she was responding to him as might a young girl faced by her first suitor, enjoying the company he offered. Companionship she'd lacked with Lyle. She looked down at her hands, clenching her fingers in her lap, and felt a moment's shame that she should so quickly set aside the memory of her marriage.

But Lyle was gone and buried, she thought, gritting her teeth. Still, she supposed she should feel some small bit of remorse, perhaps even grief at his passing. Yet, when all was said and done, she could only be relieved that he was no longer here to berate her and make her life miserable. Her sigh was audible as she faced her own lack of caring for the man she'd married.

"What is it, Jessica?" Finn rose from the ground and moved toward her, then crouched, one knee on the ground, his big frame dwarfing her. "You look like a shadow just passed over and left you in the shade."

"I suspect I'm feeling guilty," she murmured, unable to look up at him. "Lyle's been dead less than a full day, and I can't find it in me to regret his death." Her voice caught on the words and she felt the warmth of a tear as it slid the length of her cheek to fall against her breast.

"Jessica." Finn spoke her name, almost as a sigh, and she lifted a hand, as if she rejected his comfort. "Surely you don't have regrets," he said quietly. "The man was not worthy of you. Everyone in the wagon train recognized that as the truth. He didn't have a friend among the family men, only a handful of lowlifes who liked to gamble as much as he did. And the whole bunch of them aren't worth the powder it would take to blow them away."

Jessica nodded, aware that his assessment of Lyle and his cronies was on target. "He used to get angry with me," she began quietly, "when he'd been playing poker late at night and then was too tired to get up in the morning. He said I should take my turn and walk by the ox team and let him sleep in the wagon." She looked up as she spoke, as if she sought comfort in the gentle smile Finn offered. His features were blurred by her tears, and she brushed them away with her palms.

Finn's mouth tightened as he watched her futile gesture,

for the tears would not be halted now that they had begun. "Don't cry for him," he said harshly. "He wasn't worth your tears, Jess."

"I suppose that's why it saddens me so," she said haltingly. "I loved him once—or at least I thought I did. When he came courting, he was a gentleman, mannerly and polite. It wasn't until we were married for a few months that he began drinking more. I suppose he'd hidden his vices well, early on."

"Why on earth did he marry you?" Finn asked bluntly. "He didn't seem cut out to be a family man to my way of thinking. Surely he didn't have an overwhelming love for you. At least it didn't seem so."

She shrugged. "He thought he would be well-fixed. My parents have a bit of money. We always lived nicely, and my father had his own business. I think Lyle had visions of coming into an inheritance one day. My parents had me very late in life, and I was their only child. He thought they'd support all of his schemes. And if that didn't work, he figured he'd inherit a nice amount when they passed on."

"And then it didn't work out the way he thought it would, I expect."

She shook her head. "No, it didn't. My father gave him a job, and Lyle stole from the company." She felt the blush of shame sweep over her countenance. "He was let go, and then no one else would hire him when it became known that he wasn't trustworthy. My folks wanted me to leave him and come back home."

"But you didn't." Finn's words were touched with anger, and she watched as his hands formed fists and his eyes narrowed with the force of his emotion.

"No, I couldn't." She looked up at him, remembering the day she'd made that foolish choice. "I couldn't admit I'd been wrong to marry him. But I changed my mind later, after I found I was carrying a child. Then, one day—"

Her words came to a halt as she remembered the day when Lyle had struck her down and she'd fallen the full flight of stairs in the boardinghouse where they lived.

"What happened?" Finn asked, rising to stand before her.

She looked up at him. "There was an accident and I lost my child. She was born too early and didn't live."

"And Lyle? Did he feel any remorse?" His jaw taut, Finn looked away, as if unwilling to allow Jessica to see the depths of his disgust with the man.

"No. He refused to pay the midwife who came. He said it was her fault the baby died and he didn't owe her one red cent. Then we moved away from there and I began to work for our keep in a boardinghouse. It gave us a roof over our heads, and so long as I could cook and clean, we had a place to live."

"How long were you married to him?" Finn asked.

"Four years. Four long, miserable years." She bit her lips, remembering the past months. "I thought when he brought home the deed that night, things would be different. He said we'd go to Colorado, farm the land, and he'd look for gold. The papers that came with the deed said there was a rich vein there. It was probably the first time he'd ever won such an amount in a poker game."

"So you joined a wagon train and headed out from Saint Louis." Finn's voice took on a lower, gruffer note, and Jessica looked up at him.

"It didn't take Lyle long to make that decision," she said. "We must have been leaving the day you said you saw me, that first time. That was two months ago." Her mind searched out the memory of that day. "I don't remember you being there, but then, things were hectic, and Lyle was late getting our things packed up."

"Yeah, he was busy." Finn's voice imbued the word with a harshness she hadn't expected. "He tossed you on top of the wagon seat like you were a sack of oats."

Jessica's gaze searched his face, bewildered by the anger that tightened his jaw as he spoke. Surely he had no reason to hold such a grudge against Lyle, no matter how poorly he'd behaved. He hadn't even known the man.

"It's all in the past, anyway," she said, rising and brushing down her skirts. "I survived, Mr. Carson. I'm tougher than you think." She looked to where Jonas was walking inside the circle of wagons. "It looks like Mr. McMasters is getting ready to roll. I'll have to go and sort out my team."

"No, Jessica. You'll do no such thing," Finn told her. "Just put your dishes away and scrub out your skillet. I'll have your team here and hitched to your wagon in fifteen minutes." He stalked away, and Jessica was left to watch his long legs cover the ground to where the animals were staked within an enclosure.

As she watched, Gage approached the herded beasts from another direction, and he and Finn came face-to-face, obviously having words in the midst of the docile oxen. Finley Carson was not a man to cross swords with this morning, she thought as Gage cast a look in her direction, tipped his hat in a gesture of greeting and walked back to the wagon where his partners waited. The other men were already hitching up their team and Gage turned aside, tossing odds and ends of their gear inside the wagon.

Finn led Jessica's animals toward her, his eyes seeking her out. Time was fleeting while she stood gawking, she thought, and with practiced movements, she washed out her skillet and scrubbed off her baking stone. Within ten minutes she was ready for the day, and at Finn's bidding she climbed into the back of the wagon, reaching to take the wooden box inside for storage until they halted once more.

"You forgot your hairbrush," he said from behind her, and she turned to see him in the rear opening, handing in the bone-handled utensil. "I'll have to speak my mind, I think," he said with a smile. "I like your hair that way, hanging loose down your back. It makes you look about sixteen years old."

"I'm not sixteen," she told him tartly. "I feel like an old woman already at twenty-four, and this morning every single year is weighing me down." As if to refute his remark, she gathered her hair across her shoulder and separated it into three thick strands, her fingers industrious as she formed the accustomed plait she wore.

"Don't scowl," he said with a grin. "I'd think you'd be feeling pretty special, Jess," he told her, the teasing note returning to his voice. "There's a whole flock of menfolk circling you like wolves after a pretty little red deer. You'll have your pick," he reminded her.

"I'm not in any hurry. I have two weeks to make up my mind," she retorted, and noted his satisfied smile as he turned away. The fact that at least two men were actively seeking her favor should have made her feel a bit more secure, she supposed. But instead, she knew an uneasy sensation that blighted her day.

Gage Morgan was a handsome man, and if she hadn't already been approached by Finn, he might have been able to win her over, to a point where she'd consider him more seriously. As it was, Finn was crowding her, intent on cutting out the competition, and though it made her feel womanly and worthy of attention, she didn't like it—not one little bit. For the first time in her life, she savored the feeling of making her own choices, of pondering her future and charting her course. Independence was an exhilarating thing, she decided.

After the stop for noontime, when the women brought forth cold food left from breakfast or the night before, Jessica offered Finn what was left of the rabbit stew. He forked through the bits of meat and placed several on a biscuit, then topped it with another and ate the makeshift meal while he stood beside the wagon.

"I'm sorry there wasn't more," she said. "Maybe Arlois Bates has leftovers to spare. Want me to ask her?" As a scout, Finn was welcomed at almost every campsite, and offered food from various kettles each night. He carried supplies in Jonas's wagon, but rarely needed to set up a fire of his own.

"I'm fine," Finn assured her. "I have to ride out for a while. If I see any game, I'll bring you back something for supper. Will you mind pacing the oxen for a couple of hours?"

She shook her head quickly. "No, that's fine. If you'll get my burlap bag I'll keep an eye out for chips for the fire tonight. I need to walk for a while anyway," she told him, sliding over the back of the seat into the wagon bed. He was at the rear when she made her way through the piles of boxes and bits of furniture stacked on either side of the floor, and reached in to lift her from the canvas shelter with a total lack of ceremony. He reached back inside for the burlap sack she'd left handy.

"Here you go," he said, and then hesitated as she grasped the heavy burlap. "I hate you having to gather buffalo chips," he said.

"I'm healthy and able," she told him. "I'm just lucky not to have run out of wood before this. All the other women do their share, and I'm no different."

"That's where we're going to disagree," Finn said. "You are different. In the first place, you're going to have a baby."

"All women have babies," Jessica told him. "I knew when I started out from Saint Louis that this wasn't going to be an easy trip. I'm not afraid of work, and I can certainly do my share, whether it's picking up buffalo chips or cooking or walking with the team. As a matter of fact, the responsibility is mine—all of it."

"Not anymore it isn't," Finn said gruffly. "You're going to have a man to take care of you, Jessica. I'm planning on it being me."

"I thought I had a choice in this," she said smartly. "Gage Morgan is interested in me. And I've had several other of the men looking my way."

"And you wouldn't take on any of them," Finn told her. "Maybe Morgan, in a pinch. But I'd rather you didn't consider him, either." His jaw was taut and his eyes blazed with an icy fire. "I want to marry you, Jessica. It isn't a spur-of-the-moment thing with me. I've been committing the sin of looking at a married woman with desire in my heart for the past—"

"Stop it, Finn Carson," she said, cutting his declaration short. "I don't want to hear this. It makes me feel like you've been waiting for something to happen to Lyle so you could come courting me."

"No, I didn't wish him dead," Finn told her firmly. "But I sure as hell wished he wasn't your husband. The man didn't deserve you, Jessica."

She snatched at the burlap bag and stalked away, heading for the team, the pair of them standing with their heads down waiting for the signal to leave. Finn's admission was honest, she'd give him that. And he was right—it was a sin to be looking at another man's wife. Look what that sort of shenanigans got poor King David in the Bible.

Jessica laughed beneath her breath. She was no Bathsheba, that was for sure. But she'd be willing to bet that an offer from Finn Carson was as good as she'd ever come by in this lifetime. The man was prime. Golden hair that tempted her fingers to measure its silky length, and blue eyes that touched her with tenderness.

"Can I walk with you?" Arlois approached, her own bag in hand, and Jessica smiled a welcome.

"It looks like we've been given the job of gathering up

tonight's fuel for the fires," she said, holding her own bag at arm's length.

Arlois wrinkled her nose. "I'd think firewood would be the better choice," she said. "I told David that handling buffalo dung was not my idea of fun, and he told me he'd give me fun after dark tonight."

Jessica laughed softly, a yearning for the sort of happiness Arlois shared with her David sweeping over her. She'd heard their murmurs as they walked outside the circle of wagons on occasion, had noted David's possessive gaze on his wife, had seen his hand reach for Arlois as they sat by the fire at night. They had two children, and yet there was a shine about them that made her think they still resembled newlyweds.

She'd had little of that sort of affection with Lyle. Maybe with Finn, she thought. And in her mind's eye she could envision his hand enclosing hers, imagine his body sheltering her from the wind.

"Jessica?" Arlois peered at her. "Did I upset you, talking that way about David? I wasn't thinking." Her cheeks blushed crimson, as if she regretted her impetuous remark. "I forgot for a minute about Lyle…about him being gone." She faltered and then leaned closer to hug Jessica.

"Do you miss him at all?" she asked. "I mean, I know he wasn't a very kind man, but he *was* your husband—and I'm just rattling on like an idiot, aren't I?"

Jessica stifled a laugh. "You're not an idiot," she said, admonishing Arlois. "And you're right about Lyle. He wasn't very kind to anyone, least of all me. We were married, but never close the way you are with David, or Geraldine is with Harvey."

Arlois squeezed her tightly for a second and then stepped back. "Well then, I won't apologize for being so blunt. I think you'd be better off with any one of the other bachelors than you were with Lyle." She grinned. "Although

I'm partial to Finn Carson, if the truth be known." And then her eyes widened and she groaned.

"Here comes another suitor, Jessica. And this one is scary. I'm not sure what there is about Mr. Morgan, but he's a little frightening if you ask me." She set out at a fast pace. "I'm going to do a roundabout for a while, see if I can fill my bag and make David happy." With a wave of her hand at the approaching horseman, she walked at an angle, joining several other women who were scanning the ground on either side of the train for fuel for tonight's supper fires.

"Mrs. Beaumont." Gage Morgan slid from his gelding and held the reins in one hand, then closed the gap until he walked apace with Jessica. "I thought I'd check on you and see if there's anything I can do to lend a hand." He gestured toward her bag. "I see you're going foraging this afternoon. Maybe I can bring you some wood from our stockpile instead," he offered.

"I doubt your partners would appreciate you sharing their supply," Jessica said. "I don't mind gathering chips."

He nodded, as if he accepted her refusal of his offer, and then took her arm. "I made you a walking stick," he said. "I hope you have use for it. I thought I'd ask first and then bring it by later if you like."

She looked down at his hand, and he grimaced and released her elbow, murmuring a soft apology. "I'm sorry if I offended you," he said nicely. "Perhaps I'll stop by the wagon and get the stick now. It will make it easier for you, I think."

"That's thoughtful of you," she said, unwilling to be rude, yet not wanting to be beholden to the man in any way. His gaze touched her again, dark and shuttered, as if he saw within her and could know her thoughts. His next words supported that theory, she decided.

"I wonder what there is about me that frightens you,"

he said quietly. "I don't think I've ever done anything to cause you alarm, have I?"

She shook her head. "No, of course not. I'm not easily frightened, Mr. Morgan."

"I'm sure," he said agreeably. "But nevertheless, I'd like to get to know you a little better, ma'am. But I don't want to be pushy or infringe on your grief."

Jessica met his gaze head-on. "I'm not grieving, Mr. Morgan. My marriage was not a happy one, as you have probably already guessed." Her shoulders lifted in a shrug as she continued. "I've decided that life must go on, no matter what."

"Then would my proposal to you be out of line?" he asked. "I'd like you to consider marrying me, ma'am. I know that Jonas McMasters has given you a choice of either marrying one of the single men of the group, or leaving the train in Council Grove and going back East."

"News travels fast, doesn't it?" She picked up her pace, feeling a flush paint her cheeks at his words. "I feel as if I'm up on an auction block, Mr. Morgan, and I'm not enjoying it one little bit."

"You're a good-looking woman," he said bluntly. "I'd be foolish if I didn't throw my hat in the ring. I won't be the only one trying to persuade you into a wedding ring."

"And you have a ring handy?" she asked, glancing at him skeptically.

"I'll come up with something," he told her. "If I have to buy one from one of the ladies on the train, I will."

"I doubt any of the married women would give up their wedding band for my sake," she said. "I wouldn't wear someone else's, anyway. I'd rather go without."

"That's all right with me," he said. "The ring isn't the important thing."

"I'll be very blunt with you, sir," she said after a moment. "I have two weeks to make up my mind. I've already had one offer, and I'm considering it carefully. I'll put your name in the hat and let you know my answer.''

''I can do more for you than Finn Carson,'' he said harshly.

''Really?'' She looked at him, saw the flash of anger he hid with lowered lashes and felt a shiver of awareness spin the length of her spine. She'd been wrong. There *was* an element of fear in her that responded to this man's presence. Relief flooded her as he turned aside and mounted his horse. The nod he tossed in her direction was quick and his horse spun from her, its rider obviously holding a tight rein.

She walked alone for several minutes and then heard Arlois's call as the other woman hastened to catch up. ''Wait for me, Jessica.''

With a look over her shoulder, Jessica stepped to one side, allowing her team to plod ahead, and Arlois joined her, breathless from her hasty jaunt. ''David is sending Joshua to walk by your team for a while,'' Arlois said. ''Let's climb inside and rest for a few minutes.''

Even as she announced her idea, Joshua, a cheerful youth of perhaps thirteen years, took Jessica's place by the lead ox. Arlois gripped Jessica's arm and together they paced the wagon for a few minutes, then climbed into the back as it lumbered over the rutted road. Weaving their way through the assorted barrels and boxes inside, they gained the front and shared the wide plank seat.

''Whew!'' With relief, Arlois untied her sunbonnet and lifted it from her hair. ''I'm about tired out. That sun is really beating down today.'' The breeze teased the few locks that had escaped her braid and they curled over her forehead, giving her a youthful look, Jessica thought. The woman had become a good friend over the past weeks, ever present when help was needed, offering an ear and reserving judgment.

Now she looked as though her curiosity was about to

burst the boundaries of good taste, and Jessica took pity on her. "No, I didn't accept the man's proposal," she said with a laugh. "Not that he wasn't persuasive. He even offered to buy a wedding ring for me from one of the ladies on the train."

"He didn't!" Arlois was caught between laughter and disgust, it seemed, and she made a face. "As if any decent woman would sell her wedding ring." She tilted her head to one side. "Not unless her children were starving, or some idiot offered an outrageous amount." Her laughter won out, and Jessica joined in.

"I needed that," she whispered, wiping her eyes as her giggles subsided. "The man is handsome and even a bit dashing, but pompous doesn't begin to describe him. He told me he could do more for me than Finn Carson, as if he were offering to buy my affections." She considered that idea. "I think he'd want more from me than I could offer," she said quietly, her humor retreating as she recalled the man's anger.

"How about the other bachelors?" Arlois asked in a teasing manner.

"Most of them are still wet behind the ears, as well you know," Jessica said, "and the rest haven't had a bath since we left Independence."

"Speaking of which," Arlois said, her voice rising as if she announced something of tremendous import. "We're going to be crossing a nice shallow creek in the morning, David said. Instead of dabbing around in a bucket, we'll be able to wash clothes and get ourselves clean all over while we're waiting to cross over. Maybe even by tonight, he said."

Jessica would warrant that the creek ahead of them was the surprise Finn had spoken of this morning. Just the thought of fresh, cool, running water made Jessica's heart beat faster. "That's the best news I've heard all day," she said, already plotting her strategy. "Maybe we can gather up all the ladies and go as a group."

"Not unless we have some menfolk to watch out for us," Arlois said sharply. "I wouldn't put it past those scruffy young miners to sneak up and take a peek if they got the chance. I doubt David would let me go without him tagging along." Her eyes lit with mischief. "Of course, he's liable to sneak a peek himself."

Jessica felt a tinge of envy as Arlois spoke of her good-looking husband. She'd never had such rapport with Lyle, but the prospect might be feasible with a man such a Finn. It was a prize to be considered in the gamble she was considering.

The thought of Gage Morgan's eyes on her naked body was enough to send goose bumps traveling the length of her frame. In fact, the idea of any man catching a glimpse of her swollen belly and oversize bosom was enough to make her shudder with dread.

Even Finn? The thought rattled her and she closed her eyes. She could almost imagine his warm gaze sliding over her, his callused palms curving beneath her breasts.

"Jessica?" Beside her, Arlois spoke her name and Jessica's eyelids flew open. "Are you all right? You looked so funny there for a minute. You're not having any pains, are you?"

Jessica shook her head and dredged up a smile. Not pain, she thought. But an aching void that would only be filled by the tender care and attention of a man—though not just any man would do. Her choice was as good as made.

Even though Gage would yet pursue her, Finn Carson had already won the race.

Chapter Three

The smaller of Jessica's black kettles was steaming, its contents a savory stew, thanks to a roebuck brought down by one of the miners earlier in the day. The deer had been slaughtered swiftly, the meat passed among the wagons, according to family size, and Jessica had received a small chunk of venison from a hind quarter.

Now it simmered over the fire, having been dredged in flour and browned in lard. Half of her hoarded stash of tiny wild onions, dug from the prairie a few days before, garnished it with an appetizing aroma, Jessica having offered part of the tasty vegetables to the contents of Arlois's stew pot.

Her small store of potatoes were wizened, but she'd washed three of them and added them, skin and all, to the kettle. Hopefully, the venison would be tender—and well it might—for the deer had been a spike horn. She spared only a moment's pity for the animal, that his days were cut short by rifle fire.

Months ago she'd have been aghast at the thought of watching an animal butchered, her cooking limited to meat bought at a butcher's shop. Things had changed, she thought, her spoon mixing a blend of flour, salt and soda. She added a bit of milk, a generous gift from Harv Littleman, whose dainty Jersey cow traveled behind the Littleman wagon every day.

With two little girls along, Harv had brought the animal, knowing full well that finding feed might be a problem. Thus far, the prairie had provided sufficient grass for the cow to produce her usual amount of creamy milk twice a day, and Geraldine had offered the excess in trade for other food to those families with children who had no such milk supply. Several others had their own cows along, with the understanding that should dire need arise, the animals could be slaughtered for food.

What a horrendous idea, Jessica thought, a shiver passing down her spine. Though what difference there was between a cow and the deer she was cooking was obscure, except that the cow was a treasured family possession.

"What are you building there?" Finn asked from behind her. "Whatever you're cooking, it sure smells like home." He squatted beside her and peered into the bowl she held. "Biscuits?" he asked.

"I'm going to spoon dumplings on top of the stew," Jessica answered. "I'll need the lid for my kettle from the wagon, if you don't mind sorting through the box for me."

"I can do that," he said cheerfully, rising to step up into the wagon bed, and then poked his head from the canvas cover. "Is this it?" He held a black lid in one hand, and eyed the kettle. "There are two of them, but this one looks like it'll fit."

Jessica rose from the stump she used as a seat and took it from Finn's hand. "Thanks, I appreciate your help."

"Not nearly as much as I'm going to appreciate that kettle of food," he told her. "*And,* not nearly as much as you're going to enjoy my surprise for you."

She slid a sidelong glance in his direction. "I'll warrant I know what it is. Arlois told me about the creek even before we got here." His mouth drooped, an expression she suspected he donned for her enjoyment, and she laughed softly. "You look like a little boy who's just been denied a candy stick in the general store."

Finn shook his head. "Women. Can't put anything over on them. Here I thought I'd spring something on you, and you're way ahead of me." He settled beside her, watching as she dropped spoonfuls of the biscuit mix onto the simmering stew. "Does this mean you're not going to let me finish out my plan?"

She scraped the final bit of dough into the pot and reached for the lid, clapping it in place. "You have a plan? If it involves filling my water barrel, I'm all for it."

"Well, that, too," he said teasingly. "I spoke to Harv Littleman and Dave Bates about taking our women to the stream to take baths tonight. Are you willing?"

"Depends," she said, hesitating as the picture of clear water and a bar of soap tempted her mightily. "Will it be seemly for me to go with you?"

"You ladies can't go alone," Finn said firmly. "We'll take you down to the stream and leave you there while we stand guard. I think there are several other women who want to go along. They'll join us, and maybe their husbands, too."

"Arlois said she feared the younger miners might try to sneak a peek at us."

Finn's mouth tightened and a stern look touched his features. "Not on your life, sweetheart. It will be as private as if you were in your bathtub in Saint Louis."

"What bathtub?" she asked wryly. "I didn't have one of my own after I left home to get married. It was one of the things I missed the most."

"You should have gone back to your folks' house a couple of times a week for a bath, then," he told her, then frowned as he noted her silence and the quick bowing of her head. "What is it, Jessica? What did I say?"

"My parents washed their hands of me when I married Lyle," she admitted. "Well, not actually right then, but later, when he'd stolen from my father's company.'' She looked up at Finn, hoping he would understand why she'd chosen Lyle over the mother and father who had loved her so.

''I'd promised to stay with him, for better or worse,'' she said finally.

''And it only got worse, didn't it?'' His mouth had lost all traces of his usual good humor during their exchange and his eyes seemed to lose the sparkle she was wont to see in their depths. His hands touched hers and the bowl she held was lowered to sit on the ground at her feet, leaving her fingers free to twine with his.

''I've tried, especially on this trip, not to let others know how bad it was,'' she said with a sigh.

''Most of those who traveled nearby your wagon knew you were being abused during the last weeks,'' Finn told her, and she swallowed a protest. As though he read her mind, he nodded, a firm movement of his head. ''There was no hiding the way he spoke to you, Jessica. And more than once you wore bruises.

''It was all I could do not to shoot him myself,'' he admitted. ''Jonas told me to stay out of it, that if you wanted help, then it would be time enough to interfere.''

''Lyle was difficult,'' she said, looking down to where Finn clasped her hands in a grip so firm she thought she might never be turned loose from his hold. ''You can let go of me,'' she told him. ''I'm not going anywhere.''

''Not without me, anyway,'' he said fervently. ''From now on you'll be mine to protect, Jess.''

''I haven't said—''

''Look at me,'' he said, cutting off her words with a wave of his hand. And then as if he saw something in her expression that made him hesitate, he only smiled. ''Later on,'' he said quietly. ''We'll talk after a while, when we've eaten and taken care of the bath detail down at the stream.''

She nodded, willing to set aside their discussion. Pewter

bowls from the keg made an appearance within moments, and Jessica lifted the lid from the kettle a bit, peeping beneath to check on the dumplings. "I think they're almost done," she told him.

"I'll wash up," he said, reaching for the basin that hung on a hook beneath her wagon. "There's fresh water on the water wagon, Jess. I'll pour some in your barrel."

She nodded, shooting him a smile of thanks. "All right. I'm beginning to run low."

"We'll fill all the barrels in the morning. Jonas said there'll be time for the ladies to do their washing before we head out again and cross the stream. We'll go upstream and make sure we dip clean water while the women get lines strung and scrub their clothes. We may be here for another full day."

She sighed in anticipation of a day spent doing the small bits and pieces of household chores that would allow her to stay in one place, and then volunteered a bit of help in his direction.

"You're doing so much for me, Finn. Let me do your washing tomorrow, why don't you?" she offered. "It's the least I can do in return for your hard work on my behalf." He considered her for a moment, then nodded agreement before he turned away.

Her gaze remained on him as he headed for the water wagon, heard the murmur of his voice as he spoke to someone while he poured water from a bucket into her basin, and then watched as he returned. The man moved with a natural grace, she thought, his stride long, his shoulders wide, and his body lean and honed.

For so long a time she'd made certain not to look at another man, lest she set Lyle into a temper tantrum. It was no wonder she'd paid no attention to Finn during the early weeks of the trip west. Her instincts were for self-preservation, and one glance from her eyes toward anyone wearing trousers was all the excuse Lyle would have needed to punish her for her lapse.

Now, she thought with a sense of freedom, she could look at Finn Carson all she pleased. And it did please her, she admitted to herself. She had the right to pick and choose who she would speak with, the privilege of walking beside another woman, passing the time of day, should that be her inclination.

She turned back to the fire and lifted the lid of the kettle with a folded towel, setting it aside with care, lest she burn herself. Her large serving spoon held a dumpling and overflowed with gravy and meat as she turned it out into a bowl. Another scoop of the spoon added a potato, bits of onion and more gravy.

"Looks good," Finn said, standing at her elbow, waiting to take the bowl from her.

He sat by the fire and watched her as she served the second bowlful and then joined him, easing to the ground with care, accepting his hand for balance as she settled beside him.

They ate in silence, broken only when Finn rose to serve himself another bowlful of the stew and offered her seconds. She shook her head, and he nodded, settling down beside her again, only to nudge her with his elbow as he pointed to where two little boys ran back and forth, chasing a dog between the wagons.

"I've always wanted a dog," she said as she scooped up the final bite from her bowl. "Lyle said they weren't worth the food it takes to keep them alive."

"I'll get one for you if you like," Finn told her. "But probably not until we get to the end of this trip. Hell, you can have two of 'em, if it'll make you happy, Jess."

She laughed aloud in delight, and then quickly placed her hand over her mouth to stifle the sound. "I can't believe I did that," she whispered. "I'm supposed to be in mourning, Finn. One day a widow and already I'm carrying on as if I'd never been married. Let alone the fact that I'm to have a child." She smiled at him. "If you can get a pup, I'd appreciate it. And I'll try to be more circumspect in my behavior. No more cutting up and carrying on."

She felt the same weightless sensation she'd noticed earlier. "It's almost as if I'm set free, Finn. As if the bars have been removed and I'm no longer a prisoner."

"Well, you've about got that right," he told her flatly. "After what you put up with, no one would blame you if you had spit on the man's grave."

"Oh, I doubt that would have gone over very well," she said quietly. "There are a couple of the ladies who don't seem to approve of me. Even at the graveside, one gave me a long look and sniffed, as if I smelled really bad." Her eyes sought his, and she felt the old sense of loneliness creep closer as she spoke words that saddened her yet filled her with a new resolve. "I think they'd like to see me leave the train at Council Grove."

Finn snorted and shook his head. "A pretty woman is always vulnerable to gossip," he said. "And you're the prettiest female around. Some women can't help but keep a tight rein on their menfolk. Maybe they think you're a threat to them." He shot her a quick look. "And then there's the single men, most of them needy—some of them really looking for a wife. Why do you suppose the vultures are circling? We're all hoping you'll give one of us the nod."

"Is that so?" She took his bowl and stacked it in hers, then rose to clear up the remains of their supper.

He watched, relaxing for a few minutes, enjoying the sight of her graceful movements, the elegant line of her profile and the prospect of having her walk beside him to the bank of the stream a bit later on. "Harv said once Geraldine got their girls settled down for the night, we'd go to the stream for our baths," he said quietly. "I see her scrubbin' them up right now, and Harv's cleaning up their supper dishes.''

"I won't be long," Jessica told him. "I'll just need to clean my kettle out first." She emptied the remains of the stew into a quart jar and set it aside, then poured clean water into the black container, sloshing it around before she dumped it on the far side of the wagon. Again she poured a portion of clean water into it and set it over the fire to heat.

The bowls went into it, along with the spoons and the mixing dish she'd used earlier. Finn watched, a comfortable sensation flooding him as she methodically did her evening chores. She would wash everything in a few minutes, adding soap and using a rag to clean every surface. He'd watched her from the shadows more than one evening as she organized her campsite, aware of the aura of loneliness surrounding her. Lyle had not invited the friendliness of others, and Jessica had suffered for it.

Now she looked up, smiling as Arlois approached, towel in one hand, a bundle of clothing in the other. "We're about ready to walk to the stream," she said. "Geraldine said she'd be ready in five minutes, and a couple of the others are coming along. Can I help you, Jessica? I'll climb in your wagon and find your towel and nightgown and wrapper if you like.''

"Would you?" Jessica answered. "I'd appreciate it. I try not to hoist myself up over those boards any more often than I have to lately.''

His own towel and change of clothes were ready at the back of Jonah's wagon and Finn sauntered in that direction, nodding at Arlois as he walked past her. "You and your wife going along?" he asked another of the men, and received a nod. He felt a part of the group in a different way tonight, he realized, aware that it was because of Jessica, because of her tentative acceptance of him as a suitor.

Glancing back to where she stood with Arlois, he caught

her gaze and knew a moment of revelation. Limned in the light of the fire behind her, she seemed an almost unearthly figure. And wasn't that a strange thought.

For the space of just a few seconds he was back in Saint Louis, watching as an unknown female stood by a covered wagon and then was tossed with uncaring hands to sit atop the seat. Her eyes had met his for only a moment then, her nod a polite response to his own.

And with an ironic twist of fate, she'd been destined to be the one woman he must pursue in order to avenge Aaron's death. Marrying her would only solve part of the problem, he admitted to himself silently. If she found, somewhere down the road, that he'd courted her in order to gain possession of Aaron's deed, she would turn from him in anger and disgust. He would lose her trust should his motives be revealed.

One day, he would tell her the whole story, one day when their marriage was secured and he'd had time to prove himself to her. And if she turned from him then, he would kick himself for keeping the secret from her.

Finn clenched his jaw. It couldn't be helped. Blood had been shed, and Aaron's death must not be in vain. Jessica was an innocent bystander, but that fact couldn't be considered now. Of primary importance was possession of the piece of paper that had caused Aaron's death. No matter the cost, he would possess the deed, and Aaron would be avenged.

The group assembled quietly in the darkness, whispering among themselves lest children sleeping in the wagons be disturbed. Finn walked beside Jessica, lifting her hand to rest on his bent arm as he led her toward the stream. Around them several couples walked, the women clinging to their menfolk, almost as if this were a celebration of sorts.

"I feel as if we're going to a party," Geraldine Littleman said in an undertone as she and Harv caught up with Jessica's slower stroll. "I'm so tired of that wagon seat and walking in the dust, it'll be almost fun to wash clothes tomorrow morning."

"I hope you'll be feeling the same way when I bring you my things," Finn said in a low voice, his head bending until his mouth almost touched Jessica's ear.

She smiled at his words, glancing up at him, her fingers squeezing his forearm. Words didn't seem to be necessary, she thought, enjoying the darkness, the murmurs of the men and women who surrounded them. Just ahead was the stream, its banks lined by shrubbery, shaded by darkness that spread its cover beneath the low branches of willows that fought for space beside the water.

The men stayed at a distance while the women sought the shallow stream. "I'm glad Mr. Carson brought you along," Geraldine said as she dropped her bundle on the stream bank. "You looked so tired today, Jessica. Not that it wasn't expected, after all that happened yesterday."

Besides Arlois, of all the other females on the train, she'd been drawn to the young mother. She'd watched during the evenings as Geraldine's two young daughters wrote their sums and then begged for stories from the precious books that held a place of honor in their wagon.

"Mr. Carson was thinking of you, I'll warrant, when he walked around to the campfires, recruiting the bunch of us to come along for bathing tonight," Geraldine said with a chuckle as the women stripped quickly from their clothing. "I think he has eyes for you, Jessica."

"You think so?" she asked, thankful for the darkness that hid her rosy cheeks. Her dress lay around her ankles and now her underwear followed. "I'm amazed that any man would be interested in a woman who's carrying another man's child," she said quietly, catching her breath as she skimmed her stockings off. She bent to tuck them into the bundle she'd made of her dress and petticoat, and then straightened, glancing over her shoulder to where tall figures were shadows in the moonlight.

Naked but for her shift, Jessica felt the evening breeze flutter the soft cotton of her brief garment and she shivered. The women were vulnerable, almost nude as they shed their clothing. Another look eased her mind, for two of the men faced west, three looked toward the east, long guns in their hands as they guarded the place where their womenfolk enjoyed this rare treat. Finn was the farthest from her, Jessica realized, but if he should turn, he would be able to see her, would no doubt recognize her outlined form in the shadows, a shape heavy with pregnancy.

Her hands quickly removed the simple ribbon from her braid and as she untangled the three strands, running her fingers through her hair, she recalled Finn's words. *I like your hair that way, hanging loose down your back.* She smiled, allowing the length of it to fall almost to her hips once it was free from its confinement.

It was her only concession to feminine pride, this heavy mass of waving hair that proclaimed her a woman in the most primitive fashion. Falling around her like a mantle, it hid much of her from view until she gathered it in one hand, pulling it over her shoulder as she entered the river.

Carefully she stepped from the bank into knee-deep water, her precious bar of soap in hand, and sank beneath the surface, settling on the sandy bottom. The current was slow, and in the shallows where she bathed, the water held but a trace of the day's heat. Cooler than her body by a long shot, it was a welcome relief to her parched skin. After long moments, she rose to her knees and bent over, allowing her hair to float on the surface, then began working up suds in her hands. Even a sunbonnet couldn't keep the dust of the trail from settling on her head, and she used her nails to scrub the soap into the surface of her scalp, and then squeezed the suds through the length of hair.

The women, almost as one, washed, soft murmurs of

pleasure rising from their throats as they enjoyed the luxury of soap and water, then rising from the shallows to splash away the residue. Whispers floated above the surface of the moving stream as they laughed among themselves, and for those precious moments, Jessica delighted in the camaraderie of their kinship as women.

A call from one of the men broke the air, interrupting the soft chatter, and they hushed as a male voice bespoke impatience at keeping watch.

"That's my David," Arlois confided. "I think he's getting anxious to crawl under the wagon with me. I told him last night he smelled like a warthog."

Jessica joined in the wash of laughter, and with the others completed her ablutions in haste. Another such occasion might not present itself for several days, possibly not even before they arrived in Council Grove, and they would not ruin another opportunity by lingering overlong in the water.

Quickly they donned their nightwear and together they trooped up the rise to where two of the men waited. David Bates motioned them to walk ahead, ready to escort them back to the circle of wagons. The other men hastened to the water, and within seconds Jessica heard the splashing of bodies in the stream as the men sought the depths at the middle of the expanse in which to bathe.

David whispered a quick word in Arlois's ear before he loped back to the stream, and she laughed aloud, leading the way between two wagons into the light of the campfires. Seeking their wagons, the women were the object of male eyes from every corner, the men obviously enjoying the sight of females in various styles of robes and wrappers, their hair falling damply down their backs.

Jessica sat on her chunk of wood beside her dying fire, toweling her hair, then drawing her comb through its length, a process that involved long moments of unsnarling the waves that resisted her attempts to curb their tendency to corkscrew. Her fingers tamed it finally, and she worked hastily to form a long braid, aware of watching eyes. Then, with awkward movements, she arose and began the process of climbing into her wagon bed.

Her knee became tangled in her gown and she teetered for a few seconds, almost falling before she managed to gain the inside. Her wrapper slid off and she folded it, then tugged her feather tick to the floor, where it covered almost half the available space. Four feet wide, the wagon held all she owned, most of her belongings stacked along the sides, only leaving enough room for her to make her way from one end to the other.

Even with the chairs Lyle had tied on the outside and the heavy objects dangling beneath, the contents would barely make enough furnishings for one room once she arrived in Colorado.

Her quilt sailed wide and settled on the feather tick, and once more she was thankful she'd dug in her heels and insisted on bringing it along, even over Lyle's protests. It was her only luxury, comforting her body each night. From the river, she could still hear the men's voices, raised in laughter. Perhaps another night one of them might make his way to her wagon, might climb in to join her on her bed.

The stark memory of Lyle sharing her bed caused her to tremble, and for a moment she wondered if ever she would welcome a male presence beside her. The blessing was that she no longer had to fear a cuff from a closed fist or a slap from his narrow, gambler's hand. The sound of Dave's low voice, speaking teasingly in masculine tones caught her ear and she thought of Arlois, waiting for him to join her beneath their wagon.

The thought that she might one day welcome a man lured her beyond her fear and she envisioned golden hair and blue eyes that smiled on her with approval.

Without a moment's regret for the loss of the husband she'd buried only yesterday, she recognized the depth of the attraction to Finn Carson that had gripped her so quickly. Refusing to allow the burden of guilt to weigh on her shoulders, she thumped her pillow and nestled it beneath her head as she spread a sheet over herself.

She'd done her best to be a good wife to Lyle, and had only years of neglect and abuse to show for it. The blame for her unhappiness rested on the gambler she'd spent four years trying to please, and now she was free from the millstone her marriage had become. Her sigh was deep as she settled herself to sleep.

But in only moments she heard her name spoken in an undertone, and at the sound her eyelids flew open. "Jessica? Are you awake?"

"Yes." It was all she could manage to whisper as she crawled from beneath the sheet and made her way to where he stood, the wooden rear panel of the wagon rising between them. She knelt, leaning her forearms on the barrier, and looked up at him. He was in the shadow of the wagon, but his hair glimmered silver, and she could barely resist the urge to touch its damp length as he looked down at her.

"What do you want?" Her voice was a hushed whisper, and Finn swallowed the answer that begged to be spoken aloud.

You. Just you. Instead, he murmured quiet words of concern. Did she need anything? Was she all right?

His hand brushed against strands of hair waving about her face, and he rued the braid she'd formed to tame the heavy fall, wishing with all his heart that he might see it undone in the moonlight, might wrap his fingers in its length. He watched as her slender hands moved to settle on the piece of wood that separated them, noted how she clutched at it, and dropped his own hand to rest beside hers.

If he bent just a little, he thought…if she tilted her head just so…if only there weren't others nearby.

"I'm fine," she whispered, drawing him from his fanciful meandering. "Thank you for planning the jaunt to the stream. The women were all so pleased, and I haven't been clean all over at the same time for longer than I want to think about.''

It was silent for a moment, only the sound of fractured breathing apparent as Jessica inhaled and then allowed her breath to pass through soft lips that opened as if she would speak again.

And then she tilted her head—just so—and he bent, just a bit.

Without a twinge of regret, his lips touched hers, lingered for a moment and then retreated. ''Good night,'' he said, aware that his voice was rough, his breathing rapid, and his arousal apparent. He turned aside to walk in the darkness outside the circle of wagons. His horse was tied to the wagon he normally slept beneath, and he quickly exchanged halter for bridle and reins, and then with one leap was astride the animal.

He wouldn't be gone more than twenty minutes or so, he figured—just long enough for his body to resume its usual condition—before he sought his bed. Although his normal condition these days was one of longing for a woman who was patently still off-limits to him, at least until he could get a ring on her finger.

A woman who held a deed to property he'd vowed to retrieve the day he'd stood by his brother's grave. A woman whose husband had fired a bullet into Aaron Carson and then set off to claim his gold strike and the property surrounding it.

A woman who was unaware of Finn's dual purpose in courting her.

Jessica Beaumont. The woman he intended to claim as his own.

Chapter Four

Laundry was the order of the day, with rope lines strung between wagons, where a motley assortment of clothing was hung to dry in the hot sun. Men carried baskets of trousers and shirts, dresses and undergarments up from the stream, and their womenfolk reached high to drape them higgledy-piggledy over the lines. Those men without wives did their own or paid out good cash money to willing ladies who were not averse to accepting their coins.

The children ran wild, as if it were a holiday, and even though they were ever under the watchful eyes of their parents, they splashed downstream in the water and played tag beneath the trees. The noon meal was taken together, the womenfolk carrying food from their individual campfires to where quilts were spread beneath the willows near the water. Upstream, several of the men had cast lines into the water, and their catch lay on the stream bank.

"It feels like Fourth of July, doesn't it?" Arlois asked Jessica as she settled her youngest boy with a pewter plate on his lap.

Jessica nodded, remembering picnics from her childhood, and for a moment she was lonesome for the company of her parents, who were lost to her now. She would write them, she determined, before they arrived at Council Grove, and send the letter back to Saint Louis. By that time she would be able to tell them her news, of Lyle's death and the man who would be her husband from this time on.

"You'd think we were celebrating July fourth early, wouldn't you?" Finn picked up a drumstick from his plate and bit into it with gusto.

"That's almost the same thing Arlois said," Jessica told him, enjoying the smile he tossed so casually in her direction. She watched him eat, noting the manners he exhibited with unconscious ease. His upbringing had obviously contained the presence of a mother who taught her son well the everyday courtesies, judging from his ability to make himself at home with any company.

"I think these folks will take any opportunity to have a good time," he said, waving his drumstick in the general direction of the men and women sitting in small groups beneath the shade of the willow trees. He looked down at his plate. "I'm glad the ladies were able to come up with picnic food. I saw some of them picking berries at daybreak. Must've been for this cobbler."

"Hazel O'Shea contributed three eggs to make that," Jessica said. "They're about worth their weight in gold. Her husband had a fit when she insisted on bringing along her hens in a cage, but I'll bet he's happy now that she won that fight. He's about the only man on the train who eats eggs for breakfast a couple of times a week."

"How about seeing if we can pick up a couple of hens for you once we get to Council Grove?" Finn asked. "I can make a cage for them if there's wood available."

"Would you?" she asked. "I thought of it in Independence, but Lyle said it would be too much trouble turning them loose to scratch every evening, and they'd probably get eaten by hawks once we let them run free a bit."

"You just have to keep a close eye on them," Finn told her. "We could manage if it's something you'd like. We'll have a chance to buy some supplies at the general store there, too. The prices are high, but you'll know better now what things you need to fill in the gaps in your supplies.''

"Your hunting expedition is what made this such a good meal, you know," Jessica told him. Finn had headed up the group of hunters early in the morning while the women did their washing, and the wild turkeys and rabbits they'd shot and prepared for roasting over the fires formed the basis of the meal they shared. Along with the berry cobbler, another of the women had generously used her store of dried apples to make fried turnovers, then cut them in pieces for the children to share.

It was almost like being a part of a family, Jessica decided, and though the group would split off into different directions in a few weeks, she knew she would never forget the unexpected delights of this day.

The laundry hanging on the makeshift lines was ready to be tended by the time their picnic was finished, and the women turned back to their mundane chores as the menfolk watered the stock and carried quilts and weary children back to the circle of wagons.

It had been a joyous day, Jessica thought as she folded Finn's shirts. She inhaled the fresh scent of the prairie breeze that seemed caught up in the very fabric of each garment, then stacked them neatly on a box. As she turned from the chore with the last of his shirts in her hands she caught sight of him, striding with long, firm steps toward her wagon, her quilt across one arm, a basket of her belongings from the picnic swinging from his other hand.

"I'll take care of your clothesline," Finn said after he deposited her things inside the wagon. He reached up to unfasten the length of rope from a hook on the rear bow, and walked slowly toward the next wagon in line, looping the coils over his elbow and hand as he went.

She watched, enamored by the idea of a man doing chores for her. She'd been so long without tenderness in her days and nights. And now Finn provided that quality in abundant measure. He twisted and turned the rope, forming it into a neat figure eight, and then leaned past her to hang it on the nail where she stored it.

Her fingers faltered as she smoothed the fabric of his blue work shirt, and she tugged the collar, straightening it a bit. "You do that so nicely," he told her. "Reminds me of the way my mother used to handle the washing when I was a boy." He watched as she tucked the sleeves inside and smoothed the placket down, then lifted the stack of his belongings into his arms, inspecting the top item more closely.

"Thanks for sewing on a new button for me," he said. His brow lifted and a grin curved his lips. "I'll be spoiled with you taking such good care of me."

"It was an odd one I had and it doesn't really match the others, but it's better than nothing, I figured. And if that's all it takes to keep you happy, who am I to complain?" she teased, and then felt her stomach clench as his gaze narrowed on her face. His eyes darkened with a look she recognized as a yearning—a yearning probably for the easing of his masculine need. Just such a look from Lyle had meant harsh hands that groped and demanded her compliance to his wants.

Not so, it seemed, with this man, for his fingers against her shoulders were soothing, and his lips formed words of promise against her skin. "You'll find me easy to please, Jessica," he said. "In fact, just being with you makes me happy." He bent close to claim the softness of her cheek, and his breath was warm against her ear. His mouth formed a caress, his lips pressing against her flesh. And then she felt the dampness of open lips, as his murmur offered assurance. "All you have to do is smile in my direction."

Such foolishness. She turned her head sharply and looked into eyes that seemed not to consider such flattery as nonsense. "A smile will do it?" she asked.

"Just looking at you gives me pleasure," he told her, and she laughed, a quick, harsh sound.

"I'd put some stock in that if I didn't know how I look these days, Finn. Those sweet words would be more credible if you aimed them toward a pretty young girl, or whispered them to a woman who's been a success at pleasing a husband." She set her jaw, deliberately acknowledging her own shortcomings.

He laughed at her. The man had the audacity to touch his fingers to her cheek and then bent to kiss the tip of her nose. "You don't know what you're talking about, Jessica," he said. His blue eyes lowered slowly, touching the bit of skin exposed at her throat, where her collar was undone, and then settled seductively on the fullness of her breasts.

Heat rose to color her cheeks as his gaze measured the rounding curves of her bosom, and her lungs expanded as if they required an inordinate amount of air. His smile was slow, as her breasts lifted with each indrawn breath, and his murmur was low, words she strained to hear. He leaned toward her, brushing their bodies together, and she felt the distinct swelling of his male arousal against her belly.

"Finn?" Her voice was choked, her throat too dry to swallow, and the fire from her rosy cheeks descended to diffuse its heat throughout her body, as if a fever had taken hold and spread languor the length of her limbs. She leaned against him, unable to remain upright without his support.

"I suppose I should apologize Jess," he told her, his smile a bit crooked, as if he were embarrassed. "I don't mean to offend you, but I can't seem to help the way you affect me. Surely you're not surprised."

"Well, I can't imagine that you—"

He laughed, the sound muffling her words as he took her lips with a kiss that left her question answered beyond the shadow of a doubt. Then he was laughing no longer, his mouth taking hers fiercely, his need so powerful, so ele-

mental, she could not fail to understand the message. And
then they lurched, almost in unison, as the baby made its
presence known to them both, a tiny hand or foot poking
indiscriminately in protest.

Finn recovered first, setting her away from him.
"Enough of that for tonight, I'd say," he told her, his
chuckle soft against her ear. "I'll see you in the morning,
sweetheart." His smile returned, quirking one corner of his
mouth. "And yes, whether you believe it or not, I have a
need for you, Jess. I said I'd wait, and I will, but don't
think for one minute that you carrying a baby is enough to
turn me away."

The creek crossing was accomplished early on the next
day, and by noontime the train snaked out across the prairie, heading almost due west. The morning breeze carried
the perfume of wildflowers directly to the wagon seat where
Jessica was perched. One of the men, a miner, walked beside her lead ox this morning, having made the offer, probably at Finn's instigation she thought. And it was an offer
she could not afford to refuse, although she would soon
climb down and take her place there, walking the trail for
the early hours of the afternoon.

Her lungs filled as she inhaled deeply of the fresh air.
Flowers bloomed on all sides, and mixed with their soft
scent was the riper, richer aroma of soil, blessed by an
overnight rain. It had been a dry spring, McMasters said,
but this morning the trail held damp spots.

There'd been no sign of Finn after the crossing. Once
the wagons rolled through the shallowest part of the stream,
listing first to one side, then the other, men walking beside
them, watchful lest one should tilt and threaten to overturn,
he'd ridden off. With a jaunty wave in her direction he'd
turned his horse to the southwest and had soon been gone
from sight.

The crossing left them vulnerable, and though the Indian

tribes had been peaceful, Jonas was alert for trouble. Finn, she suspected, had been sent ahead to scout out the trail.

The day passed quickly, Jessica taking over the duty of walking by the team for a couple of hours during the afternoon, and then retiring to rest when Arlois sent her son to relieve her. The feather tick in her wagon served her well, and she spent an hour there, her body weary, her legs aching. She was less than two months from delivery of her child, if she had it figured right, and the hardest part was yet to come. It was no wonder a woman was considered unfit to travel without a man's company on a wagon train.

By nightfall, her back ached and her feet were swollen. Even with the afternoon nap giving her a burst of energy she was aware that her strength was lessening day by day. Sitting by the fire, she held her journal on her lap, scribbled a recital of the day, and then thumbed through the pages. Notes of the miles traveled, the meals she'd cooked and the sights she'd seen made up the entries of those early days of this trek, and she read them over by the flickering campfire.

There seemed to be a total absence of joy in her early postings and she could not help but compare them to the few lines she'd written of today's happenings. Names of women and children appeared there, and prominent among them was Finn's, the lone male she'd mentioned, but for the miner and Arlois's eldest son, who had given of their time for her comfort.

She closed the book, and leaned back against a keg, allowing the sounds of children and animals to lull her. The sun was below the horizon, and the shrill cry of some wild animal blended in with the protesting howl of an angry child. A chill settled down upon her, and Jessica shivered, wrapping her arms around her middle, viewing the campfire through lowered eyelids.

And then he came to her in the half darkness, his boots silent against the hard ground. Crouching next to her, he spoke her name, and she opened her eyes, welcoming the sight of a smile that warmed her. She motioned to the kettle that still hung over the fire, and he nodded, settling beside her to eat. Dipping into the contents of her stew pot, he savored each bite, then spoke quietly of the trail he'd scouted out.

"I didn't find anything to worry about," he said. "Jonas heard some rumors about one of the tribes stealing horses from a train that went through here a couple of weeks ago, but everything looks quiet up ahead to me. The Indians don't take much stock in oxen anyway. I think we're pretty safe."

Jessica nodded, content to watch him and listen to the quiet drone of his words, lulling her in the darkness. Finn poked at the buffalo chips with a stick, his attention never straying from her. It was as if they were already married, she thought, already forming a life together. Except for bedtime, when, as the camp settled down for the night, he stood beside her, offering his help. She rose and made ready to climb into the wagon.

His kiss was not unexpected, the slow, gentle mating of their lips that sent a shiver down the length of her spine. His mouth coaxed hers to open and her lips softened beneath his, allowing the patient exploration of her lips with the edge of his tongue. She'd hated such kisses from Lyle, dreaded the poking and prodding that invaded her privacy. Yet with Finn's delicate touches, she knew a different sensation, felt the rush of sweet, awakening passion his kisses brought into being.

He left her then, after lifting her with ease over the tailgate, touching her hand in a silent farewell before he lowered himself to crawl into his bedroll beneath the wagon. A sense of rightness, of well-being, surrounded her with the knowledge that he slept so near, and she closed her eyes, weariness creeping over her.

Sunshine greeted them each morning as they made their

way toward Council Grove. Water again became scarce and
they took a detour, stopping by a stream bank one afternoon, then spent the night there at the women's request.
The animals were allowed to graze overnight and then led
to the stream to drink deeply before they set off the next
morning. The water wagon carried barrels for filling and
Jessica was relieved to have hers delivered back to her
wagon, the lid firmly in place, the contents making it heavy
and cumbersome.

Finn was at hand, watching over her, appearing every
morning to ready her oxen for the day's travel, ever present
at her fire each night. She accepted him as a friend, welcomed the warm touches of his lips against her mouth and
forehead, leaned into his muscular form as his arms enclosed her in the darkness each evening—growing accustomed to his presence in her life.

They spoke little of the decision she must make before
reaching Council Grove, only of the trail ahead, of the lives
they'd left behind. And if Finn seemed reticent at times,
skimming the surface of his early years, she simply put it
down to the usual inclination of men not to discuss themselves.

And then, just two days out of Council Grove, he made
the offer she'd been expecting, issuing a formal declaration
of his intent. They had finished supper, and Jessica was
putting away her bowls and spoons into the keg where she
stored them. Beside her, Finn lifted it into the wagon bed,
and then turned to face her, both of them hidden in the
shadows between two wagons, where their last moments
together each day were spent, speaking quietly before separating to sleep apart.

"I thought I'd better remind you that I'm planning to
marry you once we reach Council Grove," he said, smiling
as he reached for her hand. He held it against his chest and
felt the trembling of her fingers against his palm. The inclination to touch his lips to her cool flesh was almost au-

tomatic, so slowly and easily had their relationship developed, and he lifted her hand, then bent to press a kiss against her knuckles.

"I wondered if you'd changed your mind," she said, looking up at him quizzically. "You haven't mentioned it again, only that once. I hadn't planned to hold you to it, Finn."

"I don't change my mind once it's made up to something, Jess. I figured you knew that."

"You know Gage Morgan asked me to consider his suit," she told him quietly. "I suspect he'll ask again before we get to Council Grove."

"And what will you tell him?" He heard the harsh tones he uttered that spoke of his anger, and saw her brows raise as he clasped her hand more tightly.

"What do you think?" she asked. "You've been looking after me, Finn. I've fed you supper every night, and you've slept beneath my wagon. I told you before that it seemed to me you were staking a claim. The rest of the men stayed clear of me. All but Morgan."

"Did he come around when I was riding out ahead?" Finn asked.

She nodded. "He was pleasant, but I don't feel comfortable around him."

"After we leave Council Grove, he'll leave you alone," Finn promised. "Once you're wearing my ring, you won't be fair game for any other man."

"I'll let you know right now, I'm not about to settle for a secondhand ring, Finn Carson. I'd rather do without." Her chin lifted as she followed her assertion with an explanation that surprised him. "Morgan offered to buy one from one of the other women for me if I'd marry him."

Finn shook his head in disbelief. The thought of Jessica's hand being graced by some other female's bit of gold was beyond consideration. "You'll be wearing a brand new ring when we leave Council Grove," he told her. "I understand there's a jeweler there, and we'll see what he has to offer."

"Really? You mean that?" she asked. "I've never had a wedding ring."

"Did you think I'd do any less for you, Jess?" He lifted her hand again, and this time his mouth lingered there. He looked up into her eyes and whispered words he'd considered long and hard. "I won't demand anything of you. You'll let me know when I can sleep inside the wagon with you. All right?" And within him blossomed the hope that his careful wooing, his small seductions each night might bear fruit.

Jessica was silent for a long moment, and he thought she held her breath. And then she nodded. "All right. That sounds agreeable to me."

"I spoke to the preacher and he agreed to marry us in Council Grove. And if there's a church we can use, I thought you might like to be wed in front of an altar."

He watched as her eyes glistened, and two tears fell to roll down her cheeks. "Thank you, Finn. I didn't expect you to think of that, but it would please me no end."

"I've asked Dave Bates to be witness for me, and I thought maybe you'd ask Arlois to stand beside you." He'd been jumping the gun a little when he presented his plan to Dave, but the other man didn't have any qualms about agreeing to the notion, only teased him about planning his wedding night.

"I'll ask her tomorrow," Jessica said. And then she stood on tiptoe and leaned forward a bit, capturing their clasped hands between his chest and hers. Her face tilted upward and she smiled. "If I say yes nicely to your proposal, will you kiss me?"

"I've kissed you most every night, Jess," he said quietly. "And I've waited two long weeks to do it properly," he whispered. "I didn't want to push you, sweetheart."

He bent and his lips touched hers, at first a familiar,

undemanding whisper of lips pressing together, of warmth and soft caresses that soon were not enough. His mouth opened over hers and he allowed his tongue and teeth the freedom to invade her mouth in the same way he ached to claim her woman's warmth. She leaned against him and he rejoiced that his hands were to be allowed the freedom of touching her ripe, fruitful body.

Held tenderly in his hand, her breast was firm, the crest hardening against his palm and he lifted it with care, measuring its weight and squeezing it with a gentle touch. His other arm circled her, holding her close, aware of the burden of her pregnancy between them. The fact that an unborn babe was her gift to him in this marriage was uppermost in his mind, and he spoke the words that begged to be said.

"Once you're my wife, this will be my child," he said. "I want you to forget that Lyle ever had any claim to your baby."

She bent her head and pressed her cheek to his chest. "I don't know how easy that will be," she murmured. "I'll have a hard time forgetting—" She inhaled sharply, and he felt compassion for the memories she carried within her.

His palm lifted her chin and he looked down into her eyes, rued the tears that again swam on their surface and fell to stain her cheeks. "One day, I'll make you put all that behind you," he promised. "I'll never hurt you, Jess."

"I may not be able to be the wife you want." As if the words were torn from her, she shuddered in his grasp. "I'm not very good at that part of marriage, I fear."

And how much of that fear could be laid at Lyle Beaumont's feet, Finn wondered? The man had much to answer for. A woman should not be made to dread the touch of her husband. Should Jessica be apprehensive about the coming days when she would become Finn Carson's wife, he alone would suffer for it, would pay the price for Lyle's cruelty.

And yet, none of that would make him change his mind. His arms hugged her close, swaying a bit, as if he would comfort her. "You'll do fine," he said quietly. "I'm not a harsh man, Jess."

She nodded, her head moving against his chest. "I'm counting on that."

Council Grove was a small town, one street running its length, storefronts on either side, with a primitive sidewalk of sorts to keep the ladies' skirts out of the mud. This morning there was no sign of the recent rain, only a rutted road that held both wagons and men on horseback. The wagons were circled on the edge of town, positioned on a piece of land apparently used before for the same purpose, if the remains of campfires and ruts from other wagons were anything to go by.

"Mrs. Beaumont." The voice speaking her name was familiar, and Jessica looked out the back of her wagon to see Morgan awaiting her attention. "Could I speak with you for just a minute?"

"Certainly," she told him, unwilling to climb down in front of him, knowing how awkward her descent would be. She settled instead on the floor and met his gaze.

He walked closer, accepting her unspoken invitation to approach, and took off his hat. The man was good-looking. There was no getting around it, she thought. His gray eyes were dark, bold and searching as he paused, seeming to gather his thoughts. And then, as if he knew it was his last chance to speak his piece, he began.

"I've asked you to consider me as your husband, ma'am. I couldn't help but notice you seem to have an understanding with Carson, but I want you to know the offer still stands." A smile touched his firm lips and his fingers gripped his hat brim. "I made a mistake when I spoke of a wedding ring, about perhaps buying one from one of the ladies. Now I've heard that there's a store in Council Grove where one may be bought.''

''Yes, I've heard that, too,'' she said, her smile genuine. ''In fact, that's where Mr. Carson plans on purchasing one for me.''

''Is there anything I can say to make you reconsider my offer?'' he asked. ''I'm willing to go wherever you like, find a homestead and settle anyplace that suits you. I've got money enough to outfit us nicely in Council Grove, if you don't have enough supplies to go with mine to make the trip.''

''And will you accept my child as your own?'' she asked. And then saw the hesitation he could not mask.

''I'd certainly try,'' he countered. His mouth firmed and his eyes became shuttered against her, and once more she thought that he was a man with secrets, and perhaps a plan that did not bode well for her. ''I understood from talk around the campfires that your husband bragged of a deed to land near Pike's Peak, ma'am. If you'll share it with me, I'd be willing to work the land and make a home for you there.''

Jessica's skin felt chilled, and pebbled at his offer. ''I don't have possession of such a deed,'' she said, hedging the truth a bit. ''I fear I will go to my new husband with nothing but the contents of my wagon and the child I carry.''

His gaze grew sharp and a disbelieving smile turned his mouth into a travesty of humor. ''You don't have a piece of paper that gives you the rights to a piece of land?''

''I have no such deed,'' she said again stubbornly. *Where Lyle put it is a secret he took with him into his grave.* She'd tussled with that knowledge almost daily for the past two weeks, and looked forward to turning the search over to Finn's capable hands.

''I see.'' Morgan appeared thoughtful. ''I'm still willing

to marry you," he said. "I'll need a wife once I get a place to live."

"Perhaps you'll find a willing woman somewhere between here and Santa Fe," she told him.

"But it won't be you?"

She shook her head. "No, it won't be me. I'm marrying Finn Carson this morning in Council Grove." She watched as he clapped his hat on his head, offered her a nod and walked away.

"That was well-done," Finn said from the front of the wagon. He climbed up onto the seat and made his way between the stacks of her belongings to where she sat. "I told you he'd make another stab at it before we got here, didn't I? There's nothing like leaving things till the last minute."

And then he bowed his head to her in a solemn gesture. "You handled him nicely, Jessica."

"Did I?" She thought of the hidden anger that had firmed the man's jaw, the dark shadows in his eyes, and the determination that hovered over him as he stalked from her presence. "I fear I've only made him angry. But I didn't lie to him."

"It couldn't be helped, sweetheart," Finn told her. He was bent over beneath the canvas top, too tall to stand upright. "You look pretty today, Jess." He offered his hand. "Are you ready to go to the store for your ring? Arlois and David are waiting for us."

Her ring shimmered in the sunlight, a simple band given to her with solemn vows accompanying its placement on her finger. *"With this ring…"* She repeated them over in her mind as she turned her hand to catch the gleam of gold. The wagon seat was padded with Finn's own bedroll, for her comfort, he'd said. Ahead of her, he walked beside the oxen as they leaned into their yoke.

Behind her, within the canvas walls, five new boxes of

supplies vied for space with her remaining foodstuffs, and tied securely to the north side of the wagon was a cage carrying four laying hens, plus a rooster, who was a bit frustrated with the crowded conditions. Finn's plans included building the lone male a cage of his own at the first opportunity.

His bargaining skills had made her smile as the farmer outside of Council Grove fought for the best deal he could get. Finn had made him throw in the cage and a large sackful of feed, to be used on those days when the chickens couldn't be turned loose to forage. The bed of the cage held a nest in one corner, and even now, the biddies were jostling for their turn to settle there.

He'd bought canned fruit, a real treat, to be used sparingly, and then told her they would stand the empty cans up on a tree limb for her to aim at during a session of target practice, assuring her that she should learn to use a gun. Stubbornly he'd convinced her of the need, and she'd agreed to give it a try.

All in all, it had been a most satisfactory day, she decided, waving as Geraldine came into sight, waiting up ahead beside the trail for Jessica's wagon to roll past. As it reached her, Jessica held out her hand and Geraldine climbed up to join her on the seat.

"I wanted to talk to you back in Council Grove and didn't get a chance," she said. She looked ahead to where Finn walked beside the oxen and then leaned closer to Jessica.

"I'm so glad you chose Mr. Carson. I was afraid that Gage Morgan's good looks would sway you. The man is persistent, I'll give him that, but I think you got the better of the two. The rest of the bachelors didn't stand a chance with you. We all figured that out, and I think they all knew it, too, once Finn set his sights on you."

"Morgan's a good-looking man, but he doesn't hold a candle to Finn," Jessica told her. Her gaze dwelt for a long moment on the tall, slim-hipped figure who walked before them. "He's as good-looking as Morgan, just in a different way. More importantly, he's kind and generous." She waved a hand at the extra supplies behind her, tied in place inside the wagon. "You wouldn't believe the stuff he bought for us in Council Grove. I agree with you. I know I made the right choice."

"Well, he's getting a bargain, too," Geraldine said, lifting an eyebrow with good humor. "He's got a ready-made family, and chances are you'll have a boy. First babies usually are boys, you know," she said confidentially. "And besides that, you're far and away one of the prettiest women I've ever known, Jessica. I'd say he got himself quite a good deal."

"I hope he thinks so," Jessica answered, even as she wondered what Finn's thoughts were. He'd been quiet after the return to the wagons, working in silence as he sorted out their new supplies and packed them amid the wagon's contents. But even though they spoke little, he was all that was kind and considerate as he readied Jessica's seat for the afternoon's journey and saw to her comfort.

"Everyone's wondering how you're going to manage getting under the wagon tonight at bedtime," Geraldine said with a giggle. "You know there's no such thing as privacy on a trip like this. You'll be the object of everyone's attention."

She hadn't thought of that, Jessica realized, and her cheeks flushed as she chewed over the possibilities of the accommodations available to them.

"Finn already told me he'd sleep alone under the wagon," she said quietly, "even though I told him he could share my feather tick inside with me. He hasn't said yet which he'd rather do."

Geraldine hooted with laughter, and Finn turned his head as if he would share the joke, his smile tentative. Jessica just shook her head and he nodded, apparently understanding that the women were having a discussion that did not merit his participation. Geraldine gasped for a breath as she wiped her eyes.

"As if you need to wonder where his druthers lay," she said. "If he's not right smack-dab against you all night, I'll eat my hat. He's a *man*, Jessica."

There was certainly no doubt about that, Jessica thought, recalling the unmistakable arousal he exhibited when he held her against himself each night. Her smile was immediate as she thought of his patience. "Well, we'll work it out. I'm not sure he'll be much interested in claiming his rights, with me looking like a cross between a hippopotamus and an elephant."

"I wouldn't count on that if I were you," Geraldine advised. "A little thing like a baby between us never put a bridle on Harv when I was carrying the girls."

Jessica looked at her quickly, her memory snapping to attention. "You said the first baby was usually a boy. And you only have two girls. How do you explain that?"

Geraldine's smile disappeared and she shrugged, her gaze turning to the prairie off to the north. "I had a boy first," she said quietly. "He died after only a few days, and my mother said he was just too little to make it. He was a month early, so tiny he could have fit in a shoe box." She bit her lip, and Jessica knew tears were not far from sight.

"I'm sorry," she said. Jessica touched Geraldine's hand and her voice was soft as she spoke of her own loss. "My first time—the first baby I carried—ended before I was far enough along for it to live."

"I didn't know that, Jessica. But surely you know that those things happen. In fact, a woman never expects to raise all the children she gives birth to. My mother only reared six out of the nine she carried to full term." She frowned then, looking down at the rise of Jessica's belly. "What a thing to be talking about, and you so close to delivering your own babe. You're healthy, Jess. You won't have a bit of trouble. I'd lay money on it.''

"I don't expect to," Jessica told her stoutly. "I worry a little about having the baby before we get to the end of the trail, but I'll have help, I'm sure. And I know Finn will look after us both.''

Geraldine's gaze traveled to the tall man who walked with ease by the oxen. "I'm sure he will. You're a lucky woman, Jess.'' Her look became pensive and her smile was soft. "I almost envy you, with your wedding night before you. There's something so special about the first time between a man and woman.''

Jessica covered her shiver with a quick shift of her body on the seat. Her memory of the last wedding night she'd endured had left her with a nasty taste of marriage, and it hadn't improved much in the four years following. Somehow the recollection of those long hours managed to drape a pall of gloom on the night to come and it was an effort to smile in Geraldine's direction.

For a long moment, the idea of postponing her second wedding night gained favor.

Chapter Five

"Arlois brought supper over for us." He'd taken care of the animals quickly and now Finn stepped over the wagon tongue. Around him, campfires flared with fresh fuel, and before him, Jessica waited. Holding two stacked plates in her hand, she stood before him, her eyes unwilling to focus on his face. He'd expected as much. The woman was nervous, uncertain of what was to come.

His long legs brought him to her side in three swift steps and he took the plates from her. "Why don't you let me dish it up, and you sit down."

She looked uncertain, and then, with whispered words of acquiescence, she gave over to him, and settled down on a box to watch as he served her. The pot held a stew of sorts, probably rabbit, he thought, and Arlois had, by the looks of it, dug into her store of dried vegetables to make it appetizing. The foodstuffs, an expensive addition to their supplies, were well worth the money, recovering their original size and a somewhat fresh flavor with the addition of water. Dried, they were easy to store in a limited space.

Jessica's ladle held an appetizing serving of the wedding night feast, and Finn placed it on her plate with a flourish. "There you go, Mrs. Carson. Eat hearty." His own serving was somewhat larger and he inhaled the steam as he inspected the gift from the Bates's cooking pot.

"Are those biscuits I see on the skillet?" he asked, lifting a dish towel to look beneath it where crusty bits of bread were stacked.

"Yes, I fixed those and sent most of them back with Arlois when she brought the stew over." Jessica slid two forks from her apron pocket, handed one to Finn and speared a bit of meat from her plate with the other.

He sat on the ground next to her, preferring to look up inside the bonnet brim, rather than wondering just how apprehensive she was. Her eyes met his, then skittered away, as she made a show of scrutinizing her meal closely.

"Are you worried about tonight?" he asked. He might as well be blunt, he decided. Jessica was a bundle of nerves, and it certainly couldn't be good for the baby for her to be fretting while she ate.

"No, of course not," she said quickly. Too quickly, he decided. As if the answer was what she thought he wanted to hear, and certainly not the honest reply that would vex him or ruin the evening for them both. "I didn't think I had anything to worry about," she added, making a production of sorting through the vegetables on her plate. "You told me I—"

"I know what I told you," he said, interrupting her as she faltered for words. "And I meant it, Jess. I'm not going to jump on you and make demands. I thought you knew me a bit better than that."

"I don't seem to be thinking clearly tonight," she said quietly. "Everything has happened so fast, I feel dizzy."

"All brides have second thoughts, I've heard," Finn said with a smile.

"I don't feel much like a bride," she confessed, resting her plate on her lap, or at least what was left of it. He'd never thought too much about taking a wife, but if he had, his ideal woman wouldn't have been heavily pregnant with another man's child. Yet, somehow, that didn't cause him any amount of distress.

Perhaps the thought of finding the deed and reclaiming Aaron's mine and the property surrounding it made the situation with Jessica more attractive. Certainly he would have no problem with claiming her as his woman, baby and all. His conscience twinged a bit as he thought of the deceit he was practicing, and he was tempted, just for a moment, to tell her about Aaron, to give her the opportunity to offer him the deed on her own.

Would she? If not, he'd take matters into his own hands and seek it out at the first chance he was offered. Perhaps she truly didn't know its whereabouts. And in that case it would be up to him to find it. The search would certainly cause a rift between them if Jessica thought he'd sought her out in order to lay hands on Aaron's property.

As surely as he knew his own name, he knew that the piece of paper Aaron had died for was in the wagon, and he'd tear the thing apart if he had to. One way or another, he'd lay claim to Aaron's land, now that he'd taken Jessica as his wife.

And then he'd set about raising Lyle Beaumont's child as his own.

That thought was daunting. Finn had been certain he'd dealt with it during the past few days. Now he looked at Jessica and tried to separate her from the man she'd married. Giving her his own name was a beginning. That he would accept the baby was a promise easily given but perhaps not so readily accomplished. And he wouldn't know if he was capable of fulfilling his vow until the child was born and he held it for the first time.

Sleeping with Jessica would make their marriage solid. That was a fact he'd determined right off. He'd have to go slowly, but he certainly couldn't start any sooner. The woman was fearful, no matter how much she tried to deny it. Getting past that fear was the problem he faced tonight.

"Jess?" He spoke her name quietly and she looked up, startled, as if she'd been a million miles away, thinking a hundred other thoughts. "Can we go for a walk?" he asked. "I think we could use a little privacy."

She nodded. "All right." Her gaze was apprehensive as she looked behind her to where the prairie stretched to the horizon. "Is it safe?"

"We'll find out," he said, lending her his strength as he clasped her hand and lifted her from the box. He led her from the circle of wagons and over a small rise to a slope where the grass provided a spot for them to sit. She settled on the ground and he dropped beside her. His arm curved around her waist and she leaned against it, relishing the support he offered.

With a smooth movement he eased her gently onto her back, thick grass beneath her, and then leaned on his elbow next to her, blotting the moon from sight.

"Finn?" He heard the tremor in her voice, and her eyes searched his, as if she sought reassurance. His fingers untied the strings of her bonnet and he brushed it from her face.

"There, now I can see you," he murmured. He thought she resembled a young girl, the faint lines of worry she'd worn over the past weeks somehow smoothed away, her skin pale in the moonlight, her eyes searching his. "May I kiss you, Jess?"

"I didn't think you needed to ask permission, Finn. I'm your wife. Remember?"

He felt his lips twitch in a grin and his mouth touched the tip of her nose. "How could I forget? I made all those promises to you today, and you very sweetly said you'd do whatever I asked of you."

"I did?" Her forehead furrowed a bit, and then she laughed, a soft sound that pleased him enormously. "That's right, I did. The words were love, honor and obey, as I recall. That wasn't very smart of me, was it?"

"No, but marrying you was about the smartest thing I've ever done," he said. "I got me a pretty wife, a pair of oxen and a wagon full of stuff." His pause was long as he touched her lips with his, a longer, more intimate caress. "That's not all I got, Jess. I'm claiming the rights you gave me when you walked into that church today. I want to touch you. Does that bother you?"

She shook her head. "No. I expected as much. I'm just pleased that we don't have the whole lot of them watching you kiss me."

His arms trembled a bit as he recognized that she hadn't totally understood his meaning. Her mouth looked so soft, so tempting, her lips parted just a bit as if she would speak. But words weren't what he was interested in right now. Possessing her in whatever way she would allow was uppermost in his mind, and he bent over her again, claiming her with his mouth, his lips forming to hers in a kiss she accepted readily.

She inhaled and he took the opening she unwittingly offered, his movement swift, his tongue invading the tender tissues inside her lips. She tasted of coffee there, but her skin held the essence of soap and water, a clean, fresh scent that became her. For a moment she held herself inert, as if wary of the seductive gesture—as if she feared a greater degree of intimacy.

Yet there was no fear in Jessica's mind. Anticipation, rather than fear, flooded her as she savored the feel of Finn's tongue against her own. She lifted her hands to touch his face, feeling the prickle of whiskers against her palms. The warmth of sun-kissed skin was beneath her fingertips, and she heard the groan he uttered as he left her lips to nuzzle the side of her throat.

"I like the way you kiss me," she whispered. "It never felt like this when…" Her voice trailed off as she hesitated over the speaking of Lyle's name. "You make me shiver, Finn."

He chuckled beneath his breath as he pressed damp, openmouthed caresses the length of her cheek and then against her temple. "Are you telling me I'm doing this right?" he asked, his words laced with gentle humor.

"Yes." She almost hissed the single syllable, turning her face up, hoping to capture his mouth against her own. He obliged, as if he knew her thoughts, and she was lost in the warmth of lips and teeth and tongue that explored her mouth and savored each particle of flesh therein. He kissed her as though there was no end to the night, as if they existed in a moment of time that had no beginning and no end.

And she responded to his every whisper, each movement of his hands against her face and throat, as if she had never known the temptation of kisses such as these. For indeed, she hadn't. Lyle's courting had consisted of brief brushes of his lips, and his seduction of her had involved only the barest caresses necessary to have her spread beneath him and available to his masculine need.

Now she reveled in the sweet tenderness a man offers a woman he cares for, and she relaxed beneath the magic of hands that fondled her, lips that coaxed her, soft words that offered manna to the heart of a woman who hungered for love. Her body responded to him, her breasts aching, pressing against her dress as if they begged to be free of the restriction of clothing.

As if he knew her thoughts, Finn loosened her buttons, then spread the bodice wide. She caught her breath and her sigh was a soft protest, but he shushed her with a finger against her lips, and then trailed that damp finger down her throat. With serious intent, he leaned to examine the skin he'd exposed to moonlight and then bent his head, his mouth opening against the edge of her shift, his teeth tugging the fabric down to expose the rise of her breasts.

His fingers moved gently, skillfully, releasing the tiny buttons and revealing the pale skin and rounding curves that ached for his touch. "You're so pretty," he whispered, and she felt a moment's pride that he should take pleasure in the soft breasts he beheld. And then he bent closer and his breath was warm against her skin as he claimed the puckered crests.

His palms formed the sides of her bosom, lifting them for his pleasure. "You taste sweet," he murmured, his lips shaping the swollen peak, his tongue moving against the small nubbin, circling and teasing.

As if she were smitten by lightning, she shivered and moaned aloud, her breath escaping as his lips opened more fully and he suckled at her flesh. A current of heat raced the length of her body, somehow linking the tender tissue he blessed with his mouth and the very edges of his teeth, then gathering speed as it met the place where her thighs were pressed tightly together, lest they open for his touch.

His hand lowered to gather her skirt upward, and she shook her head, shrinking from the contact. "No, don't, Finn." Should he touch her there, should his fingers encounter the moisture gathering there on her woman's flesh, he would claim her, here and now. His manhood would invade her body, stretch her with his swollen flesh, his muscular frame would batter her with his weight, pounding against the child she carried.

"Jess?" He lifted his head, his hand unmoving now, one finger smoothing gently across the skin above her knee. Like a brand, she felt its heat and her head turned from him. "I won't hurt you, Jess. I'll only pet you here, bring you pleasure."

"Pleasure?" Even to her own ears, the word sounded rough. "I'm sorry, Finn. I've found no pleasure in a man's touch before. I don't expect to now."

His hand moved her skirt down to cover her legs, and he sat upright beside her, his fingers deft as he redid the buttons he'd slid from their moorings with such skill only minutes ago. "You don't want me to make love to you?"

His body cast its shadow over her and his voice was strained as he bowed his head. "Are you afraid of me, Jessica?"

She was silent for a moment and he turned abruptly from her, wrapping his arms around his bent knees. The moon seemed to hold a special fascination for him and he lifted his head, gazing into the sky for long moments. "I thought you enjoyed my kisses," he ventured, hesitating a moment before he looked down at her moonlit features. "Are you afraid I'll hurt you?"

"It always hurts," she said sadly. "Sometimes more than others. And now I have a baby to consider. I can't risk my child—" Her voice broke off in a sob.

Finn shook his head, a slow, measured movement. "What did he do to you?"

Her eyes closed and she felt tears slip from beneath her lids, tracing a path down her cheeks. The memories that returned to her mind brought pain, not a repeat of the physical pain Lyle had inflicted on her, with rough hands and teeth that left bruises in tender places, but an aching need for solace.

It swept over her, the misery of love lost, and suffering inflicted by the hand of a man who should have cherished her but had, instead, caused bruises and welts to appear on her flesh on a regular basis.

With an agonized cry, she turned to her side and wept openly, unable to bear the painful visions that swamped her mind, the anger she'd endured, the hopelessness of her life with Lyle Beaumont.

"Jess…ah, Jessica, let me hold you," Finn whispered, lying down beside her and gathering her to himself. He rocked her in his embrace, felt the pressure of a small hand or foot as it moved against his belly. How any man could abuse a woman, a creature smaller, more vulnerable than himself, was beyond his imagination. Especially knowing that she carried his child. His jaw clenched, and in that moment, Finn knew that if Lyle were still alive, he'd seek him out and shoot him where he stood.

She clung to him, her arms wrapped around his neck, her sobs tapering off to an occasional gulp. "I'm sorry," she whispered, her voice hoarse from the copious amount of tears she'd shed. "I didn't mean to turn into a cloud-burst."

"Jess, I want you to be happy with me. I want to give you a good life."

"I don't know if you'll be happy with me, though," she said, wiping her eyes with the backs of her hands. "But I'll try. I'll do my best to please you, Finn."

He retrieved the kerchief from around his neck and pressed it into her palms. "Here, use this."

She mopped her face and wadded the cotton fabric in her hand. "I don't know where all that blubbering came from," she told him. "I truly didn't mean to hurt your feelings. It wasn't anything you did, Finn. It was just the memories…" She halted, unwilling to speak aloud the things she'd endured in the name of marriage.

"Just give me a chance, Jess, let me love you. I won't ever hurt you or cause you pain. I promise."

She nodded, her face tucked into his neck. "All right."

"I won't push you tonight," he told her. "Not while you're upset and your head is filled with what Lyle did to you. I want to start fresh," he said. "I'll sleep under your wagon for a while, until you're ready to accept me."

"No," she said hastily, "I won't shame you in front of the other men. You can share my feather tick, if you want to."

He hugged her tightly and his reply was heartfelt, a husky murmur. "I'd be honored, Mrs. Carson."

They rose after a while and made their way back to the wagon, their footsteps silent against the prairie grass, only the whispering hush of an owl flying from a nearby tree accompanying them as he helped her into the wagon. "Do you want me to stay outside while you get undressed?'' he whispered.

"You can come in if you'll close your eyes." And wasn't that foolish. The man would be living with her for the rest of her life. He'd might as well see what he was getting. She offered her hand and he climbed in behind her.

They whispered, laughing softly as he lowered the feather tick to the floor, pushing a box out of the way to make room. "Is there room for all three of us?" he asked in an undertone.

"Yes, I think so." She unbuttoned her dress, turning her back to him as she stripped from it and reached for her nightgown. Beneath its folds, she shed her other clothing and then turned back to face him. "You were looking," she whispered. He nodded.

"Yeah, I was. But I didn't see much." He was in his drawers, a shadowy form in the darkness inside the canvas shelter.

"Lie down, Jess and I'll curl around you," he told her, then watched as she obeyed, tucking the pillow under her head. He stepped into the depths of the feather-filled ticking and lay next to her, shifting to his side and lifting the sheet to cover them both.

She felt his body behind her, warm and firm, the muscled length of his legs against hers, and then his left arm slid beneath her neck and he drew her closer against himself. His hand spread wide on her belly, the heat of his palm bringing comfort to the skin that was stretched almost to the limit.

"Is that all right?" he asked, his lips nuzzling her ear.

"I'm fine," she said. "Do you have enough room?" If she turned her head just a bit farther, his mouth would be against her cheek. "Do you want me to find the other pillow? It's in a sack against the wall up at the front of the wagon."

"No, we can share," he told her. His hand left its spot

to move upward, brushing against her breast and then curving around her chin. "Can you turn just a little more?"

She obliged and shifted against him, feeling the touch of warm lips against the corner of her mouth, the whisper of his breath on her cheek. "Good night, Jess," he said softly. "If you need anything, just wiggle a little and I'll wake up."

She nodded and his hand eased its way down her body again, until it rested against the rounding of her belly. Behind her, she felt the ridge of his arousal, knew a moment of panic as it nudged her, and then heard his chuckle as he acknowledged his problem.

"Sorry, sweetheart. I'm trying to behave. Just ignore me."

Ignore him? As if she could. As if her life hadn't been changed forevermore by the presence of the man she'd taken into her life and her bed. She'd not expected to feel so safe and secure within his embrace. But Finn had promised to give her time. And she had a feeling that once Finn Carson had given his word, it was as good as gold.

"Well, you seem happy enough," Geraldine said with a teasing grin. "I figured Mr. Carson would be an easy man to please." She eyed Jessica thoroughly and settled beside her on the ground. "I told my mister that it was gonna be hard for you to take another man so quick after losing the first one, but it sure don't seem to me you're in mourning."

"I don't have much to mourn," Jessica told her. "Lyle was a miserable man, more interested in his gambling and drinking than he was in his wife." She lowered her voice and leaned closer to Geraldine. "Finn Carson is kind, and best of all he seems to like me. I've had an easier life since Lyle was shot than I ever did while he was alive."

"You're a good-lookin' woman, Jessica. I wasn't surprised to see the bachelors givin' you the eye. You know

I kinda wondered about Mr. Morgan. He's a handsome fella, and I think he'd have snatched you up in a minute, given a chance.''

"Maybe so," Jessica agreed. "I doubt he'd have much trouble persuading a woman to look his way. If Finn hadn't staked his claim so quickly, things might have been different." She smiled, remembering the man's persistence. "He was determined."

Geraldine smiled as she rose and brushed off her skirts. "I see your man headin' this way. I'd better be gettin' back to our wagon. The girls are supposed to be doing their sums, but once my back is turned I suspect they're cuttin' up."

Jessica watched her go, saw the loving hands that touched two small girls and then drew one of them onto her mother's lap. Geraldine was a good mother. *I hope I can do as well.* The babe within her twisted and stretched, and Jessica's hand went to the back of her rib cage, rubbing distractedly there where tiny feet pressed against her back.

"Are you all right?" Finn's long strides carried him across the circle and he frowned as he approached, his attention apparently caught by her gesture. "Your back hurting, Jess?" He dropped to the ground beside her and she nodded.

"This child is growing by the day. I can't say I'm looking forward to having a baby be born during this trip, but on the other hand, I'm thinking it'll be easier to tote him around once he makes an appearance."

Finn didn't often speak of her child, though she knew he accepted its presence. The past week had found his hand resting on her expanding belly every night, even as he curled behind her, surrounding her with his warmth.

Now he seemed hesitant. "Do you have enough…" He paused, his brow furrowing as he if searched for the right words. "You know, whatever the baby will need to wear," he finished. "I didn't think of it in Council Grove. Maybe we should have bought some things there."

Jessica's heart was touched by his concern, and she made haste to reassure him. "I've got diapers and little gowns," she said. "I made Lyle buy me a bolt of outing flannel in Saint Louis and I've hemmed diapers ever since. I think Arlois is making me a couple of blankets. I saw her putting pieces together a couple of weeks ago, and I'm willing to bet she'll be bringing them to me before long."

"I don't know much about babies," Finn admitted. "But I'll do whatever you tell me to. I wondered about making a bed, but we don't have much room in the wagon to keep one."

Jessica grinned. "It's going to be a bit crowded if we all try to fit on that feather tick, I'm afraid. I was thinking I could put a folded blanket toward the front of the wagon, where he'd be handy during the night."

Finn nodded and lifted the iron spit, poking it at the burning coals. "How long do you figure you've got?" he asked, flicking her an inquiring glance.

"A month, maybe," she told him. "Arlois said I haven't dropped yet, whatever that means. And Geraldine told me I don't waddle like I will right at the end."

"Waddle?" Finn's grin could not be suppressed. "I can't imagine that. You're the most graceful woman I've ever seen."

Jessica simply shook her head at his words. "Now I know why I married you, Mr. Carson. You're blind to all my faults. Right now there's not a graceful bone in my body."

"Coulda fooled me," he drawled, his leer exaggerated as he nudged her knee with his shoulder.

She sat on her block of wood, looking down at him, and for a moment she was breathless, captured by the look of pure satisfaction on his face. "Are you happy with your bargain, Finn?" she asked quietly. "You're married to me, and yet all you've gotten from this arrangement is the privilege of taking care of me.''

''I'm not complaining,'' he said. ''I told you I'd wait, Jess.''

''I know.'' She touched his shoulder with her fingertips and then released a sigh. ''I don't think it would hurt the baby if we…'' Unable to speak the words of invitation aloud, she spread her palm against his nape. She felt the tightening of his muscles, knew a moment of apprehension as he turned to look fully into her face.

''You'd better be sure about it before you climb into that wagon tonight,'' he murmured, his words urgent, his tone husky. His eyes narrowed, as if he sought assurance of her offer. ''I won't hurt you, Jess. You know that.''

''I believe you.'' She felt a flush rise to cover her cheeks. ''Talking about it is harder than just doing it, I think. But I wanted you to know that I feel guilty for making you wait.''

''It's only been two weeks,'' he said gently. And then his mouth twisted into a wry smile. ''Two *long* weeks, now that I think about it.''

''You haven't been married before, have you?'' she asked.

''No. I have to admit you're the first woman I've ever wanted to marry.''

''Why, Finn?'' The man must have seen women more slender, better dressed, even prettier than the one he'd chosen to wed. For the first time, she sought to force an answer to the question.

His gaze swept over her, not lingering on her breasts or hips, or paying special mind to the burden she carried beneath her apron. Blue eyes softened as they focused on her face, and his smile was a bit lopsided, as if embarrassment made him hesitate to speak. ''I told you before, Jess. I wanted you the first time I laid eyes on you. Why is any human being attracted to another? I don't have the answer.

I only know that I've never been so tempted to slam a man
to the ground as I was Lyle Beaumont that day in Saint
Louis. All I could see was a small, slim female being
abused by a man who obviously didn't appreciate what he
had.''

Finn took off his hat and ran long fingers through his
hair, as if he searched for words to express his thoughts.
''I had no idea who you were, but I figured I'd have a
miserable time keeping my eyes off you during this trip.
Hell, I could barely stop myself from keeping my mouth
shut and my hands to myself when I heard him holler at
you.''

He bent his head and looked down at the fire. ''I saw a
bruise on your cheek one day, and I had to saddle my horse
and ride off my anger for fear I'd shoot the bastard.''

Jessica drew in a deep breath, aching to put her arms
around his shoulders, needing to offer him the only gift she
possessed. ''Finn?'' Her voice was soft, strained, and the
single syllable vibrated with a breathless invitation. Her
hands were clenched now in her lap and she deliberately
unfolded her fingers. ''Please, Finn. I need you to put your
arms around me.''

His head tilted to the side and his nostrils flared as he
nodded. ''All right, Jess. Do you want to climb in the
wagon? Or shall we go for a walk?''

Memories of the last time they'd walked in the darkness
enveloped her. He'd touched her with gentle care. His
mouth had lured her, offering a taste of passion that had
almost frightened her. His hands had been warm and knowing, giving pleasure where she'd expected none.

And then she'd turned him away. If she walked with him
again, there would be no turning back. She would become
his wife in fact. He had wanted her on that long-ago morning in Saint Louis. Now she recognized that she was ready
to be his wife, knew that his patience and tenderness had
borne fruit.

A love she hadn't known she was capable of had been born within her, and she could not refute its existence. It was time to cede to him his place in her life with the full knowledge that once she gave herself into his keeping everything between them would be changed.

Her body would bear his imprint, and her heart would never again be her own.

Chapter Six

She'd walked this path before. Not with the same starlit slice of prairie surrounding her, nor the lush layer of grasses beneath her feet. Yet this trek across the gently rolling landscape was familiar, and the goal before her was already set. She knew what lay ahead, knew the taste of Finn's lips, had experienced the touch of his hands against her skin.

She'd denied her own yearnings on that other night, not only because she doubted her ability to please him, but because of a deep-seated fear of the intimacy he had asked of her. And he'd acceded to her hesitation, had comforted her instead within the shelter of his arms.

It would not be thus tonight, she determined. Though trust was not easily given from a heart that had been bruised and battered, Finn deserved what was rightfully due him. And Jessica was, above all else, grateful to him for his patience. There existed within her a hope that this man's arms would hold warmth and a measure of pleasure, and what she gave him would be cherished.

Open country lay before her. Behind lay the safety of a circle of wagons, fast falling into the distance. It was symbolic, perhaps, that they walked together, as they had walked down the aisle of the small church in Council Grove, a man and woman, facing the moment of truth when their vows of marriage would be finalized by the consummation of their legal bond.

Finn paced his steps to hers, his hand warm against her back. That wide palm balanced her, supported her as she climbed a slight rise, and then hesitantly stepped over the crest. ''Are you all right?'' he asked as his other hand reached quickly to grip her fingers. ''I don't want you to lose your balance, Jess.''

He drew her against his side and his palm moved from the center of her back to clasp more firmly at her waistline. Or what there was left of it, she thought grimly.

Finn would expect to expose her body to his sight, would no doubt open her dress and once more touch and explore the swollen curves her pregnancy had bestowed upon her. She'd never paid particular attention to her female form, but Finn's attention had, more than once, rested warmly on her and she'd recognized admiration in his eyes.

Lyle had never been enamored by her body, had simply used it when his need arose. And where, she wondered, had that thought come from?

The two men were different, as alike as black and white. And yet, all men were similar in some areas, as she'd discovered when the women spoke together, some of them referring to their spouses as ''horny'' or ''randy.'' The words were offensive to her, maybe because they so aptly described Lyle's behavior when he sought her out in the night hours. Unless Finn was just on his best behavior, he seemed better able to control his needs, she decided. And that might bode well for their marriage.

''Let's sit down here,'' he said, interrupting her thoughts as he brought her to a halt. A quilt was beneath his arm and he released her long enough to snap it open and allow it to drift to the ground before he bowed to her in a parody of courtly demeanor and waved his arm, designating the spot where she should sit.

She lowered herself, grasping his hand as she settled almost in the center of the coverlet. In the light of a sky full of stars, it appeared nondescript, its colors seeming faded. It had been her mother's gift for her wedding, and for a moment, Jessica wondered if that lady would appreciate the work of her hands being spread in such a desolate place.

Finn stretched out on his side and reached for her hand, kissing her knuckles and then idly drawing circles on her palm. "Are you worried about this?" he asked, lacing their fingers together smoothly and lifting their joined hands once more to his lips.

"No," she murmured, denying her apprehension, noting the increase of her heartbeat as his breath warmed her fingertips. Then he drew a fingertip into his mouth. He was wooing her, his patience seeming to be without end as he fondled her hand and then nipped one finger gently, as if he would draw her attention.

"I care about you," he said softly. "I want to please you, Jess." When she was silent, he drew her closer, coaxing her to his long length. "Lie with me, please," he asked quietly. "You said you wanted me to hold you. I'd like to feel you against me—unless you've changed your mind?"

She shook her head, not trusting her voice, and, feeling awkward and unwieldy, she did as he asked. His arms were there, welcoming her into his embrace, and she was drawn close, settling beside him as his hands eased her gently to lie on the quilt. His chest was wide, his arms long, and she was warmed by the sanctuary he offered.

For a long moment, he only held her, one hand brushing her hair back, exposing her forehead, tucking stray tendrils behind her ear. Then his fingers cupped her chin, tilting it upward, and he angled his head, allowing their mouths to meet in a gentle kiss. Undemanding lips brushed hers with care, as if he savored their fullness, and she trembled at the gentleness of his touch.

His tongue touched briefly at one corner of her mouth

and she caught her breath as temptation beckoned her lips to part. Would he think her brazen if she—

The thought was captured, her mouth taken prisoner as he swept her bottom lip with the damp tip and then pressed for entry. Her lips parted, and a sigh of pleasure welcomed him to the warmth he sought.

A low sound of satisfaction vibrated from his throat as his arms tightened their grasp and he turned her to her back. Carefully he shifted to rise above her, resting his weight on his elbows, hovering over her like a dark shadow, seeming mysterious, filling her with a sense of anticipation.

He tasted good, she decided…of coffee and mint. His scent was more subtle, soap and leather combined, telling her he was freshly washed, although his clothing was that which he'd worn throughout the day. Finn's hands moved, framing her face, his thumbs caressing the tender skin of her throat. His weight captured her, holding her beneath him, and his chest moved against the rise of her breasts, as one long leg eased its way across hers.

Now he ran gentle fingers through the loosened waves at her temples and over her ears. "Can I take down your hair?" he whispered.

She nodded. "If you want to. Shall I do it?"

"No. Let me." Those long, clever fingers slid the piece of yarn she'd tied at the tail of her braid and tucked it into his shirt pocket, then returned to the unraveling of her hair. He rubbed her scalp and his fingers threaded through the dark locks, wrapping crinkled waves around his hands and then allowing them to flow freely over her shoulders and across the quilt.

As if she existed in the midst of a dream, she closed her eyes, and a murmur of contentment sounded from her throat. "I think you like that," he whispered.

She thought amusement tinged his words, but she only nodded, pampered and coddled by his attentions. "I want to kiss you, sweetheart," he whispered, even as he bent his head to fit his mouth against hers, kissing her with long, lingering caresses, as though this meeting of their lips was worthy of his total concentration. Seeking no more from her than the taste of her mouth, the softness of her skin where he nuzzled, he whispered soft words that nourished her hungry heart.

"I've thought of you all day," he murmured. "Waiting for the chance to kiss you and touch you." He blew softly on her throat where his tongue had so recently sampled the flavor of her skin.

"And now?" she asked, his words making her bold. "Am I what you expected?"

"Well…" He drawled the word and grinned. "I'd say you taste better than rabbit stew. Better than I remembered."

"I suspect you're teasing me." She peered up at his shadowed face, and found a smile touching his lips.

"A little." His hands moved to the buttons that centered her chest. "Do you mind?" His fingers loosened each white bit of mother-of-pearl and she held her breath as he found smaller specimens on the shift she wore beneath her dress. He slid each tiny circle from place slowly and then bent to touch his lips to the exposed skin.

"No," she managed to whisper. "I don't mind."

His chuckle was low and she smiled in response. "I couldn't wait to see you, Jess," he said softly. "I won't rush you, sweetheart. I just needed to find out if you're as pretty as I remembered." And then his indrawn breath told her he was not disappointed with what he discovered as he drew back the sides of her undergarment.

She felt the puckering of those dark, swollen peaks and knew what he would do next. Yet it took all of her will-power not to shrink from his lips as he kissed them. But his mouth was gentle against her skin, as if he sensed her moment of reserve. He hovered there for long minutes and then transferred his attention a bit lower, nuzzling and caressing the underside of her breasts.

"All right?" he asked, as if asking permission, and she nodded. Only to shiver as his mouth opened and the edges of his teeth touched her skin.

She jerked to one side, her trembling an automatic response to his teeth against the tender flesh, and he lifted his head, seeking her eyes in the starlight. "Jess?" She felt his hesitation, and the frown he turned upon her. "What is it? Did he…"

She nodded, a jerky movement, interrupting his query as she remembered bruises and broken skin brought about by Lyle's drunken anger one night when she'd refused his advances. Unable to speak her shame aloud, her fingers rose to cover her trembling lips. And it seemed he needed no details to understand what she feared.

"I'm sorry, sweetheart. Sorry for what he did to you. I won't—"

"No." She spoke the single syllable softly, but it was enough to halt his apology. "I won't let him spoil this for us," she said, moving her hands to his face, then sliding them to the back of his head, her fingers threading through his hair. She pressed him closer, until his lips touched her breast once more.

"Please, Finn. Show me how it should be."

He drew a shuddering breath and nodded, his head turning to the side as his tongue began a seduction of her flesh. He was slow, gentle…all the things she'd never known at the hands of a man, and she fixed her eyes on him, watching as his mouth pressed against her skin.

This is Finn. As if the words were spoken aloud, they vibrated in her mind and she clung to the promise he'd offered. His hand rose to touch her, his palm curling beneath her breast, enclosing the weight of it and lifting it, squeezing gently as he once more took it into his mouth.

He suckled there and the thread of desire strung out,

capturing her in a taut, shimmering web as his mouth feasted on her flesh, weaving silken strands of desire that embraced her and held her with shivering delight. Her hips lifted from the ground and she was aware of a sensation that was new, a heated spasm that caused her muscles to flex and her legs to part at his urging.

Finn's husky murmur caught her ear and she trembled anew at the speaking of her name. "Jessica?" As though he asked her permission, his hand moved to draw her dress upward, exposing her legs to the night air, and then he paused, his fingers edging beneath the hem of her drawers.

"I'm going to slide these off," he said, waiting only a moment before he found the tapes that tied the garment at her waist and tugged them loose. She wiggled free of them, aiding him in this venture as he eased them past the cumbersome weight of her pregnancy. Stripping them from her, he laid them aside, and the warmth of his palm rested on her knee. She felt its heat, each finger flexing against her flesh, branding her as his, coaxing a response.

She gave it with a sigh, offering no resistance as the callused weight of his palm eased her legs apart, and long fingers caressed the soft skin. His hand slipped up the length of her thigh, and she felt the brush and tug of a gentle touch against the nest of curls he'd exposed.

A fervent rush of desire held her in place, breathless and aching as his fingers plied hidden creases and touched sensitive flesh. Her eyelids were heavy, and she sighed, turning her head away as the subtle wash of pleasure poured from his fingertips to bathe her with shimmering delight.

But he demanded more, and his voice called to her, wooing her to his purpose. "Look at me, Jess. I want you to know the man who touches you."

"I've never felt so exposed, so naked," she whispered, lifting her eyes.

"Ah, but this is only the beginning, sweetheart. One day you'll come to me with nothing to hide your body from my sight," he promised. "For tonight, I won't ask that of you. Only this much."

His mouth met hers again and she lifted her arms to encircle his shoulders. Boldly his fingers traced again the protective folds of her woman's flesh, and she had a moment of fear as he trespassed to seek out the hidden place he readied for his taking.

This is Finn. The words swirled in her mind, and again she turned from the memory that had assailed her for that single instant. *This is Finn.* She sighed softly and welcomed him. Moisture formed at his bidding, easing his path, and she murmured her pleasure as he caressed the softness and then eased a gentle fingertip within.

It was an exploration such as she'd never known, his hand cupping her, his fingers curving to open her, fondling and probing as if he sought some hidden secret deep within her body. She shifted beneath his touch, her breath catching in her throat, her hips rising to silently beg his caress, and he obliged.

She opened her eyes, seeking his gaze, and knew that his passion was reined by the barest thread, his jaw taut and clenched, his throat arched. And then he bent once more to suckle her, capturing the turgid crest of her breast and holding it captive in his mouth.

And still his hand urged her to rise against his palm, his movements more insistent, his fingers sliding within her in a quickening motion she recognized, applying pressure first in one place, then another, until she knew a gathering of heat and throbbing pleasure that grew and multiplied, forcing whimpering cries from her lips.

He caught them in his mouth, then whispered his encouragement as he kissed her with urgent lips and teeth and tongue. And still his fingers made their magic on her flesh, until the heat enveloped her and she was caught up in long moments of writhing spasms of delight. She sobbed, tears flowing as she clutched at him, yearning for his possession.

Quickly loosening his trousers, he knelt between her legs, lifting her bottom and placing her legs over his thighs until she felt the thick, velvet tip of his manhood pressing within. He was achingly slow in his taking of her, yet she felt his trembling need, heard the sound of his rasping breath as he accepted the gift she offered. Pressing within her, retreating a bit, then surging forward again, he measured his firm movements with care, lest he cause harm.

His head was thrown back then, his teeth exposed, his face contorted in the light of a million stars, and she watched as he shuddered and groaned, then thrust one last time, his head falling forward as if he could not hold it erect.

"Jessica." His voice was rough as he spoke her name, yet it held an undercurrent of tenderness she could not fail to recognize.

Her arms reached for him as he lowered himself to sprawl across her, holding his weight on his forearms, his breathing labored and uneven. "Tell me I didn't hurt you," he demanded, and she was tempted to laugh aloud.

"No, you didn't hurt me," she said, filled with a joy she could barely contain. She shivered in delight as she shifted a bit beneath him, experienced a moment of aching fulfillment as she recognized the presence of his male flesh still within her body, and flexed her muscles to hold it captive.

"Jessica." He repeated her name as if he savored each syllable, and then murmured soft words she strained to hear. "You're perfect," he said. "So pretty and soft." He inhaled deeply of her skin, his nose pressed to her throat, and then slid lower until his mouth touched her breast again. His lips opened and he drew a bit of skin into his mouth, leaving his mark on her.

She closed her eyes, caught up in the rapture of his loving, knowing his touch would bring only joy and pleasure to each place he visited with his hands and mouth. He was all that was good in her life, all she'd ever yearned for in a husband. He'd not found her lacking, and for that she was grateful. That she could bring satisfaction to this man was what she had hoped for.

That he would entice her with words, lure her with tenderness and lead her on a passionate journey such as they'd traveled together had stunned her. His patience with her fearfulness and his care of her vulnerable body had enticed her to go beyond the boundaries of her past, showing her the beauty that was possible between a man and his wife.

For the first time, she'd known the thrill of being a bride, in the truest sense of the word.

The campfires were fast becoming beds of coals as they climbed into the back of her wagon. Jessica stumbled against a box and Finn caught her arm, holding her upright. "Are you all right?" he asked in an undertone, not wanting to awaken those who might be sleeping nearby.

"Yes," she whispered, sliding the feather tick down to the floor. It was unwieldy and heavy, and he grasped the bottom half, allowing it to fall in a heap in the center of the wagon. "I'll get the pillows down."

"That's all right, I can reach them more easily than you," he whispered, holding her to one side as he tugged at the heavy feather ticking. The quilt he'd carried was shaken clean already. He'd seen to it while Jessica straightened her clothing, and then embraced her with one long arm as they made their way back to the circle of wagons.

Now he watched as she quickly undid the buttons she'd only put into place minutes before. The dress slid to surround her feet and she reached for her nightgown. His hand was there before her and he tugged it from her grasp.

"Leave it on a box where you can reach it, sweetheart."

She was silent for a moment and then her whisper reached him. "But I can't go to bed in my petticoat, Finn."

"I didn't expect you to." His whisper held a hint of laughter as he felt for her, his hands encountering soft curves and rounded areas. Her petticoat tapes were easily taken care of and the garment fell to join her dress on the floor. "Lift your arms," he told her, and when she obeyed, he slid the shift over her head and tossed it aside.

The quilt covered the feather tick and he snatched up a sheet, then guided her to lie on the thick mass of their makeshift mattress. "I'll be right there," he whispered, shedding his clothing as quickly as he'd rid her of the shift.

She rolled to one side and he fit himself next to her, his hands seeking and finding the rounded, womanly form he'd taken to himself. The murmur from her lips was not a protest, but rather an acquiescent sigh, he decided as she snuggled against him. Her skin was warm, smooth to the touch of his callused hand, and he rued the harshness of his flesh as his palm skimmed over her shoulder and down the length of her arm, until he captured her hand within his own.

"Are you sure you're all right? I wasn't too rough?" he asked, his lips against her ear. She shook her head, a quick movement accompanied by a breathless denial.

"No. You didn't hurt me, Finn." Her whisper was hesitant then. "I've never known such happiness," she confessed. "I feel like a bride."

"You *are* a bride," he affirmed quietly. "You're mine, Jess. My bride…my wife."

Finn rode out at dawn astride his black gelding, a smile nudging at the corner of his mouth. Jonas grinned widely and lifted a hand in salute as he bid his scout a good morning. "You're lookin' pretty pleased with yourself, son," he said quietly, peering up beneath the brim of Finn's hat.

"I am?" Finn's shoulder twitched upward and then settled as Jonas placed a callused hand on the black horse's neck. "It's going to be a nice day," Finn announced, tossing a glance skyward. And then he met the wagon master's gaze. "Keep an eye on Jessica, will you?"

"Sure enough," Jonas answered agreeably. "She doing all right this morning?"

"Just waking up," Finn told him. "I asked David Bates's boy to walk with the team early on, and Jessica will take over after nooning." That she'd been flushed and rosy and willing to rise with him as he left the wagon in the last moments of night was a precious moment he kept to himself.

She'd offered to fix him breakfast and he'd bent instead to kiss her, promising to return when the sun was high in the sky to share the noon meal. "This being married is all right," he said in a low tone, unable to conceal the satisfaction he felt.

"She's a fine woman," Jonas said. "I'm glad she chose you, Finn." He lowered his voice and gripped Finn's reins, holding the black in place. "There's something afoot, but I don't know what's going on. Just a feeling. Keep your eyes open."

Finn touched his hat brim, and as Jonas released his grip, the gelding broke into a quick trot. The reins loosened and the horse responded, stretching his legs as if he welcomed the chance to explore the trail ahead. He'd done his own trailblazing last night, Finn thought, recalling the time spent beneath the moon and stars. A bond had been established between himself and his bride, one he intended to reinforce over the next days.

He couldn't push too hard yet, lest he cause her to be suspicious of his motives, but he'd take any advantage that arose to locate the deed and settle that part of their relationship. Acknowledging his interest in Aaron's land must wait, lest she think it had been the sole reason for his pursuit of her. But if he could find the blasted thing and see it for himself, in order to lay claim on Aaron's behalf, he'd make it a priority.

There weren't that many places in a wagon to hide such a document. Jessica seemed oblivious to its whereabouts, as if she had never actually seen it, only been aware of Lyle Beaumont's possession of it. Finn resolved to wait for a day or so before he approached her. In the meantime, he'd spend time coaxing her to himself, and that task would be far from burdensome. He looked forward to the nights to come and the hours they would spend in the darkness.

A movement on the horizon caught his eye and thoughts of Jessica went flying as he turned his gelding to the south, where two horsemen rode at an angle across the prairie. Probably men from the nearby settlement he'd seen on the map only yesterday, but their presence warranted his time. In moments they'd apparently caught sight of him, and as he watched they turned their mounts in a half circle and galloped up a rise.

A twitch at the back of his neck issued a warning, and he drew his spyglass from his pack, focusing on their departing figures. They didn't seem familiar, but one looked back over his shoulder and the blurred face was dark with a beard. He'd do well to let Jonas know that his suspicions might bear more notice.

The trail ahead was clear, with no sign of Indians crossing the rutted path they followed. Wagons had been here before them and more would follow after, the men and women searching for a better life, for land and a new start in the West. Some of the men were determined to mine for gold and silver, and Finn determined to watch closely lest any of the miners on the train had their eye on Jessica's wagon.

Lyle had bragged a bit, according to Jonas. Jessica's hand in marriage had been a prize to be sought by men who searched for gold with a passion that trampled over common everyday decency. Even more reason why the deed must be found and secured as soon as he could manage it.

Nooning was a time to take a deep breath and sit in the shade, if such a cool spot could be found. Jessica settled on her piece of log beside the wagon and unwrapped the towel in her lap. Leftover biscuits and a chunk of cheese from their stop in Council Grove awaited her, and she sliced the cheese, placing it between the biscuits she'd split in half. The sound of a horse approaching warned her of a visitor, and she looked up quickly, expecting to see Finn slide from the gelding he rode.

It was not to be. Gage Morgan rounded the corner of the wagon and snatched his hat from his head as he caught her eye. "Miss Jessica," he said, the greeting polite, his gaze measuring. As if he sought out secrets she hugged tight, he allowed his eyes to touch her hair, then her face, his dark eyes shuttered.

"I see you've found something to eat," he said quietly. "I won't keep you from your meal. I just wanted to offer my assistance if you were in need of anything. I saw Carson ride out early on, and I didn't think he'd come back yet."

"No, he's on the trail ahead, I suspect," she said, wrapping the food she held, lest it dry out before Finn arrived. "He said he'd be back at noon."

Morgan slid from his horse and dropped one knee to the ground beside her, tipping his hat brim back, the better to peer beneath the concealing edge of her sunbonnet. "Are you doing well?" he asked nicely. His glanced at the wedding ring she wore and she thought his jaw hardened as he considered that emblem of marriage. "Is your water supply holding up?"

At her nod, he looked down at the ground, and then up again quickly, catching her unaware. "If you need anything," he said, "anything at all, I'm available."

She frowned at him, disturbed by his words. "I'm a married woman, Mr. Morgan. I'm sure if there is anything to be tended to, Finn will take care of it. He won't appreciate you volunteering your services to me."

A smile touched the hard mouth and Morgan nodded. "I

understand his being a bit touchy where you're concerned, but there'll be times when he isn't around, ma'am, and I want you to know you can call on me if you find yourself in need.''

Jessica's heart sped up at his words. If Morgan thought she was in any danger, he'd do better to speak up, she thought. ''Are you referring to anything in particular?'' she asked. ''Do you think…'' She hesitated, and he sliced his hand through the air, halting her query.

''No, of course not. You're as safe as can be. It's just that a woman in your condition is hampered somewhat,'' he began. He rose and brushed off his trouser leg, looking past her to where a rider approached. ''Ah, I see Carson made it back for his noon meal,'' he said as Finn rode closer.

With a quick movement, he put on his hat and strode away, his horse behind him.

''What did he want?'' Finn asked, tying his mount to the corner of the wagon. He shed his gloves and hat and placed them next to Jessica, then settled beside her.

''Just offering his help, should I need it,'' she said, watching the man who had mounted his horse and ridden toward the wagon he owned. ''Why do you suppose he did that?'' she mused. ''He ought to know you'll take care of me, Finn.''

''If he bothers you again, I'll speak to him,'' Finn said. He followed the line of Jessica's focus as if he would gain access to the other man's motives. ''I think he's just covering all the angles, sweetheart.'' He took the biscuit she offered and bit into it as if the simple meal were ambrosia.

''What angles?'' she asked, her brows gathering at his words. ''I don't think I know what you mean.''

Finn looked up into her eyes. ''The men on the wagon train know that Lyle held possession of a deed to land near Pike's Peak,'' he said, his words causing apprehension to rise between them. ''We spoke of this weeks ago, Jess, and you told Jonas and me that you didn't know of its whereabouts. Now I'm asking you again. Do you have it?''

Jessica shook her head, bewildered by his query. "Why haven't you mentioned this before?" she asked. "You didn't say a word about it the day you married me."

Finn shrugged and took a bite of biscuit. "It was common knowledge that Lyle planned on looking for gold when you reached the end of the trail. He bragged to his gambling friends that he had a nice little homestead waiting for him.''

Jessica's heart seemed to fill her chest, beating with a staccato rhythm, and she trembled at Finn's words. "And is that the reason you married me? To get a piece of property that Lyle talked about?''

Finn's eyes narrowed as he shook his head. "No. That's not why I married you, Jess. Yes, I knew he'd talked about a deed, and you told us that yourself, but you hadn't said any more about it. I'm just wanting to know the truth of the matter.''

Jessica felt tears forming and she stood, her meal falling to the ground in front of her. Turning aside, unwilling to allow any sign of weakness, lest Finn try to comfort her, she sought out the back of the wagon. She didn't want his hands on her right now, couldn't bear the thought of his arms circling her or his body sheltering her as she wept. As though her world tottered on the brink of an abyss, she experienced a moment of pure panic.

Lyle had bragged of a deed and told her it was none of her business, and she'd allowed him to put her off. She should have sought it out after he died, searched out its hiding place in the wagon before she agreed to marry Finn Carson. Instead, she'd basked in the knowledge that a man wanted her as his bride, that Finn was willing to take care of her.

She'd thought to speak with Finn about the miserable deed, and hadn't. And of course he'd been aware of its existence from the first, had known about it when he married her. It certainly had made her a good prospect for marriage. The unfaltering trust she'd placed in him wavered as she turned aside.

Now the possibility of land at the end of the trail seemed to be her only hope for the future, a vision of property for herself and her child. But if Finn had married her because of the deed, she'd been hoodwinked after all. She leaned against the back of the wagon, her head resting against her arms and drew in deep, cleansing breaths, fighting the tears that seemed determined to fall.

"Jess, don't turn away from me," Finn said from beside her. His hand touched her shoulder and she flinched from its pressure. But he would not be deterred. "Jessica." He spoke her name loudly, and then again, in a softer, more subdued manner.

"Jessica, please look at me," he asked quietly. "I don't know what you're thinking, but you need to know that—" His voice broke off and she heard his breathing in the silence that formed between them.

He began again, more gently this time, and yet it seemed he knew better than to touch her, only stepped close and spoke in tones that would not carry further than her ear. "I married you because I wanted to take care of you, Jess. I wanted you from the first moment I saw you in Saint Louis. I've told you that already.

"Lyle stole that deed, Jess." He breathed his words into her ear. "He took it from my brother, Aaron, and then killed him for it. Believe it or not, as you please, but that's the truth. There isn't anything more I can say to convince you."

Her eyes were closed, dry now, the tears banished, and she leaned heavily against the wagon, feeling as if her legs would not hold her upright. She'd trusted Finn, given him all she had to offer.

Everything but the deed to a piece of property Finn

thought she had no right to own. She'd not seen it, had
never touched the document, only heard Lyle's words as
he described it to her.

It had been the reason for her to climb into the wagon
in Saint Louis, the lodestar that made this whole journey
palatable, that had coaxed her into the prairie crossing and
kept her with Lyle. It was her future, and for the first time
she faced the fact that it might never be hers to own. Finley
Carson had the legal right to anything she held, up to and
including her sole bit of inheritance from Lyle.

She'd been hoodwinked by Lyle, the man who had never
been honest with her during the years of their marriage.
She'd set out on this trek with the hope of a future.

The deed he sought had no doubt been the reason Finn
Carson had spoken vows with her in Council Grove. She
inhaled sharply and lifted her head, looking up at him.

"Did you marry me to avenge your brother, Finn? For
the chance to gain the deed?" His features swam before
her, as though he stood at the end of a long tunnel, and she
fought for a breath as she spoke again.

"For once, don't lie to me, Finn Carson. For once, tell
me the truth, or you'll be tarred by the same brush as
Lyle."

Chapter Seven

"*I*'*ve already told you why I married you. Because I wanted to take care of you, Jess.*" His voice had been harsh, his jaw clenching as he spoke, and things had not been quite the same since.

Now she wished for Finn to warm to her again. Lifting a hand, she brushed perspiration from her forehead. There was an overabundance of heat beneath the canvas wagon top, she decided. She'd have to settle for that.

Awkward didn't begin to describe her position, Jessica decided glumly. She was sitting on the wagon floor, her lap full of Lyle's last bits and pieces, an assortment of his personal belongings she'd shoved aside the day he was killed. Unable to face sorting through the last mementos he'd left, she'd stuffed them beneath a box of her own belongings. Now she faced the task of seeking the solution to the mysteries he'd left behind.

The deed being number one on the list. She bit at her lip as she thought of the man who'd been so much a part of her life. He'd been almost a stranger, she decided, once the first flush of married life had worn thin. Unable to keep up the sham of happiness, she'd drawn away from him almost from the first. And now she barely remembered the way he looked or the sound of his voice.

Not so with Finn. She had only to close her eyes to recall his scent, his touch, the shine of sunlight on his hair, moonlight reflected from blue eyes. She shook her head, banishing the memories of the man who had crawled beneath the skin of her heart and then left her bereft. He'd lied and deceived her, no matter what he said. Her breath caught in a sob, and she concentrated on the task that lay ahead.

Through blurred vision she recognized a receipt for food from the emporium in Saint Louis. It was smudged, only one item and the amount Lyle had paid to the owner still legible. A bolt of outing flannel was listed there, a purchase he'd held over her head as being frivolous.

He'd taunted her that day, and his words rang in her head. *It's a waste of money. There's no guarantee you'll even deliver a live baby.*

Wiping her eyes, she placed the bit of paper aside and unfolded another document. It was their marriage license, her signature delicate, Lyle's bold and careless across the textured paper. Deliberately she tore it in half. It had been a sentence of misery, one she'd just as soon put in the past.

And had she done any better the second time around? At least she'd known where she stood with Lyle. At the bottom of his list, granted, but certain of the value he placed on her. She'd given Finn her heart, trusted him with her love, and he, in turn, had been using her for his own means.

An envelope was next, still sealed, and she turned it over in her hands, her eyes widening as she caught sight of her name on the front. *Mrs. Lyle Beaumont, c/o Postmaster, Saint Louis, Missouri.* In the upper left corner was her father's name. She was stunned, angry with herself for not finding it sooner. Lyle had kept it from her all these months when she'd yearned for a message from her parents, had hidden it from her, until now.

The note she'd written in haste and posted from Council Grove might have been different, more than just a short notification of Lyle's death and her subsequent marriage had she known of this missive. Her index finger slid beneath the envelope flap and she opened it slowly. Her father's familiar hand was evident, his words stark.

This is your final chance to return home to your mother and me. We are willing to take care of you if you have the good sense to leave Lyle Beaumont. If not, we can do no more to help you. Your father.

She closed her eyes, willing the words to memory. She could have gone back, even that day in Council Grove when she'd made the choice to marry Finn. Maybe they'd have welcomed her into their home, once she explained that the letter had been kept from her for so long. Instead, she was bound to a man who now had laid claim to her and all she possessed.

Her fingers were numb as she folded the letter and placed it back in the envelope, tucking it into her apron pocket. An assortment of receipts from Saint Louis and Independence remained, and she wadded them together in her fist. No legal document met her gaze, no piece of paper that told of property at the end of the trail. If Lyle had ever had the deed he'd bragged of, he'd hidden it. She had no notion where to begin the search.

She looked up at the stacked goods at either end of the wagon. Her worldly possessions surrounded her, and at that thought she smiled grimly. Finn's possessions, she thought, her mind filled with bitter remorse.

"Jessica." His voice called her from the back of the wagon, and she held her breath, her hands filled with the trash she'd salvaged. Trash, all of it. Nothing worthwhile left of the years she'd spent as Mrs. Lyle Beaumont.

"Jessica." Finn's voice repeated her name and she stiffened her spine, turning her head to meet his gaze.

"Yes?" She knew her eyes were red rimmed, her hair

disheveled, her clothing wrinkled, and cared little that he should see her so. "What do you want?"

"Are you all right?" he asked. "We've stopped for nooning, and I thought you were sleeping."

"No. I've been going through some things Lyle left behind," she said quietly. She watched as Finn climbed into the wagon bed and crouched beside her. "There's nothing worth looking at," she told him, offering the handful of papers she held. "You're welcome to look at it yourself."

"If you say you found nothing, then I believe you," Finn said. "You have no reason not to be honest with me, Jess."

"I've *always* been honest with *you*," she said, her words tinged with bitterness. "I only wish you had returned the favor." She pulled her knees beneath her and struggled for balance, reaching to lift herself by leaning on a nearby crate. Finn's hands were there, clasping her around her middle as he rose beside her.

He was too tall to stand upright and his head bent forward as he looked carefully at her drawn features. "I know I look a sight," she told him. "I haven't felt well today."

"Let me help you down to the ground and get you something to eat," he offered, grasping her hand as he drew her toward the back of the wagon.

She shook her head. "I'll stay here. There's some cheese left, but you'll have to cut off the mold first. Arlois brought some flatbread by earlier." Neither item sounded appealing to her, but the child within her demanded sustenance and she'd force food down if she had to.

"All right," Finn said, turning from her to climb out the back. "We'll be at Cottonwood Creek by nightfall, Jess. I'll help you wash the clothes in the morning before we cross. Jonas said we'll stay there a full day."

Her heart lifted at his words. The thought of bathing in clear, clean water was enough to bring new hope to her weary mind. She'd be refreshed by the day spent with the other women, perhaps be able to sort out the small things she'd sewn and place them in order for the coming birth of her child.

She'd hidden them as she worked, lest Lyle taunt her for the hours she spent hemming diapers and stitching together three small gowns. Unable to look any further ahead than the next few days, she determined to lay plans for her future and that of her child. Unless she was wrong, the baby would be born within the month. She had that long to form her plans.

In a few minutes Finn was back, bread and cheese wrapped in a towel. "Here you go, sweetheart," he said quietly. "Try to eat it all, will you?" He watched her as she accepted it from his hand. Fingers met, his warm, hers chilled, as if her heart had not pumped her life's blood sufficiently to reach her hands. "You're cold, Jess. What's wrong with you?" he asked, refusing to release her, reaching into the wagon to place his other palm against her forehead.

"I'm fine," she told him, pulling away from the contact, angry at the need for his touch that would have caused her to lean into his strength. Quick tears burned behind her eyelids and she lowered her lashes to hide her weakness from him. But he would not be deterred.

"Move aside," he said, as if he knew that she would only willingly do his bidding if he issued the edict as a command.

She pulled her skirts beneath her and settled again on the floor, holding the offering he'd put into her hands, warming her fingers in the towel that held her food. He was beside her in an instant, his arm circling her shoulders, pulling her against his chest. "Don't argue with me, Jess," he said in a low tone. "You're cold and I won't have it.

"Though how you can be so chilled in this heat is beyond me." He arranged her on his lap, for her comfort and his own, and then urged her compliance. "Now, eat," he said. She felt the heat of his body surrounding her, suffering his embrace yet offering it a grudging welcome.

"Thank you," she whispered, as he lifted her hand and placed the bread into her fingers. Determinedly he nudged her chin and she opened her mouth, accepting the food he'd prepared. The bread was sweet, Arlois having put sugar into the dough, and the cheese was soft and warm, tasting sharp against her tongue. She chewed and swallowed and then spoke her surprise as Finn took the next bite, his mouth opening over her fingertips, his lips caressing her skin.

"Didn't you fix some for yourself?" she asked, and then backtracked, aware that her words sounded petty and unwelcoming. "I only thought—"

"It's all right," he said quickly, interrupting her words. "I'd decided to share with you until we get you warmed up a little. Then I'll climb down and fix another piece of bread for us."

"I'm all right," she said, lying through her teeth, for the body heat he contributed to her chilled flesh was only now beginning to seep into her shoulders and back. His arms slid down and settled there at her waistline, tugging her closer to him, and she allowed it, aware that it was not in her child's best interests for its mother to shiver and quake.

"You're not all right, Jess," he murmured beside her, and then bent to bite again at the bread she held. "Now take your share," he said, nudging her hand toward her mouth. "I won't have you sitting in here, shivering for who knows what reason, all by yourself, when I'm aching for the chance to hold you and keep you warm."

He cuddled her closer. "Now you'll have to feed me," he told her, his smug words whispered against her temple, his breath warm against her skin.

She gave in to the comfort he offered, curling against him, hearing his murmur of pleasure as he gathered her close. "That's better," he said, satisfaction edging his voice. "If I'd known what you were doing in here I'd have hauled you up on the seat in the sunshine an hour ago. We can go over Lyle's stuff together, Jessica. If you want me to help you dig through those boxes and crates, all you have to do is say so. I'll do anything you ask of me."

"I was looking for the deed," she confessed quietly. "I felt foolish that I hadn't searched it out before."

"I'll warrant he hid it well," Finn said gruffly. "He wasn't about to leave it lying around in plain sight." He rocked her a bit, and his mouth made a damp trail across her forehead and down her cheek. "We'll have to think about it, sweetheart. Where would a man put something he didn't want found. In a wagon this size it wouldn't be simple to keep such a thing safe. If we crossed a creek, it might get wet. If the wagon overturned, it might be lost in the shuffle. And if it were too easy to locate, anyone could sort through your things and come up a rich man."

"Rich?" she asked. "Do you really think the deed is worth an enormous amount of money? Enough to make someone kill for it?"

"Lyle killed for it," Finn answered bluntly. "And I suspect that whoever killed Lyle knew what he was doing. I'll bet you he thought he'd stand a better chance of sorting through this wagon with Lyle out of the way."

"But who?" she asked, bewilderment touching the words with despair "I can't imagine taking a life for a bit of paper."

"There are those who are desperate for such a claim," Finn said bluntly. "Any one of the miners on the train is suspect, so far as I'm concerned."

"Even Gage Morgan?" she asked quietly.

Finn was silent for a moment and then he shrugged. "I don't know. Morgan is a breed apart from the rest of that crew. He hangs with them, but he's not a part of them."

"You don't trust him, do you?" she asked.

"Do you?" he returned, tipping her head back to look

into her eyes. And she was struck by the piercing intensity of his gaze as he awaited her reply.

Her answer was long in coming and her words were tentative. "I don't know," she said slowly. "Sometimes he looks as if he can see inside my brain and know what I'm thinking, and that frightens me. Other times I tell myself I'm being foolish and he's just a man trying to be friendly."

"I'd rather he stayed away from you altogether, Jess," Finn said, and she noted with surprise the tone he employed. "He wanted you, would have been more than willing to marry you, and I don't like him looking at you as if he's wondering if he'll ever have another chance at you."

"You don't think—you don't really believe—" she said haltingly, her eyes widening as his narrowed. "Is he a threat to you, Finn?"

"Only in so far as wanting what I hold dear," Finn answered quietly. "He'd give his eyeteeth for a chance to have you. Surely you know that already."

She shook her head. "I've never thought about it, I suppose. He's always been kind to me, considerate, but he's never pushed me for any bit of…of intimacy," she finished quietly, thinking of Morgan's small favors…heating water for her morning washup, carving her a walking stick. Things that Finn didn't need to be privy to, lest he find more meaning in them than what Morgan had meant to imply.

"Are you feeling better? Now that you have a little food in you?" Finn asked, obviously desirous of changing the line of talk they'd indulged in. Beneath her bottom, she felt the hard ridge of his arousal, nudging at the soft rounding of her hips, and she shifted, ready to rise should he allow it.

"Why don't we both go on out into the sunshine?" she asked. "You can fix some more bread, and I'll cut the bad spots off the cheese." That Finn felt more than a bit of desire for her was apparent. That she was not willing right now to supply that need made her cringe from the reminder of his right to ask it of her.

"Don't pull away from me, Jess," he said, tightening his hold on her. "I won't ask anything of you. I thought you knew that already. I'm only willing to take what you give me, freely and without coercion."

"I do know that," she answered, subsiding against his chest. "I'm sorry to be so ornery. I have much to be thankful for, Finn Carson."

"You don't owe me your thanks, Mrs. Carson," he said. "You don't owe me a damn thing. But if you'll kiss me, I'll appreciate it and take it as payment for warming you and fixing your noon meal, such as it was."

"My kisses aren't all that wonderful," she said, embarrassed by his words. "I don't know of another soul who'd be interested in sharing them with me."

"I can think of a couple just offhand," he said, his voice teasing now as she lifted her chin and brought her mouth to touch his. He kissed her, long and lustily, his tongue taking possession of her mouth in a manner she could not mistake. "Let me know when you're not mad at me anymore," he said softly as he set her aside and stood up.

His hands reached for her and helped her to find her balance before he climbed from the wagon and then turned to help her down. From across the way, a man watched, another ragged miner halting by the side of his oxen to speak in a casual manner to the first. And Finn felt the appraising look as if it had been shot in his direction with the force of a rifle bullet.

He lifted Jessica to the ground and stood between her and the two men who made no attempt to hide their interest. He thought idly that they were probably jealous and wondering what he and Jess had been doing in the wagon. And yet, the heat of searching eyes burned at the nape of his neck, and he felt a chill of apprehension that touched his spine with cold fingers.

Before they'd completed their hasty meal, Jonas called
out for the wagons to roll on down the trail, and Finn took
his place at the head of Jessica's team of oxen. She walked
beside him, and he offered his arm for her comfort. She
took it with a slight smile and her fingers clasped lightly
against the skin of his wrist as they walked together. For
the first time since their words of the day before, he felt a
renewal of the truce they'd formed, knew pleasure at the
words she spoke, the casual observations she made as they
passed flowers on the prairie, and gauged the miles they
would travel before the creek ahead came into sight.

And when the afternoon turned into early evening and
the scent of fresh water reached the oxen and mules, he
heard a resurgence of laughter among the women, loud
voices raised amid the menfolk as the wagon rolled on at
a quicker pace. The animals leaned into the yokes and
traces as they put on a burst of energy, anxious for a cooling drink. And when Cottonwood Creek came in sight, the
children ran ahead, stopping only to strip from their shoes
before they walked in the shallows and splashed with joyous shouts of merriment.

"We'll stop beneath those trees," Finn said. "I rode here
early this morning to be sure it was safe."

"While I slept?" Jessica asked, looking at him as if she
wondered at his energy after such a long day. And then she
spoke aloud the words he'd already known she would offer
him. "I forget how much I owe you, Finn. How much all
of us on the train owe you and the others who do so much
for us."

"I get paid for it," he said, shrugging off her thanks.
"My horse likes the early-morning runs, and I see a whole
different world out there when I'm riding ahead and watching the trail for signs."

"Are you in danger?" she asked, and he wondered if
this was the first time it had occurred to her that many a

scout had met a sorry end between Independence and the end of the trail.

But he would not allow her to be swamped in concern for something she had no control over, and he shook his head. "Naw, not so's you could notice. My horse is fast and I know how to duck."

His grin seemed to mollify her and she sighed, turning back to peer ahead as the wagons began forming their circle. "I'll cast around and see if there's any wood to be had," she said, falling away from his side as he followed the wagon in front of them, guiding the oxen close behind David Bates's own unit.

She held the corners of her apron, bending to pick up bits and pieces of wood from the ground, the supply scanty and sparse but still worth gathering. Finn watched her for a moment and then concentrated on removing the oxen from their yoke and leading them to the enclosure that was fast being formed by several of the men, looping ropes from trees farther downstream where the animals could drink without befouling the water.

Several other women were following Jessica's example and they called back and forth, their figures but shadows in the gathering twilight. A laugh rang out and he experienced a moment's pleasure as he recognized Jessica's distinctive tone.

He'd tried to mend his fences today and received a certain amount of satisfaction as he recalled their moments together. She was dependent on him, and that was exactly what he wanted of her. So needy of his care that she would allow him to shield her from any forces that might win her from him. Tied so tightly to him that no one stood a chance of rending asunder the bonds he'd worked to form between him and the woman he'd taken to wife.

Nightfall was upon them before the campfires were lit, the stars shining from a cloudless night sky and an unusual chill in the air. The women clutched their shawls about their shoulders and gathered their children close, remaining in small groups within the circumference of the circle of wagons. Finn worked quickly to build a fire, catching the kindling aglow with a sulphur match from his supply and slowly adding bits of wood that Jessica had gathered.

A final heap of buffalo chips from a basket hanging beneath the wagon completed his task, and within minutes he'd set up the tripod and hung Jessica's stew pot over the flames. She opened a tin can of meat he'd purchased in Council Grove and added vegetables traded with Arlois for another can of beef. Water from the barrel brought new life to the dried carrots and potatoes, and in half an hour a tasty supper was ready. The coffeepot sat on Jessica's baking stone, keeping warm once it had boiled sufficiently, and together they sat before the dying embers, eating from the pot positioned between them, sipping coffee from a single cup they shared.

"It's good," Finn said, enjoying their companionship at least as much as he did the food they ate.

Jessica nodded, dipping her utensil again into the final bites remaining in the bottom of the pan. "Finish it," she said, lifting her last spoonful to her mouth. And Finn agreeably did as she told him, scraping the meat and gravy from the sides and bending to scoop it into his mouth.

"Good stew," she agreed, readying herself to rise, one hand pushing against the side of the wagon for purchase.

"I'll take care of things," Finn said quietly. "Sit still, Jess."

She allowed it, relieved, if the truth be told, at his words. Her legs ached from the long walk today, a pleasant weariness sweeping over her. She'd tried to keep Finn at arm's length, storing up her anger and pique so that she might keep it to her bosom and hold herself aloof from him. It hadn't worked. The man would not be set aside or slighted, and she didn't have what it took to turn away from his advances or ignore his kindness.

She bent toward the burning coals and held out her hands to warm them, aware of eyes that watched her from across the circle. Who it was or where they hid while they watched, she didn't know. But the feeling of malevolence chilled her and she lifted her lashes to look for its source. Several wagons of lone men were lined up directly to the north from where she sat, and she allowed her eyes to flick over the dark forms that sat before campfires there.

A lone, tall figure stood by one of the wagons, and she glanced at him, identifying him by the height he owned and the broad shoulders he could not conceal in the starlight. It was Gage Morgan, his form unmistakable, his interest in her obvious. She sat up straight and lifted her chin, not willing to allow herself to be frightened or intimidated by his watchfulness.

And then he turned aside and walked from the circle, away from the campfires, absenting himself from the laughter that rose in the night air.

"Are you all right?" Finn asked from behind her. "You seem upset, Jess, all tensed up." He placed a warm hand on her shoulder and she rubbed her cheek against the ridges of knuckles that met her movement. She heard his intake of breath and smiled a bit, recognizing the sign of awareness to her mood he could not conceal.

"Ready to crawl into bed?" he asked, his manner casual though his fingers tightened their grip on the narrow bones beneath her flesh.

She nodded, willing to seek concealment inside the wagon. Finn would follow her shortly, she knew. And his arms would hold her without a moment's hesitation, his body warming her throughout the night, no matter that she still nursed a grudge. He was all she had to cling to, and that was frightening, she decided. A man she had taken to herself and yet did not totally place her trust in.

She felt she walked a tightrope, and until the baby was born, she was needy of Finn Carson. Her eyes closed as she rose and gave herself over to his care, allowing him to lift her into the sheltering shadows of the wagon, listening to him as he cleared up the clutter of their supper meal and finally shifting to allow him space beside her as he joined her on the feather tick they would share.

"I don't want to squash you," he said with a dry chuckle, easing his way beneath the quilt, one long arm lifting her head, the better to hold her close. He was behind her and she felt the evidence of his desire pressing against her bottom, knew a moment of pleasure as she sensed her power over this man. His mouth sought and found the tender skin beneath her ear as he rose up a bit to kiss her there.

"Jess?" It was a query she'd expected, a request she knew he would not press for should she turn him away. And that knowledge made her pliable to his will as she eased herself to her back, slipped her arm to circle his neck and drew him to her.

"I'm here, Finn," she whispered, unable to refuse him what his body ached to find in her depths. His fingers loosened the buttons of her nightgown, and she felt the warmth of his hands as he fondled her breasts, heard the accelerated tones of his breathing as he drew her gown up to reveal her body to his touch.

She opened to him, her eyes closing as his fingers spread wide over her belly, as if he would speak to the child inside her in this manner. "Is he all right?" Finn asked softly, his hand easing the tension of taut skin and firm movements of the babe within her.

"He's fine," she assured him, knowing he asked permission for what he sought. "You won't hurt him, Finn."

"I'll be careful," he promised, his murmur rasping in her ear as he readied her for his taking. His hands were warm and knowing against her woman's flesh, his kisses hot and eager as he traced the slope of her breast and took the taut crest into his mouth.

"Jessica." The syllables of her name left his lips in a sigh as she rose to his bidding, felt the flush of passion he brought into being and knew the moment he gathered the moisture of her response against his fingertips.

She could not help the soft cries that left her lips, and he muffled them, burying her face in his chest as he plied her with knowing touches. And then he rose over her and with a tenderness she felt to the very depths of her being, he made her his bride once more. Easing his way with care, he knelt between her legs, measuring the depths of his thrusts and bending to conceal his face against her throat, he spent his seed within her.

It was a moment such as she'd known on other nights, and yet there was a newness about this blending of their bodies that brought her a fuller measure of joy, a deeper aching need to speak aloud the words she kept from his hearing. And as he murmured his praise for her beauty against her throat, as his whispers brought her pleasure and satisfaction, she gave herself into his keeping.

No matter that he had not been honest with her from the beginning…no matter that she had been hurt by his refusal to be aboveboard in his methods. He was her husband, and as such, she offered him her love, speaking it aloud in his hearing.

"Finn?" She awaited his uplifted head, his inquiring gaze in the darkness and the sudden stillness that made her aware that he held his breath as he tensed above her.

"I love you," she whispered, the words clear and precise so there would be no mistake in the message she offered. "No matter how angry I might be with you, no matter how much you've hurt me by the things you've done, I can't deny how I feel about you."

He murmured softly and she lifted a hand to halt his words, touching his lips with trembling fingertips.

"No, don't say anything, please. Just know that I love you, like I've never loved another man, Finley Carson." As she spoke, her tears flowed and she knew the joy of his lips and mouth against her skin as he captured the salty drops and took them to himself.

Chapter Eight

Cottonwood Creek well deserved being called a river. Flowing slowly past the spot the ladies had chosen for their wash station, it was wider than Jessica had expected, deeper than the last creek they'd visited, and held a supply of fish that had the children shrieking with delight. Four boys, barefoot, with pants rolled to their knees, held makeshift fishing poles, complete with dangling worms, and had thus far tossed almost twenty specimens on the bank, where they flopped and sucked air.

The girls ran from the sight, much to the boys' enjoyment, shuddering their displeasure with the whole scene. Two of the women arrived as Jessica watched, both of them already finished with their washing. Calling to a couple of the younger boys, they pressed them into service, and in a minute or so the fish were picked up and tossed into a washtub, thus to be carried downstream a bit farther and cleaned.

She was of the same mind as the girls, Jessica decided, shivering her own distaste at the task. She'd told Finn up front, when she first heard that fishing would supply their noon meal, that she was not a woman who enjoyed cleaning fish or slaughtering chickens, and he'd laughed, hugging her for a moment, ignoring her protests.

"Folks are watching," she'd muttered, caught up in a breathless embrace.

"Who cares?" he returned with a grin. "You make me happy, Jess. And I don't care who knows it."

She'd decided last night to take what she could get from this marriage, and if this was part and parcel of the side benefits, she wasn't about to complain. Finn had gathered up their washing and carried the square tub to the creek, Jessica following with a jar of soap bits and pieces, and the scrub board.

The women greeted her with waves of greeting and smart remarks uttered in an undertone, due to Finn's presence. "You went to bed pretty early last night," Arlois said with a grin.

"I was really tired," Jessica told her, feeling the blush climb her cheeks.

"Newly married is what you are," Geraldine said from the creek bank, leaning back on her haunches as she wiped soap from her face. She followed the remark with a flashing smile and beckoned Jessica to commence work next to her.

"Finn's gone to get me hot water from the kettle," Jessica said. "He thought it would be easier to get the clothes scrubbed if the water was warm."

"I carried my own," Polly Haskins said from her own spot on the bank. "Guess it pays to have a new bridegroom." She rolled her eyes. "Can't remember what it was like." And then she laughed aloud at her own remark.

"How long have you been married, Polly?" Jessica asked. The woman was no doubt younger than her appearance suggested, with two youngsters running around, one of them still in diapers. The child's tiny form held an odor of ammonia, as if the urine he emitted had soaked into his body, and Jessica found him to be unwashed most of the time. Still, she thought, giving the woman the benefit of the doubt, it had to be difficult to keep a baby clean under these circumstances.

"It's been five long years," Polly answered, leaning over her scrub board to work at a pair of denim trousers. "Five *long* years," she muttered, repeating her words beneath her breath. Jessica thought sadness tinged the phrase.

The woman looked up at the newest bride of the group and spoke a casual insult aloud. "Your man won't always be so attentive, girl. Take it from me, once he's got you tied down with young'uns, he'll take what's his due and leave you to cope on your own."

Arlois spoke quietly at Jessica's elbow. "Don't pay her any mind, Jess. She's having a rough time with Joseph. He's spending time with the single miners and has managed to gamble away a good share of their nest egg."

Pity welled within Jessica at the words, and she determined to be nice to Polly, no matter that it might be a hardship calling on her scant supply of patience today. Maybe she could take the runny-nosed baby into the water later and scrub him up for his mother. Or let him play in her washtub once the clothes were clean and hung to dry.

"Here's hot water, Jess," Finn said from behind her, one bucket in each hand as he awaited her pleasure. She smiled at him and dumped the soiled laundry to the ground, then spilled a good measure of her soap into the empty tub. Finn splashed one of the buckets directly on the soap and suds rose accordingly. The second bucket joined the first, and then he went to the edge of the creek and dipped them both into the water, filling them and bringing them back to where Jessica waited.

"You want this in there, too?" he asked.

"Just one for now," she told him, watching as he spilled it into the steaming tub. "Leave the other for rinsing."

"I'll fill this one, too," he said agreeably, and quickly performed the small chore for her. "Give a holler when you need more hot water, Jess. I'll be working around the wagon for a bit."

She nodded her thanks and watched as he strode back to

the circle, her eyes fastened to his straight back, the width of his shoulders and the hat he'd cocked over his forehead. He was handsome, a prime example of manhood, and she felt a sense of pride well within her. She'd told him she loved him last night, after he'd spilled his seed in her body. And as she spoke the words, she'd been wishing futilely that he'd been the father of the child she carried.

The babe would have been conceived in love, had Finn been in her life eight months ago. Now she could only hope that he would be as accepting of the child as he'd promised.

Turning back to the washtub, she sorted through her laundry and placed the white and lighter-colored garments into the water, stirring them with a laundry stick that her mother had given her. It was meant to use at the stove, stirring the bluing into rinse water and then lifting clothes from the steaming kettle. She recalled her hands burning as she had wrung out Lyle's white shirts, a sense of pride warring with anger at his shenanigans, but knowing that if his shirts were not white, and then starched to a frazzle before the iron touched their surfaces his anger would know no bounds.

Now bluing was a thing of the past, as was starch. Clean clothing was the order of the day, no matter that they might be wrinkled, never seeing the flat side of an iron. All the niceties had gone by the way once she'd gotten into the swing of living in a four-foot-wide wagon. Just having room to spread her feather tick at night was a luxury. Hard work was a way of life, and she wasn't about to complain, now that she was sharing that soft bed with Finn.

Her lips curved as she scrubbed his shirts, working hard at a stain on one sleeve. She lowered it back into the tub to soak a bit and lifted her extra petticoat from the warm water, using the strength of her upper arms to scrub it across the ridged board. It wasn't really dirty, but sweaty and the hem dusty from the trail, and in a minute or so she'd set it aside in the grass beside her.

Low voices around her rose, with the women speaking softly of the things she supposed women had discussed over washboards since the things had been invented. One complained about her husband's dirty stockings, another scrubbed and then wrung out one diaper after another, complaining about the scarcity of flannel for such necessities.

Guilt touched Jessica as she thought of the twenty-five diapers she'd hemmed already, and for just a moment she considered sharing her wealth. Finn might not appreciate it, she decided judiciously, stifling her urge quickly. And now that she thought of it, twenty-five diapers were not so very many, considering how rapidly a baby could soil them.

In an hour, she'd finished scrubbing out the loads of laundry and tilted her washtub out, watching as the water ran onto the grass. Gray and bereft of any trace of soapsuds, it looked well used, and she slopped a bit of the clean rinse water to slosh away the residue.

"I'll lift those." From behind her, Finn spoke quietly and she spun to face him, her mind concentrating on the next phase of work. He reached to steady her, and his eyes were dark with concern. "Are you working too hard?" he asked. "I don't want you wearing yourself out, Jess."

"I'm fine," she said, feeling the warmth of his hand on her arm, her sleeves rolled up, her skin damp. He was warm and a bit sweaty, his male scent appealing, she decided. "What have you been up to?" she asked as he dumped the buckets into the tub and then watched as she picked up the clean clothing and sloshed it through the water.

"Just sorting through some things," he answered vaguely, and then he walked the few feet to the stream and filled the buckets anew, once more adding them to the rinse water. "Is that enough?" he asked, and at the nod she offered, he placed the buckets beside her.

"Let me know when you've finished and I'll carry things back for you," he offered. "Just give a wave—I'll watch for you."

She felt the warmth of his concern flow over her, and with renewed vigor she rinsed the clothing, lifting it, then drowning it beneath the rinse water, until the majority of the soap had been left behind.

"He's good to you, isn't he?" Arlois commented quietly. "He watches you all the time, Jessica. I think he loves you."

Jessica laughed dryly. "What is there to love?" she asked. "I'm big with another man's child, my feet are swollen and I'm clumsy." She cocked an eyebrow at Arlois. "Have I begun to waddle yet?"

Arlois laughed and shook her head. "Only a little, honey girl. And I don't think Finn Carson cares if you do or not. If he isn't smitten to the core, I'll eat my hat. I've never seen another man so besotted with his wife."

Her fingers ached with the effort of wringing out shirts and trousers, the strength required being enough to make washday a real chore, Jessica had decided long ago. But somehow, when Finn was the one who would wear the drawers she held, it seemed a light task indeed. She thought of his taut buttocks, imagined them covered by the gray fabric she held, and grinned. He was more appealing without the covering, she decided, recalling his strength, remembering the desire he'd kept harnessed lest he hurt her or the babe she carried.

It had been long enough for Finn to have the wagon cleaned out, certainly time enough for him to have sorted through their foodstuffs and the trunk she stored her things in. He'd no doubt have found her supply of baby items, and she smiled to herself as she considered his reaction to the tiny gowns she'd sewed with small stitches, the bow she'd tied at each neckline with such care. Her head lifted and caught his eyes on her, and with a single movement of her uplifted hand, she beckoned him.

He strode quickly toward the group of women, some of them already carrying their burden back to where they would string lines between the wagons and hang the wet laundry. Sheets flapped in the breeze from Geraldine's wagon, and between the Bates's rear bow and her front upright stake, Finn had hung a piece of rope, awaiting the clothes she'd washed.

Now he reached her and picked up the washtub, where she'd placed the wet laundry. An empty pail in each hand, the scrub board under her arm, she followed him and blessed the day he'd placed the ring on her finger that designated her as Jessica Carson.

The whole day was a holiday, with fish frying over a large fire near the creek at noontime, three women in charge of the skillets that held the boys' catch. The youths sat watching, bragging about who had landed the largest panfish, and the women looked on with scarcely concealed enjoyment as the young men basked in the glory of providing the noon meal. They'd caught upward of fifty fish, and fried as they were in an abundance of bacon grease, the mingled scent rose into the air.

There were those who were not fond of fish, and Jessica was one of them. Somehow, the thought of those graceful creatures being snagged from their watery home to lie gasping on the creek bank filled her with disgust. Finn told her she didn't seem to have much sympathy for the poor hog who'd given his all for her bacon sandwich, but she declared that that was a different thing altogether.

She was teased unmercifully as they sat on a quilt and ate, surrounded by families who cherished these moments of pleasure. The children played at the edge of the creek and the women made plans for scrubbing their young ones before bedtime, when the adults would have their turn in the water.

The current was stronger than that of the earlier crossing they'd made weeks before, and Jessica's thoughts were anxious as she envisioned the wagons rolling through the depths tomorrow. Finn would have the task of finding the best place to cross, and she worried that he might be washed away should the water run high.

"I'll be fine," he assured her. "The only problem is that you'll have to drive the wagon across, Jess. I'll walk beside the oxen and tie a rope on their yoke to help control them, but the women will need to help out."

"I can do that," she said stoutly, wanting to assure him of her ability.

"Or die trying," he murmured. "You're spunky, Jess. I'll give you that. I think you'd do anything I asked of you, wouldn't you?"

"Probably," she admitted, flushing as she thought of the last request he'd made of her, during the moments they'd shared last night. It had been unspoken, only her name whispered against her ear, but his need had vibrated between them and she could not have turned him away.

"We'll need to back off from that sort of thing pretty soon," he said, as though he read her thoughts, his murmur reaching only her hearing. "I don't want to take a chance on hurting you, sweetheart."

"You won't, Finn," she told him, feeling a heated blush sweep upward to color her cheeks. "You're always careful." And then she lifted her lashes, allowing her eyes to touch the expression he wore. His nostrils flared a bit as he inhaled, his mouth twisted wryly, and he shifted against the quilt, one knee rising, the better to conceal the arousal she knew was becoming apparent.

That this man could want her with such passion was almost beyond her comprehension. Lust was the emotion she'd attributed to Lyle, but the same needs that had driven the man she'd shared her life with bore a different label when they applied to Finn. Desire rose between them and she felt its glow envelop her. Finn was not alone in the needs he felt.

The dust flew as the women swept their wagons clean, and boxes and crates were stacked hither and yon, their contents sorted through, swapping being the order of the day. Several of the ladies brought their extra supplies to a common area to bargain among themselves for the things they might need before the journey's end. The men mended harnesses and checked over the wagon wheels, insuring that the crossing on the morrow would not be cause for disaster because of untended maintenance.

Each campfire was lit by dusk, the children settled near the wagons. An air of anticipation ruled, and the women planned for their time at the creek. Several of the husbands formed a group to escort the ladies and by the time dark had fallen the wagons held small figures, lined up on the floor like so many dolls on a shelf. The thought made Jessica smile, and she tried to imagine her own child, feeling the push of tiny arms and legs within her body, lifting a hand to rub at her ribs and feet pressed there impatiently, as if the babe yearned to push its way from her body.

"It won't be long," she whispered, one hand beneath the load she bore, the other easing the ache of ribs that refused to give way.

"Soon, Jess," Finn said from behind her, his hands lifting to grip her, allowing her to lean against his body. She pressed her back against his chest and belly, arching her shoulders to allow the firm contact she craved, and he responded, his hand rubbing just beneath her waist to ease the ache.

"Thank you," she murmured. "I'm about ready to go for my bath, Finn. I only have to gather my things together."

"Where are they?" he asked, and at the motion of her hand he stepped to the back of the wagon and picked up the bundle she'd prepared. Two other women were ready and together, their husbands beside them, and with a word to Arlois, Jessica walked toward the creek.

Beneath the overhanging willows, the water was clear and glistened in the moonlight. It filtered through the trees, and in the center of the creek the flow was noticeable, the ripples catching her eye. "Stay in the shallows," Finn warned her. "You don't want to get caught in the current."

"All right," she told him agreeably, sitting down to strip her shoes and stockings from her swollen feet. "I hate to think of putting these back on when I'm finished," she said quietly.

"I could always carry you back," Finn suggested, grinning down at her, and laughing a bit as she shook her head with a quick movement. "Not a good idea, huh?"

The other women joined them and the men sauntered away, taking their places about a hundred feet from the bathing place, standing in a loosely formed circle. Their voices rose on the night air, and Jessica knew a moment's satisfaction that she and Finn were so much a part of the group of married folk.

She had stripped down to her shift, a loose garment that at the best of times hung loosely about her body. Now, with the added bulk of her pregnancy, it fit more snugly and she was uncomfortably aware of the extra weight she carried, tugging the hem down to cover her upper legs.

Once in the water, she would shed it, tossing it to the bank, and in the darkness it would be simple to be only one of half a dozen forms bathing and splashing in the shallow water. She walked down a bit, leaving her towel and nightgown on the grass, her robe folded beneath them.

The water was warmer than the night air and she relished the feel of it against her, kneeling until it washed beneath her breasts. She spent long minutes washing her hair, careful to rinse the suds away in the moving water. Next, she settled on the bottom of the creek and wet her cloth, rubbing a precious bar of soap against the rough fabric. Her hands scrubbed briskly with it, reaching all the parts that had so sorely needed a good soaking. Her eyes closed as she rose again to her knees and splashed the water across her breasts and then down her back.

Some of the women had left the creek already, and she heard their voices as they joined their menfolk and made their way back to the circle of wagons. "Jessica?" Finn's voice called her from his station beyond the trees, and she lifted her head to respond to his summons.

"I won't be but a minute," she answered, standing and reaching for her towel. Off balance, she bent to lean a hand on the creek bank and ended up back in the water. "Drat it, anyway," she muttered, her back to the bank as she lifted herself again from the sandy bottom. Her towel draped over her shoulders and she turned to climb from the shallows, only to see the tall, dark form of a man awaiting her.

"Finn?" she asked in a whisper. Surely he hadn't come down here when just twenty feet or so from where she stood two other women were dressing. And then her heart thumped against her ribs at an accelerated pace, and she felt a strong hand grip her arm. Another palm met her lips, stifling the outcry she would have made.

"Don't say a word, or your man will be dead as a doornail," a husky voice said. "We've got a shotgun aimed at him right now."

"Who?" The muffled query was breathed against his hand, and the man who held her drew her roughly from the creek and up on the bank. She inhaled and felt her stomach roll as his sour smell filled her nostrils.

"Put on your nightgown," he said, and she was thankful that he did not touch her further, only stood before her so that she could not see past him.

With hasty movements she drew her gown over her head and picked up the flannel robe, sliding her arms into the sleeves, the better to cover herself. She wrapped the towel around her head, capturing her long hair in its depths. And then, without warning, she was swung up into strong arms and carried down the bank, farther from where the other women were laughing and murmuring among themselves.

"Jessica?" Finn's voice sounded worried, and she turned her head, straining to see him. He was alone, the other men having collected their wives, and even as she watched, he started toward the creek.

A shot rang out from beside her, and Finn slumped to the ground, a dark heap at the edge of the tree line. She heard a man shout a warning from the circle of wagons, and an oath burst from the man who carried her. With jerky movements she was seated roughly upright on a horse's back, her captor climbing on behind her, then lifting her to sit across his legs.

The animal moved out without hesitation, and another horseman joined them a moment later. "Everything all right?" he asked in an undertone.

"Finn?" Jessica's mouth formed his name, and though she thought she spoke aloud, it was barely audible, her mouth almost unable to form the single word. She fought to look over her captor's shoulder, back to where several men had hastened from their campfires to where Finn lay.

Darkness enclosed her then, and her head fell forward, her heartbeat rapid, her body chilled and trembling as the man who held her sent his horse across the creek. The horse splashed through the water and then turned south, wending his way beneath the shelter of the overhanging willows.

"What did you do to her?" The voice was deep and angry and Jessica's mind grasped its intonations, aware that she recognized the speaker. She lay on the ground, her clothing in disarray, and felt hands tugging at her robe, drawing it over her legs to cover her from the night air.

"Is there a quilt handy?" the voice asked again, and at the murmured reply, grass rustled and she felt the weight of a covering settle down over her. It was tucked beneath her legs, and hands lifted her head, placing a musty-smelling pad beneath it.

"Jessica." The voice spoke her name, and she opened

her eyes, her lashes seeming unable to lift fully. "I know you're awake," he said, and then knelt beside her. She caught her breath, recognizing the broad shoulders, the dark hair, the unmistakable form of Gage Morgan.

A cry rose from her lips and she tried to sit up. His hands pressed against her upper arms and he bent over her. "Stop it, Jessica. You're all right. Just lie still."

"Finn—what happened to Finn?" she asked, aware that her words were broken, that tears were running freely from her eyes.

"He's all right. I rode back and checked him out, Jessica. Just a graze. The shot went wild, and he caught a couple of pieces of buckshot at the hairline."

"What have you done?" she asked, shivering now almost uncontrollably, drawing her legs up as if curling into a ball would keep her warmer. "Please, let me sit up," she whispered, her movements jerky, her sobs shaking her body.

Morgan sat on the ground beside her and lifted her onto his lap. She fought his touch, the memory of Finn doing this same thing only two days before still fresh in her mind. "I'm not going to hurt you," Morgan said quietly, holding her fast, his arms circling her. "You're shivering and I want to get you warm."

She subsided, aware that she could not win this battle, knowing that two other men stood nearby, watching. Of the three, the devil she knew was the least obnoxious, she decided, remembering the sour smell of the man who had snatched her up onto his horse and ridden off.

"This wasn't in the plan," Morgan said quietly. "These two got carried away, and this never should have happened."

"You knew it was time to get to the bottom of things, Morgan," one of the men said. "We saw Carson goin' through that wagon today with a fine-tooth comb. If that deed's there, I'll warrant he found it. The only thing we got on our side is the woman. He won't let anything happen to her. He's downright foolish where she's concerned.'' His laughter was low, taunting, and Jessica trembled at his words.

Morgan shook his head abruptly, a movement Jessica was aware of, and the two men stepped back from where Morgan sat. They were beneath a tree, and he shifted, leaning against the sturdy trunk, still holding her across his lap.

''He's right, Jess,'' his voice murmured against her ear. ''So long as we have you, Finn Carson will do most anything we ask of him. You're what they call our ace in the hole, sweetheart.''

''Don't call me that,'' she whispered, struggling now to break free of his embrace. ''How could you allow this to happen, Morgan? I knew you held secrets, but I thought better of you than this.''

''If you'd married me, you wouldn't be in this fix, Jess,'' he said quietly. ''I tried to do this the easy way, but there was no keeping you away from Carson. He was determined to have you, and you fell right into his hands.''

''I know a way to get her talkin','' the second man said, his words holding laughter in their depths. ''I'll bet I can have her telling us everything she knows in about two minutes flat. Give me a chance at her, Morgan.''

''I don't think so.'' The words resonated from his chest, and she felt one hand move to his side, drawing his gun from the holster he wore. She sat quietly, aware that her very safety was in jeopardy, that the two men were impatient and ready to use any force necessary to gain her cooperation.

''I don't know where the deed is,'' she said clearly. ''I looked and couldn't find it.''

''I'll just bet you did,'' the first man said. ''But little lady, we've traveled too far to let that thing slip through our fingers now. Lyle Beaumont played us dirty, leavin' us holdin' the bag in Saint Louis. I'm not about to walk away now. Not without that piece of paper in my hand.''

His voice had dropped into an ugly growl by the time he finished his threats, and Jessica shuddered at the thought of his hands on her. Morgan tightened his grip on her shoulder and bent his head. ''You're all right,'' he murmured against her ear. And then he spoke more loudly.

''This whole thing is out of hand, fellas. You made a bad move. I was planning on going through that wagon myself tomorrow if you'd waited and given me time. I had a diversion just about set up so Carson would be out of the picture for a while.''

''I'm not sure I believe that,'' the kidnapper taunted. ''Anyway, whose side are you on, Morgan? You're supposed to be our front man, and you haven't done anything yet but mollycoddle that woman. You were supposed to get your hands on the deed, remember?'' He glared at Morgan and his fury included Jessica as he walked closer.

''This was supposed to be a three-way split, and we're tired of waitin'. This is gonna end up with you walking away with the whole kit and caboodle.'' The man squatted nearby, peering in Jessica's direction, as if he wanted to get a better look at her, and she turned her face away, leaning her cheek against Morgan's shirt.

She felt his grip on her tighten as he spoke again. ''What about the big boss?'' Morgan asked. ''He's expecting his share, too.''

''And he'll get it, after we've mined enough gold. There's plenty for all of us.''

''Well, I'll tell you one thing. If she has this baby out here, she and the child could both die,'' Morgan said briskly. ''Is that what you want? A murder charge involving a woman and her baby? I'd thought you were both smarter than that. Retrieving the deed is one thing. Killing a woman is another.''

''We didn't plan on killin' her,'' the man replied. ''Just

keepin' her here until Carson was willing to give up the deed to us. He can have her back. I sure enough don't want a squallin' brat on my hands.''

''Well, if we're not careful, there'll be a whole contingent of riders showing up here by daybreak,'' Morgan said gruffly. ''I'm not sure we can outrun them hauling Mrs. Carson with us. And I'm certainly not about to dump her here without having my hands on that deed.''

''Ah, hell…what are we gonna do now?'' the ruffian asked, his anger apparent and aimed, Jessica feared, at her.

''We're going to return her to the wagon train and make her husband happy. Not to mention keeping her safe and alive.''

''She'll spill the beans. You know damn well there ain't a woman alive can keep her mouth shut,'' the man said. ''We can bury her here and wait our chance to go through that wagon up the trail a ways.''

The second man squatted nearby. ''If one of the wheels was loose and the wagon had to be left behind, we'd have a good chance of finding it.''

''And you think,'' Morgan said snidely, ''you think that Carson is about to leave his belongings behind, giving you your perfect opportunity?''

''You got a better idea?'' the first man asked glumly.

''I've already told you what we're going to do.''

''And let her blab everything she knows about us? You're a dead dog, Morgan, once she tells them you were in on this.''

''She won't,'' Morgan said quietly, and the tone of voice he employed made Jessica shiver anew. ''If she tells Carson, he's a dead man. And I think she knows better than to cross me in this.'' He bent to peer into her face. ''How about it, Mrs. Carson? Are you going to tell your husband I'm a bad guy?''

''Please, just get me back to the wagon,'' she begged, all pride vanquished by the fear that had seized her in the past few minutes. "I don't want my baby to die, Morgan. Please, don't let them hurt my baby."

For a moment she felt his grip on her tighten and heard the sound that caught in his throat. "Damn," he growled. "This is enough." And then his voice rose as he spoke to his two cohorts. "Look, I'm taking her back, and you two had better make yourselves scarce. We'll come up with something else after the train gets across the creek tomorrow. I'll meet you tomorrow night after midnight."

He held Jessica upright on his lap, his hands rigid against her shoulders. He shook her once, as if he would get her attention. His voice was loud in her ear, carrying clearly in the night air, and he made a threat that chilled her to the bone.

"If you say anything to Finn Carson, you'll regret it for the rest of your life, Jess. If he finds out that I'm involved in this, I'll kill him. I think you know that I don't make empty promises."

She nodded quickly. "Yes…all right." She would promise anything for the chance to see Finn, to be sure he was alive, that the buckshot had not caused damage to his head. Her arms ached to hold him, and the love she felt for the man she'd married filled her to overflowing as she thought of him lying unconscious and bleeding.

Morgan set her aside and got to his feet, then bent to her and helped her stand. Holding her firmly with one arm, he led her toward a horse she recognized. "Not a word," he said, his voice carrying in the stillness. "You won't get a second chance, Jessica. I don't want to kill Carson, but I will if the need arises."

Chapter Nine

Half the wagons were across the creek by the time Morgan's horse made his way past the tail end of the line. Jessica felt the center of attention as several of the ladies hurried to where the dark gelding walked apace with the slowly rolling wagons.

"Is she all right?" It was Polly, and the concern on her face was obvious as she peered up at the riders. "Can I do anything, Mr. Morgan?"

"Find Carson," he said sharply as he looked ahead, scanning the almost identical vehicles, as if he could ascertain which of them belonged to Jessica.

"He's under a tree, up ahead," Polly announced, watching as the riders passed her by. "Still out like a light."

Jessica's heart stuttered within her chest. If Finn should be more seriously hurt than she'd been told, she'd never forgive herself. It was her fault entirely, the fact that she'd moved downstream to bathe, rather than stay with the others, her failure to fight for her freedom, and finally, putting Finn in danger because of the damned deed.

"He's going to be all right," Morgan said quietly, his strong arms holding her firmly in place across his thighs. "Don't get all upset, Jessica. It can't be good for the baby.

And it certainly isn't going to help Carson if he sees you crying.''

"I'm not," she protested, and then was stunned to realize that tears dampened her cheeks.

"No, I can see that," Morgan said dryly. His arm tightened around her back and his voice lowered as they approached the line of trees along the creek. Beneath low branches, Finn lay on a quilt, her pillow beneath his head, a light covering over him. Jessica wriggled, attempting to lower herself from the horse, and only Morgan's strength kept her from sliding to the ground.

"Let me get down first," he said, the order given in an unmistakable tone of voice that brooked no opposition. And then his voice softened. "It's all right, Jessica," he said quietly and she wondered distractedly at the words he chose. It was not all right. Not unless Finn was safe.

She subsided, ceasing her efforts to slide from the horse, waiting till Morgan swung from the saddle and then reached to lift her down. If his hands lingered just a bit too long, and if his eyes searched her face with an intensity she recognized, it mattered little. Her only thought was to reach the man she'd married, and her feet flew over the grass as she sped to his side.

Falling to her knees beside him, she reached a trembling hand to touch his face. "Finn?" The single word faltered, and she repeated it, praying distractedly that he might open his eyes and smile at her. It was not to be, and she felt fresh tears blur her vision. Bending over him, she brushed a wayward lock of hair from his forehead and her lips blessed the skin she'd exposed. He felt warm, and she rejoiced that he was not awash in the icy grasp of death. As she bent to him, she felt the warmth of his breathing against her cheek and noted the faint fluttering of his eyelids.

"I believe he's waking up," Arlois said from behind her, and Jessica turned awkwardly to look up at her friend. "He hasn't moved all night, Jess. Just sprawled right where they put him.'' She knelt at Jessica's side and touched her arm. ''He looks better than you do, honey. Why don't you let me find you something to eat, or some tea to drink?''

''I'm all right,'' Jessica protested, unwilling to move from Finn's side. She brushed distractedly again at his hair and uncovered a crimson track beneath the silky strands. ''Is this where…?'' Her voice faltered as she recognized the path of buckshot that had grazed his scalp. Bending lower, she discovered a second, then a third surface wound that accounted for his unconscious state.

''He'll be all right. You'll see,'' Arlois told her firmly. ''I washed those flesh wounds myself, and they're hardly deep enough to matter.''

''They matter,'' Jessica pronounced grimly. ''I'd like to shoot the man who put them there.'' Her gaze rose and touched the grim features of Morgan. Silently, he watched her from beneath lowered lids and she glared at him, unwilling to absolve him of fault.

''I fear we won't lay hands on the culprit,'' Morgan said. ''Once I followed them and got you out of there, they were no doubt on their way to points south. I doubt they're anywhere close by.''

''Why did someone grab you and run thataway?'' Arlois asked, her voice troubled and her expression dubious. ''I'm afraid I don't understand what happened.''

''Neither does anyone else,'' Morgan said, the look he cast in Jessica's direction a silent warning.

But she would not be stilled. ''They wanted the deed Lyle was supposed to have with him when he was shot and killed,'' she said defiantly. Let Morgan stew on that if he wanted to. She was done with subterfuge. Bright enough not to incriminate the man in the happenings of the night before, she still was willing to let him know he had not put the fear of God into her heart.

''Then there truly is a deed?'' Arlois asked, her voice rising as if she had doubted such a thing existed.

"Yes," Jessica answered. "Apparently, there is. And Lyle died because someone wanted it."

"Does Finn have it?" Arlois asked, and both women were surprised when Morgan chuckled aloud.

"If he did, he'd no doubt have ridden off toward the sunset a long time ago," the dark-haired man said. "I have an idea that if such a thing exists, Lyle Beaumont took care to see that it wouldn't come to light easily."

"I don't care about a deed if it's going to put Finn in danger," Jessica said quietly. She bent again to look closely into Finn's face and noted a change in his breathing. His eyelids fluttered, and then she was the focus of his attention.

"Jess?" His voice was a bare whisper. "Are you really here?"

"I'm here, Finn. Everything's all right. You're not badly hurt, it seems. Arlois said you have three scratches on your head, and they're a little scabbed over, but you'll be fine."

"He's awake, and that's the important thing," Arlois offered.

"I've got a banger of a headache," Finn growled. "And I'm supposed to be out there tending to getting those wagons across the creek this morning."

"I think you're going to make the crossing *inside* a wagon," Arlois said firmly. "Jessica will ride with you and keep you from banging around, and David will lead your team of oxen."

Finn's eyes closed and his mouth firmed, as if he held back words better left unspoken. At his side, Morgan stepped closer and lowered himself to the ground. On one knee, his hat shading his face, he grasped Finn's elbow. "Jessica's fine, Carson. She wasn't hurt, just upset at being hauled off that way."

Finn's eyes narrowed as the man spoke, and Jessica thought anger tinged his expression and edged his words. "How did it happen?"

"Two men, who apparently thought they'd find what they wanted by hauling her away, took her. Don't know where they came from, but they sure hotfooted it down the trail once I got there and took your wife off their hands."

"I owe you," Finn said bluntly.

Bile rose in Jessica's throat at the perfidy of the man who'd brought her back and proffered her like a trophy, bragging on his own actions as if he hadn't been involved in the happenings of the night before. His eyes met hers and the warning in them was clear. *Keep your mouth shut.*

She pressed her lips together and looked away. Until Finn was back on his feet, she was the only protection he had, the only barrier to harm he owned. Her legs were weak beneath her and she sat down suddenly on the edge of the quilt that covered him.

"You all right?" Arlois asked cautiously. "You're not feeling bad, are you? No pains or anything like that?"

"No, just weary…a little sore, maybe." Dizzy would be more to the point, she thought, and hungry, as though breakfast might be welcome. "Is there a campfire anywhere? Any coffee or tea available?"

Arlois nodded. "The last fire was left lit, just for that very reason. Crossing the creek will no doubt take all morning and maybe even a part of the afternoon." She rose from the ground and rested a hand on Jessica's shoulder. "You stay right here and I'll find something for you to eat."

Jessica could only nod in agreement, and then, as an afterthought, she called after Arlois. "Bring something for Finn, too."

"He might not be ready for food, yet," Morgan said. "I'd be careful not to get his belly in an uproar."

"Spoken like a gentleman," Jessica blurted, casting him a look of contempt.

"I never pretended to be a gentleman," Morgan told her softly. "But you'd better be glad I was nearby last night when those men dragged you across the prairie. Count your blessings, little girl.''

She bowed her head, aware of vibrations that puzzled her. Morgan stood, and she was caught in his shadow as he blocked the sun from her. A chill washed over her and she reached for Finn's hand, as if it would offer her solace.

Blue eyes met hers, and she caught a glimpse of anger in their depths. ''You shouldn't have been in danger, Jess. I should have been watching out for you better. I'm sorry.''

''You don't owe me an apology,'' she whispered. ''I was wrong to move down the creek that far. I just didn't want to be—'' She halted, aware of Morgan's presence above her, unable to admit her embarrassment at being naked and vulnerable, there in the midst of the women who'd surrounded her. ''I needed privacy, I suppose.''

''Understandable,'' Morgan said lightly, as if he would remove the pall that hung over them. ''So long as no harm was done, I'll be on my way,'' he said after a moment, and rose to his feet. ''I need to be looking after my belongings, make sure everything is secured in the wagon before it takes a dunking.''

''Thanks again,'' Finn murmured, but if Morgan heard the words, he gave no sign, just walked away down the line to where the three miners he'd been traveling with were readying their wagon for the crossing. Finn looked up at Jessica and searched her face.

''You sure you're all right?'' he asked, his hand lifting to touch her cheek.

''I should be asking you that,'' she returned brightly, blinking back the rush of tears she seemed unable to control. ''I'm so sorry, Finn. Sorry I made such a mess of things.'' She inhaled sharply then, and her thoughts spilled out without hesitation. ''At least we know that there must truly be a deed here somewhere. Or else those two men wouldn't have been so intent on making me tell them where it was.''

He squeezed her hand and looked closely into her eyes. "Are you sure they didn't hurt you, Jess?"

"No, just embarrassed me a lot. One of them snatched me when I was climbing out of the creek and made me pull my nightgown on. When I saw his shadow there I thought at first it might be you, come down to get me. And then when he spoke, I was stunned. If he hadn't threatened to shoot you…" Her voice trailed off. "No, that wasn't it. He didn't shoot you. The other man must have. I didn't see him, but I saw you fall when the gun went off."

"Your robe is dirty," Finn told her, as if he would change her line of thought. She looked down at herself, aware for the first time that she was indeed a mess, her robe wrinkled and soiled from the ground she'd sprawled on, her feet bare and dusty, her hair hanging around her shoulders in a disreputable fashion. "Maybe you can get into our wagon and get cleaned up a little." And then he smiled, a faint twitch of his lips. "Although I kinda like seeing you all mussed up and soft looking."

Arlois approached then, a cup in either hand, and she offered one to Jessica. "This is tea, Jess. The other is coffee. I didn't know which you'd rather have." She pulled a towel out of her pocket and opened it, offering biscuits to both of them.

"I'll take the coffee," Finn told her, rolling to one side and levering himself up onto one elbow.

"I'll give you a hand if you like," Arlois told him, and lent her strength to his, supporting him as he scooted back to lean against the tree trunk behind him. His fingers gripped the cup with force, and Jessica was willing to bet that they would have been trembling had he not clamped them so tightly around the heavy container.

His head bent and he lifted the steaming brew to his lips, sipping a bit, and then leaned his head back against the tree. "Haven't had this kind of headache since I went head-first off my horse when I was learning how to ride," he muttered.

"How old were you?" Jessica asked, aware that for all the close quarters they'd shared over the past week, there was very little she actually knew of Finn's past. And the thought that he might need something to take his mind from the pain engendered by his wound made her press for an answer. "Did your father teach you?"

He shook his head and then winced at the movement. "No, Aaron did. He was ten years older than me and good with horses." He sipped at the coffee again. "I always wanted to be just like him," he added with a half smile. "But we went different ways when we grew older, me into the army, him into a business he bought in Saint Louis."

"You served in the army?" she asked. "How long?"

"Several years," he told her. "I was a scout, helping to find places for forts across the Southwest. I got to know the Indians a bit, and then found that I didn't like the way things were going back East. Folks are divided on a number of issues. It looks like Lincoln will be running the country, and it's my guess that a war is ahead of us."

"Lyle wanted to head west for that very reason," she said quietly. "He feared being called up to fight, I think."

"Well, when I got the chance to go to the goldfields with Aaron, I grabbed it," Finn said, his voice somber. "He'd just been given the deed to property that looked to hold more gold than either one of us had ever dreamed of."

Jessica knew bits and pieces of the story, but Finn's openness in relating the facts kept her silent as she waited for him to continue.

"When I got to Saint Louis, I found he'd been killed and the deed was gone," Finn said flatly. "I knew there were at least three or four men involved, but the only name I had was that of Lyle Beaumont." He looked up at her as if he waited for her to speak.

She shook her head. "I didn't know anything about all that," she whispered. "Only that Lyle had won a deed in a poker game."

"And then, when we'd been on the trail for a few days, I found that Lyle was your husband," Finn muttered. "And I thought if I did anything to harm him, I'd be hurting you, too." He was silent a moment, and then he plowed ahead.

"When he was shot and killed, I found myself rejoicing, Jess. And hated myself for being such a monster that I could celebrate another man's death. All I could think about was claiming you."

"And the deed," she added softly, a chill touching her as she recognized the death of her hopes and dreams that were so closely entwined with the love she felt for this man.

"And the deed," he admitted, touching his lips to the rim of the cup he held, swallowing deeply.

A voice interrupted their privacy as Jonas stalked closer, his words urgent. "Finn, we're about to put your wagon in line. I think you need to be inside it. I don't like the idea of you riding today. Your horse can be tied on the back end, or else I'll have someone ride him across for you."

Finn started to protest and then winced as he attempted to sit upright without the support of the tree at his back. "All right," he said, subsiding as if he recognized his inability to do otherwise.

"I'll give you a hand," Jonas offered, holding out a husky arm to grip Finn's uplifted hand. Within moments he was on his feet, swaying a bit but able to walk to where the wagon waited. Jessica picked up the quilt he'd been sprawled on and shook it, then folded it over her arm, following the two men.

Her legs ached, her back felt tender, and she swallowed the last drops of the tea Arlois had given her, then bit into one of the biscuits. Finn must come first for now, she decided, even though she felt bereft as she recognized the bare facts of their relationship.

He'd married her solely for the chance of regaining Aaron's possession, no matter how much he protested that he cared about her. She'd offered her love into his keeping and had not heard an answering vow from him. At least the man was honest. She'd have to give him that. For a moment she felt surrounded by strangers, all of them not what they seemed to be. Except for Arlois and Geraldine, maybe. And Polly, who made no bones about her feelings and was blunt and up-front.

She looked ahead and caught a glimpse of Morgan, and her hands clenched together beneath the sheltering folds of the quilt she carried. He was a threat to Finn and to her, she decided. For as long as she must, she'd keep him out of the picture, until Finn was back on his feet, anyway. For now her sole task was to keep Finn safe. She owed him that much.

One wagon overturned, bringing progress to a halt as the contents were salvaged from the creek bottom and spread to dry over bushes on the other side of the crossing. Its owners were thankful for small favors, aware that it might have been a total disaster. For had the wagon broken apart, they'd have been without transport, forced to seek out a settlement and delay their journey. The train must continue, or face snow in the upper regions of the mountains ahead.

That their own journey would end before they reached that point was a comfort to Jessica. Part of the group would turn south to Sante Fe, the rest north to the Oregon Trail. She breathed a sigh of relief that she would not be in their number. Most of the miners were heading for the gold and silver fields nearer to Pike's Peak, and she feared that there might be a dearth of female companionship once the train broke into three groups. But she would have Finn to look after her. Even though his motivation for marrying her left much to be desired, he was loyal, a responsible man. She would be satisfied with that.

The crossing delayed them for another full day, for the families were not willing to continue on late in the afternoon. A vote was taken and they set up camp for another night just beyond Cottonwood Creek. The ladies stayed close to camp, as if the happenings of the night before had put a damper on their freedom.

Jessica lit a fire, gathering bits of kindling from the surrounding prairie where, at some time, trees had evidently flourished, probably cut down by those who'd gone before and used for firewood. She set her skillet on the coals and ladled lard onto its surface. A brace of rabbits had been brought back to camp by David Bates, and he'd offered one of them to her for their evening meal.

Grateful for the meat, she'd washed it in the creek, David having cleaned it first, keeping the hide for himself. Arlois said he would tan the inside of the skin and use it later for slippers for her. Finn offered to show her how to stitch them together to fit her feet, a skill he'd picked up from the Indians he'd met during the previous years.

Now Jessica floured the assorted pieces and placed them on the skillet, turning them as they browned. Finn sat on the ground behind her, silent as he watched her move back and forth, preparing their supper. She'd tried her hand at the flatbread Arlois was so good at, and to her surprise it had turned out well, crusty on the outside, tender within.

A can of peaches made up the rest of the meal, and Finn reached out for the container as she attempted to open it with a knife. "Let me do that before you cut yourself," he said gruffly.

"I can do it," she protested, but he only looked at her steadily, his hand outstretched until she obliged him.

With deft movements, he cut off the lid and divided the contents between the bowls she'd dug from the keg. Harv Littleman brought by a bit of butter after the wagons settled in for the night, offering it with a grin. "Geraldine made this earlier. Thought you might like a bit of it," he said.

"I'm passing it around a little, kinda celebrating gettin' across the creek in one piece."

Jessica had accepted the treat with thanks. Butter was hard to come by, though others had traded for small bits when Geraldine used her churn. Jessica was more likely to swap out for a cup of milk, deciding that her unborn child would be nourished if she drank it on occasion. Arlois said that drinking tea would make milk in a new mother, and though that didn't seem to make sense, Jessica recognized that she was without a solid background when it came to this business of having a baby and providing for its needs. She'd do well to pick up all the bits and pieces of advice she could.

The rabbit smelled wonderful, she decided, lifting the skillet to one side and draining the scant amount of lard from it. She offered two pieces to Finn, placing them on his plate, and then took one for herself. "Should I have only taken half a rabbit?" she asked him. "Dave and Arlois have children to feed."

"You can ask them," Finn told her. "But I think he had a wild turkey, too. I imagine they have enough to eat."

She subsided and settled on her upright perch, the log she carefully dragged along every day. It beat sitting on the ground, she thought thankfully, since getting up and down was becoming a lost art these days.

Someone played a Jew's harp across the circle and another man tuned a fiddle. It seemed that a celebration was in order, and within minutes several couples danced with lively steps in the firelight, urged on by those who sat by and clapped in rhythm to the beat of the music. Children joined in the dance, the antics making Jessica smile.

"Wish you could dance?" Finn asked quietly.

"No." She shook her head. "I'm too clumsy these days, I fear."

"If I could get around a little better, I'd argue that point

with you,'' he said lightly. ''Maybe by morning I'll be back
to normal.''

''Maybe,'' she said agreeably, not willing to place a bet
on how soon he'd be riding his horse and placing himself
in jeopardy once more. She feared him leaving her sight,
she found, and ached to tell him that Morgan was a danger
to him. Only the thought that she would put him in peril
should she confess her fears made her push aside the idea.
So long as Finn was unaware of Morgan's perfidy, he was
safe. At least for now.

But should they locate the deed, and should that discov-
ery become known, they would both be vulnerable. And
with them, the unborn child beneath her apron.

Jessica watched as Morgan left his campfire. From the
back of her wagon she saw him slip between two wagons
and disappear into the night. *I'll meet you tomorrow night
after midnight.* The words he'd spoken resounded in her
ears, and she stifled the urge to alert Finn to the man's
betrayal.

Betrayal of what? she asked herself silently. He'd never
professed to be Finn's friend. And certainly not hers. In
fact, he'd never done more in her direction than attempt to
bring her under his control.

Except for last night, she reminded herself reluctantly.
Last night, when he could have turned her over to the two
men who'd taken her and then dumped her on the ground
with such a lack of finesse that she lay exposed in the
moonlight as Morgan stood beside her.

He'd been gracious enough, pulling her robe down to
cover her, even locating a quilt to warm her. Though that
hadn't done the job. Only his arms, the warmth of his body,
had brought her out of the shivering, trembling state she
was in.

Perhaps, she thought...perhaps there was in the depths
of the man some small bit of consideration, a sense of

honor. Yet, all she'd recognized during the long night was Morgan's determination to keep her from telling Finn that her supposed rescuer was knee-deep in the treachery that had involved both of them.

Several men kept watch, and none of them seemed to pay any special mind to Morgan's leaving. But then, they hadn't heard his words spoken to the two cohorts he'd left behind. Finn had watched Morgan and then turned his attention away, as if he would deliberately hide his interest in the man. Almost as though—Jessica scorned the thought as disloyal. Finn had nothing to do with the men who had snatched her up. And Morgan was certainly not a friend of his.

Yet she pondered the matter, her attention resting on Finn as he sat by the fire, noting the men he spoke with, aware of the fact that lately Morgan seemed to hover just on the outskirts of their presence. And wondered if her imagination was working overtime.

They'd gone to bed early and now she settled on the floor, leaning her head on the tailgate. Behind her, she heard the rustle of Finn's movement, knew the instant he awoke and became aware of her absence beside him on the feather tick.

"Jessica?" His voice held the roughness of sleep, the syllables of her name spoken softly in the stillness. "Are you all right, sweetheart?"

She turned her head to find him in the shadows, and forced a smile to curve her lips, lest he detect fear on her features. *I'm sitting here wondering how to keep you safe.* Words she dared not speak aloud filled her mind, and for the first time since she'd known him, Finn Carson assumed a layer of vulnerability she ached to penetrate. Each day seemed to find him stronger, more able to defend himself. Perhaps by next week his wounds would be healed and she'd be, once more, able to lean on his strength and put herself in his protective care.

But for at least tonight, she must still be the strong one, the one to keep watch, the one to assure him of her confidence in their situation. "I'll be back with you in a minute," she said quietly. "I just needed a breath of fresh air." And wasn't that the truth? She'd felt suffocated by her own fears, unable to lie beside him another minute, knowing that danger lurked in every shadow.

And so, she'd risen to keep watch, and in her anxious moments had seen Morgan disappear from the circle. Even now he was probably meeting up with the two men who stalked Finn and would stop at nothing to get their hands on the damn deed Lyle had hung around her neck like a millstone.

If she knew where it was she'd give it up gladly, make them a gift of it rather than allow it to be the reason for Finn to fall into any more danger. And yet, she decided reluctantly, he'd been the least honest of all of them, marrying her for the claim she had supposedly inherited.

Her thoughts swam in a muddle and she sighed, crawling back to the middle of the wagon, where the man she'd married waited for her. He reached to help her settle beside him and she took his warm hand in hers, feeling the returning strength that flowed from long fingers to hold her beside him.

"That's better," he murmured against her ear, covering them both with the sheet. "I missed you, Jess. What woke you?"

"I hadn't been asleep yet," she told him. "The baby's keeping me awake, I think."

"It won't be long now," he whispered, as if he would comfort her with the promise. "Once you have him, you'll start feeling better."

"Maybe," she agreed quietly, though her aching heart told her it would take more than the birth of her child to bring peace to her soul.

From beyond the circle of wagons she heard the soft

rustle of footsteps, the murmur of voices and then the undertones of a man's deep voice. A voice she recognized. Gage Morgan was returning and had apparently been met by one of the men on watch. A chuckle touched her ear and then the faint movement of someone passing by the tailgate of her wagon.

She turned her head, narrowing her eyes to look at the oval opening, aware that a tall figure filled it, only the subdued glow of firelight allowing her to recognize his identity. Morgan peered within the wagon for only an instant, and she saw the determined line of jaw and chin as he moved on. Fear struck her with icy fingers, and behind her Finn murmured a sleepy reassurance.

"Go to sleep, Jess. I'm here. I'll keep you warm."

Obediently she closed her eyes, attempting to block the vision that persisted in remaining in place. Danger surrounded them. And in the days to come it would close in until they were caught up in a betrayal she could only hug to herself for now.

The night stretched before her, the sky endless with stars enough to spare and a moon that gave light to those who plotted against her and Finn. Tomorrow would bring no answers. As well as she knew her own name, she knew that it would take several tomorrows before she could lean with certain surety on Finn's strength. And in the meantime, she must be the one to keep watch.

Chapter Ten

Finn, clearly recovered from his scalp wounds, had once more focused on her well-being, watching her closely during the evening hours as they sat before their campfire, his concern obvious. He spoke with those who passed by and halted for long moments to pass the time of day, but Jessica knew she was his first priority. As he was hers. She cursed the bridle she must place on her lips, lest a standoff between Finn and Morgan should endanger either Finn or herself.

And most of all she seemed to have turned inward, thinking constantly about her child. He became heavier with each passing day, and his movements were slower, as if he felt confined at the space her body allotted him. As she sat peacefully by the fire, she felt the nudge of a small foot beneath her heart, reminding her of his presence, and her hand went there, rubbing distractedly at the spot where the tiny lump made itself known.

"Are you all right, sweetheart?" Finn watched her steadily from the other side of the fire and she wondered at his distance. As though distracted, he'd moved from beside her, perhaps to better watch the comings and goings of the men of the group as they closed down the circle for the night.

"I'm fine," she assured him, aware that she'd allowed a long pause to fall, and yet Finn did not appear to notice her lack of attention. He was looking beyond the corner of their wagon, his eyes narrowing as though he sought out some attraction in the darkness of the prairie. And then he rose, slowly and with a yawn.

"I think I'll take a quick walk before we go to bed, Jess. Do you mind?"

She shook her head. "I'll probably climb in the wagon and wait there for you," she told him, affecting disinterest in his ploy. He was curious about something, or someone, out there beyond the circle. And again, as she had in the early weeks of their marriage, she had a moment of disquiet, as though she could not trust his motives.

He walked between the wagons and she rose, her movements awkward, certain in that moment that Finn was preoccupied, else he would have offered to help her into the wagon bed. Unfailingly considerate on any other occasion, tonight he walked away and left her on her own to gain the tailgate and heave herself inside the canvas-topped wagon.

She stood in the shadows there, moving slowly as she dragged the wooden box from beneath the wagon for a new purpose, and then faded into the darkness, her drab clothing hiding her from notice as she settled on the box just beside the wagon wheel. Willing herself to be inconspicuous, she huddled quietly, the night covering her presence.

Before her was the man she'd trusted with her very life, walking away with long strides, his movements purposeful, as if there lay before him something of dire import. Two hundred feet or so from the wagon, he halted, tilting his hat back with one hand, then resting both palms against his hips, waiting for some unknown happening to take place.

From farther out on the prairie a whistle sounded, low and melodic, as if a nightbird had sounded a seductive call to his mate. Finn straightened from his casual stance and headed with measured steps toward the top of a rise another hundred feet or so from where Jessica watched. Too far to see his face but near enough, in the light of the rising moon, to identity the man who approached him.

Gage Morgan. She rose from her perch on the box, one hand pressing against her breast where her heart beat with anguish. Was it a trap? Had Morgan decided to make a move and get Finn out of the way, the better to accomplish his aim?

If so, the meeting between the men was not heading in that direction with any degree of haste. They stood, heads together, with not a murmur of voices to disturb the air. And then she felt the pain of betrayal stab deeply into her breast, and the anguish she'd suppressed only a moment ago was doubled by the knowledge that Finn had deceived her again. Beguiled and bewitched by his gentleness, his concern, she'd given way to the man, allowing him to creep beyond the barriers she'd held fast to for years.

Through dry eyes she watched as the two men clasped hands, the age-old symbol of agreement between friends, the unspoken bargain made by men when they formed a pact of some sort. Deprived of the sure knowledge of Finn's loyalty, she watched, swamped by pain, and knew she was truly alone. The one man she'd depended on for her well-being was in cahoots with Morgan. And should Morgan prove to be the enemy, she stood isolated once more.

Silently, stealthily, she climbed into the wagon, looking back over her shoulder as Finn turned aside from his clandestine meeting and headed back toward the wagon. Hurriedly she dropped her dress on the floor and kicked off her shoes, pulling the feather tick to the floor and wrapping in a quilt to take her place there before Finn returned and found her watching.

It was several minutes before he came to her, and she'd managed to get her breathing under control, was assuming the posture of sleep as he made his way over the tailgate and into the wagon. "It's me, Jess," he said quietly. "Are you still awake?"

She was immobile, regulating her breathing, unwilling to reply lest her voice tremble, or her words betray the fear that ruled her with an iron grip. Finn stripped from his trousers and shirt and, clad in drawers, he lowered himself to the space behind her. Jessica murmured softly, as though she roused from sleep, and heard his soft chuckle, felt the arm encircle her middle as he curled against her back. His mouth touched her hair and then the nape of her neck and his whisper was low. "Good night, sweetheart."

Her eyes closed, pinching shut tightly, lest tears betray her, and she swallowed the hurtful words that crowded her throat, willing them to silence. *Sweetheart.* He dared to call her by that pet name, as if he hadn't just met with the enemy and called him friend.

Thoughts of the morrow crowded her mind, plans for escape from Finn Carson vied in her thoughts with the sorrow that held her inert in his embrace. She would clasp the pain to her bosom for tonight, and tomorrow decide on her next move. Her breath caught on a sob and she stiffened. But in the few moments since he'd found his place behind her, Finn was asleep, and she was left to spend the night hours with her fears as her only companion.

The next day brought no resolution to Jessica's ordeal. The talk on the train was of the first split to take place. A town to the south appealed to two of the families, and offered a stopping place that might result in homes for them. One of the children was ill, and the parents grasped at the opportunity to seek out a physician. Their closest friends decided to join forces with them and the next day would find them turning off for a long day's journey to the chosen destination.

They would be at risk, two families alone, with the everpresent danger of stray Indians or bandits in the area who might seek them out and wreak havoc on their small group. But the mother's instincts prevailed, and the two men felt confident that they would be safe enough, given an early start and a map furnished by Jonas to guide them across the prairie.

As Jessica heard the talk around her, she yearned for the chance to take her life in her hands and steer her wagon behind them, ached for the strength it would require to plot her own destiny. Only the knowledge that Finn would not allow such a move halted her from setting it in motion. Her intelligent mind gave notice that she was legally under his control. And watching her drive away in her wagon, leaving him behind, would begin a conflict to rival any war in the annals of history.

So she only watched, and waited, and planned instead for another way to solve her problem. As her mother had often said, there's more than one way to skin a cat. And as obscene and vulgar as those words might be, Jessica took them to heart and planned accordingly.

They sat before the fire the next evening and Jessica looked up at Finn, speaking an idle thought. "You seem quite friendly with Gage Morgan these days." She bit at a piece of fried salt pork and wrinkled her nose, then she glanced up at Finn, who was watching her with the quiet appraisal she had expected.

"Not any more than usual," he said shortly. "We speak when it's necessary. Not that we have a lot in common," he told her. "He's got his hands full heading up that batch of miners he's traveling with, and I'm a family man. Thanks to you." He nodded in her direction, a smile forming as he teased her.

She looked closely at the piece of flatbread she held and tore off a chunk, then chewed it slowly before she answered. "I just wondered about it."

He shook his head. "I don't recall spending any time with him lately, Jess. He seems to have acquired a roving eye where you're concerned, and I'd just as soon keep him away from both of us. I don't want any trouble.''

She laughed bitterly, and his eyes darkened as he sought her gaze. ''You don't believe me?'' At the small shake of her head, he rose and stalked to crouch before her. ''The man's always had eyes for you, Mrs. Carson. Hell, he even wanted to marry you a while back. To tell the truth, I don't have a whole lot of use for him.''

Jessica shrugged, apparently allowing the subject to be dismissed. ''I just wondered,'' she murmured. ''It seemed like…'' Her voice trailed off, giving Finn a chance to offer an explanation that might satisfy her, but instead, he leaned forward and kissed her cheek, a brief caress that was followed by a quiet chuckle.

''It won't be long, only a matter of a few weeks, until we're pulling into Shadow Creek, Jess. I'm hopin' we'll be able to come up with the deed by then, so we can stake our claim and set up housekeeping. Isn't that what you want?''

She nodded, forcing a smile to her lips. Finn was not going to confide in her, it seemed. His liaison with Morgan was a subject not up for discussion, and whatever their plotting together might accomplish, she was not going to be privy to the details.

On the third day, she watched as the two wagons left the circle, early in the morning before dawn had brightened the eastern sky. Several of the men and three of the women stood just beyond the circle and waved a farewell, and Jessica sat near the tailgate of her wagon, watching as Finn mounted and rode off in a westerly direction. The small group left behind disbanded then, and the men busied themselves building a campfire and putting water into a pot, along with enough coffee to choke a horse, Jessica thought grimly.

She sorted through her things quickly, finding the stack

of diapers and the gowns she'd hidden in a bundle, along with an extra dress for herself and her shawl to keep her warm. A quilt would come in handy, too, she decided, should she decide to lie down to sleep, and though it was cumbersome to carry, she decided it would be sensible to include it in her load.

A hidden store of money at the bottom of her trunk filled a canvas bag, and she tucked it into her pocket. Lyle had forced her to be deceptive, and the cash she owned had been carefully and gradually hidden from his eyes over the past years. Now it might be all that stood between her and the casting of herself on a stranger's charity once she found her way to the town that lay just over the horizon.

After a moment's thought, she located Lyle's handgun in her trunk and placed it in her other pocket where it hung heavily, bumping against her leg as she walked. Extra cartridges filled a box and she stuffed a goodly supply of them into the bundle she would carry, uncertain if she would be able to aim the gun and pull the trigger should the time come, but deciding grimly that she must be prepared for any eventuality.

The thought of the men who'd captured her being on the prairie, perhaps still tracking the wagon train, still seeking out the deed, was frightening. But even more fearsome to her was the thought that she no longer placed her full trust in the man she'd married. If she could catch up to the two wagons and hitch a ride, surely she'd find shelter in the town and be able to make a life there for herself and her child.

Last, she gathered bread and the leftover meat from last night's meal and wrapped it in Finn's extra kerchief. With one last look around the inside of the wagon she'd lived in for months, she climbed over the tailgate and reached back inside for her bundle.

A last peek around the corner told her that the men were oblivious to her presence and the three women had climbed back into their wagons, probably to snatch another half hour or so of rest. It would be all the head start she'd have, for once the train assembled for the travel day, and David Bates had hitched up her oxen and come looking for her, the fat would be in the fire and the alarm would go out.

Her legs moved at a rapid pace and she breathed heavily as she sought the first small rise where Finn and Morgan had met only two nights past. Once over that hillock, she slowed her pace, measuring her steps so as not to wear herself out during the first half hour or so. She'd have to find a hiding place soon, somewhere she could watch from, somewhere she could find concealment while the searchers looked for her.

For certainly there would be those from the wagon train who would seek her out. But as surely as she knew the urgency of her trek, she knew the train would not wait while she was found. Jonas had said that the next few days were going to be long and difficult, their extra time spent by the creek having put them behind schedule.

It would be left to Finn to search, and he wouldn't be returning to the train for several hours, probably not until the nooning. She would have only six hours or so to catch up with the two wagons and beg a place for herself with one of the families until they reached the town that lay almost twenty miles to the south.

The terrain seemed different here, with low hills and scrub dotting the landscape. Jessica rested for a moment, seeking out a hiding place and finding nothing that would withstand a casual glance. She pressed on, estimating that she'd been walking for a good thirty minutes before she halted again.

It was time to take cover, or allow herself to be found. To the south the prairie stretched ahead, and less than a mile ahead she saw the unmistakable form of the two wagons she followed. To the east there seemed to be a bit more rugged territory, and though it meant she would lose time catching up to the wagons, she turned in that direction. If searchers came to this point, they would surely not look for her to backtrack.

Over a nearby rise she stumbled into a gully and, beneath the wall found a narrow spot where flowing water had washed away the earth, forming a small depression. From above, it was invisible and suited her purpose. Should men come this far they would have to cross the gully before seeing her, and chances were that they would consider it a waste of time to move in an easterly direction.

She lay atop her folded quilt and tucked her body into the cave, drawing her legs up to form the smallest target possible. The thought of snatching an hour's rest was appealing, she decided, and with a sigh, she placed her bundle beneath her head and closed her eyes.

The sound of horses awakened her and the voices of two men made her aware that if she were to be discovered, the time would be soon. "I doubt she came this way," one of them said dourly. And the other answered only with a grunt and a muttered imprecation.

"Fool woman. Can't imagine what she was thinking of to run off that way."

"Maybe the fellas that grabbed her the first time snatched her up again," the first voice suggested.

"Well, if they did, they sure wouldn't be standing around waiting to be found."

The sound of hoofbeats resounded above her as the men turned and rode away, leaving her breathless and tense as she considered peering over the edge to seek their whereabouts. Remaining where she was seemed the best option for now, she decided, and for another ten minutes or so, she huddled where she lay before finally rising and peeking over the rim of the gully.

No movement met her eyes, except for a small dust cloud far to the west, and she gathered her things together and climbed from the hiding place that had concealed her so well. The wagons were no longer in sight, but within a half hour she'd found their wheel tracks and set off to follow.

"What do you mean, she's gone?" Finn searched the faces of the men before him and snatched his hat off, his other hand running distractedly through his hair. "How could she just disappear? Did you go looking for her?"

Either unwilling or unable to give him a decent answer, the men faced him silently. Finally one of them shrugged and shook his head. "We looked. Looked right hard for an hour and better, Carson. She wasn't to be found."

David Bates faced Finn and shook his head. "They looked until Jonas said we had to pull out, Finn. Arlois is having a fit because we went off without Jessica, but there wasn't a choice. If we don't make up some time, the folks crossing the Rockies are gonna be in trouble."

"Well, if I don't manage to find her, I'm gonna be out a wife," Finn said mockingly. "And somehow that seems a more dire prospect to me than the other."

"We did our best," one of the men said sullenly. "I don't think the woman wanted to be found. I think she ran off on you, Carson. Did you have a fight?"

Finn shook his head. "Of course not." Such a thing was out of the question. He'd never done anything to hurt Jessica, although, his conscience nudged him, he hadn't been altogether honest with her.

Morgan stepped close and took his elbow. "I need to talk to you," he said quietly. And as the other men walked away, he met Finn's gaze. "Do you think she might have seen us together the other night?"

"Hell, no. She was asleep when I got back to the wagon."

"Was she?" Morgan looked dubious for a moment. "I threatened you when I brought her back the other day. Told her if she spilled the beans that I was in cahoots with the two others, I'd kill you."

"What the hell did you do that for?" His voice splin-
tered as Finn growled the query. "What would it have hurt
if she'd said something?"

"I wanted to keep her out of it, Carson. I had to keep a
barrier between us."

"I think it's time to nail those two," Finn said harshly.
"This would be a good time to see them in jail, I'd say.
I'm tired of keeping Jess in the dark."

"We don't have proof," Morgan said patiently. "They
haven't admitted to shooting Beaumont yet, and that charge
will stick them in prison faster than the theft of the deed
back in Saint Louis."

"Well, they kidnapped my wife," Finn said sharply.
"That's a crime in any territory if I know anything about
it."

"When I take them in, I want to know for certain that
they'll hang," Morgan told him. "And until you find that
deed, there won't be any proof that Beaumont took it from
your brother."

"I've searched that wagon over," Finn said quietly. "If
it's there, it's well hidden."

"It's there," Morgan said firmly. "I'd lay money on it."
He watched Finn closely and his next words were spoken
in a desultory fashion. "When you find it, will you give it
back to Jessica, or keep it for yourself?"

"What do you think?" Finn asked. "I'm planning on
keeping Jessica and the deed *both*. They belong to me."

"I don't think she'll agree with you."

"Why not?" Finn spoke the words quietly, his focus
sharp on the other man.

"I think she's gonna be madder than hell when you
claim the deed as yours."

"Well, that's not my problem right now," Finn said.
"I've got to find her first, and then I'll worry about the rest
of it."

"Do you want me to go with you?" Morgan asked.

Finn shook his head. "I'll do this alone. I figure she probably set off to follow those two wagons and couldn't keep up. She'll be out there on the trail, and by this time I'll warrant she's tired and hungry and ready to be found." He turned away and gathered up his horse's reins.

"Don't count on that last prediction," Morgan told him. "My guess is she doesn't want to be found. I think she's decided to call it quits with you."

"You planning on picking up the pieces?" Finn asked, bristling as he turned back to face the other man.

"I'm not the man she married," Morgan told him. "I offered, and she turned me down flat."

"Just remember that." With a smooth move, Finn was in his saddle and his horse was trotting in a southeasterly direction. The animal had been ridden hard earlier in the day, and Finn knew it was wise not to push the gelding too fast. Jessica had a head start, and wasn't aching for him to spot her. She was smart and strong, and even with the heavy weight of pregnancy, she might be able to catch up with the two families who'd set off early this morning.

Maybe.

The two wagons that lured her on were no closer now than they'd been three hours ago, Jessica decided. Against the horizon, they were too far to hail, and certainly beyond her ability to overtake. Her steps had slowed over the past hour, and she found herself dragging as she plowed ahead. Her back ached, a dull, throbbing pain that was unceasing, and she clutched at it with her left palm, as if the pressure she exerted would ease its agony.

There was no choice, she decided. She had to stop and rest, needed to eat the food she'd brought with her. Her mind was focused on water, and her disgust that she'd failed to allow for that basic need filled her to overflowing.

"Damn, damn, damn," she muttered, her anger allowing her the relief of cursing her own failure.

She halted beneath the spot of shade she'd discovered, a scrubby bit of prairie shrub at her back. The sun was hot and no breeze appeared to cool her sweaty brow. Although her trek had been undertaken with hope and confidence, she lingered now on the edge of despair as she gauged the distance to the town she sought.

"More miles than I want to think about," she whispered glumly. "Probably at least fifteen or so." Surely she'd traveled four or five miles already. Her feet were pinched and swollen, her shoes tight against her heel where a blister was forming. Going barefoot was not an option. The ground was rugged, and bits of stone made it impossible to walk without the protection her footwear offered.

She sighed deeply and closed her eyes, then unfolded the bread and meat she'd brought along. It tasted stale, but she was determined to eat it. The strength it provided would allow her to continue after a few moments' rest.

"You're a fool," she murmured beneath her breath. "You should have asked for a ride on one of those wagons, and just packed your duds and left with your head held high. They wouldn't have bothered looking for you and Finn would have gotten the message, loud and clear."

Finn. His image formed behind her closed eyelids, and she almost wept as she remembered his betrayal. Her anger saved her from that indignity and she chewed sullenly at the piece of meat she'd bitten off with a snap of her teeth.

He'd deceived her, made her love him, then gone behind her back to conspire with Gage Morgan. What their purpose was seemed uncertain as she thought of their meeting two nights ago. Morgan had rescued her so nicely, and she'd fallen for his ploys, had warmed herself in his arms and been grateful for his help, even as she doubted the integrity of his motives.

And yet, with all of that, she'd feared what he would do to Finn should she speak betraying words. Caught between a rock and hard place, as her mother used to say when describing a situation without a solution. Running hadn't solved her problem, Jessica thought, but at the time it had seemed to be a viable option.

Now she sat in aching silence, considering the pain that tugged unceasingly at her back. Surely her labor could not be at hand. She had another two weeks, at least, to carry this child. The memory of the miles she'd trudged this morning rose before her, and the thought of what such unprecedented strain on her body could bring about made her fearful.

She'd walked daily by the side of her oxen, had worked hard at the everyday chores that women were wont to tackle. But the hardship of making her way across the uneven ground, carrying a heavy pack at her side, had made her weary beyond belief. She leaned her head back and sighed.

"Finn," she whispered. "Why did you fail me?" A dry laugh acknowledged the fact that her query would go unanswered and she scrabbled to her feet, picking up her bundle and facing south. Only a faint gathering of dust on the horizon gave notice of the wagons she followed, and she set off on their trail, her feet dragging.

Jessica's footprints were indistinct, Finn found. And those he could identify were scuffed, as if she found it tedious to lift her feet, managing only to shuffle along. His lips set grimly, he continued to track her path, and when he reached the gully where the soil showed the distinct print of her presence beneath the overhead, he touched the earth with his fingertips.

"She was here," he muttered, and searched the surrounding area. No prints went farther toward the east, and the earth had been disturbed on the edge of the bank, as though she might have scrambled up its surface, dragging a pack behind her.

"She headed back to the west from here," he said beneath his breath, and then mounted his horse, following the trail she'd left.

It was well after noon, if he was any judge, Finn decided. Probably more like two o'clock or so, and she'd be getting hungry if she hadn't taken food with her. Two full canteens had been slung on either side of his saddle horn, and Jessica didn't own one of her own. So water was going to be at the top of her list once he laid hands on her. He leaned to lift one of the metal containers and nodded with satisfaction at the weight of it. Even warmed by the heat of the day, it was wet and fresh.

Small patches of scrub dotted the landscape before him and he rode a bit slower, scanning the surrounding area. He pulled his hat brim low, the better to shade his vision, and walked his horse for a while. Even at this pace he was traveling faster than Jessica, given the weight she carried and the weariness that no doubt caused her steps to drag.

He'd lost track of her trail for a while, but now he picked it up again and nudged his mount into a quicker pace. He couldn't be more than an hour behind her now, he figured and looked ahead, his eyes searching for a moving dot on the horizon. If she wasn't in front of him, heading south, she had to be hiding or maybe just resting from the sun's heat in some bit of shelter.

Jessica settled herself in the sparse shade she'd discovered beneath another patch of scrub growing atop a small

rise. From here she could look back from whence she'd
come, and by merely turning her head in the opposite di
rection could see the faint tracks of the two wagons in the
distance. It would be a safe place to sleep for a while. By
the time the sun set and the moon made its appearance she
would begin again, walking through the night hours when
her need for water might not be so desperate.

Her pack under her head, the quilt beneath her, she
curled up on her side and embraced the child within her
He'd slowed his movements over the past hours and now
she wished fiercely that he might nudge her, reminding her
that he was well and drawing nourishment from her body
Yet, though she pressed against the firm rounding of her
flesh, he made no response, and she sighed as her eyes
closed in slumber.

The sound of a horse's whinny awoke her and she lifted
her head, blinking a bit as her responses became more alert
She was groggy yet aware that the sun had fallen sharply
from the sky overhead and now hovered on the western
horizon. She'd slept longer than her plan had allowed, bu
the rest would stand her in good stead, she decided.

From her hiding place she looked back toward the north
and caught sight of a man riding toward her. His horse was
black, and as she watched, the rider bent lower over the
animal's neck and urged his mount into a gallop.

Jessica's heart beat at a furious pace as she recognized
Finn's figure, and she swallowed, almost choking on the
dryness of her throat, fearful of his anger as he approached
her hiding place.

"Jessica." He said only her name as he lowered himsel
from his gelding, and then he was crouched beside her, one
hand moving to touch her face. "Are you all right?"

It seemed his anger was to be held in abeyance, she decided thankfully, and shivered as she nodded her reply.

"I know you're not cold," he said. "It's too damn hot for that. What's wrong with you?" He ran his hand down her throat and shoulder, as if to assure himself that she was not a figment of his imagination, and then placed his palm on her belly. "Is the baby all right?"

She nodded again, her mouth too dry to form words in reply. Her tongue touched her lips and found them cracked and peeling from the long hours in the sun, without any trace of moisture to soften their surface. At the movement, Finn rose quickly and turned to his gelding, reaching for a canteen.

He sat on the ground beside her and unscrewed the cap, then offered it to her. She reached for it and her fingers trembled as she attempted to grasp it. With a quick shake of his head, Finn held it to her lips and tilted it a bit, allowing a small amount of water to slide into her mouth.

She swallowed it greedily and inhaled deeply. "More, please." Her voice sounded scratchy and she winced, barely recognizing the sound as coming from her throat. "I know you're angry with me," she whispered.

"Am I?" he asked. "I think what I'm feeling right now isn't important. The main thing is to take care of you."

"More water," she said again, her hand trembling as she reached to hold the canteen closer to her mouth.

"Just a little at a time," Finn said. "It'll make you throw up if you try to drink it in a hurry." He tilted the container again and allowed the water to cool her lips, a bit of it running off her chin. His handkerchief appeared from his pocket and he dampened it, then wiped the cloth over her forehead and cheeks.

Jessica closed her eyes at the cooling sensation and felt her dry skin absorb the moisture as if it had been starved.

Finn was here, and all would be well. Maybe she could talk
him into taking her to the town she'd been determined to
find. If he was as angry as he had a right to be, he'd be
glad to be rid of her. And then she recognized the folly of
that thought. Finn was too proud to allow her to leave him,
too set on taking care of her, come hell or high water.

And for that fact, she felt a moment's joy. Even though
he'd deceived her, he'd still looked after her, and at least
until the baby was born, she'd depend on his mercy. She
sagged against him, and felt a gathering within her belly,
as if the whole, firm burden of her pregnancy had decided
to draw into itself and exert pressure on her muscles.

With a groan she lifted herself more upright, but her back
was stricken by a growing pain that traveled around both
sides and focused on the lowest part of her belly, increasing
in intensity for what seemed like an eternity. She held her
breath, unwilling to cry aloud at the suddenness of her misery, but Finn gripped her shoulders and lowered his head
to look directly into her eyes.

"What is it, Jess?" he asked tersely. "Are you in pain?"

She could only nod, biting her lip for a moment and
tasting the blood that oozed from the small wound. The
pain subsided then, as quickly as it had come, and she
relaxed once more, slumping against Finn's arm. He held
her close and she turned her face against his shoulder, inhaling the scent of horse and man combined, thankful for
his persistence in seeking her whereabouts.

"My guess is that you're going to have the baby," he
murmured quietly. "We'll have to figure out our next
move, sweetheart."

"I don't think I can travel right now," she whispered.
"I'm about done in."

"I can see that," he agreed. "But if this baby won't wait,

we'll have to set up camp right here and see what happens next.''

She felt laughter bubble up within her, light-headed now that Finn was here to take charge. "I think we both know what's going to happen next," she said. "I fear I don't know much about this, Finn."

He squeezed her against his side. "Neither do I, Jess, but it can't be a whole lot different than birthing a colt or a cow giving birth to a calf. I've helped out with animals more times than I want to count. I'll bet you I can get one small baby into the world without too much trouble."

She looked up into his eyes quickly, and found there only a calm assurance that brought peace to her soul. No matter what the future brought for them, this day would be set aside as a time when they would join forces and strive together for the safety and well-being of her child.

Chapter Eleven

It seemed the pain had taken up permanent residence, Jessica decided. The sun was below the horizon, the moon was a slice of gold in the sky, and above her, the stars cast their glitter on the surrounding prairie. She and Finn were alone on the hillock she'd taken as her own hours before, and now she looked around at her primitive surroundings with fear uppermost in her mind.

Birthing a baby was difficult at best, with other women to lend their advice and experience to the task. Experiencing these hours with Finn had made her more aware than ever of the frailty of her condition. True, as Finn said, it couldn't be much different than the delivery of an animal, but somehow, that thought failed to give her any assurance right now.

The pain encompassed her on a regular basis, its intensity increasing as each spasm took her a bit beyond the last. She felt the tensing of her belly again, and groaned aloud as she faced another session that would hold her in its grasp for more than a minute. Finn said the labor seemed to be progressing as he'd expected, each pain a bit longer than the last, growing in strength, as if her muscles prepared to expel the baby she carried.

The babe was unmoving, perhaps gathering his own

strength to aid in his journey from his mother's body into the harsh bit of territory that waited to welcome him. And within Jessica rose a fear she could not escape. Would she be able to bear the final minutes of her ordeal, or would she cry out and fight Finn's attempts to help her. Childbirth had always been imbued with mystery, and even her own experience with it back in Saint Louis had been a more conventional occasion than the one she faced now.

She felt that she might be unable to cope with what lay ahead, with the open prairie surrounding them and not a woman with her from whom to draw comfort. Her whimper of pain was involuntary as the crescendo of pressure increased. Finn's hand was warm against her belly, and he bent over her, his lips touching her forehead. He'd sacrificed his own ground cloth for this moment, spreading it beneath her in order to save the quilt from ruin.

He'd seemed to know what to do, and she was at the mercy of his judgment. One of her clean diapers was beneath her hips, keeping her from the dubious surface of the tarp she lay on, and Finn had placed another over her, as if he knew she felt terribly exposed beneath the starlit sky. And when he smiled at her nicely, as though her modesty was of small matter right now, she could only be thankful that he didn't deny her that small bit of covering.

The pain ebbed like the waves on the shore, easing its grip and allowing her to breath deeply, preparing herself for the next assault. It was not long in coming, probably no more than a minute, Finn said quietly. And as it held her in its tentacles, she felt a gush of fluid between her legs and heard Finn's voice soothing her with soft words.

"It's all right, Jess. Just your waters breaking. It has to happen before the baby can come."

"How do you know all this?" she asked, gasping as the pain receded and left her shivering.

"I told you, sweet. All female creatures go through this.

You're a healthy woman, Jess. This baby will be born before long and you'll see I was right.''

She looked up into his face. He smiled, as if to reassure her of his confidence. And then he reached for the pack she'd carried, snatching up another diaper to take the place of the wet one she lay on. "Lift your hips, Jess," he said. "Let me pull the wet one out and get some dry cloth beneath your bottom.''

She did as he said, thankful for his matter-of-fact attitude, aching to tell him of her appreciation but unable to speak as another pain followed the last with barely enough time to catch her breath. It clung to her with iron claws, and she could not help the cry of helpless anguish that escaped her lips as it reached its peak of intensity.

"I think you're almost there, honey," Finn said. "I can see dark hair. Just another few pains should do it.''

The urge to push at the pressure between her thighs was overwhelming, and she met the next surge of agony with a flexing of her muscles that offered relief. And then as the momentum eased from her pain-racked body she faced a fear such as she'd never known.

"I can't do this," she whimpered, her head turning from side to side, as if she could deny the pain and force it to subside by the strength of her will alone.

Finn bent over her, holding her face between his hands, and his lips touched her forehead. "Yes, you can, Jess. You're the bravest woman I've ever seen. Come on now. Just a little longer and we'll have a baby.''

"There is no *we*," she cried. "I'm on my own in this, Finn Carson.''

His fingers held her more firmly, and his voice hardened in intensity. "You listen to me, Jessica. We're going to raise this child together. I told you that when we got married, and I haven't changed my mind. This baby will be mine as much as it is yours. And don't you forget it. As for the rest of it, we'll work it all out once we get back to the wagon train.''

She nodded, agreeing with his decision, aware that for now she had no choice. And then an urgent agony gripped her and she was suddenly breathless with its intensity. ''I have to push again,'' she said, her voice lifting as though she cried out for help.

''Go ahead. We'll have him here in no time,'' Finn told her, and then bent once more over the child she was forcing from her body with the strength of young, powerful muscles. Muscles that were designed to do this very thing.

With a shout that sounded like a cry of victory to her ears, Finn welcomed the child she bore and lifted the infant into the air for her to see. ''It's a boy, Jess. Just like I told you.'' He grinned widely, his eyes shiny in the starlight. And then he shoved her dress higher and wrapped the babe in another diaper and placed him across her suddenly flattened belly.

She touched the small face, her index finger gentle as she stroked the wrinkled forehead. The small head turned toward her and the tiny mouth opened wide as a cry split the silence. His arms waved, fighting their way free of the diaper that restricted his movements, and small feet kicked the air as her son made his indignation known.

''Is he all right?'' she asked, anxious lest he be in pain.

''He's fine,'' Finn told her confidently. ''I remember when my little sister was born and she sounded just like that. Aaron and I were waiting out on the front porch, and we thought somebody had hurt our new baby when we heard all the racket. But my pa just laughed when he came out of the house and told us we had a baby sister. Said all newborn babies sounded that way.''

Jessica felt another spasm of pain rack her belly, and Finn bent low again. ''It's the afterbirth, Jess,'' he said as if he knew her concern. ''I need to find some way to cut the cord and get this baby on his own.''

He rose and searched out his pack, digging in its depths until he found a length of twine. Three quick slashes of his pocketknife gave him two short bits of twine, and he tied them firmly around the cord that connected the babe to the sac that had sheltered him inside Jessica's body for almost nine months. Another slash of his knife and the bond between mother and child was severed, and the tiny boy was no longer a part of Jessica's body, but a living, breathing human being.

Finn tossed the afterbirth aside and returned to Jess. "I'll bury it before we leave here," he said. "I don't want some varmint dragging it off." He leaned back on his heels and viewed her soberly. "You're bleeding some, but I think that's to be expected," he told her. "Why don't we use a couple of his diapers to make a pad for you?"

Jessica could only nod, willing to deliver herself into his capable hands, and then her eyes closed as both of her hands grasped the baby that had quieted beneath her touch. She felt Finn lift him from her then, watched through her lashes as he enfolded the tiny form in another diaper, swaddling him and holding him close for a moment before he bent to place him in his mother's embrace.

"Thank you," she whispered, aware that those two words were totally inadequate to express her bone-deep gratitude for Finn's care. But for now it was all she had to offer, and as she watched, his lips curved in a smile.

They waited until dawn streaked the sky, and Finn was thorough as he wrapped Jessica loosely in the quilt for the journey back to the wagon train. She sat by, watching as he packed the provisions he'd brought with him, sharing the water with her, although she knew he'd given her most of it. All but the generous amount he'd bathed the baby with, cheerfully washing away the residue of birth with gentle touches.

He found some dried jerky in his pouch and she chewed

on it, thankful for the nourishment it would provide. The baby nursed beneath the protective covering of her bodice, and she winced as his tiny mouth tugged at her breast. He was a sturdy little fellow, if she was any judge of the matter, and that was all to the good. He would need every ounce of strength a baby could possess in order to survive the days ahead.

"I'm ready to load you on now, Jess," Finn told her. "My horse ate pretty well and I think he'll be fine to carry us both if we take our time."

She looked up dubiously at the tall gelding. "How long will it take, do you think?" she asked. "Have we a long way to go?"

And why hadn't he uttered one word of reproach in her direction, she thought glumly. Surely he was angry with her for causing him so much trouble, and yet he bent to her and smiled, lifting her with his palm under her elbow, his other arm across her back.

She halted beside the horse and looked up into Finn's face, determined to make him speak his mind. "I know you must be angry with me," she began, only to find her words halted by the pressure of his mouth against hers.

"You don't know any such thing," he said. "I told you we'd sort things out later. For now, I just want to get you back to our wagon and settled in."

"Where is it?"

"David Bates and Harv Littleman took care of it for me. They'll share the work of tending the oxen and keeping our place in line till we get back there. All we have to do is catch up with them."

"Oh? Is that *all?*" she asked, aware that his words made the task seem small, even as she doubted that it would be as simple as his explanation decreed.

In moments they were both in the saddle, Jessica across Finn's thighs, secure in his embrace, the baby held close.

She felt safe there, sure in the knowledge that Finn would handle things for now and she could close her eyes in sleep.

It took longer than he'd thought, and Finn breathed a sigh of relief when he caught sight of the wagon tracks snaking across the prairie ahead of them. To the west, looking incongruous in its brilliance, a metal pail shimmered in the sunlight, and he tugged his hat brim down, peering at the shiny object.

Within ten minutes, he'd neared it and his grin was wide. "Jess? Wake up, sweet. Someone left us some water."

He watched as she opened her eyes and blinked sleepily. "Water?" The single word held a wealth of hopefulness, he thought. "Really, Finn?"

"That's what it looks like to me," he said with a laugh, sliding from the saddle, gripping her firmly as he lowered her to the ground beside him. "Look here, a full bucket." He lifted it and nudged his horse's head aside as the animal would have drunk thirstily from its contents.

"You come next," he told his mount. "We get ours first though." He held the canteens beneath the surface and allowed them to fill, then offered one to Jessica, holding it to her mouth, watching as she drank. Her eyes were closed, her throat working as she swallowed, and he frowned. She'd been without water for too long. If she didn't have enough in her body, the baby would suffer from a lack of nourishment.

He filled the canteen again and drank deeply from it, then offered it again to Jessica. She eyed him dubiously. "Is there enough?"

"Plenty," he told her. "They'll both be full when we ride from here." And so it would be. If he calculated it right, they'd be caught up with the train by nightfall. His horse, even with two riders, could move faster than the wagons. He had a notion that Jonas would circle the group early on, giving him time to catch up.

Jessica drank again and he noted the color that had begun to return to her cheeks. The moonlight had washed out her normal pink tones, and by the light of the rising sun, she'd seemed pale to him, her skin washed out, her cheekbones seeming prominent. Now she seemed more herself, and he felt a surge of thankfulness.

When they'd drunk their fill, he once more immersed the canteen and then let the horse finish the rest. The bucket was empty in no time, and Finn calculated how best to tie it onto his saddle, knowing it was too valuable to leave behind. Finally, a length of his twine attached it to his saddle horn, and he put the baby's soiled diapers into it, much to Jessica's amusement.

"We'll just fill it with water when we get back and you can scrub them out," he told her cheerfully. And then his eyes fixed on her face. "I'm joking, you know. I'll take care of everything for a couple of days, including keeping his diapers clean."

"Will you?" she asked, as if unable to believe such a promise. "If Lyle were here instead of you, I doubt he'd make such an offer."

"I'm not Lyle," Finn told her. "As far as I'm concerned, he never existed, Jess. That's the past, and all I'm interested in is the future." And he'd better mend his fences in a hurry, he thought glumly if he intended to keep her happy. The next couple of days might bring them to an impasse, once they got back and Morgan appeared on the scene.

They traveled at a walk, then a slow lope for a while. Finn paced his mount, even walking beside the gelding's head through the afternoon hours. "I think it will be full nightfall before we reach the train," he told Jessica as the sun began its descent late in the afternoon. "There's a dust cloud ahead, though."

"Where?" She peered at the trail before them, and he halted his horse.

"Up ahead," he said shortly, offering her the canteen

for probably the last time. It was close to empty and unless they caught up soon, she would be in trouble. The loss of blood was not significant, but the shock of birthing a baby was taking its toll.

He hung the empty canteen on his saddle horn and lifted himself to sit behind her, shifting her onto his lap. One arm supported her, his hand beneath the weight of the child she held to her breast, and as he settled her as best he could, the baby squalled his hunger cry again.

"Can you feed him this way?" Finn asked, allowing the reins to lie loose in his hand.

She nodded and opened her dress, easing the baby inside her shift and then tugging the quilt around them both. "I'm all set, now," she said, and for a moment Finn closed his eyes. The urge to speak his feelings aloud was urgent, but he kept it to himself, aware that another moment would come, when he could tell her of his pride in the woman she had become, when he was able to convince her of his need for her.

He lifted the reins from his gelding's neck and nudged the horse into a walk, then to a ground-eating lope that would make short work of the miles ahead.

The train was a dark circle against the prairie as they approached, only a lone figure of a man standing beyond the camp. He lifted a hand in greeting as they neared, and Finn was thankful that Jessica slept as Morgan took the black's bridle in his hand and held the animal steady while Finn dismounted.

He shifted Jessica in his arms and nodded, a silent acknowledgment of thanks to the man who greeted them. Morgan led the black to the roped-off enclosure where the horses had been tied for the night. As Finn watched, the other man untied the bucket and looked inside at the contents. With a grin he deposited it next to Jessica's wagon and turned back to the weary animal.

The wagon was close by and he waited by the rear, unable to lift Jessica into it. "Let me help," said another voice, and David Bates stepped closer. "I'll take her while you get in first, Carson."

He lifted the quilt-wrapped woman from Finn's arms, and as he did, the baby, who was clutched tightly to Jessica's breast, whimpered and uttered a soft cry. David's eyes lit with humor and his grin was wide. "I'll be damned," he said quietly. "I'll be damned if you don't have yourself a baby, Carson."

"Yeah." Finn uttered the single word on a sigh, and then climbed into the wagon. "Here, I'll take her," he said, bending to ease the awkward bundle from the other man's embrace. From the next wagon a woman slipped into sight, and Arlois murmured a word to her husband.

"Is she all right?" she asked quietly, and Finn whispered a reply before David could assure her of Jessica's well-being.

"She's fine. We've got ourselves a nice baby boy."

"A boy?" Arlois's shriek brought her hand to her lips as if to muffle the sound. "Let me see."

Finn held Jessica firmly, aware that she was rousing from her slumber, and whispered against her ear. "Sweetheart, Arlois wants to see the baby."

Jessica's eyes opened as her friend tugged gently at the quilt, revealing the tiny form that squirmed against his mother's breast. "Oh." It was a sound of awe, of wonder, such as Finn had never heard, but he recognized it as a mother's welcome to the newborn babe. "Oh, Jessica, he's beautiful," Arlois whispered, bending inside the wagon to kiss the infant's forehead.

"Um…" Jessica could only murmur her agreement as Finn lowered her to the wagon floor, then stepped away to toss the feather tick into place. He returned to her in a moment and helped her to her feet, taking the baby from her and placing it in Arlois's arms. "He's wet," Jessica whispered. "I need to put a fresh diaper on him."

"Let me help," Arlois said briskly, eyeing Finn.

He shrugged and departed the wagon, helping the other woman into the back, baby clutched tightly in her arms. From within came a soft murmur of female voices as the two friends whispered together, and David touched Finn's shoulder, grinning widely.

"How about a little touch of whiskey?" he asked. "I think you deserve to celebrate tonight."

Finn felt an idiotic grin stretch his mouth as he followed the other man to where a box sat beneath the wagon. In its depths a flask was hidden, and David offered it to Finn first. "Congratulations," he said, watching as Finn swallowed the strong brew.

They shared another swallow each, and the flask was returned to its hiding place. "That's for medicinal purposes only, you understand," David said judiciously. "I think this qualifies, don't you?"

Finn nodded his agreement and turned back to Jessica's wagon. "Come on," David said quietly, touching his friend's shoulder. "There's coffee left in the pot over the fire. I think those women need a few minutes to themselves. Arlois has been having a fit all day, what with leaving the two of you behind. I almost had to tie her to the wagon to get her to come with me. They'll be wanting to talk if I know anything about it."

The coffeepot held several cups in its depths and it was still warm enough to drink. The men shared leftovers from the supper Arlois had cooked earlier, and Finn discovered he was hungry. It was almost an hour before they returned to the wagon and lifted Arlois to the ground, her whispered farewells lingering in the air.

And then Finn hoisted himself over the tailgate and found his way to where Jessica was ensconced on the feather tick, the baby clasped in her arms. "Are you all right?" he asked in a low murmur.

"I'm fine, thanks to you," she told him. "Arlois couldn't believe how you delivered the baby." She laughed softly. "She said to tell you that having a baby is nothing like a horse or cow dropping their offspring."

"Yeah, I know," he answered. "But I didn't want to worry you, so I just said the first thing that I thought of."

"I wasn't really worried, once you arrived," she said quietly.

"But up till then?"

She reached to touch his face. "I'm not over being mad at you, Finn. We have a lot to talk about, but yesterday and last night I knew I was in good hands. I've never been so thankful in my life to see someone as I was you when you rode up."

He settled himself behind her and curled around her back, his arm at her waist, his hand touching the bundle that lay beside her. "It's a lot easier to get my arm around you," he said with a soft laugh. "You've lost your tummy."

"Oh, no I haven't," she murmured, holding the baby close to her breast. "It's only shifted position."

Those travelers who would end their journey in Sante Fe began the task of breaking ties with the rest of those who would go on across the Rockies. The miners and several of the others would continue on, following the river toward Pike's Peak. The Cimarron Cutoff was the line of division, since the Raton Pass offered mountainous terrain and danger to those who chanced its route.

Not that there wasn't danger aplenty to be had, Finn said wryly, no matter which way the settlers traveled. Their own route, he told Jessica would be fraught with hardship such as they'd not known on the prairie. Losing the friends she'd found during the past months weighed heavily on Jessica's mind as she contemplated the days ahead.

"I wish we'd planned differently," Arlois said, rocking Jessica's baby beside the evening campfire. She seemed to have developed a fierce, protective stance toward the newborn and his mother, and took every opportunity to hold the tiny infant.

Jessica edged her flat stone from the coals and nodded agreement, recognizing her own opinion on the matter. "Did David ever consider traveling farther toward Pike's Peak instead of heading south?" she asked. "Or is something special about that area his reason for choosing to settle there?" She slid the brown biscuits from the stone into a bowl and covered it with a cloth.

Arlois shook her head as though the questions Jessica posed had no answer, and then she changed the subject abruptly. "Those look good," she said, nodding toward the bowl of warm bread. Her lips compressed a bit, and she bent to touch her lips to the baby's forehead.

"I hate to think that I won't be able to watch him grow," she murmured. And then she looked up at Jessica, her eyes shimmering with unshed tears. "We'll probably never see each other again, Jess."

"I know. I've been thinking that same thing." Her mouth jutted out stubbornly as Jessica blurted out her complaint. "Men don't form ties the way women do. I don't think Finn begins to understand what it will mean to me to see you head south, knowing that I've said goodbye to the best friend I've ever had."

"It's going to be slow going for you," Arlois said. "David told me that the route gets worse every mile you travel toward the mountains." She looked down at the baby she held and lifted the quilt from his face. "At least I'll know that he's warm, all wrapped up nice and cozy in this."

Jessica stepped closer, feeling her heart leap as she looked down at the precious, tiny face of her son. "I didn't know enough to make a blanket for him," she confessed. "I barely managed to sew three little gowns. Hemming those blasted diapers took forever, and if it hadn't been for the odds and ends that you and Geraldine gave me, he'd have been right close to naked."

"If he'd been a girl we'd have been out of luck. Everything I brought was leftovers from my two boys," Arlois said. "He'll be in gowns for a long while yet. It makes it a lot easier to keep them dry when they're not wearing britches."

"The Indians just pad them with moss and stick them on a board," Jessica said with a grin. "I can't imagine the mess. Diapers are bad enough. I'm forever washing them and looking for a place to get them dry."

"Well, the time goes so fast. He'll learn in a hurry. My boys didn't like being wet, and it didn't take them long to discover how to keep from it."

Geraldine approached, a quart jar of milk in hand. "Thought maybe you could use some fresh milk, Jessica. It'll be good for you."

"Thank you. For right now I'll take a bit for my tea. My mama used to drink it without cream or sugar, but I've never learned to enjoy it that way." She took the jar from Geraldine and allowed a dollop of the creamy liquid to color her cup of tea. "I'm glad my milk for him came in so good," she said, lifting the cup to her lips to sip at the hot brew. Her gaze touched both women as she allowed her hands to fold around the metal container.

"I've been thinking," she said quietly, "about a name for the baby."

"I wondered when you were going to decide on one," Geraldine said. "I figured it was something you and Mr. Carson would need to talk about." She lowered herself easily to settle on the ground. "Have you got any ideas?"

Jessica shook her head. "I thought about using Finn's

name for the baby's middle one, but I can't seem to come up with a first name I like.''

"Well, I thought maybe you'd name him Finley, but I expect that's asking a lot of your husband to give another man's child his name.''

Jessica shook her head. "That's not the issue. Finn has accepted the baby as his, and I believe him.'' She looked across the circle to where Finn stood, deep in conversation with the wagon master and two other men. "I thought about calling him Jonas.''

"It's a good strong name,'' Arlois said promptly. "Jonas Finley Carson. I like the sound of that. Will you ask Finn what he thinks first?''

"Maybe,'' Jessica said. "Whatever I decide, I need to make up my mind. I want the preacher to give him his name before he turns off south next week with the rest of you.''

"Next week,'' Arlois repeated glumly. "I thought I wanted to go to Sante Fe, but the closer we get to making the split with the rest of the train, the harder it is to think about it.''

"Harv is determined that south is the direction to head,'' Geraldine said. "I don't think he'd hear of anything else. He says that gold is too hard to come by, no matter what the miners think. He's planning on setting up in business in Santa Fe.''

"What will he do?'' Arlois asked. "I didn't know he was a businessman. My David wouldn't know a cash register if one fell on his head.''

"Harv used to do barbering, and a bit of doctoring on the side.'' She looked at Jessica quickly as she spoke. "He thought about offering to help if you ran into trouble having the baby. He's delivered several, including mine.''

"I'd say he's made his plans then,'' Arlois said. "There's always a call for someone to practice medicine.''

"And cut hair and shave beards,'' Jessica said with a

grin. "I know of a bathhouse in Saint Louis where the men came and spent half the day, getting all fixed up for a night on the town. That man had three bathtubs to rent out."

"Did he hire pretty girls to help the gentlemen get clean?" Arlois asked, bending closer so that her query would not be overheard.

Jessica shook her head and then hesitated. "I was about to say no, but now that I think about it, my mama wouldn't let my father go there. Told him he could do all his bath taking at home."

Their laughter rang out, and across the circle several men glanced their way, some of them with eyes that seemed to covet the company of womenfolk, and Jessica felt a moment's misgiving as she met the gaze of Gage Morgan. His face was in shadow, but his eyes gleamed in the firelight and she felt the weight of his appraisal on her.

"He'd still like a chance at you," Geraldine told her, flicking a look in that direction.

"Who?" Denying her knowledge of his interest in her was futile, she realized, but even with Geraldine, Jessica refused to admit to the chill she felt when the man looked her way.

"You know who," Geraldine said sharply. "He's always had a yen for you, Jess. You want to keep a close eye on Finn's back. I don't trust Morgan, no way."

"I think he gave all that up the day I married Finn," Jessica said stoutly.

"Don't count on it." Arlois chimed in quietly, and her eyes were filled with concern as she spoke the warning. "David said he thinks Morgan is hiding something behind that smooth front."

"Like what?" Jessica asked. "Does he think he's a danger to me, or Finn?"

"No, I don't think so. Just that he's sure Morgan is not what he pretends to be."

And wasn't that the same thing that she'd decided a long

time ago? Jessica thought, casting a quick glance at the man they spoke of. He watched her, a subtle, barely noticeable flash of dark eyes visible beneath the brim of his hat, but she felt the impact of his observation and shivered.

"I think I'd better take that baby and get him settled for the night," she said, deciding that the inside of the wagon was a better place to be right now. Nursing her son in the light of a campfire was not her first choice. There were always men observing and, though she threw a blanket or diaper over her shoulder to conceal the baby's form, she knew that anyone watching had to be aware of what she did.

"Climb in," Arlois said, "and I'll hand him in to you." She lifted the baby higher and kissed his soft cheek, eliciting a wiggle from his tiny body. "Hey, little Jonas. Are you ready for your supper?" she asked softly, and as she rose and prepared to give him to his mother, a tear slid down her cheek.

"I will hate not seeing him after next week," she said. "I'm almost ready to think about another baby myself."

"You'd better consider long and hard about that," Geraldine warned her. And then she grinned. "That long and hard part is what gets you in trouble though, now that I think about it."

The three women laughed again, sharing the risqué remark, setting aside the gloom that had invaded their moments together. And it was only when Jessica settled herself in the wagon and nursed her child that she allowed her own tears to flow.

Chapter Twelve

Finn's arm circled her waist in a possessive gesture and Jessica glanced up at him, only too aware that his purpose was obvious to those around them. The first wagons heading down the Cimarron Cutoff were rolling past them, and nearby, the miners and three other families stood silently, aware that this moment was one of finality. They would likely never catch sight again of those who left, and the remaining group would be banding together, whether or not it was a welcome choice.

Those who were heading toward Oregon had moved in that direction days ago, taking a seldom-used trail that would connect with the more well traveled wheel tracks farther north and to the west. Seeking the safety of a large group, they'd stayed as long as was prudent with the group and finally made the break, the men eager to move on, the four women who traveled in the small train apprehensive but willing to do as their men asked.

Now Jessica's eyes strained as she watched Arlois's departure from her life, and waved again as the smallest of the Bates children lifted a hand in farewell. Arlois refused to look back, and Jessica was only too aware that her friend's tears were flowing as bountifully as her own. Finn's arm tightened around her and she broke his hold, stalking away to walk on the far side of the wagon, where the crates of chicken squawked, guarding their small spaces, each from the other.

One of the miners called a joking remark in Finn's direction, and Jessica knew a moment of shame that she'd made him the butt of a joke. Every movement she made would be subject to appraisal by the men from this point. Hungry for a woman—any woman, Jessica thought glumly—they were plainly envious of the married men who had the luxury of soft, feminine bodies at their side.

The thought that she was looked on with lust didn't sit well with Jessica, and she cast more than one sharp look of disapproval at the men who spoke eagerly, and sometimes without lowering their voices, about what they'd find at the end of the trail. She knew there were loose women wherever single men gathered. But she didn't much enjoy thinking about those poor souls who sold themselves to any man who could afford to buy their favors.

''Jessica?'' Finn caught up with her and his long fingers circled her wrist. ''I want to talk to you.'' His voice was quiet, but the strength that underlined his words gave warning that he would not tolerate her ignoring him.

She offered no resistance, not willing to tussle with him where they could be observed by others, and only looked up at him briefly from beneath the wide brim of her sunbonnet. ''What do you want?'' Even to her own ears her voice sounded unpleasant, and she made no attempt to hide the tears she'd shed over the past few minutes.

His grip loosened, but his fingers lingered, forming a link she stood no chance of breaking, should she try. Finn was all that was kind and considerate, but now she sensed a darkness about him that stirred her. His eyes met hers with no softening in their depths, and his mouth was firm, his jaw set.

''I won't have you giving the men anything to wonder about, Jess,'' he said. ''If you think I'm talking through my hat, you've got another think coming. You're my woman, and I plan to make that clear to anybody who's looking on. From now on, you'll stay close by. I don't want to have to be looking for you if you decide to stray from the wagon.''

"I'm not about to run off, Finn," she said, hating the tremor in her words. "I just don't appreciate you flaunting your ownership.''

"I'm not," he stated firmly. And then he tipped his hat back with one long finger. "Then again, maybe I am," he said slowly. "If that's what it takes to keep you nearby, twenty-four hours a day and out of danger, that's exactly what I'll do.''

"No one owns me," she told him. "I lived that way for over four years, and I'll never put myself in that position again.''

"I own you, Jess."

She met his gaze, startled by the harshness of his tone. "I'm your wife," she said quietly, "not your favorite horse or your faithful dog.''

"That's not the way I meant it," he said, softening his stance. "You belong to me, and I want anyone who's interested to understand that.''

"Well, Lord knows I don't have eyes for any other man. I thought you knew that.''

He smiled, one corner of his mouth tilting upward, revealing his pleasure at her words. "I do. I just want to make sure that every other man in this bunch understands it.''

"No one's looked twice at me," she scoffed, aware even as she spoke the words that they were untrue. Being the youngest of the women in the group made her the target of wayward glances, but she'd determined not to allow it to bother her. And then she stopped and faced him fully. "You don't trust me, do you?''

"Ah, damn it all, Jess. Of course, I do. It's just those woman-hungry fellas traveling with Morgan and his bunch I don't trust. The other married men and I made a pact to keep a close eye on our women for the next couple of weeks. Once we get to where we're going, things will be different.''

''And then what happens?'' she asked, setting off again, with Finn beside her, his fingers still loosely grasping her wrist. They walked quickly, catching up to the lead ox, and matched their pace with his. Finn's pause was long, and then he shrugged.

''I suspect it all depends on whether or not we find that damned deed. I can't claim the land without it, and I've about run out of ideas where to look for it.''

''It's going to come down to an argument before we get done,'' she said, and was chagrined to hear him laugh aloud at her words.

''What the hell do you think we're doing right now?'' he asked. ''I knew you were a stubborn woman a long time ago, but I didn't think you'd give me this much hassle over a basic thing like your safety.''

''The thing we're fussing over is the *deed,* Finley Carson, and you know it.''

His jaw clenched as he looked at her, and she saw a determination in his face she was unfamiliar with. Generally an easygoing man, Finn had taken a stand, and she would bear the brunt of his anger.

''That deed belonged to my brother,'' he said, his words barely audible. ''You only hold it because that bastard you were married to killed Aaron for it.''

''I don't *hold* it,'' she said, denying his accusation. ''I don't even know where it *is,* in case you've forgotten. As far as we both know, we may be whistling into the wind.''

''Well, Lyle had it, and I know damn well he didn't give it anyone else, or those two men who snatched you up wouldn't have been after it.''

''How about Morgan?'' she asked quietly. ''What's his place in all this?'' Her pause was long as he seemed to be choosing his words. ''Are you going to tell me that he's on the up-and-up? Or is he hip deep in all that happened to me? And if he is, why did you walk out and meet with him that night?''

''What night?'' His gaze narrowed on her and she saw a ruddy flush of guilt rim his cheekbones.

She turned her head away, unwilling to look at him, aware that he lied to her. Her indrawn breath shuddered in her breast and she spoke the words she knew would drive a wedge between them. ''I saw you talking to him and I watched you shake his hand. As far as I'm concerned, that was a sure sign that you were in something together. And still are, I'll warrant.'' She looked up at him suddenly, and was mindful of a look of pain he could not conceal.

''You don't understand what you saw,'' he said. ''Morgan is not what he seems.''

''I figured that out a long time ago. I just wish you'd found it in your heart to let me in on all the deep, dark secrets you've kept to yourself. I might have been able to trust you.''

''And you don't now?''

She shook her head. ''It's why I left. And I still feel I'm all alone here.''

''That's not true,'' he said quickly. ''I've been looking out for you during this whole trip, Jess. You're my main concern, and you know it.''

''No,'' she said flatly, ''I don't. That deed is the most important thing in your life.''

''You're wrong again. You are. You and the baby.''

''I thought that. Once,'' she said. ''I even gave him your name, Finn. I thought it might make him more special to you.''

''I delivered him, Jess. How more special can you get?'' Exasperated, he snagged her around the middle and pulled her against himself. He'd had enough of her sharp tongue, and more than enough of her finding fault with him. His head bent and his mouth met hers with a less than tender kiss. She tried to pull back and he would not allow it, his free hand cupping her nape and holding her in place.

His chest heaved with the effort to breathe normally, and as he released her from the touch of his mouth, he felt shame wash over him. He'd never used his strength against a woman before, and now, the first time he'd done such a thing, it had been to subdue the woman he'd married.

"I'm sorry," he said quietly. "I didn't mean to hurt you."

Her eyebrow twitched and lifted in patent disbelief. "Didn't you?" He watched as her tongue moved slowly across the width of her upper lip, and felt the first twinge of a masculine arousal make itself known. She could, with one small gesture, make him yearn to touch her. With one flash of hazel eyes, she could bring him to his knees, and this was neither the time nor place to allow her such a victory.

"No." He denied it again. "I would never purposely hurt you. You're my wife." He groped for words that would impress upon her the problems inherent in the days ahead. "We're heading for some rough country, Jess. And most of the men living in the towns ahead are single, with two things on their mind. The first is gold, and the second is women. I happen to have access to both of those, and I don't plan on having to fight to keep possession of either."

"Well, at least I know where I stand, don't I?" Her chin lifted defiantly and she looked ahead, pacing the oxen and walking quickly beside him.

He released her wrist from his grip and allowed her to move from his side. "I think you need to go inside the wagon for a while. I hear the baby rousing."

She nodded and dropped back a bit, but he followed, lifting her and giving her a boost to the wagon seat. His hands stayed tightly around her waist, then slid to cup her bottom as she scrambled for footing. The temptation of firm curves and the warmth of feminine flesh beneath her clothing did nothing to cool his mood, and his frown was well in place as he took long strides to once more walk beside the team.

At nightfall the wagons formed a small circle, and for the first time, Jessica was truly aware how few they were in number. She'd known that the tally was considerably less, but only when she counted eight vehicles instead of the original forty, did she feel the cutting edge of loneliness touch her. The other women who still remained with the group made small advances, and with Polly among them, she knew she would have their support.

In fact, Finn had wandered over toward one of those wagons and spent a few minutes in conversation with two of the husbands before he'd come back and announced that he would be riding out for a while. "Something seems to be going on," he said. "I need to check it out."

"So much for sticking close," she muttered beneath her breath as she watched him saddle his gelding. The chickens clucked contentedly in their crates, and she bent to fill the feed pan through the wooden slats. Seldom turned loose to forage, they had settled down nicely in their confined space, she thought. Would that she might do the same, instead of looking for trouble.

Now she sat by her fire and felt the chill of nightfall surround her. The day had been warm, but with the mountains ahead, the elevation was higher, and the nights were becoming cooler. She huddled in the folds of her shawl and poked at the coals with the stick Morgan had carved for her weeks before. She'd used it seldom, and now she almost hoped it would catch fire and she'd be rid of it.

"You trying to burn up your walking stick?" As if her thoughts had called him across the circle, Morgan stood beside her, and Jessica lifted her eyes to his amusement. She could not find it in her heart to hate the man. He'd been kind to her, when it seemed she was beset by more danger than she'd ever known. Yet, she felt a betrayal at his hands, and it did not allow her to call him friend.

"No, I'm not trying to get rid of it," she said curtly. "Only poking the fire."

"Where'd Finn go?" he asked quietly, squatting beside her, intent on the glowing coals. "I heard rifle shots earlier and I saw him ride out in a hurry. I'm thinking something's going on south of here."

Jessica looked at him quickly. "Trouble? The men who—"

He shook his head abruptly, signaling with an uplifted hand. "No, I doubt that. I think maybe we're being signaled by someone. I wondered if Finn had gone out to investigate."

"He may have," she admitted, a spear of anxiety touching her as she thought of the danger inherent in his venture. Men were so foolhardy, she thought glumly. "He said he'd only be gone for a while."

"And left you alone and unprotected?" Morgan asked. "Or did he leave a couple of watchdogs on guard?" He cut a sidelong look at her and grinned, then nodded to where the two men watched from near their wagons. "I think he told them to put you under surveillance, ma'am."

"And you thought you'd give them something to look at?"

"I wanted to talk to you, Jess." One knee touched the ground as he settled a bit more comfortably. "I know you're angry with me, and Finn told me to stay away from you, but I need to clear up something that's bothering me."

"I don't need you here," she said pointedly. "That's about as plain as I can make it, Morgan. I appreciate what you did for me, but knowing that you're in cahoots with those no-good coyotes makes me shudder."

"I want you to know that things are not what they seem," he said.

"Well, I'm sure that's a comfort," she told him. "I hope

you and Finn will be very happy together, since you both tell the same story.''

His laughter was muffled, and she cast him a quick, unbelieving look. "I don't see anything funny about it," she said. "I seem to have missed something."

"It'll all come out in the wash," he said, rising and looking down at her. "And in the meantime—" His words were cut short by an audible shot fired in the distance. It was followed quickly by two others, both spaced as if they relayed a message.

"That's the second time," he said. "Stay here, Jess. I'll send one of the other women over to wait with you."

Jessica rose, stumbling to her feet. "Where are you going? Is Finn...'' She could not complete the phrase, could not consider that Finn might be in danger.

"I doubt anyone is shooting at him. That sounded like a signal to me," Morgan said, turning back as if his explanation might soothe her anxiety. "I'm riding out to see what's going on."

"All right," she said, bowing to his masculine judgment. Her first concern would be for her child, but the thought of Finn being in jeopardy was frightening. She watched as Morgan halted beside one of the men who'd been keeping an eye on Jessica and saw the fellow nod and mutter a few words. In moments, one of the women bustled across the clearing and approached.

"Hello, Jessica. My Bert sent me over to stay with you till your man gets back." She looked directly into Jessica's eyes and spoke. "It's gonna be fine, you know. That Mr. Morgan's a good man. He'll handle things."

At Jessica's nod of acquiescence, the woman bent to look beneath the wagon, dragging out several buffalo chips, and adding them to the coals. "We might as well stay good and warm," she said cheerfully as she sat beside Jessica. She patted the ground by her hip and offered to share her space.

"Come on and sit by me. I've been wanting to share a campfire with you for a long time, honey. Seems to me that right now is a dandy time to get to know each other a little better. Alma and Frieda are nice ladies, but I need someone new to talk to."

Jessica smiled, grateful for the offer of friendship and settled beside her visitor. She examined her memory for any other tidbits of information Polly might have dropped. "That tall boy is yours, isn't he?"

"Yeah, that's my young'un. Bertie's his name. And the skinny little one. He's Joey. Always wanted me a girl, but it never happened. Buried two other boys, and called it quits."

"Geraldine lost a baby, too," Jessica said, remembering the day when she had shared her own sorrow with her friend. She met Vanessa's gaze squarely. "And she's not the only one. I lost my first child, too."

With that, the door of friendship opened, and the two women spoke of the trials of the journey, the perils of child-bearing and the difficulties of understanding their menfolk. Beneath the small talk lay a shivering fear of what might be going on out on the prairie, but Jessica tried to bury herself in the droll wit of the woman who was so obvious in her attempt to keep their spirits high.

An hour passed, the fire burning low again, as another of the women walked across to join them, Alma Higgins, according to Vanessa. "My man rode out to keep Morgan company," the newcomer offered. "He didn't think it was a good idea for anybody to be out there alone."

And that's exactly the position Finn was in, Jessica thought. Alone. Although perhaps Morgan had caught up with him by now. A soft cry from the wagon caught her ear and she rose quickly to reach inside the tailgate for the baby. She'd tucked him in directly at the rear of the wagon, making him easily accessible should she hear him cry, knowing he would need feeding one more time before he slept soundly.

Her arms full of a small, wiggling form, she turned back to the women and surprised a yearning expression on Alma's face she could hardly bear to look upon. "I lost a youn'un about that age a year or so ago," the woman said quietly. "I was gonna come over and see him for myself when you had him, but I just couldn't bring myself to look at him."

"Shall I take him in the wagon?" Jessica asked quickly, unwilling to cause pain.

"No, I think I need to bite the bullet, so to speak," Alma said. "I buried my boy, but I've had a hard time ridding myself of guilt. I keep thinkin' I might have done something wrong that he would not wake up that morning. The doctor said it was just one of those things. Not that it made me feel any better knowing he didn't seem to lay any blame on me."

Jessica offered the swaddled bundle she held. "Here, take him, Alma. He's not starving by any means. I think he just wants to be held for a bit."

Alma eyed her for a moment and then stood, accepting the gift Jessica offered. She sat again, close to the fire and gently lifted the fold of flannel that covered the baby's face. "He's a pretty little thing, ain't he?" she said, the words a statement of fact.

"I like to think so," Jessica answered. "I was afraid when he was born that something might happen to him, him being born out on the prairie all alone."

"Your man was there, wasn't he?" Alma asked, looking up sharply.

Jessica nodded. "He found me before things got bad. I don't know what I'd have done without him."

Vanessa laughed. "I heard Geraldine say that Mr. Carson told you he'd delivered calves and colts in his time, and that babies weren't much different."

"Well, that's what he tried to convince me of," Jessica said, remembering those moments when Finn had done his best to prepare her for the ordeal of birth, and the three women shared smiles as they considered Finn's tactics.

The quiet of the night was suddenly split by a man's voice, shouting in the distance. Three of the miners trotted across the clearing and stepped between two wagons, their movements hurried. "Something's goin' on," Vanessa said beneath her breath, and then they listened as the sound of a horse whinnying a welcome gave notice of a rider approaching.

"Accident…wagon tipped…Bates…" The words were separate and spoken in hushed tones as men stood beyond the circle of wagons. And as Finn appeared, stepping between two wagons, Jessica felt the heartrending premonition of tragedy to come.

"Jess?" he said, his frown telling her without words that the news was bad.

She rose and hurried to him, reaching for his hand and clutching it to her breast. "What is it, Finn? Are you all right?"

He shook his head impatiently and his mouth was taut with pain. "I'm fine, Jess. It's David Bates. His wagon overturned heading up a hill about an hour after they left us this noontime, and he died shortly after. The thing crushed him, and they couldn't do anything to save him."

"David? Arlois's David?" The meaning would not penetrate Jessica's mind. The thought of such tragedy was almost too difficult to comprehend, and she trembled as she tried to make herself believe Finn's words.

He clutched her shoulders and shook her, his movements jolting her from the shock she could barely withstand. And then he looked into her eyes, and his words were solemn and final. "David Bates is dead, Jess. They buried him beside the trail, and Arlois wouldn't go on to Santa Fe without him."

"Where is she?" Her friend needed her. Jessica's mind fixed on that single fact.

"Jonas circled the rest of the wagons where the accident happened, and he and another fella are bringing Arlois and her children this way. They had to repair her wagon first, but she wants to join our train."

"Where...?" She looked past him into the darkness, and Finn shook his head.

"It'll be a while. When I heard the shots, I figured something was wrong. One of the men rode at an angle and fired his rifle every half hour or so, trying to signal us. By the time I headed that way, he was only about two miles away. He followed me in."

"When will Arlois be here?" she asked, as her tears began to flow. She ached to see the other woman, agonizing already over the pain Arlois must be suffering.

"It'll be a while," Finn said. "The wagon can't travel near as fast as a rider. Probably a couple of hours or so at least. We'll make room for them in the circle when they get here."

"My man will lend a hand," Vanessa said, joining the conversation with an offer of help. "Let me go and tell him what's happened. He's stayin' by the wagon to listen for the boys."

She made her way across to where her husband stood, and Alma stood to place the baby back in Jessica's arms. "I better go let Mr. Higgins know what's happenin'," she said quietly. "Thanks for lettin' me hold your little one, Jess."

The baby clasped to her bosom, Jessica rocked silently in place, her thoughts with Arlois and the confusion and misery that must be, even now, enveloping the woman's whole being. And then she looked up at Finn, suddenly aware that grief shadowed his gaze. David had been his friend, but his mourning would have to be held in abeyance.

For now, he was faced with the responsibility of helping Arlois and her family.

Jessica spoke quietly, subduing her own pain, aware that, as a man, he could not reveal the hurt that clutched at him, as readily as could a woman. "There's coffee in the pot, if you'd like some." The offer seemed little consolation, but for now it was all she could provide, and when Finn nodded, she handed him the baby, hoping that the new life in his arms would be of more comfort than what few words she might offer.

They stayed put for an extra day, the women gathering around to give solace to Arlois, the men planning for some means of support for the woman and her family. One of the miners was willing to marry her, but Arlois shook her head at the suggestion.

"It was all right for you," she told Jessica. "When Lyle died it was no great loss, and I don't mean to speak badly of the dead when I say that. David was my whole life, and I can't even fathom taking another husband."

Jessica could only nod, understanding her friend's logic, but also aware that the road ahead was fraught with danger, and just getting Arlois's wagon to the end of their journey would be a miracle in itself. "Well," she began, her mind working quickly, "your boy can take over walking beside the oxen. And the rest of us will just have to pitch in and lend a hand wherever we're needed."

She saw Finn's eyes roll as he listened from behind Arlois, saw the firm set of his jaw, and understood his dilemma. "You'll need to give it some thought," he told the grieving widow. "Once we get to where we're going, you'll need more help than any of us can spare."

"I'll find a bit of land next to the river and settle there," Arlois said stubbornly. "We can live in the wagon until we can build some sort of shelter, and I think we'll be in time to plant a few things. I've got some money to tide me over till spring anyway. David and I talked it all over, night after night, and I'm going to do what he'd want me to.''

Finn shook his head. ''I hear what you're saying, ma'am, but the reality is bound to be different from what you and David were expecting. You'll have to live on a piece of land for five years before it's yours. Improving it takes a man's strength.''

''My oldest boy is almost full grown,'' she told him. ''And I'm young enough and strong enough to work hard. We'll make it. You just help me get that far, and I'll not ask any more of any of you.''

Finn bowed his head in defeat, then turned to the miner who was willing to join his life with that of the grieving widow. He'd stood aside as Arlois spoke her piece, and only shrugged, accepting her decision. ''She's one stubborn woman,'' he said quietly. ''We'll just have to bide our time and see what happens.''

The Arkansas River closely paralleled the trail, providing water and making the journey easier on the small group. Several of the miners, men who had, up until now, been at the very bottom of Jessica's list of decent prospects for the widow's hand, began to shape up nicely. Their talk was more subdued, as if being in the presence of mourning had put a damper on their masculine humor.

Even those who had not paid particular mind to cleanliness brought Arlois their washing to do, and paid her well. Where they got their money was immaterial, so far as Jessica was concerned. The fact that Arlois was the beneficiary of their quiet rivalry was more to the point.

They'd slowed their travel, due to rougher terrain as they approached the Rocky Mountains. But once they passed the turning of the route toward the Raton Pass, a notoriously treacherous trail, they began making their days longer, circling their few wagons at dark. As if the mountain ahead lured them into its shadow, they pushed their oxen harder, and due to the abundance of water, the grass grew taller, providing much needed feed for the animals.

Matters between Jessica and Finn were at a standstill, their conversations stilted, their nights spent side by side, with little touching, only that required by the limited space in the wagon. His arm was beneath her head every morning when she awoke, and it irritated her that she could never recall being held close to him, only knew that once they were both awake they parted silently for the day.

He was quietly determined, it seemed, to continue on as though nothing had gone awry in their marriage, and she was equally set on steering clear of him, basking in the knowledge that she'd been sinned against. That Finn had not been honest with her stuck in her craw, and she held the grudge tightly to herself, allowing it to grow apace with the miles they traveled.

The air was chilly as they set out early one morning, and Jessica sat on the wagon seat, huddled in her shawl, watching as the oxen leaned into their yoke and headed west. Finn looked up at her from his place beside the lead ox and pinned her in place with a stony look.

"You all right?' he asked, yearning for the closeness they'd shared so short a time ago. "Is the baby sleeping?"

She only nodded, and he felt the urge to haul her off the wooden seat and lower her to the grass. If they'd been alone…

He imagined the scene. Jessica flushed and angry, himself holding her to the ground, his mouth hungry against her throat, his fingers nimble as he separated buttons and buttonholes. And then the sigh of surrender she might offer, the damp, lushness of her lips as she accepted his kiss—

He knew her body was not ready for such an invasion, even should the opportunity arise. That thought alone made his desire for her an aggravation he must live with for a while longer. Perhaps the act of loving, once Jessica agreed to its resumption, would help to put back together the pieces of their marriage. He could only hope so.

"Finn?" Arlois scampered beside him, and his reverie was broken by the hesitant sound of his name spoken into his right ear.

He shot her a glance, knowing his face looked far from friendly, and as he watched her cheeks reddened with embarrassment. "I know you're busy, just getting started for the day, but my wagon is wobbling. Badly," she added, and as he watched, her eyes filled with helpless tears.

He swallowed the curse that would have been uttered aloud if she'd been a man, but his innate good manners directed that he put aside his foul mood and draw his team to a halt. He'd led out this morning, directing Morgan to the end of the line of wagons, and now he stepped away from the team and signaled the other man with an uplifted arm.

From his position almost a hundred yards to the rear, Morgan waved and called to another of the miners to take his place. His horse was saddled, tied to the back of the wagon, and in mere seconds, the man had gathered the reins and was riding at a quick trot to join Finn.

"What's wrong?" he asked, a frown drawing his brows together. His gaze flicked toward Jessica, who had slid from the seat to comfort Arlois, and Finn hid his momentary surge of anger. That Morgan should so blatantly keep an eye on Jessica was a constant bone of contention between the two men, but Morgan merely smiled at Finn's accusations when he presented them in a direct manner.

Now was no time to argue the point, and Finn repeated Arlois's complaint, adding his own opinion. "I think Arlois's wagon probably has a loose wheel. We don't dare go on until it's tightened, or we'll be in a mess farther down the trail if it comes off. I'll bet that's what happened the day Bates—"

He halted midway through his sentence as he caught a

glimpse of Arlois's face, her mouth pinched tightly, her eyes shiny with an emotion he recognized. She was a grieving widow, and his careless assumption had brought back in full measure the day of David's death.

"I'm sorry, Arlois," he said quietly. "I didn't think."

She shook her head as if it were beyond her ability to speak aloud the words of pardon he asked. And then her forehead rested against Jessica's shoulder and her body trembled as she wept in silence.

Morgan cast a long look at Finn and lifted his shoulders in a helpless gesture, then turned his horse back to where Arlois's son stood beside the oxen who drew the wagon. He lowered himself quickly from his horse, approaching the boy with a smile.

"I hear you've got a problem," he said, placing a wide palm on the youth's shoulder. "Let's take a look."

The boy nodded and pointed at the left side of the wagon and then put the oxen into motion, allowing the vehicle to move six feet or so. Even from where Finn stood, the problem was obvious, and relatively simple to repair. Morgan looked up and grinned.

"Nothing to it," he called out. "Come give me a hand, Carson. We can fix this in no time." He looked up at Arlois's son again and apparently asked for tools. The lad nodded quickly and climbed into the wagon, reappearing almost immediately with a canvas-wrapped bundle.

By the time Finn made his way to Morgan's side the job was begun. Two of the miners stood by and supervised, adding small asides that brought laughter from the men. And then they wrapped up the tools David Bates had brought along for just such emergencies, and the boy returned the collection to his mother's wagon.

Morgan walked back to where Arlois and Jessica stood as Finn spoke a final word to the youth who was trying so valiantly to fill his father's shoes. Distracted by Morgan's tactics, Finn finally nodded approval of the lad's conduct and gave him an offhand salute, accompanied by a friendly grin.

And then he walked to where Morgan was in conversation with the two women.

"All set?" Morgan's eyes glittered with amusement as he faced Finn, and the air of antagonism was thick between them. As if he taunted the man who led the train on this portion of the journey, Morgan touched his index finger to his hat and bid the ladies a good day.

"We need to get rolling," Finn said shortly, and watched as Arlois hastened to her wagon, choosing to walk beside her son. Jessica turned back to climb atop the seat, and Finn halted her progress by speaking her name, a sound that caught her ear and caused her to turn toward him apprehensively.

"What is it?" she asked, hesitating as she would have found her seat once more.

"I want you to walk with me," he said. And then his voice softened. "The baby should sleep a while, shouldn't he? I think we need to talk."

"All right." She shrugged lightly, as though she were pacifying him, her look in his direction one of patience beyond measure.

It irritated him more than he could express, but he gave it a shot anyway. "I don't appreciate your attitude," he said bluntly. "You'd think I was the enemy, or worse, the way you act."

"Really?" She smiled sweetly. "I can't imagine what makes you say that."

"If you had any idea what I'd like to do to you right now, you'd change your tune in a hurry, Mrs. Carson," he said softly, in a tone of voice that should have warned her of the temper he was fighting to restrain.

"Really." This time the single word signified astonishment, and she accompanied it with a lifted brow. "Are you trying to frighten me?"

"Is it working?" he asked smoothly, and watched as a flush rose to touch her cheeks. And then rued the words. "I'm sorry. That was unkind, Jess. I'm in a rotten mood and I'm taking it out on you."

"You don't scare me, Finn," she answered, walking beside him, yet separate. "I learned from a man who had the art of intimidation down to a science. His methods were harsh, but at least I knew where I stood." She looked at him directly and he saw the pain in her eyes.

"With you, I feel like I'm groping in the dark. I trusted you. With my child, my earthly possessions and my..." Her pause was long as her gaze searched his for endless moments. "I trusted you with my body, Finn. And you didn't fail me there. You've been good to me, and I gave you all I had to offer. But you lied to me, and I'm not sure I can forgive you for that."

His pain matched hers, he decided, groping for words of reassurance that would silence her doubts. But the rules of this game must be obeyed and he could only hope that one day Jessica would understand and be willing to forgive his duplicity. His shrug was eloquent as he accepted her censure, and his mouth tightened as he fought the words of explanation she demanded.

For now, it was a matter of trust...trust she was unwilling to give.

Chapter Thirteen

Shadow Creek was about as typical a mining community as any he'd ever heard of, Finn decided. The moving water flowed from higher in the mountains, wending its way past miners' shacks and tar-paper shanties, their inhabitants intent on panning as many hours a day as the sun would allow.

Farther up the creek, where the land became more lushly overgrown with trees and bushes, folks had staked out homesteads and families were working to improve their piece of property. Summer was fully upon them and the ground had been worked, late gardens being planted and then fenced in a haphazard fashion to keep the wild creatures from the tender green shoots that held promise of food supplies for the coming winter.

Finn parked the wagon beneath a grove of trees not far from the running water, and in a few days had set to rights the contents, repairing items that had been damaged by the perils of the journey, and sorting again through the various boxes and crates they carried. Jessica watched, aware that his temper was on a short fuse, that he was frustrated by the time they wasted here. Without the deed in his hand, Finn had no way of claiming the land his brother had been given, and it galled him that things were at a standstill.

"I'm going out visiting," he told Jessica early on the third morning since they'd made camp here. "I'll see if I can find anyone who remembers the old man who sent Aaron the deed. That might give us a better idea of where to start."

Jessica shrugged, bending over the baby, intent on bathing him within the shelter of the wagon. Finn leaned on the tailgate and watched, and she felt him focus on her face. Stubbornly she refused to meet his eyes, until he called her name in a low, yet compelling tone.

"Jessica. I think we need to talk. Things are going to hell in a handbasket between us, and I'm not willing to allow it to go on this way."

She felt a moment of satisfaction at his words, and then her conscience nudged her. "I know I haven't been of much use lately," she said, lifting the infant and wrapping him snugly in a towel. Her fingers massaged his head, where dark curls clung damply to his scalp.

"You're fine, Jess," Finn told her. "Things have been kinda rough on both of us." He reached out to touch the baby, his fingers gentle as they ruffled the silky hair. "He's beautiful," Finn said. "Looks like you, don't you think?"

She nodded. "His hair is darker than mine, but it'll probably lighten up." She looked up at Finn. "I think he resembles my father, and he's a handsome man." That her fondest hope seemed to have been fulfilled brought a smile to her lips. Little Jonas bore no resemblance at all to Lyle, and Jessica considered that a blessing.

"We're going to need to get supplies right quick," Finn told her. "I noticed that the can of lard we bought in Council Grove is almost empty, and the flour barrel is pretty near down to rock bottom."

"What's left isn't much good," Jessica told him, wrinkling her nose. "I found weevils in the bowlful I made biscuits with this morning. I had to pick them out before I could start, and it made me queasy to think about them being there in the first place.''

"How about if we clean out the barrel real good,'' Finn said. "Then we'll go to the general store in Shadow Creek and stock up.''

Jessica felt pleasure wash over her as he spoke. "Wouldn't that be fun?'' she said, thinking of various items she would put on a list. And then she lost her smile as another thought occurred to her. "Can we afford it?''

Finn nodded. "We're a long way from being rich, Jess, but we have enough money to live comfortably through the winter months. I'm just concerned about getting to where we're going and setting up housekeeping.''

"There's a cabin there already,'' she said. "I hope it's in good enough shape to do for a while.''

Finn shrugged. "If it isn't, we'll add to it or tear it down and start over. I won't expect you to live in a shack.''

"We'll need some furniture, Finn,'' she told him, warming to the plans he proposed. "I have bits and pieces, but we'll be eating on the floor and sleeping there, too, I fear.''

"I'm sure I can put together a table and buy enough nails to get a framework for a bed for us. We can use rope to hold your feather tick in place. There's a sawmill in town, and they'll have lumber for sale.''

Jessica looked at the man she'd married, silently marveling at his kindness. Lyle would have put her comfort at the bottom of his list of things to tend to. Finn seemed intent on providing for her without delay.

He leaned on the tailgate and his look was sober. "Jess, we're going to have to tear this wagon apart to find that deed,'' he said. "I've tried to come up with ideas, but my mind keeps running into dead ends. I crawled underneath once and searched out anyplace Lyle might have hidden it on the framework. I thought maybe it was sealed up and stashed someplace where the sides and bottom of the bed meet, but nothing turned up.''

"Sealed up?" she asked, wondering at his words. "How would he do that?"

"I thought he might have wrapped it in oilcloth to keep it dry when the bottom of the wagon got wet. You know, when we crossed the streams."

"Wrapped it in oilcloth?" she asked. "Could he have put it at the bottom of a box of supplies, someplace where we haven't looked?"

Finn shook his head. "I've emptied every box in the wagon, sorted through them all and found nothing." His eyes narrowed suddenly and she turned her head, following the direction in which he looked. "The flour barrel," he said, his words a whisper.

"Did you fill the barrel back in Independence?" he asked, "or did Lyle take care of it?"

"He did," she answered, remembering the day Lyle had been angry and chased her from the wagon while he transferred the flour to a new, clean barrel. "The original barrel leaked, he said, and the flour would be open to bugs and we'd have a mess all over the inside of the wagon if he didn't buy a new barrel."

"And you didn't watch him do it?" Finn asked. "I'd have thought he'd give you the job. I can't imagine Lyle doing household chores."

"I was surprised at him myself," Jessica said. She looked again at the barrel in question. "Can we dump it out now?"

Finn shook his head. "Too many folks around. After a while, I want you to empty as much as you can into a couple of flour sacks. When I come inside this afternoon I'll tip the barrel and clean out the rest. We can make a fuss about the mealy worms if we need to."

He seemed reluctant to let it go at that, Jessica thought, and she felt her own anticipation rise as she thought of what they might find. "As soon as I finish feeding the baby I'll begin," she told him.

"I'll meander around while you take care of him," Finn told her. "And then we'll go to the general store later today." His eyes were sparkling with good humor, and Jessica knew a moment of pleasure at his excitement. "We'll figure this out yet," he told her.

She leaned against the tailgate and watched him stroll away, noting the width of his shoulders and the length of his stride. Unease touched her as she thought of the past days and weeks since Jonas's birth. Finn had been patient, demanding nothing of her, and she'd withheld all but the most perfunctory gestures of affection from him. He deserved better than that, she decided, recalling his body warming her at night, his arms holding her securely as they curled up in sleep on the feather tick.

She would offer him the comfort of her body, allow him to find pleasure in their bed once more. And her smile grew smug as she thought of what his touch would bring to her. And then she frowned. What if Finn had decided that she wasn't worth the trouble of wooing her again? He'd been angry over the past weeks, and she wasn't sure she had the knowledge it might take to coax him from his mood.

Today had given her hope that things might once more be on an even keel, though, and she sighed deeply as she set about doing as he'd instructed her.

The second ten-pound flour sack was full and she'd been bent over the edge of the barrel, her bottom wiggling as she scraped the remaining flour. The light was dim inside the wagon and she peered closely at the tiny insects that had taken up residence in their supply of flour. A shudder passed from her nape to the base of her spine as she managed to get her feet solidly on the wagon bed again.

"Might I ask what you're doing?" Morgan stood behind her, amusement rife in his query, and Jessica cried out, a startled sound.

"I didn't know anyone was watching," she said, confusion tingeing her words. "You sneaked up on me, Morgan."

"Not really. I've been standing here admiring the view for a couple of minutes," he told her, "wondering what you were up to." He stuck his head inside the wagon and frowned. "What's so interesting in that barrel, Jess?"

She pressed her lips together and shivered as she displayed the scoop she held. "Weevils and mealy worms," she told him. "Hateful things."

Morgan shrugged. "Everyone has them at this stage. Don't you have a sifter?"

She shook her head. "No, I've just been picking them out for the past couple of weeks."

"I'd be happy to lend you one of the gold pans we have in our wagon," he told her. "That'll work almost as well as a flour sifter. A whole lot easier than the way you're doing it."

"That would be good of you," she told him. She glanced over at the wagon he stayed in, thinking dubious thoughts about the probable condition of its contents.

As if reading her mind, Morgan smiled. "I'll even scrub mine out for you, if you like." He looked past her. "I hope you're not planning to tip that barrel by yourself, Jess. I'd be glad to lend a hand."

"No," she said, shaking her head quickly. "Finn will help me when he comes back. I'll wait for him. He told me not to try emptying it alone."

Morgan's gaze narrowed on her and his nod was slow. "If you say so."

The man was too perceptive by far, Jessica thought. He looked as if he were reading her mind, and she waved a hand at him, as if she would shoo him from his spot. "If you're going to find me a pan to sift this flour with, I'd appreciate it, Morgan."

"You don't think your husband will be riled up by me helping?" he asked.

"No, of course not," Jessica told him. "I don't think he even thought of sifting the flour, and I certainly didn't have the equipment to do it." She caught a glimpse of movement just beyond Morgan's shoulder and bent closer to seek out who it might be. Arlois stood several feet away, looking uncertainly at the man who filled the opening at the rear of Jessica's wagon.

"Arlois?" Jessica called her friend's name and Morgan glanced back, stepping aside to make room for the woman.

With an apologetic glance in Morgan's direction, Arlois moved closer. "I just wondered if you needed help with the baby," she offered. "I don't know how much longer we'll be together, and I wanted to spend some time with you."

"Are you planning on moving on up the creek?" Morgan asked nicely, doffing his hat as Arlois looked up at him. "Someone said there are a few prime pieces of land about five miles out of town. I thought maybe you would be heading that way."

Arlois nodded uncertainly. "I was hoping to speak with Mr. Carson about that," she said. "I wondered where you would be settling, Jessica, and if you thought it was a possibility for us to neighbor."

"I'd heard that Tom Lansing is looking to head upstream himself," Morgan said quietly. "I think he's hoping to find some land not too far from you, Mrs. Bates."

"I'm not in the market for a husband, sir," she said sharply. "I've only been a widow for a few weeks, and looking for another man is the furthest thing from my mind."

"I'd say it might not be a bad idea," Morgan told her, his tone allowing for no dithering. "This is a rough life for a woman alone, and if you're planning on homesteading, you'll need a grown man to protect you. You could do worse than to give Tom a chance."

Arlois's eyes filled with tears and she looked down at

the ground. "I can't do that," she whispered. "It would be a sacrilege to take another husband so soon after David's—"

As if she couldn't voice aloud the finality of her husband's death, her words broke off and she shook her head.

"Your husband is dead, ma'am," Morgan told her. "That's a harsh thing to say, but it's the truth, and if we were on the trail, you'd be forced to choose a husband from among the single men, so long as there were willing candidates."

"Well, we're not on the trail any longer," Arlois told him, lifting her face without a care for the tears that stained her cheeks. "If I have to take a husband, I will, but for now, I'm going to try it alone." She looked back at Jessica, and her smile seemed to hold not one iota of cheer, Jessica thought.

"Do you need a hand?" Arlois asked, renewing her offer. "I can keep an eye on the baby while you tend to your chores."

Jessica shot a baleful glance at Morgan and then bent a kindlier look on Arlois. "I can always use help," she said, recalling her refusal of Morgan's offer only minutes ago. Allowing the man to dump out the remnants of her flour might result in a disaster, she thought, should Finn's suspicions be correct. "Mr. Morgan has offered to clean up his gold pan for me to sift out the flour," she said sweetly. "I'm sure he was just on his way, weren't you, sir?"

With a look that told her he was on to her tactics, Morgan put his hat on squarely and nodded. "Won't take long at all, Miss Jessica," he said smoothly. "I'll be back."

The two women watched him saunter off and Arlois spoke first. "Are you sure it's a good idea to be friendly with him? I'll bet you that your husband will be very unhappy when he finds out you've been spending time with that man."

"Maybe a little jealousy will be good for him," Jessica

said with a laugh. And then she lifted the baby, fresh and sweet smelling, into Arlois's arms. "I need to make a list," she told her friend. "Finn will be back shortly and he'll be ready to go to the general store and get supplies."

Arlois looked a bit sheepish as she offered a suggestion. "Do you think he'd mind if I tagged along?" she asked. "I really don't relish walking around in Shadow Creek on my own. Just being with you and Finn would make me feel safer, I think."

"Another reason you need to think about a man of your own," Jessica told her.

"What are you up to?" Finn stood over her, hands on his hips and a frown on his face as he watched Jessica working beside the wagon. She'd found her largest bowl and was shaking Morgan's pan over it, watching closely to be certain that no tiny insects made their way through the fine screening.

She looked up at Finn and blew a stray wisp of hair from her eyes. "Just what does it look like?" she asked.

"Where'd you get the pan? It's not one of mine," he told her.

"Well, aren't you right up to snuff?" she said, as if she resented his right to question her. And then she sighed and tossed the final bits of flour and captured insects aside. "Morgan brought it to me. He scrubbed it out and offered to let me use it. Made sense to me, after I'd spent half an hour picking bits and pieces from the first bagful."

"There wasn't any need to push yourself, Jess. I told you I'd help you when I got back." He glanced into the wagon bed and frowned. "Where's the baby?"

"Arlois took him over to her place," she said. "She said she wanted to give me a break."

Finn nodded. "Has she said any more about accepting one of the miners as a husband? I know of at least two of them who'd be more than willing. Women are hard to come by out here, especially decent women."

"She's not interested," Jessica said shortly. "And *she* has a choice," she added pointedly, shooting a glance in his direction.

"What's that supposed to mean?" he asked. His hands slid into his pockets as he awaited her reply and he nudged her a bit. "If you hadn't been in a bind, would you have turned me down?"

"I can't really say," she told him with a lofty smile. "I was between a rock and hard place, as you well know, Finn. Who knows what I'd have done if there hadn't been pressure brought to bear?"

"Are you sorry?" he asked quietly, reaching for her and tugging her into his embrace. He bent his head and she turned her face aside.

"Don't, Finn. We're right out in plain sight."

"And you think I care?" he asked, lifting a hand to her nape, turning her head so that she must face him directly. "You're my wife, Jess. I don't care who knows I care about you, and I sure don't mind if the rest of the men around here get the message that I've got a claim on you."

"Is that what it comes down to?" she asked softly. "That you've laid claim to me and all I own?"

He shook his head, and a smile touched his lips. "Hardly," he said. "What it comes down to is that you're my wife. We share and share alike in everything we hold. I've provided money to outfit you over the last few hundred miles and we've slept on your feather tick at night. Once we come up with that damned deed, we'll share that, too."

She tried to jerk from his hold, but he held her fast. "Look at me, Jess," he said harshly. "You need to get this straight, once and for all. My brother died because of that piece of paper, and I'm his sole heir. It belongs to me now, whether you like it or not."

"Well, that's plain speaking, I'd say," she said bitterly.

"In case you've forgotten, my husband died because of that *damned* deed, too. And by all rights, it should belong to me. I've been willing to grant you a claim to it, but I'm tired of you rubbing my nose in your kindness, *allowing* me to be part owner of that property."

He was exasperated, and his words drove home his mood. "You just don't get it, Jess. Lyle didn't have a leg to stand on. He was a man without morals or ethics, and he apparently killed Aaron without hesitation. Then the men Lyle was in cahoots with shot him down in cold blood, probably because he was dealing from the bottom of the deck where they were concerned. And those two crooks may still be out there somewhere, hoping to get their hands on that deed. I can't believe they've given it up."

"Well, thank you, Mr. Carson for explaining all of that to me. At least I know right where I stand in all this." She felt a flush climb her cheeks as she bit off words that were designed to anger the man who held her fast. "You married me, took advantage of me, and now you're planning on claiming my child's inheritance."

Finn shook her, only once, but it was a gesture that she hadn't expected. "You listen to me, *Mrs. Carson,*" he said, his words closely echoing her own. "I'm willing to take care of you for the rest of your life, and the child along with you. I'm planning to share my inheritance with you, but that's as good as it's gonna get, lady."

She hung in his grasp, her legs suddenly weak as she took the brunt of his anger. *"Lady?"* She repeated the title he'd given her with a sound of derision, and watched as his face took on a flush.

"You are a lady, Jess. I didn't mean that in any way hurtful to you. I respect you, even if I'm madder than hell at you." And with that he dragged her closer and offered her a kiss unlike any other he'd given in the past. His mouth was hard and forceful, his tongue catching her unaware as she gasped for breath. Strong arms circled her and she was drawn up against him, her body aware suddenly of the muscular man she'd married.

His lips gave her no chance to breathe, his tongue and teeth took her mouth roughly, and she was left to gasp for air as he invaded those hidden places like a marauder in search of bounty. He held her against himself and she felt the ridge of his arousal against her belly, knew a moment of panic as she wondered just how far he was planning to take this encounter. The wagon was beside them, and if ever Finn Carson had ached to claim his marital rights, she was dead certain that time was now.

She should be angry, she thought, her mind spinning as she sought to accept his dominion. It would do no good to fight him off. She'd only look foolish to any onlookers, given Finn's strength, plus the anger that drove him. And so she yielded to him, allowing her body to meld with his, gripping his shirt with trembling fingers and opening to his taking of her mouth, an action that imitated the consummation he was more than ready to complete.

Then, as if he came to his senses and recognized the futility of their position, his fingers tightened on her, and she heard a soft utterance muttered against her lips. "Damn." It was probably as near to an apology as she'd ever get, she decided, and as his hands released her, she leaned against him for just a moment longer.

"Jess?" He whispered, and raised his head to peer down at her uplifted face. "I hurt you, didn't I?" His hand cupped her cheek and she felt satisfaction at his action. It was regret she saw reflected in his eyes, and she shared in the feeling.

"No, you didn't hurt me, Finn. I made you angry, and I shouldn't have pushed it."

"I had no right to force myself on you," he muttered.

"You didn't," she countered. "You kissed me." Her tongue touched her upper lip and she watched his focus follow the movement. "It's your right, Finn. You're my husband."

"I'll never take you in anger, Jess," he promised, his index finger brushing the tender flesh he'd caused to be swollen beneath his touch.

"I know that," she said simply. "I've walked that road, Finn, and there's no comparison between you and Lyle."

As if he ached to hold her close, he closed his eyes and thrust his hands deeply into his pockets. And with a gesture that was spontaneous, she stepped closer and placed her forehead against his chest, her arms circling his waist and holding fast to him. She felt the indrawn breath he could not control, heard the soft sound of his feet moving to either side of hers, and knew the embrace he could not deny himself.

"Thank you," he murmured, bending his head to touch his mouth against her temple. "I'll try to be patient, Jess. I won't lose my temper again." And then as if he considered that promise and found it to be beyond his capacity to keep, he chuckled beneath his breath. "I'll *try* not to lose my temper," he amended.

She leaned back to look up into his face. "You didn't tell me yet if you discovered anything about Aaron's benefactor."

"His name was John Penrod," Finn told her. "I remembered it from the letter Aaron wrote me. So I asked around and found that the man died months ago. He's buried up the creek a couple of miles, right near the property he claimed. No one seemed to know who he left the deed for his place to, and there've been a couple of miners panning there. But they'll pack up and move on once we occupy the site."

He looked down at her then, and his frown was forbidding. "What did Morgan want with you when he came by? Besides offering his pan for you to use."

"He offered to help me tip the barrel over and clean it

out. I told him you were going to do it as soon as you got back. Then Arlois came up and we got to talking and he went back to his wagon, and pretty soon he brought me the pan to use." She shrugged as if the matter was of little concern.

"Was he in the wagon?" Finn asked, and looked relieved when she shook her head.

"Are you about done with sorting through that flour?" He looked down at the bags she'd tied with bits of twine. "Let's dump out the rest, Jess. I think you've managed to salvage enough of it."

"All right," she agreed, and then watched as he set her aside and climbed into the wagon with easy movements. Rolling the barrel to the tailgate, he waved his hand at her.

"Step away, Jess. This is going to be messy." She did as he asked and watched flour dust billow from the container as several cups of the residue hit the ground with a puff. Finn tilted the barrel back and peered within, then placed it on the wagon bed and reached for her.

"Give me your hand, sweetheart," he said quietly, and he scanned the surrounding wagons and the men who milled about on the short road that led to the middle of Shadow Creek. With ease, he lifted her over the tailgate and waved at the barrel. "Take a look."

She peered within and shrugged. "What am I looking for?"

"See that brown bit of paper on the bottom?" He motioned past her, pointing at a flat piece she had barely taken note of. The same color as the bottom of the barrel, and liberally dusted with flour, it was difficult to discern at first glance. "I think we've just struck gold, Mrs. Carson."

They sat before the cooking fire, speaking in low voices as Jessica leaned closer to shift her baking stone into the coals. "I can't believe it was there all along," she said for the third time. "Why didn't Lyle let me know?"

"He was probably afraid you'd snatch it and run off, Jess. The man didn't trust another living soul, so far as I can tell. How he thought up the idea of getting it in there without you knowing anything about it is a surprise to me."

"I told you, he wouldn't let me near while he changed barrels. Said I was too puny to be of any help." She laughed dryly. "It was the only time I remember that he acted considerate of me."

"I don't know why I didn't think of it earlier," Finn said, his disgust apparent. "It was the perfect place to hide it. All wrapped up in a piece of oilcloth, it would have withstood anything but being washed overboard if the wagon should have had problems crossing a river."

"Now what?" Jessica asked quietly.

Finn settled his gaze on her. "Now we make plans. We'll locate the claim and check out the cabin that's on it." He leaned over to turn the spit, and juices dripped onto the coals, sizzling and wafting the scent of roasting rabbit toward them. The spit was new, Finn having bought it from a blacksmith in Shadow Creek, and Jessica looked on it gratefully, now that cleaning her skillet was no longer a dreaded task.

"The bread's about done," she said, "and I've put corn in the fire to roast." Coming by earlier, Polly had given instructions for the corn, directing Jessica to soak it in salt water for an hour before she buried it beneath a layer of coals.

The chance to eat fresh vegetables was a treat. Settlers up the creek brought their produce to Shadow Creek, swapping it out for staples at the store, and the corn was the first of the season. Nights were cool in the foothills of the mountains, but the days were hot and sunny, perfect weather for gardens, Finn said.

Yet, he'd grinned and shaken his head when Arlois spoke of planting peas and beans in the tiny patch of ground she'd claimed for a campsite. Grimacing and admitting the unlikelihood of such a thing coming about, she'd decided instead to use her time while in Shadow Creek doing laundry and mending for the men who spent long hours panning for gold. The fact that she was also the focus of more attention than had ever been aimed in her direction in her entire life wasn't making her unhappy, so far as he could see, Finn decided.

But that wasn't all bad. At least it was keeping her mind off the loss of her husband, and that circumstance definitely had brought her situation to a head. The woman needed a man to take care of her, whether she would admit it or not.

Tom Lansing was plinzing around, lingering for an evening in the clearing where Arlois had set up housekeeping, and Finn would almost guarantee that the miner was waiting for an opportune moment to press his suit for her hand. Arlois had taken pity on him, inviting him for the supper meal, and Tom was sitting as close to the woman as he dared, even as he directed the younger boy's attempt to whittle a whistle from a piece of wood. The man had Finn's sympathy.

Arlois, on the other hand, didn't appear to be in any hurry to settle her future. But however she chose, she needed to be under cover by the first snowfall, and that involved building some sort of shelter for both her family and their animals. Tom had a claim a mile or so up the creek, and Finn knew the man was itching to spend his time there, instead of trotting back and forth to pursue the reluctant widow.

"You know what?" he asked, drawing Jessica's attention from the baby who was wrapped securely in a blanket beside her.

"No. What?" Jessica asked distractedly as she tucked the blanket over Jonas's head. And then she looked up at Finn. "Have you decided yet what we'll do next? Is that what you've been sitting there stewing over?" Jessica asked him in an undertone. "Do you need to go to the claims office to register for a change of ownership?"

Finn's brow lifted in surprise. "How did you know that?"

"I eavesdropped one day and overheard Lyle tell someone he'd have to do that before he could lay claim to the land."

"Well, he was right," Finn told her. "I'll do it in the morning." He'd shoved the deed inside his shirt once it was unwrapped and examined, and now his hand unconsciously ventured to touch the place where it lay. He shot her a glance filled with promise. "It looks good, Jess," he said softly. "The assayer's report shows a high degree of gold in the nuggets Mr. Penrod brought in from his claim. We might have to chase off the poachers, but I'll guarantee they haven't begun to touch the main vein. If they had, we'd know it. The assayer would have the information as to where their gold was found, and he knows who claimed this piece of land."

"You mean Mr. Penrod?" she asked, and Finn nodded. "How can we prove that the claim is ours then?"

"I have the letter Penrod sent to Aaron," Finn told her. "That's all we need." He glanced over the area and nodded to where Tom Lansing was standing now beside Arlois's cooking fire. "I thought about asking Tom to work with me on the claim, and I'll lend a hand with his. Would you have a problem with that?"

She grinned. "I know what you have in mind, Mr. Carson. I do believe you're matchmaking. You're thinking if Tom works with you and Arlois decides to park her wagon on his piece of land, things would work to Tom's advantage."

"And to Arlois's, too," Finn said. "She—"

"I know. I know." With an uplifted hand, Jessica halted his declaration even before he was able to speak the words. "She needs a man to take care of her."

She dropped her chin to rest against her knees and turned her head to look across the fire at him. "And is that why you married me? Or at least part of the reason?"

"I told you a long time ago why I married you," Finn said soberly. "I took one look at you in Saint Louis and lost my head. I don't know what I'd have done if Lyle hadn't been the target for those friends of his. Probably tried to talk you into leaving him."

"You wouldn't," she said, aghast at the idea of turning her back on her marriage vows. "I couldn't have done that."

"Maybe not, but I might have considered dragging you off across the prairie and laying claim to you one way or another, Jess. I don't think you have any idea how badly I wanted you that day. I might have set aside all my lofty ideals and lowered myself to snatching you up like those two crooks did."

She looked at him from the corner of her eye and felt a flush climb her cheeks. "You know, I think you might have done just that very thing, Finley Carson. To tell the truth, I didn't think I could ever inspire that sort of passion in any man."

He laughed aloud and the sound was a seduction in itself. "You have no idea of what you've inspired in me, Jessica. But one of these days very soon, I'm going to show you."

Chapter Fourteen

Finn's stride was long and filled with purpose as he made his way to the assayer's office, and an additional air of jubilance accompanied him on his return trip to the wagon where Jessica waited, offering feed to the chickens and gathering up their eggs from the coop Finn had put together. His early-morning trek drew the attention of the men who occupied wagons and tents nearby, and their curiosity was palpable as he neared the camp. From the satisfaction gleaming in his eyes, Jessica knew that his purpose had been fulfilled.

Her thoughts were made fact as he snatched her up and held her before him, grinning widely. "It's done," he said triumphantly, and then tilted his head back as he lifted her high, the better to share his triumph. She shrieked as her feet left the ground and her hands clutched at his shoulders for balance.

"You idiot. Put me down, Finn, before you drop me." And then she recognized the vindication this moment contained for him. "You finally feel that Aaron has been avenged, don't you?" she whispered.

Finn sobered and allowed her to slide to the ground before him. His mouth twisted in a crooked smile as he nodded. "Yeah, I guess I do." His arms enclosed her for a moment and she felt his warmth seep into her flesh. With reluctance he allowed his hands to slip to her waist and shot her an exultant grin. "I'll pack us up and we'll be ready to move on up the creek within the hour. It's been a long time coming, Jess, but knowing that those men don't stand a chance of laying hands on Aaron's claim has made this whole thing worthwhile."

"Well…" She allowed the single syllable to hang between them before she stepped back, escaping his touch. Her lips resisted the smile she forced into being, and for a moment it trembled on her lips before she turned aside. "I'm pleased that you've found this experience rewarding, Finn. And I'm happy for you that your brother's property will be in the right hands."

"Jess?" As if he'd just recognized her mood, he touched her shoulder. "We're going to work this claim together. You know that. The best thing that's ever happened in my life took place the day I married you."

"Really?" She turned her head to look back over her shoulder at him. "Maybe so." A shrug emphasized her meaning as she walked away. "I don't recall you being nearly so happy about the results of that bit of business as you are right now."

The oath he uttered beneath his breath echoed in her ears as she turned back for a moment and picked up the baby. "Let me know when you're ready to leave," she said. Her eyes burned with unshed tears as she walked toward Arlois's wagon. Tom Lansing stood beside his horse, apparently ready to ride upstream, and he touched the brim of his hat as Jessica approached.

"Trouble?" Arlois asked quietly as Jessica stood beside her.

"Nothing new," Jessica said. "I just wanted to tell you that we're pulling out as soon as Finn packs the wagon and gets the chickens gathered up."

"Now?" Arlois's voice trembled on the word, and her

mouth opened and then closed, her gaze touching quickly on Tom. Close enough to overhear the two women speak, he only nodded at Arlois, and then strolled toward Finn.

"Can I lend a hand?" he asked, and then as the two men exchanged words in a quiet conversation, he clasped Finn's hand and shook it, his smile speaking for itself. "Well, damn," he said after a moment. "That's good news, Carson."

"Whatever the good news is, I don't think you're doing much rejoicing," Arlois said dryly. "What's the problem?"

Jessica shook her head, unable to voice her hurt aloud. "I'll get over it," she said, hugging the baby to her breast and stealing a look at Finn's somber face.

"I don't know what to say," Arlois said. She lowered her voice. "Tom just asked me to move with him. He wants me to put my wagon on his claim."

"Are you going to?" Jessica asked. And then, before she could contain the words, she spoke her opinion aloud. "You won't get a better chance, Arlois. Tom's a good man, and he's willing to do right by you, Finn says."

Arlois pressed her lips together for a moment and then sighed. "My oldest boy doesn't like the idea."

"And where will he be in ten years or so?"

"Probably off on his own," Arlois admitted, and her lips curved. "He'll walk off and make a life for himself, and I'll still be a widow woman, all alone, if I don't do something about it, won't I?"

"You'll still be sought after, probably," Jessica said. "But why waste ten years of your life if you think Tom will take care of you? What do you think David would want for you?"

Her eyes filled with tears as Arlois spoke impulsively. "You know as well as I do that David loved me, and he'd want me to have a man to look after things."

Jessica nodded. "And so?"

"I've had a hard time thinking about loving someone else," Arlois admitted. "But I have to admit that the winter nights are gonna be cold, and as much as I loved David, I'll miss having someone to look after things."

She bent to her cooking fire and rescued a skillet where fatback sizzled, tilting it to pour the excess grease on the ground. "Have you eaten?"

Jessica nodded. "Early on, before Finn went to the assayer's office.

Arlois caught her breath and her words were whispered. "Did you find the deed Mr. Beaumont was supposed to have? Did Finn get it put into his name?"

"Yes, to both questions."

"You don't look very pleased about it," Arlois ventured. "I would think this makes a big change for you and Finn. You know, having a deed all registered and the claim ready to work."

"It's hard to accept that my main attraction has been my inheritance from Lyle," Jessica said sharply. "I knew I'd have to have help working to pan gold and making the cabin fit for winter, but the whole thing has turned into what Finn wants, and his rights."

Arlois seemed stunned by Jessica's words. "I don't think I understand what you mean. He's your husband, Jess. And by law, he owns everything you have. Surely you understood that before you made your vows in Council Grove."

"I wasn't thinking very clearly back in Council Grove, if you'll recall. But I knew that piece of paper was all that stood between me and starving to death at the end of the road."

Arlois laughed aloud. "You never stood a chance of going hungry, girl. There was a whole slew of men looking at you, and they weren't only thinking about a deed you might or might not have in that wagon of yours."

Jessica dismissed the comment with a wave of her free hand. "You know what I mean. The one thing that really appealed to Finn was my possession of the deed. His brother, Aaron, was given it back in Saint Louis, and Lyle won it from him in a poker game. A crooked game, is my guess. And then Aaron was shot and killed, and Lyle told me we were heading west to mine gold.'' Jessica shook her head. ''You've probably heard all this already. I think everyone on the wagon train knew more than I did.''

''Finn feels it rightly belongs to him, doesn't he?'' Arlois asked, getting down to the issue at hand.

Jessica's lips trembled. ''You know he does. And where does that leave me? I was handy to have around and grateful for his help, and he knew that deed was somewhere in my wagon. Once he found it, my child's inheritance was gone.''

''Don't you trust the man to take care of you? You just gave me a whole long lecture on taking on Tom and letting him run my life. Is your choice any different?''

Weighing her response, Jessica hesitated a moment and then felt a masculine arm slide around her waist. She looked up at its owner and caught a glimpse of banked anger in his eyes.

''I need you to give me some direction, Jess,'' Finn said, nodding a greeting at Arlois. ''You'd better come back to the wagon and see if I've got things the way you want them while I've got Tom handy to help.''

Unwilling to dispute his demand, she nodded and whispered a farewell to Arlois. She allowed Finn to lead her back toward their wagon. ''I'm sure you can handle this by yourself,'' she said quietly.

''Maybe,'' he agreed, ''but I want you and the baby inside and the wagon ready to roll. There are too many eyes watching this morning, and I have a feeling that all of them aren't friendly.''

''Do you think those two men—''

Finn cut her off, shaking his head. ''I don't know, but there are enough places to hide that someone could be keeping an eye on us and we'd never know it. If you see anyone who looks familiar, sing out and let me know."

She halted in her tracks. "Where's Morgan? He saw those men, Finn."

"Did he?" His arm tightened around her and he urged her toward the tailgate.

"You know he did. Don't think you're fooling me any more with your games," she said. "You and Morgan have been playing hide-and-seek ever since we left Missouri. Between the two of you you've managed to—" Her jaw clenched as she suppressed the anger she could barely contain. "Don't lie to me anymore," she said. "And don't tell me it's not what it seems to be. I've heard that before."

"Morgan is trying to put an end to this," Finn said bluntly. "He wants those men in jail as badly as you or I do, and he's just about to round them up."

Jessica held Jonas up against her shoulder and closed her eyes. Arms enclosed her and Finn's mouth touched her temple. "I want you and the baby safe," he said quietly. "Now, get in the wagon. We'll be ready to roll in a few minutes."

He'd sorted out their belongings, tied the crates of chickens on the side of the wagon and was ready to fasten the yoke on the oxen. Jessica headed toward a crate near the front of the wagon, clutching the baby against herself as she edged through their combined possessions, watching Finn lead the oxen from where he'd staked them over the past days. Within minutes the animals were in place, and Finn turned the lead ox toward the road that headed west from Shadow Creek.

Open country surrounded them within minutes, the clutter and bustle of the small mining town left behind. Ahead of them, the white caps atop the mountains glistened in the sunlight, and Jessica marveled at the thought that snow was able to exist in the midst of summer. The wonder of high peaks and slopes of evergreen trees that rose to cover their

foothills held her spellbound and she felt a resurgence of
hope that this might be the beginning of a new life.

Jonas stirred, suckling at his fingers and she bent her
head, enticed by the small sounds he made, the sweet scent
of his breath and the knowledge that in this one accom-
plishment she had been successful. Opening her bodice, she
brought his mouth closer to the sustenance he required, and
he nuzzled her breast, lured by the smell of her milk.

For this child, she would allow Finn to hold full sway
of her future, she realized, because if any one thing was
true, it was that Finn felt responsible for Jonas. Whether or
not he would grow to love the baby was a question she
could not answer. Perhaps it would never come to pass, she
thought, but how anyone could resist the appeal of this
child was inconceivable to her. She slid to the floor and
leaned her head back, aware of the rough road they traveled, anticipating the end of this final leg of the long journey.

The claim was marked by stakes, with numbers painted
down their length. Narrower at the front, then widening to
encompass what seemed to be an enormous area to Jessica,
it was a piece of wilderness that seemed raw and untamed.
About three hundred feet from the creek stood a small
cabin, seeming primitive and ramshackle, its only attraction
the crude shelter it offered from the elements.

Bypassing the wide streambed, Finn headed toward the
shack, hoping glumly that its interior would outshine the
visible dilapidation of log walls and a lack of windows. He
drew the wagon close to the single door and looked up to
find Jessica climbing over the seat, ready to descend to the
ground.

"Let me give you a hand," he told her, his hands reaching for her waist. Lowering her to stand before him, he
purposely injected a touch of humor into his words. "Not

exactly what we were hoping for, is it?'' And knew he had failed miserably in his attempt to lift her spirits.

''We'll make do,'' she said quietly. ''I'm not a child, Finn. I know how to work, and I'm not afraid of the future here.''

Relief flooded him at her words. He'd known Jessica was strong, had seen her struggle against a situation that might have overwhelmed a lesser woman, and recognized that she would not falter now. ''I'll help you all I can,'' he said. ''We'll need to get this place tight before bad weather sets in, and I've got to spend as much time as I can panning in the stream.

''The first thing I need to do once we get unpacked is to build some sort of pen for the chickens. If they don't have shelter at night the hawks will get them.'' He looked beyond the wagon seat. ''Is Jonas asleep?'' At her nod, he led her to the sagging door and forced it open. They stepped over the threshold, and the scurry of some tiny creature broke the silence. ''Probably a mouse,'' Finn said. He looked upward at the rafters. ''I thought there might be birds in here, too, but apparently there are enough trees around the cabin to hold them all.''

Jessica looked at the floor, then stepped from the doorway, allowing the light to invade the interior of the small structure. ''It could be worse,'' she said flatly. ''I don't see any snakes.''

''I think,'' Finn ventured, ''it would take more than a snake to scare you off, sweet. I've seen you in some pretty tough spots over the past months, and I'm not worried about your ability to cope with this place.''

She looked as if she were ready to roll up her sleeves and pitch in, he thought. And as the image appeared in his mind, he saw her fingers unbutton her cuff and begin the task of baring her forearms for the tasks ahead. ''Help me carry things from the wagon,'' she said, ''beginning with something to put the baby on or in.''

In one corner of the single room a simple framework had been constructed, and was covered with a cotton mattress, half of the stuffing exposed, the floor littered by its debris. "We'll clean that up first," Finn told her, "and then sweep underneath it before we bring in your feather tick." Three long strides took him the width of the one-room structure and he tugged at the mattress, pulling it free of the sagging rope support beneath it. "I'll drag this outside and bring back your broom."

Jessica crossed to where a fireplace stood on the opposite wall, bending to peer up the inside of the chimney. "This doesn't look too bad," she said. "Your spit will fit in here just fine. All we need is some wood and the box of matches, and I'll put together something to eat."

In another corner a dilapidated cupboard sat at an angle and she bent to look beneath the ragged bit of cloth that dangled from two nails. A wooden bucket lay on its side and a nest of tiny pink mice curled within. Bits of the mattress stuffing surrounded them and Jessica shuddered visibly as she reached for the container.

"Want me to get rid of that?" Finn asked, and was not surprised when she shook her head. The mattress lodged in the doorway and he pushed it through to the outside and grasped it by one corner.

"I can handle mice," she said briskly, appearing in the doorway carrying the bucket. "What I can't cope with is fixing that door so it will close and figuring out a way to cut a hole in the wall so we can let some light in here."

"What will you cover a window with?"

She looked at him and her mouth twisted wryly. "I'll bet you can find some waxed paper or a piece of glass somewhere in Shadow Creek. I'll leave that up to you." Holding the bucket, she sailed past him, toward a patch of brush where she emptied the family of mice to the ground.

"You're a cruel woman, Jessica Carson," he said, relishing the sight of her hips as she sashayed back to the cabin. Her glance in his direction let him know that she was not about to be bested in their ongoing battle.

"Just go get my broom," she told him. "I've got work to do."

By late afternoon they had carried the bulk of their belongings into the cabin, and Finn moved the wagon until it sat close to the outside wall of the cabin and near the door. He nailed chicken wire to the cabin and the back of the wagon, put two posts to form corners and then covered the open top with more wire. The chickens clucked contentedly in their domain, and he threw in a double handful of grain for them.

"The rest of this can wait," he told Jessica. "So long as the food and the bedding are inside, we'll be all right for tonight. Are you finding everything you need?"

"There's not much to find," she said bluntly. "We've got food for a few days, and I picked up enough firewood close at hand to make do for now. The big kettle is full of soup, and I've stirred up a batch of johnnycake to bake on my stone."

He stood in the doorway and looked at the results of her day's work. The dilapidated cupboard had been shored up with a chunk of wood beneath one corner, the bed was made, Jonas occupying its center, and a makeshift bench, put together with pieces of board and firewood held her assortment of bowls and dishes. "You need a shelf or something to hold that stuff," he said.

"I'm going to stack crates and boxes in the corner for now," she told him. "That will hold most everything but our clothes. My trunk should take care of those, and it'll fit under the bed during the daytime."

"What about Jonas?" he asked. "He can't sleep on the floor the way he did in the wagon."

"No, he'll be at the back of the bed or between us."

"The back of the bed," Finn said firmly. "I don't want to chance rolling over on him." His eyes warmed as he touched her shoulder, and she caught the flare of desire he made no attempt to conceal. "Besides, I need to have you next to me, Jess. You warm the cockles of my heart, as my mother used to say."

"Really," she said dubiously, and then her smile appeared. "I think I'd like your mother."

Finn looked up from his chosen spot in the stream and allowed his eyes to linger on the woman who reached high to snag a pair of his denim pants from the clothesline. A rope strung between two trees held trousers and shirts and a whole string of diapers, pinned neatly and blowing in the breeze. And then the slender female bent to place the pants she'd so quickly and deftly folded into the basket at her feet. Her bottom was clearly outlined, her dress blown by the accommodating wind that exposed her lower legs as she bent over.

His heart snagged in his throat as he watched her, his eyes narrowing as she lifted a hand to brush a lock of hair from her face and then reached once more for another bit of his clothing. She'd scrubbed everything over a washboard just hours ago, and he'd been hard-pressed not to gape as her body swayed in time with the motion of her hands moving across the galvanized surface.

Panning for gold was a profitable business only if a man could concentrate on the job at hand, he decided. And being exposed constantly to the movements of the woman who seemed to be holding him at bay these days was keeping him on edge and drawing him from the task he'd set for himself. Gold nuggets were here to be found, and if the number he'd already taken to the assayer's office were anything to go by, he stood to be a man in danger of having a dandy bank account.

"Finn?" Her voice beckoned him, the sound carried on the wind, and he lifted a hand in response. "Dinner's about

ready,'' she called, then picked up the basket and walked
toward the cabin.

He watched her walk through the doorway and thought
for a moment that the sun had gone behind a cloud. His
smile was mocking as he looked back down at the pan he
held, and the derision was aimed at himself. The woman
had him in a bind. On the surface, all was well. She cooked,
cared for Jonas and kept the cabin as clean as was possible,
given the primitive conditions she was coping with.

The problem was his. Jessica was oblivious to his aching
need for her, flitting around the cabin in bursts of energy.
Her newly restored waistline and the fullness of her bosom
lured his gaze each morning and night, at breakfast and
supper alike as he watched her putting together and serving
up the meals they shared.

She was a bit reserved but outwardly friendly. Her attitude was ever cheerful but nonchalant, yet with Arlois she
exuded a sense of delight that was lost as soon as the other
woman took her leave. Her smiles were cordial, and he
found he wasn't satisfied with her courteous demeanor. She
kept him fed, his clothing presentable and his dwelling
place habitable, and yet she held him at arm's length.

Only in the hours of the night, when she was asleep,
with all her defenses down, was he able to bask in her
warmth. For then she turned to him, wrapping herself
around his back or twining her legs with his or allowing
him to hold her against himself, lost in well-deserved slumber. Upon awakening, she moved away from his warmth,
quietly and carefully climbing from the bed they shared—
yet did not come to—as man and wife.

Surely it was time, he thought, for her to be healed from
childbearing. Yet she made no mention of resuming their
relationship, and he feared he would be rebuffed should he
approach her.

His steps dragged as he trudged toward the cabin, his

mind focusing on the woman who now was probably placing his dinner on the table.

His eyes found her as he stepped across the threshold and he drank in the picture she presented. A faded cotton dress, bare feet peeking from beneath its hem, clothed her body. And beneath that covering was a combination of skin and bones and flesh he'd give a year of his life to hold close, preferably while lying down on the feather tick, with her wide-awake and willing.

Crossing to the basin she'd prepared for him, he scrubbed at his hands, although they were already as clean as six hours in the cold, running stream could make them. He splashed his face with the warm water she'd provided and then reached for the towel she'd placed in a handy spot.

"It's only stew," Jessica said. "But I made flatbread to go with it." Bending to scoop the hot bits of bread from her baking stone, she presented another view of her rounded calves, her dress pulling up nicely. He turned aside, acknowledging the heat that seemed to be permanently located in his lower parts these days.

And then, as she placed the steaming bread on the table, he took the folded towel from her hand and tossed it on his chair. Her eyes widened as she looked up at him and her mouth opened.

Right handy, he thought as he scooped her against himself with one arm, his own lips matching hers, his open mouth swallowing her protest.

She was warm, her skin glowing from the heat of the fireplace, but her body was resisting him, unwilling to be molded to his, and he set about resolving that problem. His hand curved against her throat and he allowed her no quarter, acknowledging the thrust of his manhood as she wiggled against him. Her hands clapped against his shoulders then, and she pushed against him, drawing in a breath of air through her nostrils and growling unintelligible words in her throat.

"Hush," he said, lifting from her mouth for only a moment. "Let me, Jess. Please."

Perhaps it was the softly spoken entreaty, the single word that begged her indulgence, or maybe she'd had a change of heart. Whatever the reason, her fingers curled into fists and slid downward. The soft sound that met his ears was barely a whimper, almost a sob, and he brushed her lips with tenderness, held her with a gentleness that was hard to come by.

He kissed her, inhaling the fragrant womanly scent she exuded. His hands slid the length of her body, reveling in the firm lift of her breasts, then the narrowing of her waist, finding purchase where they would, finally enclosing her hips with his palms. He dug his fingers into the resilient flesh, drawing her against the needy portion of his masculine frame. She'd tasted the stew, for its flavor was on her tongue. Her hair was soft, carrying the scent of rainwater, and his mind recalled the image of her bending over the wooden bucket only yesterday as she'd scrubbed at the long, dark locks.

Somehow her hands had crept beneath his arms and were spread against his back, their warmth encouraging his suit, and he felt a growl of satisfaction emerge from his lips. It echoed between them, and he felt pure desire nudge at him with tentacles of fire.

She inhaled sharply, as if she'd been running full-out and only now was able to draw in a breath. "Finn?" Bewilderment coated the single word, the speaking of his name, and he shushed her with a shake of his head and a brush of his mouth against hers.

His hands loosened against her flesh as he spoke, and he recognized the strength he'd used. "Did I hurt you?" he asked. "Have I left bruises?" He felt a wash of relief as she shook her head. He bent his neck until his forehead touched hers and his words were whispered between them.

"I need you so badly, Jess. I know you've only just had the baby, but—"

"He's seven weeks old," she said, interrupting his confession. "I've been all healed up for weeks, Finn." Her eyes were soft in the dim light inside the cabin. "I won't deny you your rights. I think you know that."

"Hell's bells. I'm not talking about rights here, Jess. I'm asking you to make love with me. If I have to demand your respect, command you to put your arms around me or kiss me or respond to me, then I'll go without."

"I respect you, and I think I just now showed how much I enjoy your kisses," she said quietly. "I'm trying to be a good wife."

"I can't fault you. You are a good wife, but I need more than clean clothes and a meal on the table three times a day."

He watched as her teeth clenched and her nostrils flared. "You don't trust me, do you?" he asked. "You can't give yourself to me when you don't trust my motives."

"I'm not sure that's the problem," she said. "I'm more than just your wife, Finn. I'm Jonas's mother and he needs me. Probably more than you. But he needs a father, too, and you haven't touched him in a week."

Finn frowned, considering her words. "You think I don't care about the baby?"

"I don't know. Do you?"

"You don't know?" He felt his temper rise. "Damn, I was there when he was born, Jess. I saw him before you did, and I'm the one who wrapped him up and handed him to you. How could I not care about him?"

Tears filled her eyes as he watched, and her mouth trembled. "I know all that. You've said those things before, but I keep thinking that he's not really your child. I've given you the responsibility of taking care of him and of me, and if you aren't chafing from the pair of us hanging around your neck, I'd be surprised."

"Well, I'll have to tell you, girl, you have me totally confused." He stepped back from her and slid his hands into his pockets, his desire quenched as if he'd been doused by a pail of cold water. "You think I don't care about Jonas. You think I'm reluctant to be responsible for the pair of you. And, instead of talking about it, you've withdrawn from me and treated me like I have a case of the clap."

"Finley Carson. What a way to talk."

"I don't know any other way, Jessica. That's about as plain as I can make it. I'm just a poor, dumb husband trying to work a claim and get you some decent shelter put together before winter sets in. I'm tired and I'm hungry, and I'm horny as hell most of the time lately."

One hand rose to cover her mouth and he closed his eyes. He'd really done it now with his ranting and carrying on about his lack of loving. He'd might as well face the music, he decided, cautiously opening his eyes to focus on her face.

"I know you work hard," she said, biting at her lower lip as she paused, her shoulders trembling as if she was about to burst into tears. "I know you're tired and hungry, and I've suspected for the past weeks that you're ho-hor-horny—" Her voice broke, and laughter bubbled up from within her to burst forth from behind the hand that was totally inadequate to conceal her smile.

"Jessica. Damn it, Jessica. Don't stand there and laugh at me."

"I can't help it, Finn. We've been looking at things from two different directions here, and I'm afraid it's mostly my fault."

"Well, the problem that's bothering me the most is definitely your fault," he said sourly. "And if you're not careful, I'm going to toss you on that feather tick and do something about it."

"Not right now," she said primly as laughter danced in

dark eyes that glowed with promise. "Jonas is sleeping there."

"Jonas is always sleeping there," he returned glumly.

"They have laundry baskets a bit larger than mine at the general store," she told him. "I'll bet he could fit in one just fine. I don't know why I didn't think of it before."

"I'll build him a bed as soon as I can," he told her. "But if you think a new laundry basket would work, I'll go downstream to Shadow Creek and buy one after I eat."

"I think it would work," she said solemnly, picking up his bowl and scraping his stew back into the kettle. "Let's start out fresh here." She stirred the contents of the kettle, scooped out a generous helping for him and placed it on the table. "Eat it, Finn. I'll fix mine in a minute."

The bread was still good and warm and she had butter, traded from the general store for a dozen eggs she'd taken them. In moments she was across from him, occupying the small bench he'd put together from scrap wood at the lumber mill. Odds and ends of furniture were appearing every time he visited Shadow Creek—the table they sat at the first thing he'd purchased—and the small cabin was beginning to take on the appearance of a home.

Finn finished in short order and rose. "I'll be back before you know it," he told her. "Keep an eye out for strangers, you hear? You know where the gun is if you need it."

Jessica nodded. "Arlois might come by later on. She said she has something to tell me."

His brow lifted. "You think she's going to marry Tom?"

"I wouldn't be surprised. He's persistent enough for two men. And he's been working hard at building a lean-to for them to use until he gets wood for a cabin."

"I told him I'd help when he was ready," Finn told her. "I'll stop by there and see how things are going. I'm going to need his help before long." He crossed to where she sat and bent to kiss her, his mouth firm against hers, his hands pulling her from the bench as if he could not leave without holding her close.

"I'll be back before you know it."

"I'll be here."

Chapter Fifteen

The laundry basket served its purpose well, and before darkness fell Jonas was nestled nicely in its depths. A folded quilt beneath him, the quilt Arlois had made him offering warmth atop, he slept undisturbed as Jessica straightened up her house. It took little time, just banking the fire and pulling the trunk from beneath the bed so that they could sort through their clothing for tomorrow.

The window was covered with waxed paper, allowing light to enter during the day. Finn had made a set of shutters to cover it from the inside at night, and they were already in place. The door swung back and forth on hinges, shiny and efficient, looking somehow incongruous against the weathered lumber. It was home, Jessica decided. Nothing like what she'd shared with her parents, or with Lyle for that matter, but a shelter from the dangers of the night and a haven in which she could sleep unafraid.

Finn was restless, it seemed, walking outdoors for a while, checking on the oxen and his horse. He fed the chickens an extra measure, brought in three eggs and then stood by the table and watched Jessica as she knelt before the trunk, removing her nightgown from its depths. She looked up, wondering at his silence, and found herself the focus of his attention, his eyes dark with a message she could not help but recognize.

"Where do you want the eggs?" he asked, and she almost laughed aloud, so prosaic was the query, so far from what the man was really asking.

"In the bowl on the cupboard," she said, turning her head to watch as he took the three steps necessary to do as she bid. "Are you coming in for the night?"

"Yeah. Do you need to go out again?" He crossed to the door and bent to remove his boots, then awaited her reply, his hand on the heavy wooden portal. He'd dug a pit and put together a rough sort of outhouse, promising her a better job of it when the weather turned cold and he could no longer work the stream from sunup to sundown.

"No," she said. "I'll be fine."

The door closed and the candle she'd placed on the table glowed afresh, as if each corner of the cabin must be touched by its light. Finn's face, though, was in shadow, his hands fisted on his hips, even the gold of his hair subdued. He was tall, and from her position on the floor, kneeling near the bed, she thought he looked dangerous and determined, a man to be wary of.

Yet, being the focus of his desire gave her the same feeling of power she'd felt once before, when he'd needed her body with such desperation. She'd given her heart to him that night, and offered herself into his hands. She would do the same tonight. With no need for him to beg anew for her favors, or admit his need of her. *If I have to demand your respect, command you to put your arms around me or kiss me or respond to me, then I'll go without.*

He would not go without, she determined. Rising in a fluid movement, she placed her gown on the bed and took the necessary steps to reach him. His face was warm beneath her palms and his eyes narrowed as she curved her fingers around the back of his head and drew it downward.

She kissed him, a soft, warm meeting of lips that brought pleasure to her. His own mouth was hard, and his jaw clenched beneath her touch, as if he held himself aloof— and she would not have it.

"Please, Finn. Kiss me the way you used to." Her eyes meshed with his, as her mouth formed the words in a whispering plea.

"I don't want you to do this because you think it's your duty, Jess," he said, his eyelids half-closed, his nostrils flaring as if he'd inhaled her fragrance and found it to his liking.

"I'm not much on doing my duty," she said quietly. "I prefer calling this a way to let you know that I care about you, Finn. And I need you."

The last phrase she uttered hung in the air between them for a long moment, and then his arms reached for her, lifted her, clasping her against his body, his mouth doing as she had bade him. His lips covered hers, taking the sweet warmth of her to himself.

If the woman was being honest, Finn thought, then he'd be a fool not to take her up on the offer. She tasted like desire, like passion unfilled, and his body responded as it had that first day back in Saint Louis, when he'd caught sight of her and known the full meaning of *need* for the first time in his life. One hand slid to her bottom and held her against his arousal, and he rued the layers of clothing that kept him from the soft flesh he craved.

Rocking her against himself, he walked to the bed, skirting the laundry basket, careful not to disturb it. A small rug lay on the floor, a remnant of her early life in Saint Louis and he stood her on it, then with a speed that appeared to stun her, he stripped the clothing from her body.

She was lush, her breasts full, the crests dark and swollen. The curve of her waist drew his gaze and he held her back from him, allowing his eyes to feast on the hollow of her throat, the rise of her bosom and the roundness of her hips.

"You're beautiful, Jess," he whispered, aware that his voice was husky, roughened by the passion he could barely contain. Turning her before him, he bent to touch his mouth against the tender nape of her neck and felt the shiver she could not control. It was akin to the trembling of his hands, he thought, as he took down the braids she'd wrapped around her head. In moments, he'd run his fingers through the long tresses, separating the strands and allowing them to fall over her shoulders and down her back.

His hands on her shoulders, he turned her back to face him, his eyes fastened on the pure line of her profile and then into her eyes. They held his, wide and watchful, and he wondered at her silence. Had he frightened her? Startled her with his handling of her?

"I won't hurt you, Jess," he whispered, his voice stronger now. And she nodded, her head barely moving as her lips assured him, a smile lifting her mouth in a seductive manner, as if she were enjoying this encounter, and only wondered where next he would lead her.

"Stand still," he said quietly, removing his hands from her and tending instead to the buttons on his shirt. She watched him, her tongue touching her upper lip, her hands ready to linger in the golden curls on his chest. Fingers spread wide, she moved her palms over the exposed skin he offered, and the shirt slid to the floor behind him.

With no hesitation, she worked at his belt and he offered a deft touch, loosening it and then unbuttoning the trousers it held in place. Her palms slid to his hips and she maneuvered beneath the soft cotton of his drawers and sent them to the floor.

"Sit down," she told him and, befuddled by her actions, he obeyed. The woman was writing the rules as she went along, he decided, and he could not find it in his heart to mar this moment. Jessica knelt before him, and beneath the layers of fabric, she worked his stockings free and scooped them from his feet. The trousers and drawers were a simple matter to lay aside, and he found himself exposed to her on a new level.

He'd been in an aroused state before, and had more often than not done nothing to relieve his problem. Now he could only watch as Jessica examined that part of him, her hands clasping him, examining the length and breadth of his manhood, as if it were of prime interest to her.

"You need to stop that, Jess," he whispered, his throat dry, his heart pounding at a rapid clip. "I'll be all done before I even get you into bed at this rate," he said bluntly.

"Really?" She tilted her head to the side and smiled fetchingly. "We wouldn't want that to happen, would we?" And then she rose and he could wait no longer. Snatching her to himself, his head leaned forward until his face was cushioned by the lush curves of her breasts. Her neck bent, allowing her forehead to rest against his temple and he felt her breath touch his ear, heard the whisper of his name.

His mouth opened against the flesh he nuzzled, and he left openmouthed kisses on the lavishly rounded flesh she offered. "I can't do what I'd like to, Jess," he murmured, his lips barely touching the dark crests. "For now, these belong to Jonas." He looked up at her, catching a glimpse of dark hair and shadowed eyes. Her lips were curved indulgently, offering trust and a promise of pleasure.

"Lie down with me," he said softly, and she obeyed, moving beyond him to the back of the bed, pulling the quilt over herself. "You won't need this for now," he told her, lifting it from her hands to toss it at the foot of the bed. "I want to see you, Jess."

"I'm not that much to look at, Finn."

The memory of nights past when he'd taken her with care, guarding against putting pressure on the baby she carried, entered his mind and he could only shake his head.

"You've always been lovely in my eyes," he said. "I wanted you when you were ready to have a baby, and I want you now." He bent his head and his lips took hers in a gentle mating, his hands touching with care the tender flesh he yearned to cover with his own.

"I've never been able to get really close to you, sweetheart," he murmured. "Jonas took up a lot of room. Tonight will be different." His mouth touched her cheek, left a trail of kisses across her throat and beneath her ear and he inhaled the sweet scent he found there.

"Did you bathe tonight?" he asked. "I smell soap."

"This afternoon, while Jonas was asleep and you were at the stream," she told him. "I used the washtub."

"How did you fill it?" he asked. "Those buckets full of water are too heavy for you to lift, Jess. You should have called me in."

She only shook her head and raised her arms to capture him, fingers entwined in his hair as she drew him close. "Maybe I wanted to surprise you. I thought if we were going to…you know—"

He grinned at her, loving the combination of feminine seduction she employed and the innocence revealed by her hesitation to describe what was to come. "If we were going to make love?" he asked, capturing her face between his palms and bending to continue the kisses he'd begun only moments past.

She nodded, allowing her eyelids to flutter shut, and he felt his heart hammer in his chest as he watched the rosy hue of breasts newly aroused, their crests taut and firm. She was perfect, this woman he'd married, and though they faced the certainty of problems ahead, tonight he would make her understand that their marriage was strong enough to withstand any peril from without the walls of their home.

She sighed as his mouth pressed damp kisses on her flesh, smiled as he cupped her breasts and caressed them with a gentle touch, and then as if she savored the aching tenderness he bestowed on her body, she moaned beneath her breath, a whisper that told of pleasure at his hands.

Sweeping his palms to her waist, he admired the newly formed contours where once there had been no definable curve. Then he eased his hands lower, measuring the width of her hips, bending to kiss the flesh where slender white wheals proclaimed the stretching of her skin where Jonas had lain for long months. And as his lips caressed the tiny scars his fingers curled beneath her bottom. She rose to his touch, and her voice whispered his name. In an instinctive movement, her knees lifted, welcoming him to the cradle of her womanhood.

"Jess..." He looked up. His whisper called to her and she responded, her palms curving against his face for a moment before her fingertips brushed his lips. He drew them into his mouth and held them there, and she smiled, her eyes opening to grant him a glimpse of desire in their depths.

He rose to hover over her, his hands more bold now, his fingers seeking her response and with a shiver he hoped was of anticipation she clung to him, drawing him against herself. "Not yet, Jess," he murmured. "Not yet."

Leaving no place unvisited, he explored her body, luring her ever closer to the goal he had set, his mouth tasting the sweetness of her flesh, his fingertips arousing her passion and urging her response. She gave it, unstintingly, her soft cries rising to his hearing, her enchanting whisper calling his name, tempting him beyond the limits of his control.

Fingernails pressed against his shoulders then, and as her knees captured his hips, he sought and found the haven she offered, sliding to its depths, possessing her as he'd never thought to share himself with a woman. Their coming together while she was yet carrying Jonas in her womb had been joyous, but his natural caution had forced him to take special care, lest he hurt her or the child she bore.

Tonight there was no such need for hesitancy. As if they

had been formed for just this joining, their bodies united, melding into one, skin touching skin, muscle against soft curves…man against woman. The ultimate mating of male and female, as it had been since time began. Finn groaned aloud, shuddering as he possessed her flesh, his hands clutching at her shoulders, holding her fast for his taking. And she responded, her legs around him, her arms gathering him to herself.

He spent his seed within her and felt her response, knew the tightening of muscles deep within as she drained him of his masculine essence. And found, to his delight, the depths of peace and comfort he had long craved. His head fell to rest on the pillow beside hers, his breathing slowed and he shuddered as the perspiration that dewed his skin responded to a draft of cool air.

That same draft caused the guttering candle to flare once, and then the darkness overtook them. Finn reached for the quilt and drew it over them, unwilling to leave the warmth she offered, yet aware that his weight was pressing her into the depths of the feather mattress. He stirred, his body shifting as he reluctantly moved from her, and her hold on him tightened.

"Please, Finn. Don't go yet," she whispered, her mouth opening against his throat, her words a husky entreaty he could not refuse.

"I'll crush you," he murmured, wishing he could see her face, his lips exploring once more the swollen lines of her mouth. A mouth he could very well become addicted to, he realized. She was sweet, warm and soft to his touch, and he feared greatly that his heart had been given to her care. Such a gradual process, one day sliding into another, during the past weeks and months, that he had barely noticed the evolving of his enchantment with the woman.

From the day in Saint Louis, when he'd first recognized his desire for her until this moment, he'd become more and more enamored by her strength, her loveliness and her generous spirit. That first, immediate surge of desire had turned, over the weeks, to a deeper yearning than he'd ever known. And that yearning had become a love that overwhelmed him with its power.

If she loved him in return, it would be all he could ever ask of life. And if he had to coax that love into being, if he were forced to spend time without end in bringing her to that same state of being as he, he would work to attain his goal.

He sighed against her temple, his mouth open, the better to savor her essence and the texture of her skin. The room was dark around them, the woman was warm beneath him, and for this moment at least, her heart was beating in time with his.

Gage Morgan stood before the open door, his tall form outlined by the early morning sunlight behind him, and Jessica looked up from the table in surprise.

"I didn't mean to startle you," he said quietly. "I looked for Finn down by the stream, but he doesn't seem to be anywhere about."

"He's gone to see Tom Lansing about helping him with this claim in return for Finn swapping out his time to build a cabin," she said, wishing for a long moment that she didn't feel cornered in her own house.

As though Morgan recognized her discomfort, he stepped back from the door and waved a hand at her. "Come on outside, Jessica. I won't be long."

She nodded and crossed the threshold, then halted, watching him and finding no flaw in the easy smile he offered. "What is it?" she asked. "I'll be glad to tell Finn you were here."

"Just let him know that I'm leaving," he told her. "Tell him I think the danger is over. The men who were trailing the wagon train seem to have given up their hope of snatching this claim. Once Finn registered with the office in

Shadow Creek, it became his, all legal and binding. If those men are half as smart as I think they are…'' His grin gave away his opinion of the crooks, and his shoulders lifted in a dismissive shrug.

''Well, let's just say that they haven't been around. In fact, I haven't seen any sign of them for the past two weeks, and trust me, Jess, I've kept an eye out.''

''Finn said you were going to have them arrested.'' She heard the belligerence in her voice and lifted her chin, her words an attack on his purpose.

''If I find them, I'll do it myself,'' he told her.

''You? And how will you manage that?''

He slid his hand into his pocket and brought forth a folded piece of tanned leather. With a swift movement, he held it open to reveal a badge. She leaned closer and read the identifying word.

Marshal. Her eyes flew to meet his and her mouth tightened. ''You could have told me this before,'' she said accusingly. ''What was the big secret? Did Finn know?'' She viewed him through a veil of scorn. ''Why didn't you do something about all this mess long before now?''

''We wanted to be sure we could nail them and put them away for a long time.'' He sighed and lifted his hands in a gesture of penitence. ''There are several others involved in this ring of criminals, Jess. These two answer to a higher authority, and in the long run, that's the man we're after.'' His mouth was taut and his eyes revealed the anger he did not seek to conceal from her.

''There have been others who lost their claims, all through this area, and in California. The gang is widespread, and bringing in these two men may still be our best chance at nailing the man at the top.''

''And you think these two have disappeared?'' She knew her tone smacked of skepticism, but the constant worry of the past weeks brought her doubt to the forefront.

''They're out there,'' he admitted. ''But unless they're

invisible, they aren't in Shadow Creek. I tend to believe they've notified their boss and are awaiting instructions from him.''

''And you think they'll hightail it out of this area?'' Disbelief tinged her words, but she was so caught up in the knowledge she'd been deceived by this man, and Finn, as a matter of fact, that she threw discretion to the four winds.

''You were in on it with them from where I was standing,'' she said. ''How am I supposed to believe you now?'' And then she thought of his care of her, the rescue he'd effected that night on the prairie.

''They *thought* I was in on it,'' he said, correcting her with a slash of his hand. ''Finn knew all along what was going on. He was with me from the beginning.''

''He didn't act like it most of the time,'' she said defensively, her doubt fading.

''He didn't want me courting you, Jess. He knew I'd marry you in a heartbeat, and he was determined to have you for himself.'' His mouth twisted wryly and he smiled, a sad, bitter gesture that held no humor. ''I'm a lawman, first and foremost, and the chance of me taking a wife never was an issue before this.''

''Well, it was never an issue as far as *I* was concerned,'' she said, retaliating quickly.

He nodded, an acceptance of her edict. ''I know that. You were Finn's from the beginning. That's why the rest of the men pretty much stayed clear of you.''

''I still don't understand why you both kept me in the dark,'' she said. ''I don't know that I can forgive that.''

''Finn and I had to operate separately, for the most part,'' Morgan said. ''If there'd been any hint of my part in this, it couldn't have worked out the way it did. I'd never have had a chance to bring you back to the train that night. As long as those two thought I was in on it, and that I had the favor of their boss, I could keep up with what they did.''

"And now you think they've vamoosed? Given up on the whole thing?"

His face was grim as he hesitated, and then he nodded firmly. "I wouldn't be pulling out if I thought otherwise." He slid his hand into his pocket, returning the leather folder to its place. "If you'll tell Finn I came by, I'd appreciate it. He looked past her, into the shadowed interior of the cabin. "Is the baby doing well?"

"Yes. He eats and sleeps mostly. But he's growing every day."

"He's a lucky little fella," Morgan said softly. "He'll grow up knowing that you and Finn love him."

And didn't that tell her something? she thought, as she nodded her agreement. The man was alone in the world, as alone as the male creatures that roamed the wilds, those masculine beings that held no truck with permanence. There were those who moved from one place to another, like desert nomads, seeking and never finding peace for their souls. Perhaps Morgan was of the same breed...a loner through and through.

He tipped his hat, strode purposefully toward his horse, which stood nearby, reins touching the ground, and with a lithe movement was in his saddle. The horse turned at a touch of the reins against his neck, and Morgan shot her a last, penetrating look as he rode toward the stream. As she watched, his mount forded the shallow, running water and set off at a trot.

Jessica shook herself, wondering at the sadness that overcame her. He was to be pitied, she thought. Alone and lonely, needy of companionship but probably unwilling to admit the lack of it in his life. Turning to the cabin, she entered the door and shifted her attention back to her bread dough. Finn's gift of a small oven she could place in the coals was awaiting its first use, and time was wasting.

Her first warning of his return was the sound of his voice, and she peered out the open door. He rode into sight and she called his name in greeting, then stood in the doorway, watching as he rode closer.

"Morgan was here," she said, hearing the cool tone she could not conceal.

"Was he?" As if the news were of little matter, Finn shrugged, then slid from his horse and approached. "Tom's said he'd lend a hand. We're going to spend mornings at the stream and afternoons both of us cutting trees for a cabin," he said, satisfaction gleaming from his eyes. "We've decided to start tomorrow."

"You don't sound very interested in news about your partner in crime," she said.

"Partner in crime?" He grinned. "You mean Morgan? What's that supposed to mean?" And then he halted before her, his hands already reaching for her. "What happened?" he asked quietly.

"Morgan showed me his marshal's badge," she said. "He said you were both trying to protect me and keep me safe."

"He's right," Finn replied. "What else did he say?"

"That you were both in cahoots from the beginning. That you were working together to catch the men who shot and killed Lyle. That he was leaving…now, today."

"Leaving?" Finn's brow creased. "Does he really think the danger is over?"

"Seems to think so," she told him. "He said there hasn't been any trace of the two men for a while. He thinks they gave up and moved on once you filed the deed for the claim and it was put in your name."

"I'll be surprised if that's so."

"Is that why you told me to keep the gun close by?" she asked.

"You're angry with me, aren't you?" Finn's eyes seemed to see within her and found it not to his liking.

"Yes, I'm angry. I'm downright mad, Finn. You deceived me all along, pretending not to know about Morgan, warning me against him and yet giving me reason to doubt you. You led me on a merry chase, marrying me and using my need for you.''

''Morgan is the lawman, Jess. I'm only the brother of Aaron Carson, the man who was robbed and murdered. It was up to Morgan to call the shots, and I was ready to do whatever it took to make things happen.''

''Even expose me to danger?'' she asked.

''That never should have happened. The fact is, I thought you'd learned your lesson after that night. And then you set off across the prairie all alone, on foot and almost due to have a baby. You were damn lucky you didn't die out there.''

''That would have solved one problem for you,'' she said cuttingly. ''You'd have automatically owned my wagon and its contents.'' *The deed included.* Silently the words stood between them, and for a moment she rued the petty message she'd tossed in his face. And yet, her aching heart was hungry for reassurance.

''I love you, Jess.'' As she watched, his eyes softened, his hands reached for her and she was drawn into his embrace. ''No matter what else you believe, know that I love you.'' The words were spoken through clenched teeth, and he bent to kiss her as if it were imperative that he impress on her the certainty of his claim.

She was held tight against him, on her tiptoes as he drew her upward and laid siege to the softness of her lips. It was not a subtle taking of her mouth, but a demand that she believe his assertion. Jessica stood silently, allowing the caress, unable to respond to his coaxing.

''You're really gonna hang on to this, aren't you?'' he said flatly, lowering her to the ground, holding her until she caught her balance. ''No matter what I say, even if I tell you a hundred times that I love you, you're gonna carry a grudge.''

His jaw formed a rigid angle, as if he gritted his teeth

against words better left unsaid, and then he turned away, only to whip around to face her once more. "Didn't last night mean anything to you, Jess? Couldn't you tell how much I care about you?"

"You were...*horny*," she said softly. "You said so yourself. I was handy, I suppose, or at any rate there was something about me that appealed to you."

"Yeah," he muttered, his hand snatching his hat from his head and slapping it against his thigh. "You were *handy* all right. You gave as good as you got, Jess, and you know that for the truth. I didn't force myself on you."

Honesty seared her conscience with a finger of flame. "No, you didn't force me, or talk me into it, Finn. I needed you last night. I've missed you holding me and loving me."

"Then what's all this about? You know how I feel about you, but we're back to the trust thing, aren't we?"

"Are you sorry you deceived me?" she asked.

He shook his head. "I'd do it again if I had to. Morgan called the shots, I told you. I did as I was told, and my job was to look after you and keep you safe."

"All right, I understand your part, Finn. But I don't have to like it."

"No, you sure as hell don't," he growled. "But I'll tell you, I'm tired of never knowing where I stand with you. I thought we had things all straightened out."

"Dinner will be ready at noon," she told him, turning back to the cabin. "I'll call you in."

He stalked off across the long stretch of grass leading to the stream, and she looked back over her shoulder to watch his progress. Maybe she should have let it go, accepted that he'd done what he thought was best. Her shoulders slumped as she crossed the threshold. Once more they were on the outs, and this time it didn't look like Finn would be making any effort to heal the breach between them.

Chapter Sixteen

The day dragged by, the sun seeming to stand still overhead as Jessica worked inside the cabin, then carried the heavy tub outside to wash Jonas's diapers and hang them to dry. She pinned them on the line, aware of Finn's presence as she completed the task. Then, before she could lift the heavy tub to dump the water, he was beside her, moving her to one side as he lifted it with ease and emptied it farther from the house.

"I could have done that," she said, waiting for him to return the tub to her.

"I suppose you could," he replied. "But I did it. I told you before, the tub's too heavy for you to handle when it's full of water."

"Thank you," she said grudgingly, her good manners winning out over the tendency to sputter at his opinion of what she could and couldn't do without harm to herself.

He stalked off to his interrupted work and she dragged the tub to the back door, turning it upside down on the ground before she went back inside. The baby awoke then, and what with nursing him, changing him again, and lying beside him on the bed until he went back to sleep, she found herself dozing off.

Supper was a silent affair, and Finn went out to feed the

stock and bring the oxen in from where he'd staked them for the day. "I'll take them with me to Tom's tomorrow after dinner," he said quietly when he came back in. "If you don't mind, I'll ask him to eat here to save time before we start cutting trees. I figure the oxen will come in handy to snake the logs back to their clearing."

She lifted her shoulders in a shrug and wiped the table dry with a dish towel, then looked up quickly as he spoke again. "He said he'd bring Arlois along with him in the morning. She wants to talk to you."

Her heart lifted at the thought of having another woman with her all morning long, especially when Arlois was the female in question. "That's fine," she told him. "I'll make enough dinner for all of us."

Her nap kept her awake far into the night, and even the warmth of Finn's backside pressed against hers as he slept did not relieve the chill she felt. Guilt was like a blanket over her, and its weight held no comfort. She rose at dawn and added wood to the fireplace, blowing on the banked coals to coax the flame to life. Behind her, Finn dressed and left the cabin, and returned just as she put breakfast on the table.

She thought to please him, frying up a panful of sausage gravy, white stuff that held chunks of seasoned pork, to go along with the simple fare of everyday biscuits. A dozen of her precious eggs were worth the price of the sausage at the store, and along with fried eggs and fresh biscuits, she thought the meal might be construed as a peace offering. Finn split the last biscuit, using it to mop up his egg yolk.

"Good breakfast," he said, almost as if he begrudged the words of praise. He glanced over at the fireplace where the new oven resided. The biscuits had baked and risen nicely in the new oven, and Jessica thought of how Finn's gift had lightened her chore of baking.

Tempted to thank him again for it, she hesitated at his

dour look. It decided her abruptly, and she kept her mouth shut. At least being on the outs with her hadn't dampened his appetite any. But the lack of a hug as he left the cabin squelched her attempt at good humor.

Arlois arrived before the chores were finished, and the two women greeted each other with squeals of delight, hugging as if it hadn't been only a few days since they had last met. The baby was duly admired, and Arlois held him as she spoke of the rocking chair Tom had carried inside. That awkward piece of furniture had traveled across the prairie tied to her wagon, and now it seemed she was ready to lend it for Jonas's sake.

"You need it worse than I do right now," she said. "I'll take it back when Jonas is too old to be rocked."

Jessica was hard put to hold back tears at the generous gesture, but managed to set her reluctance aside long enough to sit down with the baby in her arms, sending the chair into motion with a nudge of her toe against the floor. "I'd love to have one," she said. "My mama always kept a rocker in the parlor."

"I'll warrant Finn would order one for you from the general store," Arlois said. "He'd do most anything in the world to make you happy, Jess."

"Not lately," Jessica replied, her head bent as she felt hot tears wash across her eyes. "He's upset with me. And to tell you the truth, I'm still mad at him, too." She looked up at Arlois, seeking an ally.

"Morgan came by and let the cat out of the bag. The man carries a badge. It seems he's a marshal, and he was in cahoots with Finn all during the trip from Saint Louis. They never let on that they knew each other, and between them they sure fooled me."

"And you're feeling real put upon, aren't you?" Arlois's smile was crooked and Jessica thought it held a good amount of sympathy. But her next words put paid to that thought. "I'm sure Finn was looking out for you, Jess. Men have different codes to live by than women. If the law was involved, then maybe he could only do as he was told.''

Jessica's chin lifted and anger brought an edge to her words. ''After he married me, I would think I deserved to know what was going on.''

''Men don't think the way we do, Jess. David didn't always tell me everything either, and I don't remember my father ever giving away any secrets.'' She grimaced a bit as if she remembered things better left forgotten. ''I think I decided when I married David that I'd just take him like he was and enjoy what we had. All men are a pain in the patoot once in a while.''

''But not when it comes to a life-and-death thing,'' Jessica said vehemently. ''I trusted Finn.''

Arlois persisted. ''And he seems worthy of that, from where I'm standing.''

Jessica felt her shoulders slump. ''I'm tired of arguing with him. I just want things to be on an even keel between us.'' She shot Arlois a glance of speculation. ''You really think I should just trust him blindly to do what's right for me and the baby? Is that what you'd do?''

''That's what I'm about to do with Tom,'' Arlois confessed. ''I feel kinda like this is what David would want for me. I miss him dreadfully, and I suspect I'll always remember what we had together, but Tom is taking hold and looking after me.'' She lifted her eyebrows as if surprise had touched her with a wand. ''You know, I think I'm getting to enjoy his pampering. David always depended on me to be strong, and for the first time in my life, I can lean a bit, and it's a comfort.''

''When will you get married?'' Jessica asked.

''Maybe in a couple of weeks. Tom said as soon as he can get the first logs laid for the cabin he's going to ask some of the men to lend a hand for a day. If he and Finn can drag enough logs in from the woods, it won't take long

to put it together. And then we'll ask the preacher in
Shadow Creek to marry us.''

"I'm happy for you," Jessica said. "I think you're doing
the right thing."

The new oven was duly admired and put to good use as
Arlois readied a venison stew for roasting in its depths.
Three hours would be long enough, they decided, to turn
it tender and tasty with the addition of wild onions for
flavor. And when the men came in after noontime for dinner, it was ready.

Finn's look held a hint of regret, Jessica thought, and she
made a special effort to touch his shoulder as she served
him at the table, then sat beside him and allowed her palm
to rest on his thigh. He shot her a glance, and his eyebrows
raised, but the hand that covered hers was warm and his
fingers wove themselves between hers in a satisfying fashion. The muscles beneath her grip tensed, and she recognized the quick intake of breath he made no effort to conceal.

So easily it was repaired, she thought, this breach in their
marriage, and she bent her head for a moment, thankful for
Finn's willingness to mend their fences.

The men headed off downstream, the oxen before them,
yoked and ready to work. Arlois climbed into the wagon,
and Jessica stood in the doorway to wave a farewell. "Are
you sure you won't come along, Jess?" Arlois asked, lifting
the reins.

Jessica hesitated a moment, tempted by the suggestion,
and then shook her head. "I'm going to cook something
special for supper tonight, maybe see if I can bake a cake
in the new oven."

"All right," Arlois said easily. "I'll see you in a day or
so. The men sharing time like this is going to make it easier
for you and me to keep up with each other, isn't it?" She
snapped the reins over the horses' backs and the wagon
rolled off.

An hour later, Jessica was deeply engrossed in a notebook of recipes her mother had written out for her on a day many years before. Nostalgia swept through her as she read the notes scrawled in the margins, hints for success in cooking meringue and a basic recipe for pound cake that seemed a likely choice for Finn's dessert tonight.

A shadow dimmed the light from the doorway and Jessica looked up quickly, startled by the silent approach of her visitor. One look at the man who watched her from cunning eyes brought a soft cry from her lips, and she jumped up hastily, the chair falling on the floor behind her. Jonas was sleeping in his basket, and she snatched him up, holding him against her breast.

"Well, well, look at what we have here," the visitor said quietly. "Just the person I've been hoping to run into."

Familiar features brought a chill to Jessica's spine as the man stepped into the cabin, and she shuddered as he approached her with grim purpose in every movement. Behind him the second man waited on the doorstep.

"What do you want?" Jessica asked, her voice trembling, already knowing the answer to her question.

"The gold your man has been taking from the stream, for starters. And you can bet your bottom dollar we'll find it, if we have to tear this cabin apart, lady. And then you're going to write him a letter telling him if he wants to see you again, he needs to go into Shadow Creek and change the name on the deed to this claim. He can either play the game with us or lose both his wife and the brat he took on when he got married."

"No one is going to believe Finn would do such a thing," Jessica said quickly. "I'll give you the gold, gladly, if you'll just leave here right now." She paused, hoping they would take the bait, aware that a loose board beneath the table hid the cache where Finn had placed a goodly portion of nuggets he'd accumulated over the past few days.

"Where'd he hide it?"

His gaze pierced her and Jessica felt a chill touch her spine. It was no time for stalling, she decided, and pointed beneath the table. "Under that board."

In moments, a canvas sack was clutched in the man's hand and his eyes had the gleam of greed as he held it high.

"Can't you be satisfied with that?" Jessica asked quietly.

"This is just for starters, lady," the crook said, tossing the bag to his partner.

"But if he changes the name on the deed…" She hesitated. "Whose name would he put on it?"

"We'll tell you the name when you get busy writing your note to him. And just to be sure he tags along behind us, you're gonna tell him we'll drop you and the baby off the top of the pass just south of here, if he don't show up by nightfall," the first man said. "He'll do it, or let the mountain lions and bears have a chance at you."

Jessica thought rapidly, and her words were skeptical. "And when he does that? What then? All he'll have to do is tell the sheriff what happened, and you'll both be in jail."

The second man grinned. "Yeah," he said with a shrug. "But since Carson isn't going to make it back alive once he sets off to find you, it won't matter much. And if you don't want to write the letter to him, we will. I'll bet six bits he'll be hightailin' it to town in no time flat to get that deed changed."

"Don't count on it," Jessica said sharply. "This claim is the most important thing in the world to him."

"Well, when we let him know that his wife and baby are needin' to be rescued, I'll lay odds that it won't take him long to come lookin' for you." Satisfaction was alive on the man's features as he picked up Jessica's chair and pushed her toward it. "Either you write it, or I'll take that baby and leave you here."

Jessica grasped the tiny form tightly. "He'll die without me and you know it."

"Yeah." A leer twisted his mouth in an ugly parody of a smile and his hand dug into her shoulder. "Sit down, Mrs. Carson, and write your man a note."

The sheet of paper was liberally spotted with tearstains but the message was clear. Jessica's handwriting spelled out the stipulations, leaving no doubt in Finn's mind what his choices were. Either he changed the deed to Mort Green's name, or Jessica and the baby would be left to die in a mountain pass. And according to a postscript, written in an unfamiliar, scrawling hand, someone would be watching him to be certain that he did as he was told. A copy of the new deed was to be brought with him.

"How the hell did this happen?" Tom asked, his anger visible as his hands clenched against his sides. "They just walked in here and took her?"

"Must have surprised her," Finn said. "I'd told her to keep the gun handy, but we both thought it was pretty safe. Before Morgan left town, he told Jess and me both that those two men hadn't been seen hereabouts for the past weeks." He bent his head, inhaling deeply as if his lungs were craving air.

"I should have taken her with me this afternoon. Hell, I should have known right off something was up when you brought me back in your wagon. My horse isn't staked out. They must have taken him, too."

"What are you going to do?" Tom asked. "I'll take you into Shadow Creek, but if you change that deed—"

Finn looked up quickly and cut off Tom's words. "I'll leave a note for the sheriff. I don't dare stop by his office, in case they're not bluffing and they've left someone in town to watch me. And if I have to, I'll give them the damn claim. I want Jess back," he said, his voice ringing with a truth that brooked no denial. "I can find gold somewhere else, but there's only one woman for me, and I won't take the chance of losing her.''

"You've got no guarantee that they'll let you go, Carson," Tom said bluntly. "Once they have their hands on the deed, you'll be a dead man."

Finn nodded. "That's probably their plan, but I have to take the chance that I'll be able to sneak up on them, maybe get Jessica out of there without them catching on."

"I'll go with you," Tom said firmly. "I'll follow along behind, maybe snatch them red-handed."

Finn hesitated, reluctant to accept the offer. "I'm asking you to risk your life if you go along, Tom. You've got a woman and her kids depending on you now."

"Arlois would kill me herself if she thought I'd let you ride out alone," Tom retorted.

"Yeah, and that's another problem. I'm going to have to find a horse to ride. My guess is that they put Jessica and the baby on mine and led them along behind."

"We're wasting time standing here talking about it," Tom told him. "Get what you need and close this place up."

Her knees were sore from gripping the sides of Finn's horse, the only thing holding her in place the saddle horn she clutched with one hand. But the baby slept, probably enjoying the rocking motion of the horse she rode, Jessica thought hopefully. They'd gone in a roundabout fashion outside of town and headed south, making no attempt to hide their tracks.

"What if he don't change the name on the deed?" the larger of the two men asked the other.

"He'll change it. It's the only way he'll get the woman back."

"I told you. He won't come after me," Jessica told them, fighting tears that already mourned the baby she held. "Please, just take my baby back to town. I don't care what you do with me, but this baby hasn't done anything to deserve this.''

"He was born, lady. He's Beaumont's kid, and that's his tough luck. Now shut up, or we'll find a nice handy place to drop you over a cliff and then wait for your man to come following us.''

And they would, too, Jessica thought dejectedly. Obviously life was of little value to them, with the exception of their own. Finn's horse followed docilely behind the second man, and she clung tightly for balance. She looked back over her shoulder when it seemed the men up ahead were intent on their plotting, but except for a dust devil far to the north, she saw nothing that might indicate a rescue effort.

"They're not too far ahead," Finn told Tom, pointing at fresh tracks where several horses had dug up the soil as they'd plowed their way up a hill. "Maybe we'll catch a glimpse when we top this rise.''

"I'll stay back," Tom told him. "If you see anything, I'll go round about and keep you in sight if I can." He halted his horse and waited as Finn's mount scrabbled up the foothill before them.

In a few minutes, Finn brought his horse to a halt and looked south at the rough ground that bore faint tracks where three riders had passed by. A trail snaked up a steeper rise ahead and he narrowed his eyes, attempting to make out small figures that moved against the rough terrain. There wasn't much doubt in his mind. Jessica was on one of those horses.

That he was visible, silhouetted against the horizon, was a given. They'd be watching for him. He turned back to where Tom waited and lifted his hand cautiously.

"They're up ahead?" Tom called, and Finn nodded.

"I'll cut to the north and ride along the edge of the tree

line,'' Tom said. "Give me a few minutes head start before you ride on.''

Finn waited, knowing he presented a handy target, but gambling that the men he followed wanted to see the altered deed before they made a move. The note he'd left for the sheriff gave him hope that help would be on the way, and his only regret was that Morgan had ridden out of town only that morning. He could have used the lawman at his back.

Impatient with the delay, he swung down from his saddle and made a pretense of examining his horse's hoof, then squatted beside the animal, tilting his hat brim a bit, the better to shade his vision. The sun was already touching the top of the mountains in the west, and soon the path would be more difficult to follow. He watched the three small figures ahead, aware that they had slowed their pace. Either they were having difficulties with the trail, or perhaps Jessica had slowed them down.

Jessica looked back again, torn between a yearning for Finn to be following them and the knowledge that his life was in peril because of her. "He's back there,'' one of the men said harshly. He lifted a scope to his eye, and his lips thinned in a grimace. "Looks like his horse has a problem with a shoe. Carson's stopped. I'd say he's pickin' at a stone or something.''

"Do you think he's alone?'' the second man asked. "I'm thinking I'd feel better if we'd heard from Morgan before we started this.''

His partner laughed. "Morgan's hightailed it out of town. I think he gave up on the deal once Carson laid claim to the deed.'' His leer touched Jessica and he jerked on the lead line, causing her mount to lurch into movement. "We got the woman. We don't need Morgan. He's too softhearted, anyway.''

"You got what it takes to kill a kid?'' The other man

looked dubiously at Jessica and the baby she held. "I don't want any part of that, Mort."

"You'll do what you're told. Once we hit that vein, we'll clean up and be on our way. There's too many miners up and down that stream for the law to worry about one man who rode off and never came back." He reached back and touched his saddlebag, grinning as he gloated over its contents. "There's enough gold in here to make this whole thing worthwhile. It won't take no time to make a fortune."

Jessica swallowed her anger and frustration with difficulty. Finn had worked long and hard for that bag of nuggets. Not to mention all they'd gone through to get across the prairie. If Finn was killed because of her... She could not bear the thought, and determinedly set aside the fate these men had in mind for her, and concentrated on something she might do to thwart their purpose.

Glancing back again, she found no trace of Finn, until a movement caught her eye and she made out a figure on horseback. Seemingly in no great hurry, he nevertheless was gaining ground, and she heard one of the men ahead of her laugh.

"I could pick him off from here," he said, lifting his rifle to his shoulder.

"I want my hands on that deed first," Mort said. "We got time." He nudged his horse into a quicker pace, and Jessica clung tightly to the saddle horn, holding the baby with aching arms.

They crowned a peak, and for a moment the wind caught them, chilling her to the bone. And then their mounts picked their way down a rocky slope and she knew they were lost to Finn's sight. Ahead, a stream cut through the tree line to the west and then crossed the trail they followed. Trees grew alongside its banks, and Jessica kept a lookout for a sheltered place where she might persuade the men to allow her to stop for a few minutes.

"I need to feed the baby," she called out. "He's gone past time for him to eat, and he's getting restless."

"You can do that while you're riding along," Mort told her. "We're not stoppin' for that."

Jessica injected a note of pleading in her voice. "I really need to get off this horse for a few minutes," she said. "I won't be long."

As if he read her meaning, Mort looked back at her, his expression grim. "Once we cross the stream, we'll give you five minutes to yourself," he said. "But we keep the kid while you do your business."

"All right," she acceded quickly, and concentrated on the rough trail ahead. A movement to her right caught her eye and she lowered her head toward the baby and then shifted her gaze in that direction. There, where the tree line merged into the pines, where the stream bent its way southeast, another glimpse of color appeared for just a moment.

Her heart beat more rapidly. Perhaps Finn had been able to bring help with him. Maybe Tom or even the sheriff were shadowing their trail from the woods to the west. She bent her head, her lips touching the baby's head, whispering soft words that spoke the message of her heart, a petition for Finn's safety and that of her child.

In less than five minutes they were crossing the shallow stream, and in the shadows beneath the trees on the far side, the men dismounted and turned to her. Mort reached up, grasping her roughly about the waist and hauling her from the tall gelding to stand on the ground. Her legs trembled beneath her, and she leaned against the horse's front shoulder.

"Give me a minute," she said. "I've got cramps from holding on so tight." Her thighs felt sore, the muscles protesting the long ride, and with a suspicious look, Mort hesitated.

"Don't play games with me, lady. You got about ten minutes to get what you need to do done. If you want to waste time standing here and feeling sorry for yourself, that's up to you. You're gettin' back on that horse as soon as they're watered and we're ready to ride on."

"You gonna let her take that baby with her?" the second man asked Mort.

Mort looked around the area and shrugged. "There's no place for her to go from here." He shot a look at his partner. "Unless you're volunteering."

Jessica straightened and walked away, her legs moving with an effort, her eyes scanning the brush for a likely spot. Only one area held promise, where bushes seemed taller and branches drooped close to the ground. She'd been truthful in her plea for time alone, and after depositing the baby on the ground, she sorted out her clothing and hastily tended to business.

Jonas was fretting by the time she was able to pick him up and she hushed him, holding him over her shoulder as she stepped from the protection of the shelter she'd chosen. A soft murmur caught her attention and she paused, her breath catching in her throat. Again it came, and she turned cautiously, lest the men be watching.

"Jessica." The whisperer called her name and she trembled, recognizing the voice.

Tom. Looking down at the ground at her feet, she took a careful step, then another. "Jessica, come here," Tom murmured, his voice so low she barely caught the words. Her feet seemed unable to move, yet in a moment she'd changed direction and was heading toward his hiding place.

A voice called her name, a curse ringing out. "You can't get away," the man shouted. And then from beside her the sound of a gun split the air and she fell to the ground, sheltering Jonas beneath her. She lifted her head a bit, conscious of Tom moving toward her and then he was sprawled almost atop her, offering the protection of his body.

A shout from the men by the stream was followed by

splashing water and the sight of both men attempting to slide their rifles from behind their saddles. The horses milled and whinnied, attempting to reach the water, blocking Tom's view of his target.

Down the hill, beyond the melee before her, another rider appeared, and she recognized Finn, knew at a glance the width of his shoulders and the dark hat he wore. Bent low over the horse's neck, he rode at a reckless pace, catching the two crooks unaware. Mort cursed loudly, finally able to reach for his rifle, and in that instant Jessica heard a shot from over her head.

Mort dropped where he stood, his gun at his side, and the other man snatched at his own weapon in a last-ditch attempt. As he turned to lift the long gun, aiming it wildly at Finn, Tom fired again, his bullet hitting its target even as Finn leveled his own weapon on the still-standing kidnapper. A red stain blossomed on the man's shoulder, another appeared on his leg, and he dropped the rifle and sank to the ground.

Jessica heard the whimper of the child beneath her and she shifted, allowing him the freedom to fill his lungs and protest loudly at his treatment. It was a wail of distress such as she'd never heard, and for a moment she feared she'd crushed him as she fell. The quilt fell from his head and she caught a glimpse of eyes squinted shut and crimson cheeks as he squalled his anger aloud.

"He sounds mad," Tom ventured from beside her. And then as Finn splashed through the stream, riding his horse at full tilt, Tom rose and waved a hand in welcome. "It's about time you showed up," he said. "Thought I was gonna have to clean up this mess by myself."

Finn ignored him, his full attention on Jessica, reaching her as she struggled to her feet, and clasping her against himself. Her face was buried in the folds of his heavy shirt and the baby protested loudly at the indignity of being squeezed between them. "Jess." He spoke her name as if it were with his last breath, as though he'd reached for and sought some prize he'd thought beyond reach. His mouth was against her forehead, his hands widespread against her back. Then as Jonas uttered another squawk, Finn inhaled sharply and his words were tempered with fear.

"The baby—is the baby all right? He's crying, Jess. Did they hurt him?" He pushed her away a few inches and his hands fell from her to gather the infant to himself. "I should have aimed to kill," he muttered darkly. "If they hurt Jonas, I swear I'll—"

"He's all right," Jessica said sharply. "Really, Finn. He's just mad because he's hungry and we squashed him in between us when you hugged me."

"You're sure?" As if he could not quite believe her assertion, Finn held the baby before his face, scanning him as he searched for damage to the precious piece of humanity he'd claimed as his own. "He's red as a beet, Jess. Did he get too much sun?"

"He's mad, Finn," she said, rescuing Jonas from Finn's clutching fingers. The baby nestled against her throat and rooted against her skin as he caught the scent of his mother's milk. "In a minute, sweetheart," she crooned, and cuddled him close.

"These two are out of commission," Tom called from near the stream. "What do you want me to do with them?"

"Load them on their horses. We'll take them back to Shadow Creek. Unless the sheriff catches up with us in the next little while." He looked down at Jessica. "Why don't you sit under that tree and nurse the baby, get him quieted down, while I help Tom with cleaning up the clutter?"

She nodded and did as he asked, shivering with relief. Finn returned to her and brought with him a coat from the bundle he'd tied behind his saddle. Draping it over her shoulders, he wrapped her in its folds and she smiled her thanks. Jonas settled down to nurse with a will and as she watched, the dead man was slung over his saddle and the wounded criminal was hoisted onto his horse's back. His whimpering protests went unanswered but for a threatening look from Tom as he discovered the canvas sack of nuggets beneath Mort's body.

"I believe this belongs to you," he told Finn, and then grinned as Finn gave little notice. "I can see how high gold rates with you," Tom teased. "You're more interested in that pair over there than a small fortune in nuggets." He looked at Jessica and winked broadly.

"I've already got a fortune," Finn told him. "Had it before I got to Shadow Creek. Too bad it took me till today to find out its value." He shot a glance toward Jessica and she saw in his eyes a look she found hard to interpret. As if he could not bring forth the words he wanted to speak, he only shook his head. "I'll talk to you when I get you back home," he promised, and she hugged to herself the message he'd left unspoken.

An hour later they were traveling in a line, the two kidnappers between Tom and Finn, Jessica settled sideways on his lap, she and the baby wrapped in the warm coat. Ahead, several riders called out a greeting, and within minutes the small caravan was surrounded by the sheriff and three other men from town. "I guess you didn't need us after all," the sheriff said, eyeing the two prisoners. "What went on out there?"

Jessica spoke up quickly. "These men took me and my baby, Sheriff. They were going to kill all of us, Finn included. And all for a piece of land."

"Well—" The sheriff grinned at her. "If you're tryin' to defend your husband there, Mrs. Carson, you needn't bother. Nobody's goin' to cry much over a couple of crooks. Even if one of them is still alive, he won't be for long, once the judge gets done with him." He looked up at Finn. "Did he get hold of that deed?"

Finn shook his head. "No, didn't get close enough to touch it."

"Did you change it like they wanted you to?" Jessica asked.

Finn grinned at her. "Not a chance. Once I thought about it, I decided it was my ace in the hole. I planned on using it to bargain for you if I had to. The sheriff knew what was going on as soon as the fella in the assayer's office took him my message. I was counting on this bunch showing up in time to rescue us."

"Well, we'll take these fellas in hand and let you folks find your way back home," the sheriff said with a grin. "I think that woman of yours looks like she could use a good night's sleep, Carson."

Chapter Seventeen

The little church in Shadow Creek was filled almost to capacity, and dusty miners sat side by side with townsfolk who'd gussied up for the event. The piano borrowed from the saloon across the road played a rousing version of a ballad as Arlois and Tom walked together down the center aisle. On the front bench, in a place of honor, Finn and Jessica beamed their approval of the wedding about to take place.

"Will the witnesses step forward," the black-clad minister requested, eyeing Finn as he spoke. Taking Jessica's arm, Finn escorted her to stand beside Arlois and he moved to flank Tom. A enormous bouquet of wildflowers threatened to overflow Arlois's embrace, and her eyes were glistening with happy tears as she smiled in Jessica's direction. In lieu of a bouquet, Jessica held Jonas, his eyes wide as he observed those gathered around him.

"I reckon the baby can serve as witness, too," the preacher said cordially. "Though I doubt he'll be able to sign the registry afterward."

"I want him here with us," Arlois said in an undertone. "I'm claiming an interest in him."

The ceremony was short, the kiss lengthy, as the minister instructed the groom in his obligation to the bride, and then the two couples left the church in a flurry of good wishes. They paused outside the front door and waited for the congregation to follow them. From the threshold the preacher called out an invitation to a party beneath the trees in the churchyard, where his wife stood ready with several of the ladies from town to serve the guests.

Polly watched with a big smile, her husband beside her giving out handbills to everyone, advertising his new blacksmith shop. "We decided there was more sure cash dollars in shoeing horses than in freezing your arse off in a mountain stream hoping to find gold," she said with a hearty laugh.

"Depends on where your claim lies," Finn said, shooting a triumphant glance at Jessica. He'd only this morning deposited an enormous amount of gold in the assayer's safe, and once the money changed hands, his bank balance would soar. Long days spent in the pursuit of gold from Aaron's claim were paying off. Unless Finn missed his guess, there was enough to be found in the stream and beneath the ground, where he suspected a vein lay beneath the surface, to last him and his family for the rest of their lives.

The party was noisy, the men raucous and uninhibited, and the ladies delighted to have an occasion to celebrate. Several men slept beneath trees before the sun dropped behind the majestic mountains to the west, and weary children were deposited in wagons for the ride home. Finn and Jessica found themselves in the back of Tom's wagon, the canvas top having been taken off and used for covering a lean-to for his livestock.

The ride home was long enough for Jessica to become sleepy and Finn held her close, lifting the combined weight of his wife and the infant she held from the rear of the wagon when they reached the clearing where their cabin stood. With a wave of his hand, he sent Tom and Arlois on their way, the two boys perched behind the seat on crates.

The cabin was dark, but Finn lit the candle near the door, and then pulled down the kerosene lantern he'd installed over the table. "Hang on, Jess," he said softly, so as not to awaken the baby. "I'll get his basket ready for him."

Leaving her on a chair, he fluffed the pillow they'd given the baby for a soft mattress and then gathered the child from his mother's arms and placed him carefully in the basket. His big hands were gentle as he covered the tiny form and tucked the quilt around him.

Behind him Jessica waited, and he closed the door before he turned back to face her. "You all right?" he asked, leaning against the heavy portal. She was weary, but radiant, her eyes shining in the light from the candle. Her hair gleamed softly as the lamp overhead cast its glow upon her, and he thought he'd never seen so beautiful a sight.

She was his, his alone. He savored the thought, then stepped closer and knelt before her. Gathering her hands to lie in his palms, he looked down at her fingers, tracing them with his own, then turned them to see the calluses she bore from the everyday chores that made up her life here in this place.

"You deserve better than this, Jess," he murmured, lifting her hands to press his lips against their palms. One, then the other, were given the homage of his lips and he heard her whisper of protest as she shifted in the chair.

"I have everything I ever wanted, right here with you," she whispered.

"It's not enough," he told her, "but it will be better soon, sweetheart. We'll have a bigger cabin by the first snowfall, I promise you. Maybe we'll just add on to this one for now, but a year or so down the road, I'm going to build you a nice big house farther back from the stream, up on the hill."

"Can we afford it?" she asked, reaching to tilt his face upward, then bending to touch her mouth to his.

"Um…" His reply was lost in the blending of their lips, and then he laughed softly as he stood before her and pulled her from the chair and into his embrace. "We have more money than I ever dreamed of, Jess. One of these days, when this part of the world is filled with cities like Boston and Philadelphia and New York, our children and their sons and daughters will have a legacy from this piece of land."

"I can't fathom that," she told him. "All I ever wanted was to be happy with someone who would love me and be good to me."

"I'm trying to be good to you," he said, his gaze touching her with a passion he could barely contain. "And I love you more than I ever thought I could love a woman."

"Do you? Truly, Finn?" she asked, yearning overflowing her eyes as tears formed and dampened her cheeks.

"I only want to take care of you and Jonas for the rest of my life. And if all goes well, we'll add to the number of children beneath our roof," he promised. "I want a house full of little girls who look like their mother and a couple more boys to lend a hand once we get a barn built and some livestock brought in."

"We have chickens already," she reminded him. "And Polly's on the lookout for a cow for us."

He laughed softly. "Those chickens were more trouble than they were worth, hauling them across the prairie. But I'd probably have bought you a whole menagerie if you'd asked for it that day in Council Grove. As to a cow, we'll probably be needing one, especially once you stop nursing Jonas. I figure we'd better plan on learning how to milk it." His arms enclosed her more tightly and he rocked her in his embrace. "Do you think it's time for bed, sweetheart?"

"I wouldn't be surprised," she said agreeably. "Now that Jonas is sleeping through the night, I may be able to—"

Her breath left her in a rush as he snatched her off her feet and into his arms. "You won't be sleeping for a while tonight, Mrs. Carson," he said, his voice roughened with a desire that he'd kept pent up for the past several hours. "I have plans for you."

His touch was gentle as he rid her of her clothing, and his kisses followed the path his hands took, admiring her curves, leaving her breathless and trembling as he spent his passion over the length of her feminine form. He stood finally, lifting her to the center of the bed and joining her there in mere moments.

She was what he'd yearned for, the center of his life, the very epitome of all he'd ever dreamed of in a woman. And now, with the force of a man bent on seduction, he coaxed her response to his caresses and brought her to peak after peak of fulfillment. She clung to him, begging for his possession, her arms enclosing him, her fingers grasping at his shoulders and back.

"I love you, Jess." It was a pledge he gave unstintingly as he acceded to her plea, blending their bodies with care, reining in the urgent need that set his blood afire and threatened to escape his control. His muscled arms flexed about her, holding her close, bringing her with him to that place where their souls met and lingered, where their hearts touched, and where their bodies knew a pleasure so profound they could barely contain the joyous delights it lavished upon their flesh.

He whispered it again and heard her response murmured in his ear as they lay in a tangle of arms and legs, content for the moment in the center of the bed. Breathless and damp, their mouths meeting again and again, as if the thirst for pleasure could not be quenched, as though their hunger for each other would never be satisfied. And when at last they curled together, Jessica murmured her love for him once more, as if she could not tell him enough of the passion that filled her being and spilled over to saturate the man she had married.

"How long have you loved me?" he asked, idly wrapping a strand of her hair around his finger, unwilling to drift off to sleep and thus end this day.

"I don't know," she answered after a moment. "Maybe it came about so gradually I barely noticed. Or maybe it was when you helped me birth Jonas. Or perhaps the first time you loved me, out on the prairie, beneath the stars." She stirred and turned to face him.

"And you, Finn? When did you first love me?" she asked, her palm curving against his cheek.

"In Saint Louis, I think," he said quietly. "At least that was the beginning. I knew you were the only woman I'd ever wanted so badly. There was such a need burning inside my soul I could barely abide the pain of it. And then when you said you'd marry me, I knew that heaven had opened and allowed me a glimpse of paradise."

She smiled at him in the faint glow of the candle that had all but burned to its base. "I didn't know you were so eloquent, Finn."

"Only with you," he told her. And then bent to her again, holding her in thrall to his kisses and caresses, taking her once more on a journey that would transport them to that place where lovers dwell.

September 1864

Abigail Elizabeth Carson was born early on that September morning, making her entrance with barely a whimper on her mother's part, but with deep sighs of relief from the man who stood by as an observer.

"It was easier, I think, when I was the one calling the shots," Finn said as Polly and Arlois tended his new daughter. He held Jessica close, and their whispers blended as they celebrated this most significant of days. Although Jonas would always be a child born into his hands, and a boy who had filled Finn's heart to overflowing with a father's love, this little girl was the first infant born who would carry his life's blood in her veins.

He heard the toddling footsteps of his son as Tom led Jonas into the bedroom, and opened his arm to accept the boy onto his lap. "You have a sister," he told the two-year-old. "Her name is Abby. Do you like that?"

Jonas tilted his head as if he considered the idea, and then grinned as though he found it agreeable. "Abbeee," he mimicked after a moment, and then leaned to kiss his mother. "Mama," he said loudly. "Get up."

Finn laughed at the boy's demand. "Your mama is going to stay in bed for a day or so, son. She's tired out."

As though he decided his demands were in vain, Jonas slid from Finn's lap and returned to Tom. "I don't think he's much impressed with the new arrival," Tom said with a laugh.

"How about you?" Jessica asked, her voice weary. "Take a look and see what you think of her."

Tom dutifully crossed the room to where Arlois bathed the tiny little girl and examined the pink bundle knowingly. "So that's what a girl looks like," he murmured, and bent to touch his lips to the downy head. "Hope you've taken a good look, honey," he told Arlois. "When ours gets out of the oven, I'm hoping for a duplicate of this one."

"You'll take what you get and like it," Arlois said, frowning with mock dismay at him. And then she smiled wistfully. "I hope it's a girl, though. It would be nice to give you a son, Tom, but I really want a girl."

"I've already got two sons," he told her gently. "Couldn't love David's boys more if they were my own flesh and blood." And then he basked in the warmth of her gaze.

"I know exactly how he feels," Finn said as he smiled

at Tom's words of commitment to his wife. "I have something for you," he told Jessica then. "I've been saving it for a long time. My mother told me it was to be given upon the birth of my first child, and I've kept it tucked away in a package with my father's watch ever since that day."

"I never knew that," Jessica said, her eyes wondering as he left the bedside to open a dresser drawer.

He found what he sought and returned to her, a small box in his hand. Offering it into her keeping, he sat beside her again and watched as she opened the lid. Within the velvet-lined container lay a silver locket, embellished with a blue columbine, painted in delicate detail. Jessica opened it with care and found two tiny miniatures, a man and woman, whose eyes seemed to be focused on each other.

"Your parents?" she asked, her voice soft as she touched the two faces with the tip of her index finger.

"My parents," he confirmed. "But we're going to change the pictures, Jess, just as soon as I can arrange to have an artist brought in from Denver to paint them for us. I want you and me in it, for our children, and our grandchildren to follow. I'll keep my parents' pictures and we'll do something else with them, but this is going to be an inheritance for Abigail to pass down the line, perhaps to a niece or granddaughter someday."

"Can I wear it?" Jessica asked. "Just for a while, and then I'll put it away and keep it as an heirloom."

"No, you'll wear it as long as you live, Jess," he said firmly. "An heirloom should be seen and appreciated. *Cherished* might be a better word," he added. "As you'll be cherished, sweet—for the rest of our lives together."

She nodded in agreement. "All right, Finn." She looked at the pictures again and her smile was sad as she held the gift in her hands. "I'd like to know your parents."

"Maybe someday we'll send for them," he told her. "Now that we're planning to build a bigger house, we'll have plenty of room for them to visit. Or even stay if they'd like to."

"This house is big enough," Jessica insisted, continuing an ongoing tug-of-war over the size of the home Finn was determined to give her. "We have three bedrooms and a nice kitchen added on the back. What more do we need?"

"Ah, Jessica." He shook his head. "You still don't understand, do you? Your husband has one of the richest mines in the territory, and he delights in providing for you."

"You've always provided for me," she said stubbornly. "From the first day we met, until now, you've taken care of me."

"Because I love you, Jess," he said softly. "I almost lost you three times, and each time I recognized anew the need I have for you in my life.

With a smile, she accepted his homage and as he gathered her into his arms again, she sighed with contentment and leaned her head against his broad chest. He looked down at her as her eyes fluttered shut, sleep overtaking her, and the morning sun reflected from the locket she held in her hand.

He covered it with his own, and though his vow of dedication to this woman and their children was silent, it held a promise that would last for all the years to come.

* * * * *

Be sure to look for the final book in the
COLORADO CONFIDENTIAL *series,*
ROCKY MOUNTAIN MARRIAGE
by Debra Lee Brown,
coming in March 2004,
only from Harlequin Historicals.

Turn the page for a sneak preview…

Chapter One

Colorado, 1884

"It's a saloon?"

"Yes, ma'am. The pride of Last Call. Draws customers from Fairplay to Garo." The driver hefted her trunk from the buckboard and set it on the ground under a young oak, in front of the steps leading up to the entrance.

There had to be some mistake. Her father had owned a cattle ranch, not a…a Dora couldn't breathe. She gawked at the gold leaf lettered sign above the swinging doors. *The Royal Flush. Established 1876. William Fitzpatrick, proprietor.*

"The best damned gambling house in the state, if you ask me." The driver tipped his hat to her, then climbed atop the buckboard to depart.

"W-wait. Please." She plucked her father's letter from the small, leather-bound diary she always carried with her, and read the first shakily written paragraph again.

If you're reading this, Dora, I'm dead. Seeing as you're my only living kin, I'm leaving you the place. Lock, stock and barrel, it's all yours.

She gazed out across the high-country pasture surrounding the opulent two-story ranch house turned saloon. A few stray cattle grazed in the meadow below the original homestead. Nowhere were the herds she'd expected, or any evidence that her father had made his fortune in cattle.

Several outbuildings were visible behind the house: a barn, what looked like a bunkhouse, and a few small cabins nestled between naked strands of aspen and oak. It had been a ranch once, by the look of things.

"I guess you'll be running the place now. Good luck to you, ma'am." The driver snapped the reins and the horse sprang to life.

Running the place?

"Wait a moment. Please!" Dora ran after the buckboard. "You're not just going to leave me here?"

"You want to go back to town?" The driver pulled the horses up short. "Before you even get a peek at the place?"

The sun had already dipped well below the snowcapped peaks in the distance. Spring columbine checkered the rolling grassland as far as the eye could see, but winter's chill still frosted the air. Dora pulled her cloak tightly about her as she glanced back at the bustling business her father had never once mentioned in his letters to her.

Horses stood in a line, tied up at the long rail outside the saloon. Buggies and buckboards and other conveyances were parked along the side. A corral flanked the building, where other horses were feeding. Presumably they belonged to customers, *regulars* she believed the term was.

Soft light spilled from the entrance of the saloon and from windows draped in red velvet. Tinny piano music, men's voices and coquettish laughter drifted out to meet her. Fascinated, Dora took a step toward the entrance, then paused to consider her predicament.

"Ma'am?" the driver fished a pocket watch out of his vest. "Got to get these horses back to town. Are you coming or staying?"

Not once in her twenty-five years had she ever been inside a saloon. God would strike her dead, her mother had been fond of saying when she was alive, if Dora so much as set foot in one.

''Last chance, ma'am.''

Last chance.

She heard the driver's words, the snap of the reins, and the buckboard rattling back down the two-mile stretch of road to the mining town of Last Call, where her only hope of securing proper accommodations for the night was to be found.

But Dora was already on the steps, her gaze pinned to the swinging doors, her eyes wide with excitement, her stomach fluttering. Lock, stock and barrel, she thought as she tucked her father's letter carefully away between the pages of her diary.

She placed a gloved hand on one of the swinging doors and pushed. A heartbeat later she stepped from her comfortable and orderly existence into a new world. By some miracle, God did not strike her dead after all.

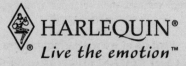

PICK UP THESE HARLEQUIN HISTORICALS AND IMMERSE YOURSELF IN THRILLING AND EMOTIONAL LOVE STORIES SET IN THE AMERICAN FRONTIER

On sale January 2004

CHEYENNE WIFE by Judith Stacy
(Colorado, 1844)

Will opposites attract when a handsome
half-Cheyenne horse trader comes to the rescue
of a proper young lady from back east?

WHIRLWIND BRIDE by Debra Cowan
(Texas, 1883)

A widowed rancher unexpectedly falls in love with
a beautiful and pregnant young woman.

On sale February 2004

COLORADO COURTSHIP by Carolyn Davidson
(Colorado, 1862)

A young widow finds a father for her unborn child—
and a man for her heart—in a loving wagon train scout.

THE LIGHTKEEPER'S WOMAN by Mary Burton
(North Carolina, 1879)

When an heiress reunites with her former fiancée,
will they rekindle their romance or say goodbye
once and for all?

Visit us at www.eHarlequin.com

HARLEQUIN HISTORICALS®

From Regency romps
to mesmerizing Medievals,
savor these stirring tales from
Harlequin Historicals®

On sale January 2004

THE KNAVE AND THE MAIDEN by Blythe Gifford

A cynical knight's life is forever changed when he falls
in love with a naive young woman while journeying
to a holy shrine.

MARRYING THE MAJOR by Joanna Maitland

Can a war hero wounded in body and spirit find
happiness with his childhood sweetheart, now that she
has become the toast of London society?

On sale February 2004

THE CHAPERON BRIDE by Nicola Cornick

When England's most notorious rake is attracted to
a proper ladies' chaperon, could it be true love?

THE WEDDING KNIGHT by Joanne Rock

A dashing knight abducts a young woman to marry his
brother, but soon falls in love with her instead!

Visit us at www.eHarlequin.com

HARLEQUIN HISTORICALS®

HHMED34